# Halcyon

Harbingers, Book II: Child of Sea

Jane M. Wiseman

Shrike Publications

Albuquerque, New Mexico

Shrike Press
Albuquerque, New Mexico




Book Layout © 2017 BookDesignTemplates.com

Halcyon/ Jane M Wiseman. -- 1st ed.
ISBN 978-1-7328141-3-4

For Will and Wallace

*Some say that Alcyone, grieving for her love lost to storms at sea, cried out to the gods. So touched were they by Alcyone's tears that they turned her into a bird, the kingfisher. When the kingfisher is flying, the seas are tranquil. Such days are known as halcyon days, and "halcyon" is another name for kingfisher.*



Thank you!

# The Stormclouds/Harbingers Fantasy Novels

### Stormclouds: The Prequel Series

Book I, *A Gyrfalcon for a King*

Book II, *The Call of the Shrike*

Book III, *Stormbird*

### The Harbingers Series

Book I, *Blackbird Rising*

Book II, *Halcyon*

Book III, *Firebird*

Book IV, *Ghost Bird*

## Betwixt and Between: The Companion Series

Book I, *The Martlet is a Wanderer*

Book II, *The Nightingale Holds Up the Sky*

And now:

*Dark Ones Take It, being the origin story of Caedon and his brother Maeldoi, the Dark Rider*

New series! **Planestriders**, bridging the gap between our world and the plane of the Stormclouds/Harbingers novels. The first, *Witchmoon*, is coming soon!

All available in paperback and for e-readers.

# The Known World

1 The Sceptered Isle
2 The Western Isle
3 The Eastern Baronies
4 The Ice-realm
5 The Southern Primacy
6 The Fire Isle
7 The Lyre Lands
8 The Cold Lands
9 The Burnt Lands
10 The Realm of the Asp
11 The Mountain Fastnesses
12 The Trade Route Fortifications

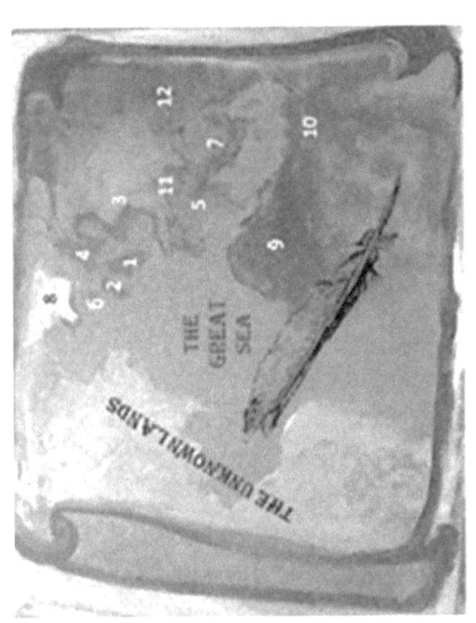

# Contents

# Child of Earth, Child of Sea

*Come all you mothers, listen well to me!*
*Come to catch your elf child, elf child, elf child,*
*Chase your naughty elf child*
*underneath the sea.*

That's what I sang at the village fire in the big hall on the last night, the last good night we had. All us women were gathered around the hearth while our men exchanged farm tips with each other by the door. Everyone was laughing and joking. This song, especially, made the women laugh. It's an unsophisticated little ditty, nothing like the ones that must be popular at court. We were as far away from the courts of kings as we could get, Wat and I.

I thought at the time that my song had no dark undertones. I was wrong.

Our little village seemed a charmed place, sheltered from the dangers always lying in wait underneath the Spheres. Maybe some sort of warning should have risen from the hidden place inside me, summoned by my music. But that night, song failed me.

The gathering was one of the last purely happy times I spent with other peasants like me. I might not have been born a peasant, but I was reared as one, and now I found myself living that life once more, singing a simple song to simple people, glad to be among them, glad to feel safe and loved.

The song is a cautionary tale. It's about a woman who gave birth to an elf-child who ran away to live beneath the waves, and every verse is sillier than the last. What that mischievous child got up to! How her mother scolded!

I loved living in the little village. I should have known better.

Living there meant laughter, good neighbors, good food, singing only for pleasure, not in the service of some sinister plot—experiences I hadn't enjoyed lately, especially not in the last few difficult years.

Wat and I had lived in the village for only a few seasons now, but we were starting to feel like we belonged. Not like strangers come over the water. They should have been wary of us, those good people. They were not. They were kind and generous folks who had no notion of the darkness rising up beneath the calm surface of their lives, a dark tide of events as monstrous as the fabled sea creatures said to menace this coast.

No hint of any terrible thing marred our happy time. Just the pleasures of the evening, uncomplicated and hearty. With my rebec and my voice, I was made especially welcome. Then home in the dark to our own small cottage at the edge of the village we went, Wat and I, laughing and shivering and pulling our cloaks around us in the cold. Our eyes must have been bright with the ale we drank.

Once we reached our doorstep, everything changed. The hazy feelings of good food and drink vanished in an instant. I felt it through to the marrow of my bones, as if the temperature of the air had dropped beyond frosty and brisk to a dead cold. The feeling was an old too-familiar dread. My hidden place opened to me, a threshold into the deep corridors and windings inside. This happens to me. A darkness comes on me. I almost never get any warning. Or not much. Not enough.

I put out a sudden hand, grabbing Wat's cloak.

By now he knew what I meant when I did something like that. We knew each other well by now, Wat and I. He stopped and gave me a sharp look in the moonlight, his body going tense under my hand. I looked to the shadowy doorway, and Wat's eyes followed my gaze. He nodded almost imperceptibly.

I stepped ahead of him, seemingly casual. When the killer leaped from the shadows, I swiveled hard into him, my knife already in my hand. Before the man could act, Wat stepped behind him and had him in a lock about the neck. Wat was fast, his arm pressed down on the man's throat, throttling off any cry.

This stranger thought he had surprise on his side. But no. We did. I finished him off with a brisk flurry of stabs underneath his rib cage. He didn't have the chance for much of a struggle.

We stood over his corpse. Both of us were breathing hard. Wat bent to push aside the man's hood. He examined the man's oddly tranquil face in the moonlight, but we knew we'd see nothing unusual about him. We knew we'd find nothing in his clothing or about his person to tell us who he was or why he'd come. But of course we did know why he'd come.

I reached automatically to check my rebec, to make sure it hadn't been smashed. How I'd ever find another one in this remote, rough place— Thank the Children it was fine.

Wat got to his feet. "They've found us." His voice was soft.

"I'm tired, Wat. Really tired. Can we think about it tomorrow?"

"Of course. It will be days before they realize this fellow didn't perform the duties they assigned him. Days before they send someone else. I need to get rid of the body, though."

I nodded. A bloody body covered with stab wounds would be pretty hard to explain to our decent neighbors.

"Go inside where it's warm," Wat said, putting a steadying hand on my shoulder. He knew I hated it. Killing.

I reached down for a clump of grass to wipe off my knife, then re-sheathed it in the scabbard I kept always strapped to my calf, concealed under my kirtle. I wearily shoved my way into our tiny stone house to collapse by the hearth ring.

It was a bad moment. Until that time, we'd been happy. Through the sodden gloom that comes to me in the aftermath of violence, I tried to hold on to that good feeling. In winter the nights are long this far north. But I had Wat beside me. That's all that mattered. It's a comfort to me still, thinking now about our life there together for those few seasons of peace in the little village, even though that period of our lives was cut short. The memories make me smile, and maybe they help reconcile me to all the ugly events that happened afterward, even understand about my sister Jillian and what may have become of her.

My feelings about Wat are easy to describe. I love him more than life itself. My feelings about Jillie are difficult. I searched for her, and then through the mercy of the Children I found her. Now I've lost her again, the only family I have.

I'm a woman who has lost her family. Although, as I thought past that pain, I realized that in the years since my parents died, Wat had become my family, and Wat was a man who knew about loss. That's one reason for the strong connection between us. Not the only one.

During our interlude of peace in the little village on the cliffs overlooking the sea, Wat came home each evening from trying to eke out a living on our rocky piece of farmland. He, as is the tradition in these parts, was responsible for everything over the threshold, like other men, while I, like other women, was responsible for everything within. We didn't believe that should be the way of it, but we wanted to blend in. We needed to blend in. So that's how we behaved.

At night, we could shed these restrictive lives we led. They were simple lives, and we both loved them in a simple, easy way. Compared to the struggles we'd endured, we found them somehow deeply satisfying, as if it meant we were ordinary people living ordinary lives. I think both of us yearned for that, even though, under the Nine Spheres, it didn't appear to be true and seemed like it never would be.

At night we'd snuggle down into the sheepskins piled on our big bed. The bed stood facing the hearth-ring in our one-room stone cottage. We built the fire up high from the pile of turves, and we lay warm and content in our nest while the winds blew about the house, howling like demons.

"Not much of a farmer," Wat was saying ruefully. "Or a grave digger." He was examining the calluses forming on his hands. He'd come in after candle measure or so, and now he climbed into our bed.

"Pull those hands under the fleeces," I told him. "You're letting freezing air under." I laughed at him. "Not born to be a farmer, huh," I said, pushing the gravedigger part aside.

"Neither was your father, but he managed to make a living for your family," Wat said.

*Just barely*, I thought to myself. Not that I realized it, growing up poor on my parents' tiny farm in the Riverlands across the water. My father was an earl, my mother fine and beautiful. But they'd had to flee Audemar's tyranny and try to live as poor folk, hiding out from the king's assassins.

Until the assassins found them.

Now Wat and I were living the same kind of life, on the run from the king's assassins. It was the life I was born to. A melancholy thought. I was beginning to think happy evenings like this one made up for the constant worry. But now the assassins had tracked us to our refuge.

"What did you do with the body?" I gave in to reality. It was not a matter I could easily shove away. I tried to keep my voice steady. I knew I was on the verge of tears.

"Under the shed," he mumbled. In the firelight his eyes looked haunted, sunken.

"Wat, you're exhausted. I'm so selfish. I was just thinking about me." Wat had been gravely injured several years ago in a fight with Caedon, our enemy. Coming back from a hurt that severe was still wearing on Wat.

He pulled the fleeces around us both and gave me a kiss. "You're worrying about me. But anamcara, I've been bothered about you. You're looking thin and pale these days."

"Always trying to protect me. Look. I'm tough," I said, shrugging off the fleeces and showing him my muscles.

"You've always been tough. Come back down under here where it's warm."

"I'm the one who gets to fret about you right now," I told him. "You're not allowed to fret about me."

"I know, but—" He stopped, looking over at me, and I felt a chill that had nothing to do with the cold.

"What is it," I said, trying to still my heart's pounding. The hidden place inside me was opening. It's as if I were standing at the lip of a deep well, looking down many fathoms into darkness. I shook myself slightly, bringing myself back to the present moment.

"A messenger came yesterday," Wat said, his voice quiet.

I sat up again, abruptly, the fleeces sliding from my shoulders. "You didn't tell me."

"I didn't want to worry you."

I didn't carp at him for not telling me sooner. Instead I asked the question I dreaded he would answer the way I thought he would. "What did the messenger say?"

"You can probably guess."

"Diera needs you."

"Yes," said Wat. In the flickering firelight, the fine planes of his face were tense and drawn. My heart caught in my throat when he looked like that.

Now Diera had summoned him to her side, Queen Diera the First. Wat and I had seen her crowned monarch of the Sceptered Isle, and then we'd had to flee across the straits to the Western Isle from the mainland to escape her traitor uncle Audemar the Usurper. That's when Diera had had to go into exile in the Eastern Baronies, across the Narrows from our homeland.

"Diera's coming back at the head of an army," Wat told me now.

"And she needs her Queen's Companions." My hand found Wat's under the sheepskins and held on tight.

Wat is another of Diera's uncles, even though they are almost exactly the same age. Officious-minded people would call him her half-uncle, since Wat is bastard-born. He and her full uncle, Avery, were the two in her family who had saved her from the terrible fate Audemar had planned for her. Audemar is Diera's uncle, too, but he has behaved toward her like a rapacious stranger.

As many know, in spite of Audemar's efforts to suppress the news, Avery died in the rescue attempt. Audemar's henchmen savagely butchered him. Diera survived.

Tears rose to my eyes as I thought about that chaotic, bloody day. I loved Avery. It bit at me that in spite of doing everything I could, playing my own part in the rescue as well as I could, as we all did, Avery still fell to the evil planned by his own brother.

In the aftermath of his death, our situation was complicated, Wat's and mine.

Audemar successfully eliminated most of his entire family, his father Ranulf the Fourth's bastard children included, one by one, all his rivals for the throne, even the most unlikely, such as Wat's six-year-old brother. Avery was the last. He killed them all, except for Diera and Wat, and that wasn't for lack of trying.

Wat lived in spite of the best efforts of Audemar's fellow conspirator Caedon to cut him down.

Caedon makes my blood run cold. He is accounted the finest swordsman of his generation. I've seen it myself. The rumors aren't wrong. Caedon should have killed Wat when Wat went up against him. But in the contest between them, Wat employed some skills Caedon wasn't expecting. Even so, Wat lost that duel. At least he didn't lose his life.

The Children stood by him, and They stood by us. Or maybe luck.

The only person more depraved and evil than Audemar is Caedon. That's what I think about it. I know what it's like to end up in Caedon's hands.

I know what it is to feel the searing pain of Caedon's branding iron. I'll wear his brand to the day I die, and many, seeing it, will think that legally makes me his bondswoman. I keep that brand concealed.

Thank the Children I got out. Thank the Children Wat lived.

And Diera escaped. Her crowning was a beautiful moment. At her coronation, Diera honored Wat by elevating him to Queen's Companion, with the magnificent sword to prove it. She honored me, too, in the same way, and gave me a rich dagger emblazoned with the harbingers of Earth Child and Sea Child. Now I keep it hidden away in a safe place, but from time to time, I take it out and run my fingers over it. On one side of the hilt, in chased gold, is the blackbird, harbinger of the Earth Child. The Child of Earth watches over Diera and Wat, as She watches over all inheriting the sacred blood of Ranulf. And so the blackbird is the sign of the Rising against Audemar and Caedon.

But on the other side of my dagger's hilt is the fisher bird. My own Child is the Child of Sea, and the fisher bird is Her harbinger.

Because we are Queen's Companions, Wat and I need to ready ourselves to fight at her side when Diera summons us. We knew the summons would come, maybe not quite so soon. But we did know it was coming. We'd decided between us that when it did, he would go and I would stay. He is formally trained in arms and the skills of battle, while I am not. And Wat is Diera's near kin. They think of each other as sister and brother.

So now, as Wat and I lay quiet together in the firelight, he told me that Diera had issued her summons. I understood. Wat and I knew that meant I would have to stay behind in the Western Isle if we wanted to keep our farmstead. Practically speaking, I would have to be the one to stay. I can hold my own and then some in a guerilla action, and I've proved it. I was the person who got Diera out of Caedon's hands, after all.

But Wat and I also knew that in a pitched battle, I'd be useless. So we decided that when the summons came, Wat would be the one to answer it. I agreed to this plan.

But I didn't have to like it, Wat leaving me and sailing off to the mainland on some dangerous mission without me by his side.

After he told me, I sat blinking into the firelight, trying not to fall apart.

"Your hands are freezing, anamcara," Wat said.

Anamcara, "soul mate." It's a word from this remotest part of the realm. I loved it when he called me that. He pulled me back down under the fleeces with him. For a little while, we forgot all about Diera and her summons. We forgot about the assassin we'd just sent to a bloody death. We just thought about our hands on each other's bodies, our lips, Wat's long self against mine, and how we fit together as if we were born to it. I do believe we were.

Later that evening, as I lay with my cheek against Wat's shoulder in a rosy sleepy glow, I tried out some of my own new-found words on him. "Is ceol mo chroí thú," I told him. We were both trying to learn how to fit into this new place, the Western Isle, where we had found refuge, a place we were trying to turn into home.

The Western Isle had been its own separate realm, not so very long ago. The Sceptered Isle's King Ranulf the Fourth (Ranulf the Good to us of the Rising) had conquered it. Ranulf, Wat's father. As a young man, my own father had fought in Ranulf's name to subdue this vast savage western island. Avery had fought, too, and Wat's older brother Johnny.

I had the secret notion the people on the isle whose land was taken from them weren't likely to call Ranulf "the Good." I had a sneaking sympathy for these people, even though I knew I and my family had been on the other side. As for Wat, Ranulf was his father, after all. I hadn't discussed my uncomfortable feelings about these dispossessed islanders with him.

Living here, though, both of us had learned a lot, not just about different lands and different people but about power, maybe. How power that benefits some people can perhaps destroy others. Lying beside Wat in the firelight, I thought about that, how you can't just march around thinking your ways are the right ways without thinking hard about how your own ways may damage others.

People are different in the Western Isle. They talk differently. When they spoke to us in our language, Wat and I had a hard time understanding their accent, and they have a strange language of their own. They are forbidden to speak it, but everyone does anyway, especially in these remote villages here on the westernmost coast. Now I said the new words again, trying to get the sounds of their strange language exactly right: "Is ceol mo chroí thú."

"And what does that mean?" said Wat. Beside him, I could feel the tension falling away from his body. He pushed my hair back off my face and leaned in to kiss the corner of my mouth.

I laughed and kissed him back. "They tell me in the village it means something like, 'You are the music of my heart.'"

"That would appeal to you, wouldn't it?" said Wat. We lay gazing into the firelight. I ran my fingers through his close-cropped hair, the color of barley ripening in the field. "I was starting to get used to it long," I said. "I liked it long." When we crowned Diera and Wat was knighted, Wat had let his hair grow long, as he'd worn it in boyhood at Ranulf's court. He held it back off his face with a leather thong, and I loved to loosen that thong and play with his hair as it fell across his face. But now it was short again, the way peasants wear it. The way he'd worn it when we first met. In our little village here, we were acting the role of peasants again and had to look the part.

He smiled and curled a lock of my own hair around his finger and drew me to him for another kiss. "I'll be leaving within the sen'night," he said, after a moment. "I want you with me, but—" He looked over at me, his eyes worried. "And now the stakes are higher. Much higher."

I knew. If we both went, our work on the farm would come to nothing. The farmstead would be declared vacant, and when we returned, someone else would be the owner of our house. We needed to keep our holding here. Diera had sent us here to create a refuge in case the Rising needed a base remote from Audemar's reach. If we left, we'd forfeit all we'd done here, little though it was.

But Wat was right. Now the stakes were higher. Now Audemar, or maybe Caedon, had found where we were hiding. Wat had to leave, and I would have to face these assassins on my own.

I slipped out of bed, threw on my kirtle and a warm cloak, and started banking the fire for the night.

"You know I can take care of myself, Wat," I said.

Wat lay looking at me in the firelight. "I'm thinking of a plan," he said after a while. "A plan to keep you safe while I'm gone."

"I don't need anyone to keep me safe."

"You're a goose, Mirin, you know that? We all need help keeping safe in these times, around these people. I'm not leaving here if I don't think you'll be safe."

"Wat. You know that as long as Caedon and Audemar are in the world, we'll never be safe. You know that, don't you? Yet we have to keep going."

"As safe as possible," he insisted.

The stubborn set of his mouth made me smile at him in spite of myself.

"I'm going to let Ivor know to watch out for you," he said.

"Ivor," I said. "He's as big a rascal as any man I've ever met."

"He got us to this isle, didn't he? He didn't betray us, did he?"

I sighed. If it would make him feel better about leaving me—"Very well," I said. "Tell Ivor."

I had nearly finished my small tasks around our cottage. Every so often I caught Wat's eye, and we smiled at each other again. We didn't need to say much. Strange, how a man who started out reluctantly taking on my care, and training me to be a spy and assassin, could now be this to me. Especially when, for a time there, I thought of him as an older brother, and he clearly thought of me as a pesky young sister.

*But now we are this to each other*, I whispered to myself.

I held out my hands to the fire, and a secret glow spread all the way through me. During our long and difficult years on the road together, spying for the Rising, we had learned hard things about each other, and about ourselves. We had been very young in a world that robbed us of childhood. Through terrifying and unsettling ordeals, through mistrust and the hard process of learning to trust, we had both grown up. And as we did, we found we were meant for each other, Wat and I.

Before I came back to our bed, I took my rebec from its place on pegs by the door and sat down on the bench before the fire. I stroked the rebec's well-loved form, admiring the carving of the fisher bird on the neck, and also the tailpiece, which my father had cleverly fashioned into a blackbird.

Wat's older brother Johnny had taught me to play. Every time I picked up my bow to tease shimmering tones from my instrument, I prayed to the Children I'd be worthy of my father's making and worthy of Johnny's teaching. My rebec and the music I played on it had traveled with me to so many places and stood with me through so much danger and sorrow that by now it had almost become a person to me. A confidante. A teacher. I say almost. I know what Johnny would say. He'd say it is all those things, and more, a connection to the hidden place inside me, the wellspring, what my father called my second sense.

Taking it to the hearth with me this night, I played a new song I had learned from the women in the village. It was a well-known song in these parts, a place where fishermen set sail into unknown rough waters, and it told a story.

> *I saw the old moon yester night*
> *with the new moon in his arms;*
> *if you sail out to sea, my love,*
> *you'll never more come home.*
>
> *Now good Sir Ceyx, he loved his wife,*
> *and she was Alcyone.*

*He'd drive his ship to gates of hell*
*but he would come back home.*

*Weep, O weep, Alcyone,*
*by waters wap and wan,*
*hold out your silver mirror,*
*hold up your golden comb.*

*Oh long she sits in tower high*
*at window o're the sea.*
*Come back to me, my own dear lord.*
*But never more will he.*

*I saw the old moon yester night*
*with the new moon in his arms;*
*If you sail out to sea, my love,*
*you'll never more come home.*

*O forty leagues off rocky strond*
*'tis fifty fathoms deep;*
*And there lies good Sir Ceyx adrowned,*
*Alcyone's heart to break.*

*He calls her ghostly on the wind,*
*and then she knows he's gone.*
*I may not live, O Child take me.*
*My grief it is too strong.*

*The Children, they look down from high*
*with pity in their gaze.*

They change her into Halcyon,
the bird that stills the waves.

Halcyon, oh fisher bird,
wife forever true,
weep for me and fly to me,
and I will weep for you.

I saw the old moon yester night
with the new moon in his arms;
if you sail out to sea, my love,
you'll never more come home.

A few days earlier, when some of the other village women had been admiring my rebec, one had exclaimed in excitement, and then the others had joined her. They were all looking at the carving on it. Long ago, my father had incised the fisher bird twining around the neck of the rebec, its beak pointing upward.

"We know a song about the fisher bird," cried one of these women, one of the many sisters of my friend Siobhan, and then the others had clamored to teach it to me, the song I was singing now.

It's a beautiful song, but sad. After I finished playing and singing it, I laid my rebec and bow aside on the bench, threw my apron over my head, and burst into tears.

"Mirin, anamcara, what is it?" Wat was out of bed and by my side in an instant.

I jumped off the bench and came back with a fur robe for him, wiping the tears from my eyes. "You'll catch your death."

"I'm not that easy to kill," said Wat.

"So it seems," I said, and managed a wavering smile. Caedon had done his best to kill Wat, and Wat had the long, wicked scar to prove it.

"What is it? Sit here and tell me," said Wat.

"It's that song, only. It's so sad."

"Listen, Mirin. I'm not going to die at sea. I'm coming back to you," he said. "You'll pray to the Sea Child for my safe return."

I am a Child of the Sea. Wat, though, is a Child of the Earth. The Sea Child is not his friend. Not necessarily. That thought sent a shiver up my spine, but I tried not to let Wat see it.

"I'm a lot more worried about these assassins than any disaster at sea," Wat told me. "I'm going to work out the plan with Ivor before I leave you here by yourself."

"I can take care of myself," I said again, forcing more confidence into my voice than I was feeling.

Wat gave me a shrewd look. We were both actors. That's what we'd done, as we traveled around the country, spying. We'd passed ourselves off as performers, and we'd both gotten good at it. But Wat knew. He saw right through me.

"Before I leave, I'll get Ivor to promise to meet you and decide on the details," he said.

As for me, I sent up a quick prayer to the Sea Child for Wat's safe return, and a plea to the Sea Child to give me warning of danger, even though I'm not a praying woman. I thought luck would have more to do with it, the chances puny mortals take when they head out across a cruel and powerful and unknown element like the sea. And the chances they take when they go up against a calculating enemy.

Luck and chance. When it came to aid, though, I had a sight more confidence in the powers the Sea Child granted me than I did in any uncertain protections Ivor might offer, the creature. But I knew if I let Wat see how little confidence I had in his family's crabbed retainer, he might never leave. And Wat needed to leave. Part of me wanted him to see my uncertainties and stay. That part of me didn't want him to leave. That part of me was afraid.

I knew he had to.

I'd also learned, as I played out my role in the Rising, that deep inexplicable forces exist in this world of ours.

There's something no one knows, something I keep to myself. Diera doesn't know it. Not even Wat. Everyone knows I saved Diera, but no one knows how. No one knows the blackbirds showed me how to find her. No one knows how my music called them to me. I don't even know how music, mine or anyone else's, could do a thing like that, and by now, I don't even try explaining. The blackbirds don't speak to me now. Sometimes I wonder if they ever did. Sometimes I wonder whether I dreamed it all. But I did find Diera, and she is our queen, so I know what I experienced was real.

Deep inside me, the gates of my hidden place began to open as I returned to bed with Wat. I turned shuddering away from that inner darkness. What I glimpsed there was too disturbing. Part of me, the waking part, didn't want to know.

# Chapter Two

# Anamcara

What's happening?" I asked Siobhan. She was craning her neck to see across the market square. I sensed something was wrong. Siobhan was my neighbor as well as my friend. She lived on the farmstead closest to ours, although her house was the last in the village lane, and ours was all the way on the other side of the townlands, across the village fields. Today Siobhan and I had made the trip to the near-by market town together. She was there to look over a pig she and her husband hoped to buy, and I had carefully saved for a new iron pan.

There was a big stir over on the other side of the market square. Voices raised. Laughter. But not happy laughter. Jeering. Siobhan looked startled.

By now, it was nearly a full turning of the moon after Wat's departure, secret, in the night. He and I had spent several days preparing, once we'd gotten Diera's summons. I had pulled warm clothing from our big chest and mended any rips. It would be cold out on the seas. I baked some barley cakes for him to take with him, and put together some potions he might need if he were taken sick. After his ordeal at the hands of Caedon, he was still much too thin. I had supplemented our meager income from the farm by practicing my skills as a healer during our time in the village, and I had a stock of herbs ready to hand.

Meanwhile, Wat tracked down his old family retainer, Ivor. Ivor was the man who had arranged our passage to the Western Isle after Diera's coronation. He had traveled with us. But when we arrived, Wat had released Ivor from his service. It wouldn't do for a poor farmer to arrive in the village with a servingman. Wat had given Ivor a bag filled with coin, and Ivor had headed off to Sliagh, the biggest town on this rocky western peninsula of the isle. Ivor set himself up there as a blacksmith.

I knew Wat kept in touch with Ivor. I was pretty sure Ivor was doing some spying for Wat.

I didn't ask Wat much about their arrangement. The problem was, I didn't trust Ivor. He was an evil-looking fellow, foul-smelling, gray rank locks spilling out from under his wool cap, and a terrible disfiguring scar running down the side of his nose.

"He got that scar fighting in the wars over here," Wat told me. "John told me once Ivor liked it over here. He's glad to be back here." Ivor had accompanied Wat's older brother, my beloved teacher Johnny, when Johnny and Avery and my father Drustan had come to the Western Isle as young men to fight in Ranulf's army.

I tried hard not to dislike the man. It wasn't his fault he was hideously ugly. Although, I told myself, it was his fault that he was dirty. But there was something about him I found repellant, something beyond the dirtiness of him. I couldn't put my finger on what it was. Even Wat had to admit that the man was only indifferently honest. He cheated his customers at the smithy, people said. I believed them. I didn't like having to put my trust in such a fellow. I didn't like it that he knew who we were. I didn't like thinking about the price on our heads and how attractive that might seem to a man like Ivor.

But Ivor knew people. He knew how to arrange things. He knew sailors who didn't ask too many questions, and how to book passage on their ships.

The night of Wat's departure filled me with difficult emotions. Wat and I waited until full dark. There was no moon that night. We gathered Wat's supplies together, and he took Diera's beautiful sword from its hiding place and sheathed it at his belt. I bent to work the belt buckle, trying not to let Wat see the tears that kept squeezing out and trickling down my cheeks.

He reached out a hand and ran it through my hair. "Like spun bronze," he whispered to me, and then he'd caught me into his arms. He kissed the tears away, and we were embracing as if we'd never be able to let go of each other.

But it was time. We pulled our cloaks around us. Quietly, we pulled the door to the cottage closed behind us and skirted around the village to the main road. My eyes gradually adjusted to the dark. The night was beautiful, thousands of glittering stars thrown across the frosty interior of the crystalline sphere that was their home. We made our way in silence through the dark of night toward Sliagh, but we hadn't gotten very far down the road before we found ourselves walking arm in arm. We both kept needing to touch each other.

As we neared Sliagh, we turned off onto the steep, stony path that led down to the harbor. A dark shape waited for us by the side of the road.

"Stay here," Wat breathed in my ear. He advanced to the figure cautiously, but it was Ivor, as they'd planned. Wat motioned to me to join them.

"Mistress Mirin, 'tis good to lay eyes on ye after many a moon has waxed and waned," said Ivor in his high nasal voice as I came up to them.

"Good even to you, Ivor," I said.

"Ivor has arranged passage," Wat said to me. "The cog rides at anchor below in the harbor."

My heart froze over. Here is where we'd say goodbye.

But Wat was continuing to talk, explaining the plan he and Ivor had worked out. I didn't have time to wail and throw myself into Wat's arms, as part of me wanted desperately to do. I needed to listen.

Ivor would check with me once at every full of the moon, Wat was saying. As soon as Wat got safely over the water, Wat would send word to Ivor, and Ivor would bring word to me. Ivor would dress as a peddler to avoid suspicion when he came to our village to bring me this news. Ivor would keep his eyes and ears open in Sliagh for any activity at the small fort, really just a dusty collection of dilapidated buildings thinly manned by Audemar's soldiers. Ivor could come and go there, because he did some blacksmithing for the soldiers' horses. Ivor would know if any stranger arrived. Ivor would track anyone leaving the fort to travel in the direction of our village. Ivor would come to warn me if he saw any such activity.

I nodded along.

"Ivor has asked around," said Wat. "He thinks maybe a moon's turning ago he saw the man sent to kill us."

"Aye, Mistress, the very man. Didn't think much about it at the time, but now, looking back on it—"

"So Ivor will watch for any other activity like that and come to warn you if he notices anything," Wat finished. He turned to Ivor. "You've heard nothing about the assassin?"

"Nay. Them there at the fort didn't know the man. Thought he might be a mercenary. They started asking around, when he didn't come back. But they didn't go off searching for him."

"Maybe that will be the end of it, then," Wat said. "But maybe not. The two of you must watch and be careful." He seized me by the arm and leaned down to me. "Be careful, anamcara."

"I will. I promise."

"If you see anything out of the ordinary, get word to Ivor. Send someone to give him this." Wat pressed something into my palm, something hard and smooth. "He'll come to you as soon as he gets it."

I knew without looking what the hard little object was. One of the obsidian blackbird amulets, symbol of the Rising.

I couldn't help myself. I couldn't keep a sharp note out of my voice. "What good will that do?" I said. "By the time Ivor gets it, I'll have dealt with the problem myself."

Wat's voice was patient, coming at me out of the dark. "Suppose this . . . problem . . . needs to have a grave dug for it?"

"I could dig it," I said. I was feeling stubborn.

"Mirin. Anamcara—"

"Yes, Wat. I'll send for Ivor."

"I'll help 'ee, Mistress Mirin, see if I don't," said Ivor.

Wat raised my hand to his mouth and kissed it.

But Ivor's whining voice intervened. "Young master, tide's turning."

"I must go," Wat said, pulling me close. "The Children keep you," he murmured at my ear.

I raised my face to his, and I knew the tears were starting from my eyes again. I was glad he couldn't see them in the dark. He knew, though. He brushed them from my cheeks with his hands and kissed me fiercely, deeply. Then he tore away from me.

"Ready," he told Ivor. The two of them crunched away down the path from me. I stood listening until I could no longer hear their footsteps. Then I turned and made my way back to the village, getting there just before first light.

I let myself into the cottage, threw myself onto the fleeces of our bed, and sobbed myself to sleep. Full morning, pouring through the chinks of the thatch, woke me. A shameful thing for a farm wife.

Many days went by with no word.

Finally I couldn't stand it any longer. Under the pretext of looking for a rare ingredient to use in my potions, I headed off to Sliagh to speak to Ivor. I didn't find him. The other man at the smithy said he'd gone to the countryside to burn charcoal for the bloomery. I headed in the direction the man sketched out for me, but I didn't find Ivor. The charcoal burners I did find all said they hadn't seen Ivor that day. Late in the afternoon, as I went back through town, I passed by the smithy, but it was locked tight. So I made my way forlornly home, footsore and foolish.

At least no more assassins came.

I tried telling myself that hardly enough time had passed to hear news back from over the water. Yet I worried. To still the worry, I made myself keep busy. Siobhan was a good neighbor to me and brought me all the gossip from the market town a fair distance away, a good candle measure's walk, although not as far by half as Sliagh.

Now here we were at the very same town on market day. Siobhan and I had walked here together this morning. I was arranging bunches of herbs on a cloth I'd laid out before me in the market square, hoping to sell the little bundles to offset the expense of the pan I hoped to buy, and I was trying hard to concentrate—should the dock go here and the marjoram there? Or the other way around?

But a murmuring and jostling caught my attention.

Siobhan was craning her neck to see over a knot of villagers. "I'm not sure what's going on over there," she said now. A little crease appeared between her straight brows. "Something odd. That strange man over there, he's saying something about the wrong gods, how we worship the wrong ones."

The two of us were at the edge of a crowd filling the market square. On the central stone, where Fergus the day watchman usually proclaimed the town news, stood a stranger. As the crowd parted, I got a good look at him. He was dressed in long ochre robes.

I put a hand to my mouth. "The Lady Goddess," I said.

"You know this god of his?"

"My mother worshipped Her."

"That's all right, then. You come from over the water, and so does he, this man on the stone. That must be what you do over there, with your strange ways. Worship this goddess."

"Oh, no. I worship the Child of Sea," I told her.

It wasn't a lie. Not quite. The Child of Sea really is my Child, even if I have trouble believing in Her. Or in any god.

"But why is he saying we shouldn't worship our own gods?" asked Siobhan. She really was puzzled. She really didn't know. They'd all been sheltered over here from the worst of Audemar's tyrannies. "Why?" she said again, when I didn't answer.

"I suppose we'll find out," I said, thinking quickly. "Sounds like he's about to tell us." No need to drop the hard truth down on Siobhan if I didn't have to. Besides, it was too complicated and ugly. "My mother never thought such a thing," I said. "At least I think she didn't." At Siobhan's quick look, I clarified, "My mother died when I was a half-grown girl. But I never heard her say such a thing of the Lady, that Her ways were the only ways." I was telling Siobhan the truth about that, at least.

The man on the stone harangued us. "I say to all of you here assembled, it is treason to worship these so-called Children of yours. The Lady Goddess is the only true God. This is a decree from your king."

My heart sank. Some in the crowd were grinning and beginning to edge away out of the square. Others were outright laughing at him. Clearly they thought this stranger might be a bit out of his head. But I knew what it meant for him to be here. It meant that Audemar's troops were nearby. Wat and I knew they were already on the eastern edge of the island, closest to the mainland where the Sceptered Isle's forces were strongest. That's why we had deliberately sailed around the tip of the is-land to the westernmost coast, where rocky fingers of land stretched out into the sea. Nobody knew much about Audemar and his edicts out here. Of course we knew about his small outpost in Sliagh, but it didn't seem very important. The peace we had found here on the peninsula, even in the short time we'd been here, healed us from years of hurt and attack. Or so we'd thought at first, before the assassin. Before Diera's summons.

The square was emptying out, neighbors exchanging jocular remarks at this stranger's outlandish demands. *Oh, well,* I was thinking. *Here it is at last. This priest will have his say, but then he'll leave us to our own devices again.* Surely we weren't important enough for Audemar to spend much effort on us. We were too remote from the centers of power.

But I knew real terror when those same departing townspeople began crowding back into the square, closely followed by mounted soldiers in the scarlet of Audemar.

"We should go," I whispered to my companion. It was too late. All of us were herded into the center of the square. I could only send up a prayer of thanks to the Sea Child (or maybe to luck) that Wat had gotten away before this. I knew he'd be instantly recognized. I doubted I would be. But then . . . I glanced down at the mark on the inside of my left wrist. There was that. I pulled my sleeves well down over my hands.

The soldiers chivvied us into long lines. We waited in the queue to talk to an officer, probably a man from the little outpost in Sliagh, who had upended a barrel and had pulled a joint stool to it. He sat there at the head of our line, taking down information and issuing slips of parchment. I groaned inwardly, remembering the constant asking for and receiving of these pieces of parchment on the mainland, the control of the people, the suspicions and corrupt practices bred of the usurper-king's system.

There in the market square I began to worry. What would I need to say, when it was my turn before the king's official? What was the man asking? I tried to listen to what the others were required to say, but I was too far back in line.

At last there were only a few people ahead of me.

"Angus," said a man I knew by sight, giving his name to the official. "Angus, blacksmith, in the lane behind the tavern."

"Angus 'Smith," said the official, writing it down on his list. "And are you a loyal subject of His High Majesty, King Audemar?"

No fool, Angus said he was. He was issued one of the slips of parchment, told he'd have to show it to any soldier or official of the king who asked for it, and dismissed.

It was almost my turn. I imagined announcing myself as Lady Mirin of the High Sea Cliffs, Queen's Defender, wife of Sir Walter, named The Steadfast and Queen's Companion by Queen Diera the First, enemy of Audemar the Usurper. That made me smile to myself. Mirin was a common-enough name in this area. I could use Mirin.

Then I realized with a chill that these people were looking for us, me and Wat. I couldn't use my name. I decided on the spot to give them a false name. Cara, short for anamcara. But what should I say about Wat? A name like Wat cried out, "foreigner." A name like Walter cried out, "interloper." That's because even back across the water, Wat's mother was a foreigner, scorned by the others at court. She'd given her two oldest children names common among her people—John and Walter, but then, prudently, she'd given her third child a name all of us could recognize. Aedan. Not that it helped him or his poor mother when the killers came.

But here a name like Wat, like Walter, would attract instant attention. And Caedon was looking for Wat. I couldn't use his real name.

I was jolted out of these anxious thoughts as I reached the head of the line.

"Are you a married woman?" the official at the table asked me.

I nodded yes. I had a fresh worry now. I didn't sound like I came from these parts, not at all. If I opened my mouth and the wrong sounds came out, how suspicious would he get?

"Where is your husband?"

"At sea," I said, trying to mumble the words. "Fishing."

"Then you'll have to answer for both of you and make sure he comes to us for his parchment, when he's back."

I nodded.

"Are you both loyal subjects of his High Majesty King Audemar?"

I nodded again.

"And your name?"

"Cara, of the farmstead across the fields, in the village on the cliffs."

"Goodwife Cara Farmer," said the official, as he wrote it down, seeming not to notice my different accent. "That's what I've written, Goodwife," he explained, showing me the paper.

I knew then he thought I couldn't read. I decided to keep it that way. I nodded.

"You can make your mark here." He dipped his quill in ink and handed it to me.

I looked at it in bafflement. *Here's where all that acting comes in handy*, I beamed silently at Wat. Those days we had spent on the road performing. And spying.

The official sighed, taken in by my act. He put the quill in my hand and guided it to make a straggling x on the paper. Luckily my right hand, not the left, with the brand.

"And your husband, Goodwife? What is his name?"

"Kenning," I said. It was the only thing that came to mind. Kenning the Juggler had been Wat's stage name, when we were vagabond players.

With a chill, I realized Sir Caeden knew that name. But that didn't mean Audemar knew it too, I consoled myself.

The official merely nodded.

Even if the name meant something to somebody somewhere in the royal administration, it would mean nothing to this man. He was just a flunky stationed at a tiny outpost. He would hardly bother to communicate it up the line to his superiors. He wouldn't know to do it, even if he were on the look-out for someone named Wat, and here Wat's stage name would sit on some dusty list that no one was likely ever to look at again.

The official told me what he had told the others. I'd have to show the parchment to any agent or official of the king who asked for it. "Next," he said.

Now that I had my parchment, I could hand it to the soldier at the head of the lane leading out of the square toward the sea cliffs and our farmstead, and I could go home. I wasn't going to bother trying to sell my herbs or buy the pan, not after this.

I looked around for Siobhan but didn't see her, so I headed off in the direction of home.

I hadn't gotten far before Siobhan caught up with me. She must have felt the same about the wisdom of staying around to look over the town's stock of pigs. She wanted to get out of there and home to safety, too.

Now, though, she gave me a strange look.

I felt my heart sinking. She had been right behind me in line. She must have heard me give the King's official a false name. Now I'd have to explain myself to her. The fewer people who knew about me and Wat, the safer for us. The safer for them, too.

Unless they were betrayers. *Eight for the foul betrayers.* I remembered with a chill the line from the song Wat's brother Johnny had taught me.

"Mirin," Siobhan said hesitantly. "Is that really your name, then? Or is it—"

"Mirin is really my name," I told her. "I made up a false one for the king's official. Wat calls me anamcara, so . . . Cara. That's what I told him."

I glanced over at her. The big question *Why?* was written all over her face. It was worse leaving her that way than telling her something, so I tried.

"Siobhan . . . the reason Wat and I came here is because Wat was in trouble, over there on the mainland. It's hard to explain, because here, nobody worries very much about the king and all of his laws. But over there, it's different. A neighbor can take against you and denounce you, and the officials don't ask questions. They pay the neighbor the reward, and they punish the person he denounces. It's not fair, but it's the way things work over there."

"What did they think Wat had done?"

I told her the truth, just not all of it. "He'd done it, all right. Me too. We worship the Children. And that's forbidden."

"Oh," said Siobhan. "You told me that, but I didn't think—"

"And now it's happening here. That's why that priest was in the square, the priest of the Lady Goddess. To give everyone here fair warning. Change your god, or something bad will happen to you."

"Do you think those soldiers were looking for the two of you?" Siobhan's eyes were huge.

"I don't think so. We're nobody very important. But I didn't want to risk it."

Siobhan took my left hand and turned it over. My sleeve had hiked up. I thought of pulling away from her, but I didn't.

"I've noticed this," she said quietly. "Is this a part of your troubles?"

"Yes," I said.

Siobhan nodded and pressed my hand warmly. She pulled my sleeve well down over my brand.

That made me feel better. I didn't think Siobhan was a foul betrayer. Now I felt even more sure of it.

"So if they come asking me about you and Wat, I'll just say you're Cara and he's Kenning?"

"Yes." I tried to smile. "That's a private joke between the two of us. It will make Wat laugh."

She looked over at me silently as we trudged along. "I don't think it's a laughing matter. It scares me," she said finally.

"I don't want you to get into trouble," I told her. "Just say you don't know us, if anyone comes asking." We walked for a while longer in silence. "But I don't think anyone will," I added.

"Is Wat really fishing? At this season? We've all been wondering where he is. Malicious tongues have been saying—" She stopped and gave me a sidelong guilty look.

"What have they been saying?" I asked her, more intrigued than offended.

"Some say he left you because . . . Well, you know . . ."

I wasn't paying attention. I started to worry hard. Had the official noticed too that no one would be out fishing at this season, or was he too stupid and unfamiliar with the ways here?

"No. Nothing like that," I answered her, hardly aware of what she was implying, what those wagging tongues had been saying. "Wat had to go back across the water. He had to see about his niece."

"Isn't that dangerous?"

"Yes, but it couldn't be helped. She's in trouble. She worships the Children, too. Wat had to go to her."

Again Siobhan pressed my hand. "He's out there on those rough seas. You must be so worried."

"I am," I said, and I didn't have to lie this time, not even a little.

"Especially now," said Siobhan, and that strange expression had returned to her face.

I looked over at her inquiringly. She put her hand to her mouth. "What?" I said.

"Mirin. You know you're going to have a baby, right?"

# Chapter Three

# Child of Fire

How could I have missed the signs? I must be ad-dle-witted. After all, I'm a healer. A good one. But I never thought about what my own body was trying to tell me. I knew my courses had not been ex-actly ordinary, but in difficult times like the many seasons of my imprisonment by Caedon, and during the difficulties of our escape to this place, with all of the hard-ship and privation, they hadn't been regular for a long time. So I hadn't thought very much about it.

And I hadn't thought at all about the village's one or two idle gossips and what they might have made of Wat's sudden disappearance. They whispered that Wat had run off and left me. They whispered it was because the child I was bearing was not his own.

*Such silly stuff,* I thought now. I shoved it out of mind. When I met those gossips in the village lane, I gave them a cordial nod of greeting and went on. I wouldn't give such folk the satisfaction of seeing that their gossip bothered me.

But it did bother me that I would be having a baby while Wat was so far away and in such danger. Maybe Siobhan was wrong. Maybe it was not so. I tried to explain away the changes in my body.

It was so. Siobhan was right, of course. She had five children and six sisters, four of them married. She knew all the signs. And she was clearly right. I was pregnant. The coming fortnight and more, and the noticeable changes in my body, proved it.

During those long turnings of the moon, she was kind to me. Beyond kind. Now I treasured her more than ever. She'd walk up the road from her own farm, bringing me nourishing soups and stews. And her oldest sister Maire was the village midwife. Maire came to visit me, too. They were both encouraging. As the moon waxed and waned and waxed and waned anew, I started to dwell on Wat's absence. I couldn't help it.

He had been gone so long, and there had been no word. None at all, despite Wat's promise to send news as soon as he could. No word from Ivor. That rascally fellow never did appear at my doorstep pretending to be a peddler, as we'd all agreed, and the two times I'd made the trek to Sliagh to look for him had come to the same fruitless end. *So much for trusting that man,* I thought. But my anger at Ivor paled beside my fears for Wat. So many things could have happened. His ship could have foundered and sunk. And if he had made it safely to land, he could have been killed in Diera's war.

I was starting to grieve and pine.

I kept replaying, over and over again, the last day we'd spent together, how we'd sat together in the firelight, my head resting on his chest. How, in the dark of the moon, I'd helped him pull on his cloak, helped him fasten it with his golden brooch.

My own father had made that brooch. As a sign of their solidarity, he had made one for each of the six main instigators of the Rising. Each brooch depicted six small golden figures walking tall together. *Six for the six proud walkers,* Johnny's song rang in my mind. Fingering each of the figures as I helped Wat fasten the brooch to his cloak, I named them to myself. It was a comfort to me, naming them.

*Drustan,* my father, Earl of the High Sea Cliffs and Avery's friend from childhood.

*Prince Avery,* next in line for the throne after his oldest brother Artur's assassination, the murder of Artur's two young sons, and the disqualification of the middle brother Audemar because of his treachery.

*Conal*, Avery's best-loved companion.

Happy-go-lucky *Rafe*, a man with a hidden side, a secret I never learned the nature of. Wat knows about it, though. Wat never talks about it. Almost no one knows this, but Rafe and Diera were deeply in love. People keep saying she needs to find some powerful man to marry, but then I think of his violent death before her very eyes, and I see why she can't bring herself to marry. If I had watched Wat die like that, I don't know how I would ever have gotten past it. And then, I thought. There was something haunted about Rafe's eyes. He had known deep sorrow and trouble. I was sure of it.

I fingered the six gold bars as I helped Wat with the brooch.

*John*, Avery's bastard half-brother and lifelong friend, and Wat's older brother. He too was one of those Six. Beyond that, Johnny was my own dear teacher and mentor.

Finally, Johnny's young brother Wat, the last to join them and now the only survivor. *Wat*, I whispered to myself. *Wat. Wat.*

After I had finished fastening the brooch at his shoulder that night, reluctant to take my hands off him, Wat held me close and kissed me. And then we had headed out into the night, down to the harbor past Sliagh.

I thought about that night over and over, especially those last moments. Wat's mouth on mine, the wheedling, whining voice of Ivor. *Tide's turning.*

"Mirin, dear heart," said Maire to me at her most recent visit. "You mustn't take on so. It's not good for the baby."

"I know," I whispered. "But I miss Wat so, and I'm so worried about him." We'd forgotten all about "Cara" and "Kenning." The priest of the Lady Goddess was long gone, and no one else had come by to enforce the king's edict. I only remembered to find my slip of parchment where I put it for safekeeping in a fissure between the stones of our wall so I could bring it along with me when I had to make the long journey to Sliagh. No one in the village made me show my paper, or even in the market town, Lady be thanked—because if I had had to, my false name would have raised uncomfortable questions. But at Sliagh, they did ask for the parchment.

Now I was too uncomfortable to make that journey. I wanted to. Maybe I'd find Ivor. Maybe he had news. I was too far along, though. I didn't dare leave the village. Maire thought she knew when I'd maybe give birth, but none of us knew for certain, of course, no matter how experienced.

I was sick with worry about Wat, but also worried about the farm. It was past time to do the planting, but I was so ungainly I had a hard time getting out in the fields. I didn't want to mention this to Maire. She and Siobhan were already doing so much for me, and they had their own worries. One of their other sisters was a priestess of the Child of Sea, and she'd had to go into hiding.

While our village wasn't very much affected, Audemar's men garrisoned just outside Sliagh had become more active. His official there had taken over the town beadle's building and was beginning to enforce Audemar's laws the way he thought those laws should be enforced—not the usual ways in these parts, the long-held mixture of faint lip service paid to the king's law coupled with a strong body of local practice going back to their grandfathers' and their grandfathers' grandfathers' time. I called to mind the official as I'd seen him on market day, when he'd had me mark the parchment with my X. Some stolid nondescript sweaty fellow. But now he was in charge.

One day, as I looked out over the fields from our dooryard, I decided I'd have to do the planting, or the baby and I would starve. I made my way out to the shed to see what implements we had. I remembered that when I was a child, our whole village turned out for the plowing. The plow was brought over from the place it had been stored for the winter, and the village men would all help out. I remember watching my father following the team of oxen, guiding the plow so that its blade would bite down into the newly warmed soil. And then back over the furrow, to gouge it deeper. And back again. My father the earl. I knew him as my father the unsuccessful poverty-stricken farmer. He never complained. I blinked back tears, remembering his tenderness toward all of us, and thinking of how brutally he and my mother had been cut down on our own doorstep.

As for Wat and I, the two of us were likely to prove just as unsuccessful as my father. Wat and I had no ox. I thought of our old ox Millicent with longing. Millicent had pulled our player's wagon from one town to the next. At each, we had set up a stage on top. Wat juggled. I sang. And Wat passed secret messages to the members of the Rising. Later on, so did I.

After Diera's coronation and exile, when Wat and I had escaped to this remote village, we arrived after planting season. The former tenants on our place had done a poor job of it with their assigned furrow, so we had had to make do with little.

What now? Did all the village men work together here as they had done in my childhood village far across the water? I looked around me in despair. Our shed was bare, or nearly so. I saw a hoe that I remembered using the year before, and little else. There was a rough bench in the shed. I sank down on it, suddenly exhausted. My eyes roved over the bareness of the shed, avoiding the rucked up soil in the corner where, I knew, the assassin's body lay buried. I must have sat there a long time, my mind wandering.

I shook my head to clear it. From outside, someone was calling my name. I hoisted myself off the bench and went to the door. It was Maire and her husband, Seon. Maire rushed up to me. "What are you doing out here, cara?" she said, using our name, mine and Wat's, not realizing. I couldn't help it. I teared up. "Now then, come to the fire and warm yourself. It's still chill out here. You need to be off your feet." She led me toward the house. Over my shoulder I saw Seon looking things over. "Seon is here about the plowing," said Maire. "It's time for our fields to get plowed, you know."

"I do, but Wat and I have no ox," I said.

"Yes, but the village team is here to do our furrows—Siobhan's, ours, yours. Wat helped out with the feeding of the team, as all of us have, and when he left, he made sure he paid good coin to keep your place in the field rotations. Seon and the others are bringing the oxen and plow over today. So don't worry, Mirin. Your job is to stay healthy and have that baby. Later you can get out in the fields and work with the oats and barley. There's plenty of time for that."

I was overwhelmed with relief.

"You know," said Maire, peering at me and pinching my cheek down to look into my eye. "You're very agitated, aren't you? I'm thinking your time is almost here. That's what we women do, start fretting about undone tasks, start bothering around, especially when our time draws near." She placed her hand on my belly. "Oh, my," she said. "The baby has dropped. Are you having any pains, cara?"

"Nothing much. A few twinges," I said.

"Pains in your back?" she asked.

I nodded unwillingly. Now that the baby was about to be born, I didn't want it to happen. I was a little bit crazy, I suppose. Deep down, I thought, *Stay inside me where it's safe, little baby.* Foolish thinking. Nothing was going to stop nature taking its course with me.

As I let Maire examine me by my hearth, I thought back to my apprenticeship with Old Cwen, the healer. We did help pregnant women and women giving birth, but we weren't midwives. The midwives called on us for the potions and cures they needed. What they did with them after we handed them over was a mystery to me. I'm sure Old Cwen knew all about it. I think she'd been a midwife when she was younger. I knew little. I knew what was about to happen to me, but not the finer points.

"This baby wants to come out into the world," said Maire. Her words filled me with dread. "It will be fine, Mirin. You'll see," said Maire, placing a reassuring hand on my arm.

Maire was right about the baby. The next day, I began to feel the pains in earnest. She had been so sure of it that she insisted on staying the night with me so I wouldn't have to go trekking across the fields to Siobhan's house to send word. Siobhan came later in the day, and a few other women. They made me as comfortable as they could. I was frightened.

"No need to be scared, cara," said Maire, after poking around my body. "You look to be doing exactly what the Children made you to do."

"It hurts," I whispered.

"I know, but you can breathe in a certain way to get through the pains." She showed me how. It did help. The waves of pains kept coming and got harder. There was a crisis point where I really didn't know where I was—everything distilled into a single endless moment and a single endless task: getting through the next wave. Then, when I thought I couldn't bear it one more moment, my body took over. I swear to the Nine it turned itself inside out.

The women gathered around to soothe me. I heard a lusty cry. Soon they were cradling my daughter into my arms and smiling at me and giving me little nudges of encouragement. I put the baby to my breast, and she began to nurse.

"A strong girl!" Maire exclaimed. "A strong healthy baby from this strong mother."

"What will you name her?" asked Siobhan.

I was lying back in the fleeces, exhausted and happy, while they cleaned me and the baby up. They took her from me briefly and swaddled her, then handed her back. I lay with her in the crook of my arm, gazing down at her. I had no idea what I'd name her. Anyone would think that all this time I should have been thinking of names, but I hadn't. I'd had too many worries. I think I almost didn't believe in her. Until now. And here she was.

I put out a finger and touched her on her tiny nose, marveling at the delicate eyelashes, the rosebud of her mouth. And her hair.

And her hair.

I looked up at my friends and neighbors blankly. "She has red hair."

"She's one of the Fire Child's own, for sure," said Siobhan, squeezing my hand. She reached over and pulled a corner of the swaddling down so I could see my baby's shoulder. "Here's Her mark." A birthmark stood out on my baby's fair, delicate skin, a mark that looked like a flame.

But I was astounded. No one in my family had red hair. No one in Wat's, I didn't think. Wat and his brothers were as blond as could be, ranging from Avery's tawny to Wat's, the color of ripe barley out in the fields. Only Diera was dark-haired, and her father, the murdered crown prince Artur. Audemar, they say, is fair-haired. Wat told me once that his little brother Aedan had had hair as golden as his mother's. As for my side of the family, my father's hair was dark. My mother's hair was a light, lovely honey shade, and so was my sister's. I'd always thought of my own hair as mouse-brown and dull, but Wat used to run his fingers through it, calling it spun bronze.

*Used to.*

I got weepy then. But I needed to think of a name. A name for a red-headed girl.

"Keera is a good name for the Fire Child's own. It means *fiery red*," said Maire.

"I'll call her Keera," I said quickly, blinking the tears back.

Siobhan put her hand on the baby's head and spoke a few quiet words, praying to the Children. She commended my daughter to Fire Child and Sea Child, naming her Keera and dedicating her to the Children.

One of the other women had cooked up a nourishing gruel for me. After making sure my baby and I were well, they all quietly took their leave. Maire promised to come by daily until I got my strength back.

After Keera and I were alone together, I sighed out a prayer of my own to Sea Child and Fire Child, thanking them for the blessing of kind neighbors. I hardly ever prayed. This time I did.

But Keera and her flame-colored hair. That was a mystery. I started to worry. Suppose Wat thought the child was not his, when he came home? Suppose Keera and her red hair gave the village gossips new reasons for their suspicions, despite the loyal support of Siobhan and her family?

When Wat left, he hadn't known I was having a baby. I remembered the time we stopped trusting each other, and the disastrous results. What would he think when he got back?

When he got back.

*If he got back.*

I held Keera close to me in the firelight and worried and pondered and thought. I was too weak to get up and go after my rebec, hanging by its strap on a peg by the door. That's what I usually did when I was troubled, play my rebec. Now instead I sang to Keera, sang her a lullaby. She opened her blue eyes and gazed into mine. I thought I'd never known such love. Her eyes wandered to a spot just past my shoulder and a tiny frown creased her brows as she fastened her eyes there. She looked fascinated.

"What are you looking at, baby?" I cooed to her. Her eyes came back to mine. Should babies be able to do this so early, focus on something this intently? Mine could.

I realized I knew little of babies. I realized I'd have to learn, and learn fast.

I began singing to her again. But pretty soon I was singing that sad song. *I saw the old moon yester night with the new moon in his arms. If you sail out to sea, my love . . . I* couldn't finish the verse for crying.

Then I stopped.

Keera was crying too. But not because she was sad.

This child was hungry. I was a mother now, and I had work to do.

# Midsummer Moon

By midsummer, Wat had not returned. Sometimes I thought about traveling to Sliagh to see if I could hear any news of the war, but the risk was too great. Besides, Ivor had disappeared. As the moon waxed and waned through its turnings, officious parties of scarlet-clad soldiers and officials were showing up with Audemar's edicts and pronouncements, even in our little village.

Meanwhile, Keera was growing lusty and strong. She had not known a single day of sickness. Her lungs were great. She'd let out a howl the moment she was hungry.

"Are you going to be a singer, too, my darling?" I'd say to her, crooning and cuddling her while she nursed. I'd sing songs to her. When I rocked her in the cradle Seon had brought over for her, one that his and Siobhan's own babies had used, I played soft lullabies to her on my rebec. I avoided the sad song, the one about the halcyon bird. I believed in luck, not demons, but still a superstitious shudder would run up my spine when I sang of drowning and shipwreck. If, around the village fires, anyone started spinning tales of the blue sea-demons out beyond the rolling breakers underneath the cliffs, I turned away and found some task to keep me busy and out of earshot.

Yet I kept fingering the carving my father had made so long ago on the neck of my rebec. The fisher bird, the sign of the Sea Child my protector. I hadn't known the other name for my protector bird was halcyon, after the grief-stricken wife Alcyone, the woman in the song. I did know the fisher bird was a good spirit of rivers and seas, not the demonic naiad that people in my old village used to think such birds were, in disguise. Around here, the people didn't know about naiads, but they did have stories of frightening sea-demons called murdúchann who would lure you to your death beneath the waves. And there were stories further north and east, stories about the malevolent Blue Men of the straits. Of course I didn't believe these stories.

Did I?

The daily round of village life went on. I was able to offer my skills as a healer to several in the village, and I felt it was payment in kind for the generous treatment Siobhan, Maire, and their sisters had given me during my own time of need. The other people of the village looked on me with a friendly eye. I felt the irony of it. I was nineteen years old. Only five years earlier, my own mother had played a similar role in the village where I grew up, in the Riverlands on the mainland, where she and my father lived as refugees from Audemar's violence and cruelty.

Now it was my turn to seek refuge from his malice.

The gentle round of village events gave me solace. I'm sure my poor mother must have experienced something similar. Alone and with a baby to take care of, I withdrew from many of the activities that Wat and I had enjoyed together. As spring made the turn into summer, I got out less and less. I realized I was becoming a kind of recluse. I didn't want to go anywhere or do anything. Keera was my whole world.

But Midsummer's Eve was a big event in this little village. Siobhan walked over across the fields to make sure I knew to come to the celebration. The celebration rotated from village to village of the Hundred, and this year it was our village's turn to serve as host. All of the villages in the Hundred would assemble in the fields stretching between my isolated little cottage and the first houses of our own village. "It's important to gather around the Midsummer Eve bonfire, so that the crops will grow and the harvest will be bountiful," Siobhan told me. "It's especially important for you, because it's the Fire Child's celebration, and Keera needs to be there." I wasn't sure I believed that. Maybe Siobhan just wanted to get me out and around people. Still, I agreed to go, and to bring Keera with me.

I put Keera in a sling across my chest on the day when the summer sun rose high in the sky and never did seem to set. As I walked with her under the luminous sky of Midsummer Eve across the fields to the big cleared place of celebration just outside the village, I picked up downed branches and twigs to add to the fire. That's what Siobhan had told me to do.

Everyone gathered for the lighting of the fire, and everyone brought fuel to feed it. Keera's eyes grew big at the sight of the flames, and she held out her chubby little hands to the warmth. The whole village feasted. Family after family from our own village sent a child or wife or husband over to me and Keera, where we sat on the green, to bring us good things to eat. I was touched. But something about their kind behavior chilled me, too. This is what people did to comfort widows. I was losing hope of Wat's return, and as I could see in their faces, they too believed he would not be coming back. Some of them believed him dead. Others, I could tell, thought he'd abandoned me.

As the flames burned bright and families huddled close, one after another of the most accomplished musicians rose to sing. A few had instruments. One man had brought his pipe. Another had a small finger-drum. I sat plucking the strings of my rebec softly. Siobhan came to sit with us, me and Keera.

"Play for us," she urged me. Of course she and the other women had heard me play and sing. Some of the men must have, too, at our friendly gatherings. But I'd never stood before all the assembled villages in the Hundred to perform.

I put aside my shyness and did it. Handing Keera to Siobhan, I stepped before the fire. I glanced over at Keera, where the firelight played over her small face. She turned her eyes to mine. I could swear she knew what I was thinking and what I was about to do. Siobhan jiggled her on her knee and gave me an encouraging smile.

I was oddly nervous. Me, a professional performer! I hadn't played for a crowd in quite a while now. But as I drew my bow across the strings of my rebec, the old feeling came rushing back as if it had never left me. I was filled with a kind of power. I began to play. As I played, I sent up a prayer to Sea Child and Fire Child. *Sea Child, bring Wat back to me across the waves. Fire Child, bring this poor babe's father back to her.*

And now I opened my mouth to sing, and the words poured out of me. I sang with all my heart. I sang fearing the tears would run down my cheeks, but I couldn't care about that. I had to sing.

> *I saw the old moon yester night*
> *with the new moon in his arms;*
> *if you sail out to sea, my love,*
> *you'll never more come home.*

While I sang, the fire began to burn low. As I finished, villagers in twos and threes came up to the fire to gather some of the ashes. Tomorrow they'd scatter them on their fields to ensure a good crop. Few left without stopping to tell me how much my song touched them, and to lay a friendly hand on my arm.

The last were Siobhan and Maire. The light had finally faded to a kind of silver twilight, but now a fat bright moon had risen beyond the sea cliffs, shining its benign countenance over us all. In the moonlight and the dim light of the embers, young men leapt over the fire to show off their courage, and young women did, too, to make sure they'd be fertile.

Siobhan and Maire both pulled me into their arms and held me close. They were moved, and they saw how moved I was.

Then they stepped back, and we three stood in the waning firelight, three friends who had been through an ordeal together, bringing new life into the world, and had come through it unscathed. The object of our admiration slept soundly as we gazed at her, her tiny face puckered up rosy in the dim red light when Maire pulled aside her covering to exclaim softly over her perfection.

Siobhan looked past us to the leapers at the fire and laughed. "I'm thinking many of those men showing off their courage may well attract the eyes of many of those women hoping for fertility. I'm thinking it's more than the bonfire will do the job for them. But now," she said, turning back to me, "Come with me and Maire. A lucky Midsummer's Eve we have this year, the moon shining so bright. We're going in search of Child's Flower." At my look of confusion, she explained. "It's a tiny golden flower, good for healing. You see it all about. But some say, if you pick it during the full of the moon, the healing will be even better. And a full moon at Midsummer's Eve? Luckier still, the best of all. You're a healer, Mirin. You need some of these lucky flowers for your potions."

I settled Keera more securely against me in her sling. Arm in arm, we women picked our way over the furrows in the bright moonlight to the edge of the forest in search of Child's Flower.

I came back home with a pouch full of the precious herb. Keera had slept peacefully through the entire thing. We women exchanged a Midsummer Eve kiss, and I watched Siobhan and Maire head back across the field to their own cottages. Now I pushed open my door and knelt to nestle Keera in her cradle.

I made ready for bed myself. The glow I felt from the evening was fading now. It was a cold bed I crept into, without Wat. I thought I'd never get used to it, not finding his long body there beside mine. I thought of the terrible years I spent away from him in Caedon's cell, all the misunderstandings and bitterness of those days. Then a joyous reconnection. Now this emptiness. I fell asleep with the tears not yet dry on my cheeks.

The next morning I woke and nursed Keera. I put her into her sling and prepared to go out into the fields to weed and hoe, and to shoo away any troublesome birds or animals intent on taking my crop for themselves. In the doorway, I shaded my eyes. A movement from across the fields caught my attention. Just three men stumbling their way over the furrows in my direction. I paid them little mind. As the embers had died the night before, a lot of drunken carousing had broken out. So now I thought these men were only revelers making for their homes to sleep off their Midsummer Eve's headaches. I figured they'd probably just roused themselves from the furrows where they had dropped in a stupor late last night.

I made my way out to our own furrows, jouncing Keera on my hip. She made soft cooing noises at the rustle of the barley, beginning to stand tall. I was examining one of the ripening heads when something about the men nearing me put me on alert. I squinted against the light, resting on my hoe. That's when, shading my eyes, I made out the bright scarlet of the cloaks.

Soldiers. I stood frozen for an instant, my heart pounding. Soldiers. A vision of the red-cloaked men who had cut my parents down outside our cabin in my childhood village flashed into memory.

I whirled and hurried back toward my cottage, clutching Keera to my breast. *So much for my second sense,* I thought grimly. It had given me no warning this time. I barred the door behind me and put Keera in her cradle. She fussed at the unaccustomed flurry. I only hoped she wouldn't start to bawl at the wrong moment. Darting to our one window, I saw the stumbling figures coming nearer.

Now I threw off overdress and kirtle, pulling on a pair of Wat's trousers and one of his tunics, wrapping a long woven belt several times around me to keep the trousers from tripping me. I hiked up one trouser leg to reveal my scabbard that I kept always strapped against the outside of my right leg, and I pulled out the long knife I kept concealed there. Not Diera's precious one. I kept that one wrapped in a hiding place dug out beneath the far wall of our cabin.

But this knife, the one in my scabbard, was the one I kept honed and ready for business. I reached for a short sword Wat and I had hung over the door. With the sword in my left hand, the knife in my right, I sidled along the cottage wall to the window, so that I could peer out without being seen. I was frightened, yes, but my training had taken over, shoving the fright someplace deep inside, where it couldn't get in my way.

Three of them. Three red-clad soldiers, one walking tall, the other supporting his wounded fellow. They were almost to the cottage.

Could I take three? Torrin and Lorel, my companions in the Rising, had trained me well in the art of the knife, but during this last peaceful year, especially during my pregnancy, I had gone woefully out of practice. I reminded myself of the enforced practice Wat and I had had with our would-be assassin. Still— I looked again out the window slit— three of them.

Maybe these men only wanted shelter for their wounded comrade. Maybe I could offer it, and then they'd go. No violence. But in the moment I was thinking this other choice through, I realized I couldn't risk it, not with Keera there in her cradle. I'd heard too many stories about what such men did when they came across lonely undefended cottages.

I made a snap decision many would call dangerous. They'd be wrong. I knew what I was doing. Quietly, I unbarred the door.

The soldiers came onto the beaten dirt around our cottage and looked about them. One of them ducked into the shed where we kept our tools and came back out. "No one here," I heard him call out to the others.

"Smoke rising from the roof hole," said another. "Someone in there."

"Only a woman, that woman we spotted across the fields," I heard another of them say. Their voices were loud. They were just outside.

*They're going to come in here*, I thought. Three of them. But one is wounded, and I have the advantage of surprise.

I moved to the door and stood behind it.

As the first one shouldered his way in, I darted from behind the door and drove my knife upward underneath his rib cage and twisted the knife into the meat of him. I knew the spot. I could smell him, the sweaty maleness, and then the fear and horror. And then the sickening sweet smell of blood. He fell, making a strange gargling noise, my knife with him. I tossed the short sword from my left to my right hand, silently thanking our old companion Conal, one of the Six, for all his drilling. Some might think I should have been offering up a prayer of thanks to the Children. I offered up instead a prayer of thanks to my dead mentor Conal.

The fellow supporting the wounded soldier came in after the first man. He blinked stupidly into the dim interior of our cottage, his eyes dazzled at the quick change from bright sun. When he saw me crouched in front of him, he gave a bark of surprise. He was trying to extricate himself from his wounded comrade and reach for his own sword when I slashed him across the face. As he lifted an arm to fend me off, I drove the sword under his armpit, and he too fell. I sliced down across the place in his neck where I knew the lanes of blood ran, the ones that spurt red blood that can't be stopped, and his life's blood spattered me. He went sagging down across the doorway. Now I stepped across the two bodies to the wounded soldier, who had fallen against the door frame, his eyes wide. I slashed him across the neck, and the red blood spurted from him, too.

I moved so silently and so fast that Keera didn't let out so much as a wail.

Now I stood heaving over the three bodies, the heavy iron smell of blood mingling with the stench of their piss and bowels. Beyond them, out the door, I could see slashes of scarlet beginning to come into the fields.

*Nine Spheres*, I thought. *I can't take on Audemar's entire army.*

Reaching down, I wiped off the blade of my sword on the nearest dead soldier's cloak. I reached overhead to grab down Wat's spare baldric off its peg, then harnessed the sword across my back, slanting to the left, where I could reach for it fast with my right hand. I belted the baldric under my arm and buckled it. Then I worked my knife free of the first soldier, who still lay twitching and dying on the floor. *Why won't you die?* I said to him. I don't think I said these words aloud. I had to move too fast to be horrified by him. Or by myself.

I wiped the knife off on him and settled it back into its scabbard, making sure it was securely fastened to the outside of my right leg. I adjusted Wat's trousers to hide it. Then I ran to Keera and scooped her up into her sling. Now she did wail. I'd have to get out. I'd have to try to run for it.

Again I thought of my parents. The scarlet soldiers, burning down our cabin at home. The bodies of my parents. They'd tried to run. They were trying to shield Jillie, and it slowed them. *Your father was the best we had.* Torrin's words came back to me then. *He wouldn't have let some common soldier cut him down. But he had your mother and your sister to protect . . .*

I pushed the memory away. I knew I had to try, for the sake of my daughter. For Wat's sake, if he were still alive somewhere.

What I didn't know was this. The soldiers hadn't come for me; they hadn't even come to commit crimes against some random defenseless villager. They themselves were fleeing. Here's what I was witnessing: the aftermath of a terrible battle, Audemar the usurper against his own man, his best general, turned against him. That man was Caedon, my old enemy.

Caedon's forces had landed in the same moonlight that had illuminated our village singing and dancing, the night before—landed in the bay underneath the sea cliffs. Then his men had silently quick-marched inland, scything up behind Audemar's army encamped outside Sliagh. At dawn, they'd attacked. The surprise attack decimated Audemar's army out here on the frontiers of his realm.

I expect at court everyone told some rousing tales of heroism and chivalry about that battle.

I was there. I saw how it really was.

The survivors of Audemar's broken army were fleeing across the fields, trying just as hard to stay alive as I was. Their clothing was just as blood-soaked as mine.

I knew I couldn't outrun an entire army. Instead, I tried to blend in. I ran with them, my breath coming in ragged gasps. I tried to keep to the fringes of the running men, looking for any opportunity to peel off into the trees, but so far we were still in the open fields.

Some fellow behind me caught up with me and grabbed me by the shoulder, nearly pitching me forward into a furrow. I realized then that, in trying to keep Keera safe as I ran, I wasn't thinking about my sword and drawing it to defend myself. Or my knife, either. I thought at the time that this same impulse probably killed my parents.

I've thought about it since, though, and I've changed my mind. Being burdened with Keera probably saved my life, because it forced me to use my wits instead of my weapons. Back at the cottage, the weapons had given me the advantage. Out here, I had none.

"Girl, what in the name of all the Dark Ones are you doing here?" the man said, shaking me roughly.

"I'm Gruffyd's bondswoman," I told him, one knee into the soil, trying to catch my breath, trying to shelter Keera. I reached up my left hand to him, showing him Caedon's brand burned into my wrist. I took a chance he wouldn't recognize it. If he was Audemar's man, he probably wouldn't. "This is his son." My acting skills kicked in. I wove an entire story around this imaginary soldier, Gruffyd, right there on the spot. "Gruffyd is wounded. We got separated. I'm trying to catch up to him, bring him bandages and his extra sword," I told him over Keera's outraged howls. I checked her quickly. She seemed fine, probably just frightened by my jarring fall into the field.

The man who'd stopped me heard my accent. Somehow he believed my story. The brand helped, I suppose, because every army has its camp followers. I knew many of the more well-off soldiers in Audemar's army brought bondswomen along to look after them and comfort them in bed.

"Run, then," he told me. "Caedon's men are just be-hind us." He sped past me.

That's when I knew. The civil war between Audemar and Caedon had erupted into our own peaceful fields. I stood frozen with terror for a moment. Then I scrambled back to my feet, ignoring the stinging of my scraped knees and palms, and sent up a prayer to the Sea Child. This man had believed me. He'd believed in my fictional Gruffyd. The Sea Child was on my side. Or luck, more likely. I might not be so lucky next time.

We were coming off the fields and toward a wooded area. As soon as I could, I headed into a thicket and bent down, gasping, a hand to my side, trying to catch my breath and hoping I hadn't been noticed. I had to think. If these men were running as fast as they were, that meant the man who'd grabbed me was right, Caedon's men were just behind.

Caedon's men. I remembered what kind of people they were, the kinds of things they knew. If they caught sight of Caedon's brand, they might understand what it meant. Whether they did or not, I knew that if these pursuers caught me, it would be over for me. Over for Keera before she'd even had a chance to live.

How much shelter would this thicket give us? I looked around in a panic.

Keera was beginning to wail again. A mammoth tree towered at the edge of the thicket where we crouched, and it was hollow. I leaned down to grab up a branch and poked it into the hollow to make sure no serpent or other noisome creature was within. Then I dragged more downed branches and foliage over, to make a quick sort of barricade before the opening. Anyone who peered into the thicket wouldn't see the hollow, barricaded with leaves and greenery, or not so easily, not unless they were looking closely. I crept inside, pulling the barricade back over the opening after me.

In the dim green, I pulled up my tunic and nursed Keera. That quieted her. Her tiny mouth worked. I gazed down into her face as her eyelids fluttered and then closed. I nestled her close. Then I leaned back against the inside of the tree-trunk, enveloped by the funk of mold and foliage and damp, cradling Keera and trying to still my breathing and my pounding heart. That's when I realized. I had left my rebec in our cottage.

There was no help for it. We'd survived, and the rebec was gone. Diera's beautiful dagger, too. I put these things, mere objects, resolutely out of mind. This moment, this present moment, was the important thing. We had to get through it, Keera and I.

We dozed for a while, propped up in our makeshift shelter. Loud noises woke us, screams and groans. Keera begin to whimper again, so I put her to the breast. I'd seen enough of war to know what I was hearing. Caedon's men had caught up with Audemar's. Caedon's men were finishing off the wounded and the slow. Now was the most critical time. They'd be looking for hiders and stragglers. The butchery seemed to go on forever as I cowered with Keera in our place of concealment. Several times there were blundering and slashing noises at the edges of the thicket where we hid. I unsheathed both weapons and laid them within easy reach. In the end, though, silence settled back over the fields. Caedon's men were rushing on after the retreating army they'd defeated. These fields were behind them now.

I couldn't count on being alone, though. The thicket was a good hiding place. Others may have found it, too—Audemar's soldiers, the few lucky ones who had escaped the carnage. It was twilight now. Several times I heard crashing in the underbrush and shrank back further into my hollow, making sure Keera was secured against me in her sling and that my weapons were ready to hand.

It grew darker. Even then I waited. I didn't want to flounder around in the deceiving midsummer twilight. But I knew the moon was soon to rise, a blessing with its light and also a curse.

I knew it had risen at last when the leafy covering of my barricade gave off an eerie green glow. Trying to make as little noise as possible, I began shifting the branches aside. Keera sound asleep against me, I crawled from the hollow and steadied myself against the tree trunk. Working the kinks out of my cramped legs, I stumbled to my feet. Keera made a small noise, but she didn't wake. I rocked her gently in her sling.

Everything was still. I crept to the edge of the thicket and stood looking out over the fields stretching between me and the village. It was hard to make sense of what I was seeing, at first. There was a heaving, wavering motion over the entire field. I thought *Ghosts of the dead*, but that was silly. As I waited and watched, I realized what I was seeing: wolves, foxes, other animals, worrying at the corpses and ripping them apart. Carrion creatures.

They were busy. They wouldn't bother me. I edged my way down the fields, circling back toward the village the long way around.

Before I'd gotten close, I knew what I was about to find. The feeling of dread grew stronger the closer I came. I smelled smoke.

When I stepped into the outskirts of the village, I was the only one there in the moonlight. A few bodies lay half in, half out of still-smoking cottages and cabins that the retreating soldiers had fired. We were lucky, Wat and I, that our cottage was on the remote edge of the village overlooking the sea cliffs. Otherwise I knew Keera and I would have been among the slain. I had had warning. They'd had none. As I reached Siobhan's cottage, I braced myself. I could tell one of the bodies huddled there was Siobhan. I could tell by her long streaming hair, silvery in the moonlight. I made my way over to her and reached down to touch her, just in case, but she was cold. Across the lane, bodies strewed the yard around Maire's cottage as well. My friends. My neighbors. People who had become dear to me lying dead and stiffening. I crouched for a long time beside them, paying them tribute in my mind and heart, holding Keera close to me. In that place of death, she slept peacefully against me in her sling. If not for Keera, I think I would have sat there forever, sat until I turned into stone and weathered away with the others back to the earth we were all of us shaped from.

But there was Keera. I forced myself to rise. Stifling the sobs rising into my throat, I made my way across the tongue of field that separated our cottage from theirs. Smoke rose from our stove-in thatch. I felt numb. For five years, this had been my life, one burned out cottage after another, starting with the place where I grew up.

Ghosts were not haunting our fields, but I felt like a ghost myself, the only moving thing in a landscape of death and destruction.

I paused at the door to our cottage, startled at the little pile of bodies there. Then understanding jolted me. These were the soldiers I'd killed. I, Mirin Far-Meadow. Lady Mirin of the High Sea Cliffs. I was part of the death and destruction. I pushed past the bodies into the interior of our cottage. Everything there was ruined and burnt. Everything but one object.

A shaft of moonlight illuminated it as it hung on its peg, untouched. My rebec.

A shiver ran up my spine. How could this be? But I reached over, retrieved it, slung it over my shoulder, and stepped back out of the cottage, back over the bodies of the three dead men. No point in looking for anything else. All of our clothing, everything we had, the furs, the fleeces, the bedstead—all was a black, smoldering pile. Diera's dagger was without a doubt safe in its hiding place, but I left it there, hoping to come back for it someday. I never have. It's probably still there. Someone in ages to come may find it buried under the rubble of my cottage's stone wall, who knows? May find it and wonder what such a rich and beautiful object was doing in such poor and squalid surroundings. I committed it to Sea Child and Earth Child in tribute to its beautifully etched fisher-bird and blackbird, and murmured a thanksgiving. I threw in Fire Child just to make sure I'd covered them all. True, there's also the Sky Child, but where She dwells is a mystery beyond the vastness of the Great Sea to the west, and I don't know much about Her.

I did know one thing, the only important thing. Keera and I were alive.

And now where would I go? I asked myself this. With no real goal in mind, I headed in the opposite direction of the armies.

As I looked back over my shoulder at the still-smoking village, only one thought comforted me, the comfort of certainty. If I hadn't killed those soldiers, they would surely have killed me. Child forgive me, I didn't know that when I struck out at them. Was Wat ever coming home to me? I didn't know. But the families of those three, somewhere across the water missing their men? Those men were never heading home to the love of wife and child.

It does something to you, when you see a lot of death and you're very young. Maybe it had hardened me in destructive ways. Taking a last look back at the ruined little village, I realized I didn't know. I realized I wanted a better place for my daughter. I realized that she and I lived in a hard world where that better place might never come to pass.

It was going on dawn as Keera and I picked our way down the lane away from the village. Behind us, the first of the carrion birds were just beginning to settle on the corpses to feed.

# Hope and Despair

I'd been on the road for a few candle measures. Getting past Sliagh, I now saw, was going to be more difficult than I imagined. The camps of Audemar were not empty, as I had supposed. Instead, they were newly occupied by the army of Caedon.

Still, hundreds and hundreds of refugees streamed down the roads and lanes leading to and past Sliagh, so I could only hope Keera and I would blend in. My heart sank when I saw, outside Sliagh, several wagons blocking the roadway and soldiers in black, Caedon's color, with Caedon's golden wolf's head insignia on their shoulders, checking the parchments of those traveling past. Some of the travelers were being herded into a small area, guarded.

I thought about what those parchments said. *Are you a loyal subject of our High King Audemar?* his official had asked on that day so many turnings of the moon earlier. If the answer was yes—and it had to be yes—the villager signed the paper or made a big x, as I had.

The Dark Ones must be laughing at that. Anyone who'd answered yes was now marked as a traitor to Caedon.

I didn't have my bit of parchment with me. I had left it behind in the cottage. Was that a good thing, or a bad thing? Or both?

I didn't want to find out. I started looking around for some concealment, trees, whatever it might be, so I could make my way around the town rather than straight past it on the roadway.

Someone ahead of me had the same idea. I stopped and squinted against the sunlight, watching the man ease his way toward the edge of the road. And off it. And across a little cleared area toward some woods. As I watched, a detachment of mounted soldiers swept out from the checkpoint and rode him down. They caught him and bound him and hauled him along toward the checkpoint. He was half-running behind them on his rope, half-being dragged.

I saw I'd have to take my chances at the checkpoint.

*No one should pay me any mind*, I thought. *I'm just a lone ragged woman with a baby.*

*In men's clothes*, I reminded myself. *Blood-soaked.*

Then I realized. Although I had left the shortsword behind me in my burned-out cottage, knowing how obvious it looked and how much it had slowed me down during my flight across the fields, I still had the knife strapped to my calf. I bent down, as if to adjust something, and then squatted on the verge of the road, nursing my baby. No one paid any attention to me. I undid the sash belting my tunic high and kicked it behind me into the weeds. Now Wat's big tunic billowed down almost like a kirtle. Under cover of that, I worked my knife's sheath off my leg and discarded it, with its knife, too, in the same weed patch. I felt a hard pang of regret. It was a good knife, well balanced and sharp, the weight exactly right for me. But there was no help for it. It would endanger me, and Keera, too, if I were caught with it. I wriggled out of the trousers and left them behind as well. I almost looked like an ordinary woman now, a bare-legged woman in a baggy kirtle, maybe a poor beggar woman with no other clothing to her name. *Good*, I thought.

I got up, strapped Keera more closely about me in her sling, and strode quickly away, not looking back. No one cried after me. No one noticed.

*Time for some first-class acting*, I told myself.

When I reached the checkpoint, one soldier was pushing everyone into a line. I waited, trying to look obedient and vacant.

When my turn came, I stepped up to the soldier in charge and stared into his face.

"Name?" he said.

I said nothing.

"Name?" he said again. "Your parchment?"

"Cara," I said in a wispy voice.

"Mistress, are you bleeding? How did this happen?"

I just stared at him.

"What do we do with this one?" he said over his shoulder to one of his fellows. "No parchment. Has a baby. Lots of blood. Look at the rags she's wearing."

"What this one must have seen," said the other soldier, maybe a bit more sympathetically. "Her whole family might have been killed before her eyes. Left her like this."

The first one nodded. I thought then they'd wave me on, but the second one stopped and stared harder. He lifted my left wrist and turned it to show the first one my brand. "Someone's bondswoman," he now said. "Come with me, goodwife." At least he didn't appear to recognize whose brand it was.

Again, I just stared at him. He grabbed me by the arm, although not very roughly, and half-led, half-pulled me over to an enclosed wagon at the side of the road. "Another bondswoman for your collection," he called to the man at the back. Between them, they got me through the canvas flaps and into the wagon, where they pushed me down onto a rough bench. Two benches ran the length of the wagon. They were packed with people. Men, women, children. And there we waited.

Keera began to fuss, and I tried to nurse her. But I had no more milk. I hadn't eaten in two days. As I sat there trying to soothe her, I began worrying that she might starve. I started to stand up, to try to make my way to the back and look out through the flaps, to ask for something to eat, but a hand shoved me back to my place on the bench. The man sitting beside me didn't look at me, just down at his feet, which were bare. "Don't, mistress. You'll call down a beating on yourself, maybe on us, too. Just wait," he said softly. "That's all the likes of us can do, wait until they find our masters or give us new ones. Maybe take us off and sell us for the coin."

"But my baby—" I began.

He just turned away from me and wouldn't say anything more to me.

We waited all that day with no bite to eat, nothing to drink. By the end of the day, the thirst was getting to me more than the hunger; more than both, the fear of what would become of Keera. First she had cried, lusty wailing that everyone ignored. Finally she settled into a continual low whimper. Now nothing at all, and the fear in me rose and rose. Yesterday, I'd worried about her urine-soaked

sling and what it might be doing to her tender skin. Today, I shivered with terror because her sling had become
stiff and dry.

Late in the day, the wagon began to lurch forward.
Through the gap in the flaps, I saw we were being taken
into Sliagh. There we were unloaded like so many head of
cattle. We were marched into a log enclosure where we
milled around. Some sat on the ground. I was feeling
weak, so that's what I did, too. Keera was silent. I cuddled
her close, whispering in her perfect rose-petal of an ear
how much I loved her. I wanted to whisper how I'd always
protect her, as I had done during our flight across the
fields, but now I couldn't manage even that much.

People started to arrive, looking us over. They were
masters who had lost their bondservants. A few left with
some of the ones in the enclosure. Not many. I figured
most of us were lost for good. Either our masters had
been killed or they didn't know where to look for us. Probably a number of us were bound to people in Audemar's
army, and of course they wouldn't come looking, if they
were even alive. Like Gruffyd, the imaginary master I'd
conjured up when I had taken flight and needed to explain my brand.

I wanted Gruffyd, or someone like him, to come into
the enclosure to claim me. Anyone. Anyone who would
feed me so I could feed Keera. I didn't care who it was or
whether they thought they had any legitimate claim to

me. *Anyone? Even Caedon?* a mocking voice whispered to me. To save my child's life? Yes, even that.

The mocking whispers continued. I started worrying I was beginning to see things that weren't there. Maybe I was going out of my head. My vision was swimming. *You must not faint. What would happen to Keera then?* the voices said.

I found a place over by the logs of the enclosure where I could lean against something solid.

Soon after, new people came into the enclosure. Well-dressed people, mostly men. As they circulated among us and examined us, I realized these people had come looking for bondservants; that we'd be given to these people. In the state I was then, I wanted that to happen. I tried to make myself look more alert, look more like someone some master would want, not a starveling who would promptly die on him.

Now here's the strange thing. Throughout the entire ordeal, I'd kept my rebec slung over my shoulder. I hadn't dropped it. No one had taken it from me.

"What about this one?" someone was saying. He cast a shadow over me and Keera. I shaded my eyes and squinted up at him.

"Oh, this one? No one knows who owns her, and she can't tell us. I think some bad thing happened to her. We found her like this, covered in blood. She can't say much. We think it's the shock," said another someone. I had seen this man walking the stockade. He appeared to be in charge.

"She has a baby," said the first someone. His voice sounded dubious.

"That's two for one, good sir. Feed her, and she and the infant will soon be doing well," said the man in charge.

"What's that she has?" The first someone leaned down to finger my rebec. I pulled it protectively away. I couldn't help myself.

"That's some kind of fiddle. We think she's an entertainer."

"Hmm. That would be an asset. Maybe I'll take her."

The two seemed to be agreeing on my fate, when footsteps announced that a third had walked up. I kept my eyes down, on Keera.

I heard a sharp intake of breath.

"Don't give that one away, good masters," said this third someone in a nasal, whining voice.

I froze. I knew that voice.

"Oh? And why not, may I ask?" That was the voice of the man in charge of the stockade.

"See that? That fiddle thing? Someone has been asking after a bondservant with a fiddle. Someone important wants that one, I tell 'ee."

My heart sank.

"What is your name?" said the man in charge, bending low over me.

"Cara," I muttered.

"That's not her name," the third someone said, the man with the high, whining voice. Ivor. "She's a little liar, she is. She does that, masters. Pretending to be high and mighty. Now pretending to be lowly. But look there, the general's own brand."

*General? What general? Caedon?*

The voice of the first man: "I do believe you're right, fellow."

*Take me! Take me, Master First Someone!* I was pleading, inside my head.

"Step away from this one, my masters," said Ivor. "I'll take her over to the manor. The general's been looking for 'ee." This he said directly to me, bending down until his face was right in mine. A smile twisted his lips. I stared up into his eyes.

"Traitor," I whispered to him. His smile widened.

Beyond Ivor's shoulder, the man in charge of the stockade peered down at me too. "You know that, do you, my man?" he said.

I looked up now from one to the other of these men, the man in charge and the one who wanted to take me with him. I tried to make myself look helpless, pleading. That wasn't hard to do. It took no acting skills at all.

The second man, the one who had wanted to take me, said to Ivor, "You've the right of it, I see. I'll look at some of these others." He walked away toward another knot of wretched captives in the stockade.

Ivor reached down and grasped me by the wrist. "I'll take her to his lordship, that I will," he told the man in charge. I tried to pull away from Ivor, but he gripped me harder, so hard I nearly cried out.

But the man in charge of the stockade was frowning at Ivor with distaste. "That you won't," he said to Ivor. Over Ivor's outraged screech, he said, "This woman is my responsibility, fellow. You can't just walk in here and take my captives."

"She's valuable, that she is. I'll take her," Ivor insisted.

"If she's valuable, all the more reason for me to keep her," said the man in charge. He put a hand on Ivor's shoulder and walked him protesting to the gate of the stockade. To a guard at the gate, I heard him say, "See this fellow doesn't come in again."

The man in charge of the stockade strolled back over to me and looked down at me where I sagged in relief against the logs of the stockade. "Valuable, eh," he said. He gave me a skeptical squint. "That I doubt. But we'll send you along with the others. Let his lordship's people sort you all out."

I didn't say anything. Anything I might say could change this man's mind, and I didn't want him to change it. Being sent away with dozens of others seemed a far safer fate than being taken away by Ivor. I stared down at

Keera. My rage against Ivor was building out of control. I felt my hands beginning to shake. I didn't want this man to see the ferocious anger I knew must be plain for all to see in my eyes.

Someone else came up to the man then, thank the Nine Spheres. As they moved away from me, I heard some of their muttered conversation. "Everyone in the Hundred coming in here hoping to grab a bondservant or two to sell for the coin . . ."

*Ivor*, I thought to myself, first with scouring rage and then with despair. If Ivor was ready and eager to betray me, what had he done with Wat on that night he was supposed to be securing safe passage across the sea? No wonder Ivor had never come to me with news. There might not have been any news to bring. He might have arranged for Wat to be killed, for all I knew.

*Wat can take care of himself,* I reminded myself. But it was little comfort. Wat trusted Ivor. I never had. Now I realized my second sense had been trying to tell me something dark about Ivor. But I hadn't paid enough attention.

As these thoughts besieged me, one of the stockade's people in Caedon's black hauled me up by the arm and led me to an open wagon where others were sitting on benches. This man got up on the wagon seat, urged his ox forward, and we jolted away down a road heading from the town up into the hills.

I closed my eyes. It was nearly twilight when we came to a manor up above Sliagh. We were unloaded and herded into a small stone shed. There they fed us. Small bowls of gruel for each and a single bucket of water with a dipper for all. I put my finger into the gruel and held it to Keera's lips. Her rosebud of a mouth worked. She sucked my finger. I did this again and again, saving some for myself in case I could make more milk for her, and I drank as much of the water as I could.

For the first time since early morning, she looked up into my eyes and began to squall. I put her to my breast, just to comfort her, and then I gave her more of the gruel.

*Three turnings of the moon, and I'm weaning you.* How I hated that. I cuddled her to me. She was eating. She would live. That gave me hope.

Now Keera had quieted. She was content. Everyone in the small crowded room was leaning back against the stone walls, preparing for an uncomfortable night, so I did the same. After all, I had spent many seasons in one of Caedon's cells. I could do it again if I had to, as long as Keera was eating.

Several days went by. I grew dirtier and more despairing by the day. But Keera was eating. She was growing stronger. I was even able to nurse her a little bit again. Not enough to keep her alive. My milk for her was drying up. But there was the gruel.

I learned from my fellow bondservants that we were indeed locked up in Caedon's manor here on the isle. During an earlier incursion into the heartland of the island, Audemar had taken it for himself from its owners and had had these owners executed. Now Caedon had driven Audemar from the island and had made the manor his.

In the chess game of the civil war he and Audemar were fighting, Caedon had taken possession of the island and had turned the entire north of the mainland into his stronghold, while Audemar held the south. Smaller realms on the edges of the mainland, such as the independent northern isles, had allied themselves with one or the other. And now the Western Isle was Caedon's.

Audemar appeared to be the one at a disadvantage. He was fighting on two fronts—Caedon to the north and west, and the forces of Diera and the Rising on the east. "What news of Diera's army?" I asked several in the stone shed, but no one seemed to know. After my first few attempts to gain information, I decided I had better stay quiet. I didn't want to identify myself as a sympathizer with the Rising. I still hoped for a chance to escape Caedon's notice. Surely he was too important now to look into the identities of a roomful of lowly unwashed bondservants. If I were lucky and kept my head down, he might never know I was here.

The very next day, little by little, the room emptied out. The master of Caedon's fields arrived to remove five of the lustiest men in the group. A woman in charge of domestic affairs at the manor came a few candle measures later to choose two of the women and depart with them. I looked after her hopefully. To be inside Caedon's manor, a place where Caedon himself might easily spot me—that was a frightening thought. More frightening still was not knowing how I'd take care of Keera. She was stronger, but I could see for myself she wasn't out of danger.

The woman didn't choose me. At the end of that day, I and a few of the others were the only ones left.

I fed the gruel to Keera that evening and was able to nurse her a little. I was preparing us for sleep when two of Caedon's servants came into the shed. One was the man who seemed to be in charge of us. One was a man I'd never seen before.

"See that woman?" said the stranger, pointing me out. "His Royal Highness wants to see her tomorrow early."

*His Royal Highness?* What in the Nine Spheres? But then I realized with dread he was speaking of Caedon, who had styled himself king now.

The servant in charge of us nodded, then closed and barred the door, as always, leaving me to stare into the dark, trembling over what bad thing the morning would bring.

I don't know what that thing might have been, because only a little while later, I heard the grating sound of the bar being drawn back from its brackets. The same servant, the one in charge of us, looked in, holding a rushlight high. "Is that the one, young master?" he said, pointing me out to the man with him, a tall man wrapped in a cloak.

"That's the one, I'm certain of it," said this tall man, speaking out of the sharp shadows cast by the rush light. As far as I could tell, he was a complete stranger to me. "What is your name, girl?"

"Cara," I said.

"Ah, yes. I remember now. That's the one," the stranger told the servant.

"Very well, then," the servant said. "There must have been some mistake. Knowing your good service to His Highness, I am sure you have the right of it. You may take her."

"Come with me, girl," said the stranger. "That's my own bastard," he remarked to the servant as I got to my feet, clutching Keera to me.

The servant peered down at Keera, then up at the stranger. "Oh, I see," he said, nodding.

The stranger guided me by the elbow out of the shed. He led me over to a wagon and helped me in. Then he climbed to the seat and took up the reins. As he did so, he bent down and gave the servant some coin, and the servant pulled his forelock respectfully.

"I thank you, Master Stefan," said the servant.

The servant's rushlight fell more directly on the stranger now. I stared over at this Master Stefan, and I saw what the servant had seen. Master Stefan's hair was fiery red. Like Keera's. Yet I had never set eyes on him before.

I didn't care. I felt a rush of relief. We were heading away from Caedon. That's all that mattered to me. If this man thought Keera was his baby, she'd be his baby.

Keera and I drowsed in the back of the wagon, I'm not sure for how long. By the time we reached another manor house, the moon was high, although not as full as it had been on Midsummer's Eve. The house, I saw, was not quite as grand as Caedon's but grand enough. It stood at the top of a hill overlooking the sea. In the silvery twilit midsummer night, I looked it over, wondering what was about to happen to us, me and Keera.

Master Stefan helped me down. I gazed up at him, baffled. "Time for questions later, Mirin. It's Mirin, isn't it?"

I nodded, a bright hope springing in me. Stefan must be part of the Rising, and they had found me and rescued us, Keera and me.

I was wrong.

"Time first to get you cleaned up and fed." He looked at me with distaste. "They nearly killed the two of you.

Starved and filthy." A servant had come from the manor's big doors to look after ox and wagon. "Send Goodwife Berit out to take charge of these two." Then he turned to me. "I'm your brother. Dark Ones take that Caedon. Father and I will see you tomorrow." He stepped into the house, leaving me gaping and stunned on the doorstep until Goodwife Berit bustled out and took Keera and me inside to baths, nourishing food, clean clothing, and later, sleep in a bed more luxurious than I had lain in for many a year. I didn't think I'd be able to sleep, but I did, the sleep of the exhausted and the safe.

# Chapter Six

# The Garden

In the morning, I sat with Keera in the big bedroom and sang to her, and nursed her. I didn't really have milk to give her any longer, but it comforted us both to try. I forced myself not to think too much about the puzzling events of the day before. I was away from Caedon. That's all that counted. Now I'd wait to see why this man thought I was his sister.

Of course I wasn't. My family had had only two children, two daughters. I was one, and Jillian was the other. Jillie was off with Diera across the Narrows in the Baronies. At least I hoped she was. When Diera had gone to war, moving with her army back across the Narrows to the Sceptered Isle, surely she would have left Jillie safely behind in the Baronies. Our parents had had no sons. But if this man, Master Stefan, thought he was my brother, and if that would keep me and Keera safe, I'd agree to any fantastical mad thing he'd tell me.

Just the same, a nagging thought kept intruding. *What about Keera's hair? Her fiery red hair? What about that?* I tried to drive this thought out of my head. It was merely a coincidence, I told myself. Somehow, it had led this man into a misapprehension. A misapprehension to our advantage. Now I'd simply have to wait and see what he and his father had to say to me. If they realized their mistake, though, and gave me back? The thought sent such chills up my spine that my teeth actually began to chatter.

The woman, Goodwife Berit, reappeared at the door to my room soon after, forestalling these morbid thoughts. She told me Master Stefan and his father awaited us in the main hall of the manor. She showed me to the hall. Cradling Keera in my arms, I made my way after her impressive starched and bustling figure.

Master Stefan and an older man, his father, I supposed, were seated in chairs together at the far end of the hall. Goodwife Berit made her curtsey to the two of them and backed out of the room. Between the two men and the place I stood with Keera in her sling, a low-banked fire in the hearth ring helped ward off the early-morning chill. I curtseyed as well.

"Come closer. Come over here to us," Master Stefan called to me. I complied. "Here they are, Father," he said to the older man.

This man, his father, was tall, like his son. His hair was white with evidence of having been as fire-red as his son's (as Keera's) and swept in two wings off his face, which was lined and severe. His green eyes were deep-set, his nose craggy, his expression forbidding. He regarded us without speaking.

"Shall I leave you together, Father?" Master Stefan said at last.

"No," said the older man, a curt, bitten-off syllable. We all stared at one another, a strange frozen tableau. Finally he spoke. "You have some of your mother in you. How are you called? Mirin?"

"Yes, sir," I said, making him another curtsey. As an afterthought, I added, "Master." After all, I was their bondservant, or so it seems they thought. When no one said anything further, I said, "You knew my mother?"

"Of course, girl. Elsebet is my wife. She's your mother, girl."

My parents' loved faces rose in my memory. "My parents are dead. Elsebet, my mother. Drustan, my father. You're not my father."

"Indeed, but I am," said the old man calmly.

"No," I insisted.

"And this is my grandchild. Give her to me."

"No," I said.

In two steps, Master Stefan strode to my side and wrested Keera away from me. I screamed, and so did Keera. Master Stefan gave my daughter to the old man, who gazed down at her, squalling furiously in his lap. "That's my grandchild," he said, and he handed her back to Master Stefan, who handed her back to me.

I cradled her away from them, terrified.

"Then it's true, what we've heard. Elsebet is dead. There's one problem we won't have to handle," said the old man to his son while I stared at him in horror and hatred. "Take them away now," the old man told his son, nodding toward us.

"Yes, Father," said Master Stefan. He waited while his father painfully rose from his chair. Goodwife Berit arrived unbidden and helped him out through a door behind him, leaving me, Keera, and Master Stefan alone together.

"I'm your brother. That's your father," he told me.

"No," I repeated, setting my mouth in a stubborn line.

"Let us sit here, and I will explain, since Father has left a lot unsaid." He moved to the big rocks ringing the hearth and indicated I should sit beside him. Hesitantly, I did. "My father's wife Elsebet—your mother—ran away with the man you're calling your father. She took you

with her. You were a small child. You probably don't remember any of it. I was a near-grown boy. I remember it
well. Father sent the beadle after the two of you, but that
man got you away with him. Father made his peace with
that. You, after all, are only a daughter, while I am his son.
He didn't try to go after Mother. He allowed that man to
take you and Mother away. That's the way of it."

"No," I said. "This can't be. My husband recalls people
he knew seeing me as a child in the house of my parents.
My real parents," I said with emphasis.

"They may have seen you as a small child, but you were
born on the Fire Isle right enough. Later, Father and I
came over the water to this place in the Western Isle
when his brothers took his lands over there in our homeland."

I sat silent and astounded.

"We know where he took you both, that man," Stefan
went on. "He controlled territory overlooking the sea,
across the way over on the mainland." Stefan made a
vague gesture. "Father made inquiries. He protested to
the king. Ranulf as was. But Ranulf dismissed his plea."

I found my voice at last. "If he didn't care, because I
was only a daughter and my mother was only a woman,
why would he bother?" I argued. I wanted to argue, because deep inside, I was afraid.

"You and Mother were Father's property. Of course
he'd make inquiries. Now matters are different. Ranulf is

dead. Father gained King Audemar's assurances you would be found, and when we heard you had had a child, Father was all the more determined. Now, though, his grandchild turns out to be a girl only. But still. You both belong to him."

"As your bondservants," I said, and the bitterness edged my voice.

"That makes it easier to keep you," said Stefan. He picked up my left wrist, turned it over, and stared hard at the brand. "But now it seems Audemar has been defeated, and this new man has proclaimed himself king. Caedon. It seems this Caedon believes you belong to him instead of us. Father wanted to make sure he took you before Caedon got to you. And so you are here. It was a near thing, but good coin means a great deal still. All of those retainers at Caedon's manor, I know many of them. The former owner was a good friend of Father's."

I pulled my wrist away from Stefan and held onto Keera fiercely. "As I heard it, Audemar had that man executed."

"Yes," said Stefan. "But Father saw the way it was and made haste to assure Audemar of his loyalty. As he will now do with Caedon, if it turns out Caedon can keep himself in power. We'll see. We'll wait to see."

"And what if Caedon does prove that, and what if he demands our return, me and Keera's?"

"Who is Keera?"

"Your niece," I told him in exasperation. Then I bit my tongue. I was buying into his whole story, that he was my brother, that the tall old sullen man was my father.

*No*, I told myself. Drustan was my father. I called to mind his dear face, how loving he was to me, always. *That's my father*, I told myself. Not this man.

"Oh, Keera. I see. A name from this savage island. Never mind that. She's a daughter of the Fire Child, whatever you've called her."

"The Children are your gods?" I asked cautiously.

"Of course."

Then why, I wanted to ask him, did my mother Elsebet worship the Lady Goddess. But I didn't ask him. I said only, "Keera means fire."

"Oh, I see," he said.

"Does this mean you're not from here, then?" I asked, intrigued in spite of myself.

"No, as I said. Father is from the realm north and west of here, the Fire Isle. So am I. So are you." The man called Stefan made an impatient wave of his hand. I tried to follow along, but what he was telling me was so confounding that I found it difficult to keep track of it all.

"Your father is from across the sea? The Northern Sea?" I asked.

"Your father," he corrected. "Your father and mine." And then, "Of course, and so are you and I. We're certainly not from here, from amongst these ragged barbarians."

I shivered. From the sea cliffs by our cottage, the sea stretched to the north, vast and cold. *I saw the old moon yesternight, with the new moon in his arms. . .* "If you're my brother," I said to him, trying to keep my tone even, trying to keep from shouting at him, "you need to help me. My husband sailed south around the cape, and then to the east. I must find him."

"Certainly not," said Stefan. "Father would never agree to anything so rash, and besides, your husband must be one of those people over on the mainland. Trash." He spat.

"He is one of Ranulf's sons," I told him.

Stefan regarded me shrewdly. "Not one of the true-born sons, I'm sure."

"Avery, the rightful king before the rightful Queen Diera, named him adopted son," I said proudly.

"Ah," said Stefan. "You're one of those people. No wonder Caedon is after you." He looked at me thoughtfully. "We heard rumors, Father and I, about this husband of yours."

"You won't give me to Caedon? You won't give Keera to him?" I was suddenly fearful again.

"Certainly not. You're our property, not his, no matter what he thought he was doing with that branding iron of his."

"He thought I was some nobody, and he made me his bondservant."

Now Stefan laughed. "Oh, no, he didn't. Caedon always knows exactly what he is doing. He knows who you are, all right."

"If he did know, he thought I was my father's daughter. Drustan's," I amended. "Earl of the High Sea Cliffs."

"Oh, no," said Stefan. "He knew. If he had you, he'd be able to force Father into a bad position. But now Father has you."

"If I'm just a daughter, why should your father care?"

"Your father," Stefan corrected again. "Yours and mine."

"Not my father."

Ignoring this, Stefan went on. "Because now he has you, Father can marry you off to his advantage, of course."

"But I'm married already."

"Pfft," said Stefan. "A marriage like that, unsanctioned by your family. That can be easily overturned."

"My marriage was held on the same day as Diera the First's coronation, before her and everyone, by a priestess of the Child of Earth."

"Diera is an illegitimate ruler. Actually, she is no ruler at all. Her forces have been defeated and scattered, the few territories where she had any influence have been overrun. Audemar rules them now. This husband of yours is probably dead. He probably died in the battle. Her whole army was slaughtered. Those who escaped were caught between the armies of Audemar and Caedon as they faced off over the spoils.

"As for Diera, she has fled to the Eastern Baronies. I don't recall hearing of anyone with her who meets the description of this supposed husband of yours. She only has a few household retainers with her. Among them, I hear, your so-called sister Jillian."

"You don't know that!" I burst out. "You don't know he's dead." I was so horrified my mind skated right past the knowledge that at least my sister was safe.

"It's of no matter, whether this Walter fellow is alive or whether he's dead. He's dead, no doubt. The heralds issue names of any captives of note. This man wasn't on their list. As for you, Father will dispose of you as he sees fit."

But then the full import of what Stefan was saying about Wat hit me. I collapsed to the stone floor and lay weeping, overwhelmed with the feeling, in spite of my brave words, that Stefan was right. Wat was dead. And these two unpleasant men talked of my mother as if she had been merely a problem for them to solve, a problem that no longer concerned them, because now she was dead. It was too much. It was too sudden. I was too weak from hunger and privation, and now I was shatttered.

"I'll leave you to compose yourself, Sister. Father is expecting important guests and I have a lot to do to help him get ready to meet them. You do, too. Pull yourself together. Besides," he called back to me as he hurried away to a different part of the manor, "whether that fellow is alive or dead, any marriage conducted by priestesses of the Children is void. Audemar has decreed all married in that way must re-affirm their vows before the Lady Goddess. We're expecting Caedon will keep to that."

Stefan left me there. In a while Goodwife Berit was helping me toward my room, and I stayed there for the next few days. I did try to eat, because I knew Keera needed me strong. Beyond that, everything around me seemed to have turned a dull gray. Nothing mattered to me, only Keera. I cared about nothing. The few times I played my rebec, I found myself singing that sad song and dissolving into tears, so after a while, I didn't play it any more. I didn't sing the song any more.

Wat was never going to be coming home to me. The feeling in me was a dark mass that kept growing, suffocating me. First the overwhelming suspicion that thanks to Ivor he never even made it off the isle. Now the news that if, in spite of Ivor's treachery, he had made it to the mainland, he had probably died in battle. If only, I thought to myself, the gods really were kind. If only they'd change me into a bird, as the grieving woman in the song was transformed.

*The Children, they look down from high*
*with pity in their gaze.*
*They change her into Halcyon,*
*the bird that stills the waves.*

*Halcyon, oh fisher bird,*
*wife forever true,*
*weep for me and fly to me,*
*and I will weep for you.*

*I saw the old moon yester night*
*with the new moon in his arms;*
*if you sail out to sea, my love,*
*you'll never more come home.*

My fate was not to be transformed. Instead, it was to remain Mirin. The days and nights were long, but I had to get through them. I had to for Keera's sake.

Soon, though, the entire household was caught up in a buzz of excitement. Fylkir, my supposed father, was especially excited. That was his name. Fylkir Magnusson. Important people were coming for an extended visit, and the manor needed to be ready for them. I tried to stay out of the way, but Mistress Berit kept thrusting tasks on me, and I was required to perform them. Airing the linens. Helping with the cookery. Plucking elderberries from the hedge in the small enclosed orchard garden outside the kitchen house and putting them in baskets, careful not to crush them, so that the cook could bake them into pies.

Embroidering brilliant strips of cloth, picked out in gold thread, to be sewn on Fylkir's and Stefan's holiday clothing, on my own clothing. I had new, rich clothes to wear. I put them on without any pleasure. Embroidering was torture to me. I had never been good at it. Now I pricked my finger, I bled on the costly cloth, I snarled the thread, I endured Mistress Berit's scoldings.

Regular, straightforward sewing, that I could do. Old Cwen had taught me. She was going to teach me to embroider, too, but I had been taken away from her before I could learn much. And then Caedon's woman had tried to teach me. Six or seven years ago at least. It seemed much longer ago than that, an event in the distant past, like something that had happened to a different person, a young girl I only slightly knew.

The only pleasure I had was tending Keera and watching her grow.

In one of the out-buildings, a bondswoman knew tablet weaving, and her bands of beautiful cloth so surpassed my feeble efforts that Mistress Berit grabbed mine up one day and dumped them with an exasperated exclamation behind the dunghill out by the barn. I didn't care.

I could see the pressure on Mistress Berit was mounting, and at last I got a little bit interested. Who was so important that their visit would affect such a placid woman this way?

No one told me who these guests would be. I don't think Mistress Berit knew, either. It was all some kind of secret. When I asked Stefan, he brushed me aside.

"Tomorrow's the day," Mistress Berit told me one evening, as I was taking Keera into our bedroom to put her to bed. "I have drawn a bath for you, mistress. In the morning, you're to bathe the child, too, and see that she's dressed in her best."

The bath, at least, was a pleasure. Later I sat on the bed beside Keera, watching her sleep and combing out my long hair. *Like spun bronze*, Wat had said. I teared up. I had a gold comb, now, and a little silver mirror. *Just like the song*, I suddenly realized with a shiver. But I took no pleasure in those.

Before I was supposed to appear in the manor's great hall, Stefan came to the door of my room. He and Mistress Berit conferred together, and he handed her a small embroidered cloth bag. He nodded to me and then moved briskly away.

Keera had awakened and I was sitting on the side of the bed, playing at peek-bo with her as she kicked and gurgled.

Mistress Berit bustled over to me and handed me the cloth bag. "Your father bids you wear these," she said.

I loosened the drawstrings that held the bag closed and tipped the contents into my lap. They were two armlets of beaten gold. "Very pretty," I said without enthusiasm. I began fastening them onto my wrists.

"They were your mother's," Mistress Berit said as she hastened from the room.

When she was gone, I gazed down at them, and lifted each arm so they caught the light and I could examine the finely wrought decorations on each. My eyes filled with tears. My mother had left all these riches behind to take me away with her to a foreign land where I'd grow up loved.

Then I realized something else and felt a slow cynical smile quirk my lips. The armlets concealed my brand. Whoever these important visitors turned out to be, Fylkir didn't want them seeing that.

Fylkir was a prosperous man of high status. Rich, even. I was a rich man's daughter. No rich man's daughter bore the brand of a bondswoman. That was shameful, ill befitting Fylkir's high status and without a doubt diminishing his daughter's value on the marriage market.

As I was soon to learn, Fylkir was more than prosperous and highly placed. He was influential.

It was time. We all stood outside the manor to await our guests. We were dressed in our best, even Keera. She squirmed to be put down, but I didn't dare let her spoil her clothing, so I kept a good grip on her, and then she fussed.

"Quiet that child," Fylkir said. Then a dust cloud down the road leading up to our manor let us know. The guests were arriving.

An ornately-decorated wagon pulled by a team of oxen toiled up the hill toward us. It halted. Servants handed out a man and woman, dressed even more richly than we were.

"My lord," said Fylkir, sweeping the man a low bow. Then, likewise, to the woman. "My lady. Welcome to our house."

The man stepped up to Fylkir and clasped him warmly on the shoulder.

"What news of the north?" said Fylkir.

"My good friend Magnusson! I'll keep my news until we have time to talk it over fully, but all is well with our plans," said the man, this lord, in an accent unfamiliar to me.

"There's another guest coming, my lord," said Fylkir to the man. "Someone you need to meet. Someone it were best you meet outside the—" he paused delicately. "—outside the usual channels, shall we say." Fylkir and the man exchanged a long knowing look.

Watching Fylkir go to work like this didn't surprise me now. Fylkir was always scheming and conniving and arranging. Even I knew this. In only the short time I had lived in his household, I'd seen it. It was Fylkir's whole life.

Fylkir led the way, and we all moved into the hall. We sat on benches, and Mistress Berit supervised the bond-servants in serving us all cheese and fruit, honey mead filling our best silver cups.

After Keera had fussed some more, and the visitors—whose names I still didn't know—had exclaimed appropriately over her beauty, I was allowed to take her away again. I bore her off to our room with a sigh of relief. Now that was out of the way.

But no. Mistress Berit arrived soon after with a girl set to watch her. "You must go back out to the guests, master says."

"Nine Spheres," I muttered. Mistress Berit's disapproving stare followed me out of the room. Behind me, Keera began to squall.

I hesitated at the entrance to the hall. Other guests had arrived, and everyone was standing around and talking. As I entered, the conversations stopped.

"Here she is, my daughter," Fylkir said to a man with his back to me. The man, this guest, turned around to face me. I nearly fainted.

Caedon.

He came to me and extended his hand. I looked at it in bewilderment, as if it were an alien thing.

Fylkir strode up to me. Turning to face Caedon, he bowed. When he rose, he hissed in my ear, "Kiss his hand. Caedon is our king now."

I took Caedon's hand in mine and looked up into his face, those hooded reptilian eyes.

Caedon's mouth curved up in the slow cruel smile I had known of old. "Lady Mirin," he said to me.

I said nothing. I was not going to address this man as "your highness," or even "my lord." I bent over his hand and kissed it. I wanted to bite it instead. I dropped into a deep curtsey.

He guided me back to my feet. "How good to see you again, Lady Mirin," he said. His voice was deeply ironic.

I matched his tone, and more. If my voice had been the mordant of the metalworkers' etching barrels, he would have dissolved. "The pleasure is mine," I said. I stepped back to the others, and then I found my way to one of the benches and sat down.

The last time I'd seen him, I'd knocked him off his feet, and he'd slashed at me with his sword. I still had the scar on my arm to prove it. And on my left wrist, concealed beneath my mother's armlet of beaten gold, I wore his brand. Deeper than the long-healed physical wound, his act still burned me.

Now, from the bench, I scrutinized him. A thin gold band circled his brows. His wolfish strange amber-colored eyes flashed underneath it. He was dressed, as always, in black. He turned to the foreign man, the lord from the north, and they stepped aside to confer.

Fylkir came over to me and motioned to me to stand. "You'll treat our king with the utmost courtesy, Daughter," he said to me, privately.

"That man branded me as if I were a cow."

"Do as I say, or I'll have you beaten," said Fylkir and turned on his heel.

Soon afterward, the menservants came into the hall to set the planks of the table up for banqueting. Fylkir sat at the head of the board, with Caedon at his right and the lord from the north at his left. He motioned to Stefan to sit between the northern lord and his lady, and he motioned me to the seat beside Caedon. I hesitated, but then I sat down. Each man had brought a number of noble retainers, and they ranged up and down the board according to their ranks and importance.

A few young men of lesser noble birth sat below the salt at the foot of the table. A table was set outside for the carls and their wives, and the servants all crowded into the kitchen house. Caedon had brought quite an entourage. I was glad I'd missed his arrival.

Now I knew why Fylkir had vacated his own sleeping room and had moved into Stefan's. The king would sleep there. Caedon our king.

I thought at once of how I could manage to sneak in there and kill him. Murderous thoughts filled me. Even worse, glancing at Caedon beside me at the table, I could tell that he saw what I was thinking. I saw he was enjoying it.

"You're a vile excuse of a man," I said to him, under my breath.

He laughed out loud.

"My daughter amuses you, my king," said Fylkir.

"Indeed she does," Caedon replied.

Fylkir nodded at me and smiled, but I could read the warning in his eyes.

*Let him beat me*, I thought. Everything had been taken from me. I didn't care.

Then I thought of Keera and dropped my eyes to my trencher heaped with food. I clasped my hands in my lap, squeezing hard to keep them from trembling.

I raged when, beside me, I heard Caedon's strange, low grating laughter. Below the level of the table where no one could see, he placed a possessive hand on my thigh.

I felt that I was burning with rage and embarrassment. I felt everyone must be able to see my thoughts written plainly on my face.

But the conversation flowed on around me as if nothing at all were happening. I tried moving away from Caedon. He just tightened his grip. Now the few women at table had fallen silent. The men were doing the talking.

Caedon released me to gesture as he made some point. I looked over at him with loathing.

The talk was all about alliances. About Caedon's conquest of the west and north of the mainland as well as how much an alliance with him would benefit the Ice-realm in the far north, much more greatly, Caedon emphasized, than any alliance the Ice-realm's monarch might make with Audemar. This northern lord at our table came from the Ice-realm; he was an emissary from its king, Haakon Hardaxe. Of course I knew that King Haakon was one of the most powerful men in the world. Wat and Diera and others in the Rising had once sent emissaries to him. He would have made an ally to reckon with. But Haakon Hardaxe had brushed their suit to him aside. Haakon was a realist.

"Audemar is weak," Caedon was telling the northerner. "I'll crush him."

I gained then an appreciation of my father Fylkir's skills. By then I had reluctantly accepted Stefan's story of my true origins. I winced away from really thinking about it, though. It was as if Drustan, the man I'd known and loved as father, were killed all over again when I thought about it.

At his table, Fylkir encouraged Caedon and the emissary from Haakon to talk, while he himself took a background role. But every now and again, he'd interject something into the conversation. Always, it had to do with Fylkir's own land claims in the Fire Isle. While this land was not an outpost of Haakon's Ice-realm, it might as well have been. It was under Haakon's influence. I could see how Fylkir, making himself useful to both men, was strengthening his position with each. I found myself listening closely. But I pretended not to.

Eventually, the dinner ended, the leavings were borne away by the bondservants to divide between themselves and the pigs, and we all retired to our rooms for the night's sleep. Mistress Berit helped me out of my clothing. We moved quietly so we wouldn't wake Keera. I unclasped the armlets, and she nestled them back into their bag. Then she helped me pull my fine linen sleeping garment over my head and sailed out of the room. I stood watching her. She never curtsied to me. I felt sure she disapproved of me. Maybe she even thought I was an imposter. I idly wondered whether I could enlist her aid in running away, but already I knew she was too loyal to Fylkir for that.

And where would I go, I wondered. And why would I bother trying if indeed Stefan was right, and Wat was dead.

I lay down on the bed beside Keera, but thoughts like these tortured me. I couldn't sleep. I was too stirred up by what had just happened. Caedon in this very house, sleeping under the same roof. I began wondering how easy it would be to get into one of the outbuildings of

Fylkir's manor and find a knife. Even a kitchen knife would do. Finally I pulled my fur cloak around me and, driven by these bloodthirsty thoughts, stepped quietly out of my room, pulling the door to behind me.

As I made my way to the outer door through the dim house, I smiled at myself for the thoughts I'd harbored about killing Caedon in his sleep. Nearing Fylkir's room, where Caedon was sleeping, I glimpsed dark bundles, bondsmen bedded down outside his door. Not even the most determined assassin would be able to get to him.

I stole quietly to the door to the outside and let myself into the courtyard. No point in looking for a knife. I had my rebec, though. I thought maybe I'd be able to play very softly, and maybe that would soothe me. I sighed and made my way to the neat walled orchard, which had become a kind of refuge of mine. I decided to sit there and settle my raging thoughts. Maybe I'd be able to sleep a little, after.

I opened the gate and went in. It made a slight creaking in the darkness, but nothing that would alarm the household. There was a bench just under the pear tree, and I headed for it. The year was well past midsummer now, but I still didn't need a light. The dim light from the stars poured down into the place, and the light from a faint moon hiding behind clouds.

A hand on my shoulder made me gasp.

"Quiet, little Mirin. We don't want to rouse the house," said a voice at my ear.

With a chill, I recognized it was Caedon's.

He let me go and I shrank away from him.

"I'm not planning to hurt you. I didn't know you'd be here."

I just stared at him in the strange shadows cast by the pear tree.

"I didn't come here to hurt you," he repeated. "I noticed this place when I came in, and I couldn't sleep. You can't sleep either, it seems."

"What a liar you are. You always mean me ill."

"I mean you well, mistress, if you can only see it. Your father tells me I can have you, if I like," he said.

"I thought you already owned me," I said, the bitterness rising into my voice.

He took my left hand in his and turned it over. The clouds had parted now. In the moonlight we could both see his brand. "That's true, I do own you. Here's the evidence, no matter how that old man tries to conceal it. My mark will be on you til the day you die. I should call the law on Fylkir."

"Why don't you."

But my bravado was hollow, and he laughed softly. "You'd like that, would you?" He reached out and grabbed me by the arm, pulling me close to him as I cringed away, wondering if it would do any good to scream. *Why hadn't I tried to get that knife*, I raged at myself.

His face, shadowed under the moonlit pear tree, was much too close to mine. "Well now, Lady Mirin," he said. His voice dropped to a mocking whisper. "Let me think about your suggestion. Why don't I call the law on Fylkir. Why indeed. If I make good on my claim, I won't have your father's help with a few other matters I need him for. So it pleases me to abide by his fantasy that he's the one who owns you."

"Neither of you owns me," I told him.

"You're wrong about that. One of us does. All I have to do is pay your father his asking price, and there will be no question which one. And I can afford it. Maybe I'll do it and save myself the trouble of simply taking what's mine from that doddering old father of yours."

"He's not my father."

"You keep saying that," he said. "But you know it's not true."

How did he know what I kept saying, I wondered. And he'd known about my parentage. All along, he'd known it.

"How long have you known?" I blurted out.

"A long time."

"When you first saw me dressed as a boy in the castle where Audemar was keeping Diera?"

"Not then. But shortly afterward. I made inquiries. I found the truth. Easily."

"On the day Diera escaped you? The day you killed Avery and imprisoned me and my sister?"

"Yes, by then I knew."

"Ha. You thought you were going to marry Diera."

"That was one plan. There are many other ways it could go, and now it has."

"If you could take her, would you marry her now?"

"Of course not," he said. "She's nothing, now. You, though. You might be a prize worth paying for."

"Only if Fylkir's conniving produces any results. And we both know that's a chancy thing." I tried to squirm out of his grasp and he suddenly loosed his hold on me, so suddenly I stumbled backward and nearly fell.

"Mirin, Mirin, Mirin. You were listening. You know why I like you? You have a brain, and you're always using it. Always figuring things out."

"You have a brain," I said slowly. "And you're always using it in the service of the Dark Ones."

"The Dark Ones!" Caedon laughed. "Superstitious drivel. You're too smart to believe any of that trash, Mirin. Maybe I'll take you right here, and not pay your father a single coin. As you say, you're my property." He seized me again and shoved me against the rough wall of the garden. I tried side-stepping him, but the fur robe slipped from my shoulders and I stumbled, the garment twining about my legs. I fought to regain my balance. Even without a knife, I thought desperately, I could maybe hurt him. If I were lucky, maybe kill him.

He saw what I was doing. He moved fast to forestall me, pinning me to the wall with an elbow across my throat, a knee jamming me up against the rough stones. We stood together in that strange tableau, both of us heaving for breath.

"Master Walter trained you well, but I'm onto you now, Mirin. Don't think you can use your tricks on me this time," he hissed into my ear. He snatched the rebec from my shoulder and tossed it away from us into the grass. "None of your witch music, either, mistress." He shifted his grip and I could breathe again, but he had me by the hair now, forcing my head back. His knee drove into me, and now with his right hand he was twisting my arms behind me and holding me by the wrists.

"I'm a married woman." I felt a rising panic.

"You're a widow. I made you a widow. I did it, Mirin," said Caedon. He slammed his body against mine. My hands were pinned behind me. I struggled, feeling a kind of desperation now, but he shoved harder. Now his right hand was free; he fumbled at the neck of my nightdress while I vainly pushed back. He knotted my hair in his left hand. Our faces were inches away. I stared fascinated and horror-struck into his strange eyes. "I watched it," he said, his mouth curving up as he saw my reaction, the re-alization of what he was telling me slowly filling me with dread. Nothing in the intervening years since our last encounter had lessened his strength and agility. "I watched that man of yours die, and I enjoyed it. High time, too. This time his luck ran out. As you probably know by now, in my employ there's a man your bastard husband was unwise enough to trust."

A cry escaped me and he clapped his hand over my mouth, grinding his body against me.

I looked around myself wildly for a way out, and then back into his face.

His smile widened. "Shall I tell you the things I did to him, that bastard?" He said, close to my ear. "What I did before I finished him? I like to draw these occasions out a little bit, when I have a man like that where I want him. It would be my pleasure to tell you . . . everything." He stepped back so suddenly that I fell forward against him.

"No!" I shrieked at him.

He lunged at me then and clamped his hand over my mouth again. "There now, mistress." His breath was hot against my cheek. "Stay silent while I take what's mine." Off-balance, I pitched into the grass with Caedon on top of me. What he did next, mercifully, he did fast. He pinned my hands above my head with his left hand, wedged his knee between my legs, and with his other hand he yanked my nightdress up. I lay frozen in shock at what he'd said about Wat and half-stunned from the fall backward, while he thrust himself on me, holding me down in a bruising grip. I tried to squirm away from him, tried to get a knee into his groin, but it was useless. He had me pinned there. He knew what he was doing.

We were both absolutely silent, except for his hoarse breathing, hard and fast. I went limp, broken in mind and body. I closed my eyes while he finished. When I opened them again he was kneeling over me, cleaning himself off. He got slowly to his feet while I lay on the stones of the garden path, watching him.

He looked strange to me, standing aside from me, his face pensive in the dappling shadows cast on us by the moonlight filtering through the spears of the pear trees' leaves. "I should have done that long before," he said, wiping his mouth with the back of his hand. He reached down to help me up, an odd courtly gesture. I got to my feet, shaking my head, trying to clear it. "To tell you the truth, I like them younger, though," he said at last, examining me with what seemed like curiosity. He moved close to me again, twining his fingers through my hair as I slumped shivering against the garden wall, holding the rags of my torn nightdress around me. "You may have figured that out." He pulled me to him and ran his hands along my body as I remembered his strange behavior, long ago in Lunds-fort.

"Then why?" I whispered between cracked lips.

He picked up my left hand and turned it over, bringing his brand on my wrist to his mouth, and kissed it.

"I've marked you here. Now I've marked you elsewhere. It seems you were forgetting who owns you, Mistress Mirin Fylkirsdottir. I've just reminded you, that's all. I doubt you'll forget again." He peered into my face, his strange golden eyes moody. "I should have taken my chance years ago, when you were just a boy. I would have enjoyed that. I'll have to find my real enjoyment elsewhere, I suppose." He began to smile. "Your sister, now. That was a rare pleasure."

I stared at him aghast. Without knowing how, exactly, I was away from him and running barefoot to the house. His laughter followed me all the way to my room, ringing out into the night.

There was a stirring in the house, people sitting up and wondering what was wrong, people coming out of their rooms. I buried my head under the furs. No one came into my room to see about me, and I didn't come out.

In the morning, despite Mistress Berit's remonstrances, and the threats she carried to me from Fylkir, I didn't come out. I wouldn't. Later in the day, I heard the wagons pulling away and crunching down the road away from our manor. I stayed in my room. When Mistress Berit brought Keera to me, I waved them both off. Keera's wails filled me with guilt, but I couldn't hold her. With Caedon's stink still on me, I think I thought I might infect her.

Once the house grew quiet, I made my way silently to the well behind the kitchen house and drew up a bucket of water. One of the bondsmaids spotted me and rushed over to help me. Something she saw in my face sent her backing wide-eyed away.

Finally I could wash. I scrubbed myself until I was raw. I washed the blood from my back, scratched and scraped and bruised from the rough stones of the garden wall and the stones on the path. Then I rushed back to my room.

Finally, in the early evening, I did come out. My clothing concealed most of the evidence of my struggle with Caedon. He hadn't hit me in the face. I wondered if he abstained on purpose. Often enough, in earlier times, he'd left me with a blackened, swollen eye or a bruised cheek. Last night, he probably knew it wouldn't be a good idea for anyone to suspect what he had done to me, and he knew enough about my situation to realize I wouldn't tell. He knew I wouldn't say a word. Not to these hard people surrounding me. Caedon was calculating. Always.

Stefan was waiting for me to emerge from my room. He grabbed me by the wrist and pulled me to the manor hall, where Fylkir sat ominous in his big chair. I winced at Stefan's touch.

Keera was playing on the floor at Fylkir's feet. She screamed for me when she saw me, but Stefan thrust her into Mistress Berit's arms, and the goodwife bore her away.

"Daughter, you shamed me," said Fylkir.

"I don't care," I said. My lips felt stiff, numb. I spoke to him as if I were someplace far away, above him somehow, and he a small dot far below me, his face upturned to me as if he were at the bottom of a deep well. I couldn't feel my feet underneath me.

"You will care." He instructed Stefan to take me to the barn, where a servingman was waiting to beat me.

"Father, no. It will be a bigger shame for all the servants to see her stripped, the lady of the house."

"What do I do with a misbehaving woman?" said Fylkir to his son. His tones were aggrieved.

"Find a husband for her as soon as you can, and send her away," said Stefan. "She'll be his problem then."

Fylkir pushed himself upright and left his chair. He walked around me, his fists clenching and unclenching.

I didn't look at him. I stared straight ahead into nothing. Their words came at me from a distance. I heard what they said, but I didn't understand them. It was as if they were speaking in some language I didn't know.

"You lost our chance with the king, girl," he grated at me. He came close to me and was near yelling. His spittle spattered my face. "He was minded to take you off with him, but no. Mistress Prideful wouldn't come out of her room."

His words finally penetrated through the bubble of silence that encased me. I burst out laughing. Even I was startled by the bitter sounds that spilled from my mouth. There was a bitter taste in my mouth as well.

I do believe Fylkir would have beaten me himself, right then, had Stefan not intervened.

"Father, no. Don't exercise yourself." He led Fylkir back to his high carved seat, casting a look of consternation over his shoulder at me, and settled the old man in, drawing furs over his gnarled body. "And Father," Stefan continued. "You yourself should marry."

"I'm too old to marry."

"Of course you're not. Find a fit young woman. Have more sons. With your strong position, it should be easy."

"You're advising me to make rivals for you, boy?"

"Of course not, Father. I'll always be your heir. But a man can't have too many sons. They'll enlarge your holdings through their own marriages and be there for you if you come under attack."

They talked over and past me as if I weren't even there. In a way, they were right. Except for that single moment when the laughter burst out of me like a poison, I wasn't really there. I was somewhere else.

But that's what they did, the two of them, starting that moment. They began scheming to marry me off and find Fylkir a wife.

That was the moment my life in the household got so hard it was too hard to bear. At last I really believed it, that Wat was dead. I'd cringed from the thought. I'd had premonitions. Stefan had sown his doubts.

Now, with Caedon's poisoned words still whispering at my ear, I knew.

*I watched that man of yours die, and I enjoyed it,* Caedon had whispered. *Your sister. That was a rare pleasure,* he had murmured in my ear. *There's a man in my employ your husband was unwise enough to trust.*

Along with the terrible grief I felt for Wat, there was the sick feeling, too, about Jillie. I'd harbored my suspicions with dread, what she must have undergone in Caedon's house.

Now I knew.

On top of those two terrible pieces of knowledge there was the thing that Caedon had done to me. Layer upon layer of hurt, and this was a part of it. *I won't hurt you,* he'd said. He may have even meant it, in the moment. But Caedon is a man who can't stop himself from hurting whomever he has in his power. It is his nature.

Remembering that made the bitter laughter bubble up inside me again and spill out of me in brittle shards of sound. Finally Caedon had done the thing he'd threatened in the past but had never done. Now he had.

Stefan summoned Mistress Berit to take me away. As he hustled me to her, yanking me along in exasperation, my cloak fell aside. He stopped short and stared. My throat and neck, my one exposed arm were mottled with bruises. The bruising extended down below my neckline. Bloody scratches raked my arm. I looked Stefan in the eye. I looked through him. He stepped back, his mouth an o of dismay. Mistress Berit led me by the hand out of their presence, Fylkir's and Stefan's, while they stood gaping after me.

As she guided me with a hand on my back through the garden, I spotted my rebec lying neglected in the grass where Caedon had tossed it. I shoved away from her and went to it, bending over it, bringing it up into my arms and cradling it there. Then I allowed her to lead me away.

After that, I stayed mostly in my room, taking care of myself only for Keera's sake. Stefan kept away from us. Fylkir had nothing more to say to me.

From time to time, Fylkir would demand my presence at dinner. Goodwife Berit would see that I was presentable and wearing the golden armlets. Then she would lead me into the main hall where the planks of the dining table were set up when guests came. The old man would sit at the head of the table, with Stefan at his right. I'd be placed at his left. I'd sit there picking at my food while Stefan and Fylkir entertained the guests. No one expected me to speak.

If I were there at the table, I could be sure of two possibilities. First, that among the guests was someone Fylkir was hoping to buy a bride from, and he wanted his whole family on display. He was flaunting his prosperity, letting the family of the prospective bride see what a catch he was, even though he was a crabbed old man.

And second, that among the guests was someone looking me over to decide whether to buy me from Fylkir. Young ones, old ones, men in between. A few times I'd gaze around the table to see which one might be the suitor, but mostly I didn't care, just kept my eyes fixed on my trencher. As soon as I was allowed, I'd go back to my room and Keera.

Let them give me to some strange man. What was the difference? I was theirs now, then I'd be somebody else's. At least I wasn't Caedon's.

But Wat. Wat was gone.

# Sold

One such night at dinner, a man was there, old, nondescript, woebegone. Somehow I knew. This was the man they'd sell me to. That's what they were doing, after all. Selling me. That's what they did, these people, when a family had a daughter. Find a good alliance with some neighbor who'd exchange land or maybe even coin outright, probably both, to get that daughter and breed sons with her. Or if she were unlucky enough to have daughters, they could be sold in their turn.

Maybe I'd have a better life outside the cold household of Fylkir. By that time, I had become resigned to the idea that Fylkir was my father. By birth, anyway. Not in the spirit. Drustan was my true father and always would be. But I was curious. How had it happened that my mother had run away with Drustan, taking me with her? That was one puzzle.

Another was my own name. Stefan told me once no one could remember what his father had named me, not even Fylkir. Maybe he hadn't even bothered. That's how important girl babies were in Fylkir's world. Not important enough to name or to remember naming if you did. So he and my brother Stefan called me Mirin the way everyone else did.

Stefan told me that couldn't be my real name. "No one we know is named Mirin. That would be ridiculous. So that's not your name," he told me one day, when I was trying to probe him for more information about my mother and why she had run away.

By then, though, something inside me knew. My second sense, maybe. Drustan had named me. He had taken me for his own, his beloved daughter, and he had named me for the sea.

But still I quizzed Stefan about my mother and why she had done what she did.

"Why. Why. Why," Stefan said, finally tired of my persistent questions. "It was that man." He meant Drustan.

"That man from the mainland. He came to the Fire Isle to visit Father with some kind of proposition about something. Politics, maybe, or money. He stayed there as Father's guest. And when he left, he took Elsebet with him. That's the kind of trash he was."

"My father was not trash," I said, flushed with rage. "He cared enough to name me and remember what it was." The rage felt good. Maybe because it was one of the few emotions I had felt at all for a season and more.

Stefan ignored my outburst and walked out of the room.

I lapsed back into the numbed state I'd been left in by Caedon. So when Goodwife Berit informed me of Fylkir's decision to marry me off to a prosperous farmer from far away to the north on the Sceptered Isle's mainland, I merely nodded.

"Get your things together, that's what Lord Fylkir bid me tell you," she said.

There was little enough to get together. My clothes, my rebec, and Keera.

On the appointed day, I sat on the bench that ran along the outer wall of the main hall, waiting with Keera in my lap to find out my fate. I didn't even know what this man looked like, beyond that brief vague impression at dinner. I didn't even know his name.

Goodwife Berit supervised the bringing in of a carved chest that, she said, contained my dowry. I didn't know what was in the chest. I eased it open to look when she left the hall. It was filled with sumptuous clothing, bed linens and furs, things like that.

Staring into it, I wondered what Fylkir had made this man, my husband-to-be, pay him to possess me. Not much, I intuited. Partly it was Fylkir's scowl whenever he looked at me. Partly it was chance things I overheard from the servants or others about the manor. Word had gotten out about Caedon and what he'd done to me. I was a widow, and I was damaged goods. My price was low.

I closed the chest and sank back down on the bench with Keera.

Soon I heard male voices outside. Fylkir, Stefan, and the man I barely remembered from the dinner maybe a full season ago came into the hall.

"Here's your new husband, Daughter," said Fylkir.

I stood and dropped the man a curtsey. He was, just as I remembered, much older than I, and very pale. Almost Fylkir's age, I thought, studying his jowls and the wrinkles of his neck.

"Daughter," said Fylkir. His tone was warning.

I dropped my eyes.

"Bring in the priest," Fylkir told Stefan. My brother left the hall briefly and returned with a doddering old man in ochre robes. I had seen him around the manor from time to time. He was the local priest of the Lady Goddess, whom we now all had to worship. Fylkir and Stefan worshipped the Fire Child, as I knew very well, but as the times demanded it, they switched their allegiance, whether it was to an earthly king or an other-worldly god. Their outward allegiance, anyway. As I knew by now, their real allegiance was to themselves and their own interests. Some of those interests lay in the Fire Isle, where Fylkir had claim to property, and some here in the north of the Western Isle.

Just outside Fylkir's manor stood a small chapel dedicated to the Lady Goddess. I thought they'd bring me there to this husband who'd bought me from them, but they didn't bother.

"Stand up, Daughter," Fylkir told me, so I did.

The priest took me by the hand right there at Fylkir's door and took the stranger by the hand as well. The priest murmured some words of blessing and put our two hands together. My hand lay limply in this husband's. Oisin. That moment was the first I'd heard the man's name. Probably Fylkir and Stefan had discussed him in front of me. Or maybe they hadn't thought to. In those days, I wasn't able to pay attention. Their words floated overhead as remote from me as the moon.

And it was done. Oisin and I were married.

Now Oisin took my hand from the priest's and led me out of the hall to his wagon, a plain wooden cart with an ox. I was balancing Keera on one hip while trying to manage a large bundle of goods I'd be taking to my new household.

"Hand me the child," said Goodwife Berit.

So I gave Keera to her as I hoisted myself up onto the wagon seat and then stepped over into the back of the cart, where the carved chest had already been loaded. I set my rebec alongside it. Oisin sprang to the wagon seat and picked up the lines to guide the ox.

Now I reached over the side of the cart for Keera, but Goodwife Berit moved out of my reach. Fylkir plucked Keera out of her arms. Keera began to shriek. Oisin clucked to the ox and the cart moved off. I stood up, and I think I was screaming. I started to climb out of the wagon, but Oisin, surprisingly strong, reached back and held me in his grip. So we rode down the hill, me wailing and struggling all the way.

At the bottom of the hill, he stopped the cart. I looked up at him with a sudden hope that he was going to turn around and bring me back to my little child. Instead, he sprang into the cart with me and tied me fast by both hands to its top rail, saying nothing to me, and then re-sumed his place on the wagon seat. I sank to the bottom of the cart in despair.

Now I saw it. Keera was another commodity Fylkir could sell. Goodwife Berit would raise her until she was old enough for him to pack off, in exchange for something valuable he wanted, coin or influence or prestige, and I'd never see her again. I railed at myself for not paying enough attention in those dark days after Caedon's attack. If I'd paid attention, I told myself, I'd have seen this coming. I'd have escaped with Keera. I would have done it. Somehow, I would have. I lay shattered at the bottom of Oisin's wagon.

I couldn't think at all beyond two thoughts, one chasing the tail of the other, around and around in an endless circle. First Wat, now Keera. Both lost to me. My heart broke in two.

I lay in a kind of stupor the entire trip to the eastern side of the island. When this man Oisin couldn't rouse me during our overnight stop halfway to the coast, he simply folded some furs around me and went into the inn for his own dinner and sleep. In the morning, the jolting of the wagon woke me.

Eventually, we reached a small port on the Western Strait, that constricted body of water separating the Western Isle from the islands clustered off the northern coast of the Sceptered Isle. Oisin helped me aboard the ferry waiting at the port, and the oarsmen pulled us across. I thought of leaping into the choppy waves, but Oisin kept a firm hand on me the entire way. He must have seen my despair.

We had only a short journey across the waist of this island before reaching another strait, one that separated us from the northwestern edge of the Sceptered Isle's mainland. As we waited onshore for the cog that would take us across, I saw the seamen milling about the pier, some raising their hands in prayer to the Lady Goddess, others making the furtive, forbidden sign of the Sea Child.

Oisin took me by the hand and led me to the edge of the sea. "We'll pray, wife," he said. I noticed his bony hand was shaking a bit. I looked up into his face in curiosity, an emotion I was so unaccustomed to feeling that I didn't even recognize it for what it was. He looked uneasily away from me. He had barely touched me or spoken to me during the journey, and I, wrapped in my perpetual fog, had barely noticed.

He looked out to sea, his eyes apprehensive. He cleared his throat. Now he fell to his knees on the sand, dragging me down after him. He raised his hands to the heavens, pulling my hand up with his. "Lady Goddess keep us safe upon these waves. Lady Goddess help us when no help is near," he prayed, his voice quavering.

*Lady Goddess help us when no help is near*, I thought. My mother had taught me that prayer.

But then, looking at him sidelong, I saw that Oisin had made the secret sign of the Sea Child too. He started guiltily when he saw me watching and yanked me with him to our feet. "There now," he said.

I looked around me, puzzled. The sea seemed calm, yet everyone acted frightened.

*Maybe we'll sink,* I thought dully. And I remembered my childhood where almost everyone I knew worshipped the Child of Earth, if they didn't worship the Lady Goddess. They were all afraid of water.

*But these people worship the Child of Sea, however much they try to hide it,* I told myself. *Water holds no terrors for these people.* I found their behavior odd.

Soon it was time to board the cog. Oisin helped me across the plank stretching from the pier to the vessel. I watched as the seamen loaded my chest of goods, the dowry from Fylkir that I had brought with me. On top of the chest, my rebec was lashed.

Now, with help from some landsmen, the seamen pushed off from the pier, and we put out to sea, heading across the strait. It was wide. On the Western Strait, we had been able to see both coasts from our small craft. Not on this larger body of water, a finger of the Northern Sea.

The seamen bustled around the cog, hoisting up the sail and making headway. But now, as the coast behind us dwindled and disappeared, a calm came rippling across the waters. "To the oars!" the ship's master bawled out. The seamen rushed to obey him. They looked panicked.

"Good master!" Oisin called to him as he strode the deck, but the ship's master paid him no heed. "Good sir!" Oisin, too, was looking nervous. "I've paid good coin for my passage," Oisin insisted. "You must answer me." But the master ignored him.

A lookout at the mast let out a strangled cry. I pushed myself up from the narrow strut where I was sitting and stared in the direction of his pointing finger but could see nothing. Oisin grabbed me by the cloak to pull me down. "Wife. Wife," he muttered. He looked terrified.

Now a murmuring rose from the seamen, and now they had left their oars to rush to one side of the ship, their voices rising to shouts of fear. The ship's master laid about him with a rope, screaming at them to get back to their oars, but they paid him no mind.

I struggled to my feet again, pushing off Oisin's clutching hand. He pulled his cloak half over his head and fell cowering to the planks at the bottom of the cog.

"The Blue Men! They're coming!"

# Witchery

The Blue Men!" As near as I could make out, that's what the mariners were screaming. Blue Men? I thought, confounded. The naiads with the blue hair, the water demons my father had always told me were only stories. Could that be what these mariners thought they were seeing, dead ahead of our vessel in the sea?

Past Oisin's horrified shriek, I stepped to the rail to look.

A short way from us, the sea was boiling. The ripples spread, and then heads began bobbing up above the waves. Creatures. They were blue, but whether they were men or not, I leave to the wisdom of others.

"They'll sing," one of the mariners groaned. "We're lost."

I plucked him by the sleeve. "What happens when they sing?" I asked, but he stood terrified, making the sign of the Sea Child over and over, and didn't answer. Now all the seamen turned to stare at the ship's master, who approached the rail and gaped beyond it at the Blue Men. He had gone pale. He licked his lips as if he were trying to speak, but only a croak came from between his lips. The mariners let out a collective groan. Some sank to their knees.

And now, over the water came an unearthly sound. The Blue Men. They were singing.

Their voices were eerie and mocking, ringing out like strange silvery bells, alien music. But we could all make out the words.

*I saw the old moon yesternight*, came their song, wavering over the suddenly still waters at us. *With the new moon in his arms*, they sang. Then they were silent.

"Sing to them, sir, or we be dead men," cried one of the mariners to the ship's master.

"I don't know it," he said, his face a mask of despair. "I don't know what to sing. I can't." But he stepped again to the rail and lifted his chin, as if he were about to try to sing to the creatures. Again, only a croak came from between his parched lips.

I looked around me. Beside me stood a young seaman, just a boy, really. His mouth gaped open and his eyes were wide with fright. I grabbed his hand and squeezed it. "Do you have a knife?" I said to him, pulling him around to face me and forcing his eyes on mine.

"Yes, mistress," he stuttered.

"Give it here," I said.

He handed it over, beginning to weep.

"Hush, now," I said. I stepped to my chest and with a deft motion sliced my rebec free of its ropes. I caught it to me and stepped back to the rail.

Again, the eerie voices came at us over the water.

*I saw the old moon yesternight, with the new moon in his arms.*

"Third time we're done," screamed one of the mariners to the master. "Sing, man!"

Again the master lifted his chin and opened his mouth. Again, no sound other than a dismal croak came out of it. He threw his hands over his face and stumbled back from the rail.

A moan of despair rose from the men. The sea boiled more ferociously, and more of the blue creatures rose to the surface. I could see them now. They were grinning, and their serrated rows of teeth looked gleaming sharp.

The hidden place inside me, dormant so long, opened to me now. I knew what to do.

I stepped to the rail and brought my bow down in a commanding motion across the strings of the rebec.

The creatures stopped their writhing and stood up on their tails in the waves, their saucer eyes astonished.

The song issued across the waves to the ship again, less mocking and more uncertain. *I saw the old moon yesternight,* they quavered, *with the new moon in his arms.*

I sang back to them, my voice carrying triumphantly across the stretch of water to where they waited: *If you sail out to sea, my love, you'll never more come home.*

A deep hush fell over the waves. The seamen, the master, Oisin— they were all cringing away from me, as terrified of me as they were of the creatures.

Now the voices came again.

*O forty leagues off Holy Isle 'tis fifty fathoms deep.*

Now I felt a moment of fear, because this wasn't the version of the song I knew. If I sang the wrong thing, would the charm break? But if they could improvise, I decided I could, too.

*And there lie all the seamen drowned, their loved ones' hearts to break,* I sang back to them.

Now they were singing again, their heads bobbing up and down in the sea, their strange eyes fixed on me.

*Halcyon, oh fisher bird of Child forever true,* they sang.

I didn't think about what should come next. I just opened my mouth and the music poured out of it.

*Sing to me and fly to me, and I will sing to you.*

One by one, the blue creatures launched themselves partway out of the water, revealing their scaley fins and tails. One by one, they sank back under, until only their bubbles of eyes floated at the surface. One by one, they blinked them closed. The roiling sea calmed. Then it became a serene silver plane, and the creatures sank beneath the surface of the sea and were gone.

The ship went completely silent. And now a cheer erupted from the mariners, and they were leaping to me and pounding me on the back and hugging me. Some of them were kissing me. The small boy-seaman stood on tiptoes to give me a shy kiss. The master stepped to me and took up my hand in his rough paw.

"Mistress," he said, his voice husky. "ye saved us, that ye did. When the Blue Men come, and they sing at ye, ye're a dead man if ye don't know what to sing back. If ye sing the wrong thing, ye're just as dead as if ye stay silent. They swarm yer ship, they take'er to the bottom, and there they feast on yer bones, that they do."

I was speechless. How had I known what to sing? The Children gave me the right words, I suppose. Or luck. I pressed his hand and smiled at him.

Then I went back to my place beside Oisin and sat down. He blinked, like a person coming out of a deep sleep, or a trance, maybe. He looked over at me, his eyes wide with shock and horror. He took the rebec away from me. I let him take it. It fell from my nerveless hands into his.

"Wife," he whispered. I didn't answer. We spent the next leagues of the voyage in silence. When the cog docked on the mainland shore, Oisin hustled me off and into the cart held waiting for us by a servingman. Behind us, the seamen shouted and gesticulated toward me, and the passers-by stopped to gawk after us.

"Get this cart on the road to home," Oisin said to his servingman, shoving me in and drawing the brocaded curtains close around us. He put his head out and I heard him say, his voice tense, "Stop for no one. Do you hear?" And we jolted away, followed by shouting from behind us.

He said nothing to me during the ride to his manor, ten leagues or more away from the coast. I tried to doze.

Finally the cart began to slow. Oisin sprang out of it. I heard him give terse instructions to someone. I heard footsteps going away.

Then Oisin was reaching into the cart and yanking me by the arm out of it. He hurried me into a dim outbuilding while I looked in puzzlement and rising panic over my shoulder at him. When we got inside, he slammed the door to. He laid hands on me, shoving me to a rail along one wall where it looked like animals might be tethered. I fell against it hard. He grabbed up a leather strap and fastened me to the rail. Then he picked up a stout stick and began to beat me. In the dim light filtering into the place through a narrow window, I saw his face distorted by fear and rage.

I screamed out in protest, and then in pain. Eventually, my throat raw from screaming, I sagged down from the strap and he stood back, dropping the stick, breathing hard. He left me then, and I half lay, half sat, still bound to the rail, until the next morning.

A servingwoman woke me then. She opened the door a crack and peeked in. Wera was her name, I later discovered. The bright slash of sunlight made me squint through swollen eyes at her. I couldn't speak. My whole face was swollen. I moaned.

"Good sweet Lady," said Wera. She unbound me from the rail and sat down on a small stool beside me, a pail at her side. She dipped a cloth into the water in the pail and carefully, painstakingly washed the dried blood off my body. She pulled my clothes in strips away from me. Finally she helped me stand and pulled a clean kirtle over my head.

"Lean on me, mistress," said Wera. Half dragging me, half-leading me, she took me to a bedchamber and put me to bed. I slept for a full day, maybe. It's hard to remember.

When I woke again, Oisin was by my bedside. I shrank away from him.

"Wife," he said. "If you practice witchery, I must beat you. Don't do it again. Stoning is the sentence for witchery."

"I saved your life," I whispered. "I saved all of your lives."

"The penalty for witchery is stoning to death," said Oisin. His mouth was set in a stubborn line. "Luckily, I got us away from the port before someone could accuse you. Now no one can claim I haven't done my duty. I've disciplined you. I think the law will see it my way. I think you're safe, wife." Then he muttered, "I think I'm safe."

He left me then. I drowsed in that room for several days. Wera brought me something to eat from time to time. When I could stand and move around again, Oisin showed me my new household just as if nothing harsh between us had ever happened.

He led me around the yard of my new home. It wasn't as imposing a place as Fylkir's, not by a long sight, but it was comfortable enough. He showed me what he expected of me as housewife, the cooking and cleaning and direction of the two bondservants on the place.

"And I'll beat you if you don't do as I say," he concluded. He said this without heat, but he took me to the outbuilding, shoved the door open as I cringed back, and pointed out his stick leaning against the wall in a corner. "That's how I managed my first wife Griselda," he told me. "She and I got along just fine, once that was clear between us. But then she died in childbed." He had no children, he told me. He expected me to give him some.

That's how all these men managed their women, it seemed. I wondered dully if that's how it had been in the Riverlands village where I'd spent my childhood. It was certainly not that way between my parents. My mother and my true father, Drustan. They'd shared everything with each other. I'd never seen Drustan raise a hand to my mother Elsebet, ever, except in love.

That night, my husband Oisin moved me out of the little room where I'd been staying and brought me to his bed. I closed my eyes and let him do whatever he needed to do, trying not to cry out when he ground down on my bruised body. That seemed to be enough for him.

And so day succeeded dreary day.

For the first time since Wat's older brother John taught me how to play and my father had made me an instrument of my own, I couldn't bear to touch my rebec.

Oisin seemed inordinately proud of it, though. He hung it in a place of honor in the hall of the manor house. When guests came, I'd watch him pointing it out to them as I silently served them the dishes I had cooked.

"She brought it with her," he'd tell them, nodding his head in my direction. "She can't play it, but it's a pretty thing, isn't it?"

The guests would admire it, admire the skillful carving. My father's hands had made it and had carved the beautiful images. My true father, Drustan. I remembered well his clever hands fashioning it. And I remembered Johnny teaching me to play his own rebec. I remembered Elsebet, my mother, always singing. I remembered the tenderness between my mother and father, as my little sister Jillian and I played at their feet in the firelight.

While the guests admired the fisher-bird my true father had carved on my rebec, and the vines and flowers, and the blackbird cleverly fashioned as the tailpiece, I'd busy myself clearing away the dishes and helping out with the scouring and washing afterward. Anything to get out of the hall, to get away from the beloved sight of it.

And I wondered, too, at Oisin's words. *She can't play it,* he told everyone. Yet he'd heard me play it to charm away the Blue Men. Had he somehow blocked that dread incident out of his mind? Or was he just making sure any stories certain drunken mariners might be telling around the local taverns would be disbelieved? If he was so worried about accusations of witchcraft, why wouldn't he hide the rebec away? It was a mystery. I didn't know the answer. Thinking about it exhausted me. In the end, I found I really didn't care why he behaved the way he did.

All my songs had dried up in my throat. I barely spoke. My words had dried up, too.

Late the next year, I gave birth to a baby boy, but much too early. The baby didn't live a day. I turned my face to the wall. I couldn't weep. I couldn't feel.

Oisin took it hard. If I had had any human sympathy left, I would have felt for him. But I had none. None for him, and none for myself.

I was weak. I'd lost a lot of blood. Oisin sent healers in to me, but they weren't much use. They prayed to the Lady Goddess over me. That's how I learned that Oisin had become a loyal subject of the king, whoever he was at that time and at that northwestern edge of the mainland. Audemar? Caedon? I supposed it was Caedon, but really, I neither knew nor cared.

Only one good thing came of it. The healers insisted I be moved to a small room by myself.

I felt myself wasting away. I thought I'd die, and I looked forward to the peace that would come with death. Maybe I'd be reunited with Wat across that river. Maybe. I didn't really know. But at least I'd be rid of this burdensome life of mine. To hasten it, I started refusing to eat.

In the stupor where I lay, fantasies flitted across the screen of my self. *What if,* I asked myself. *What if you had given yourself to Caedon?* I had no illusions Caedon would have actually married me. He just wanted to regain control of me. In the end, though, I doubted he would have paid Fylkir to do that. He'd already given me his object lesson in control, and that seemed enough for him. He saw exactly what I myself had seen about Fylkir. Fylkir was rich and ambitious. Fylkir had claim to lands in the Fire Isle. But Fylkir's ability to reclaim his lands depended on whether he could get men like Caedon to support him. Caedon needed a sure thing. He needed to marry into firmly established privilege and influence. Otherwise, why do it? He needed to add power on top of power.

But all that day I had hidden away in my room, I could have instead made myself pleasant to Caedon, even begged him to take me away with him. I could have lured him, that night in the garden.

If I had given myself to Caedon, I could have gone away with him. No one is able to be vigilant all the time. Sooner or later I would have found the opportunity I needed. And I would have killed him.

I saw something else. Caedon understood what I hoped to do to him. He wanted the challenge of it, my wits against his.

He wouldn't squander a marriage to get it, though, or even a chest of gold. Caedon the realist.

But in the end I also knew something else. I knew I'd never willingly let Caedon put his hands on me again. Not for all the missed opportunities in the Nine Spheres.

It tortured me to think of the things he'd had done to Wat. What he'd seen as Wat died. When I thought of it, I moaned in agony. Oisin or one of the bondservants would come running, but I just turned my face to the wall when they did.

I remembered too well what Avery had told me. How Caedon had imprisoned Wat's brother John. Then how he'd had John tortured. Debased. Killed. And how Caedon had watched. There was something twisted inside Caedon.

I remembered too well Caedon's words to me in that room of his, such a civilized room, lined with books. *I killed the little brother. Then I killed the older brother. Now I'm going after the other one, and I'll have the whole set, all three of those bastards.*

*Now he has the whole set,* I thought. His words in the garden kept coming back to me. *I like to draw these occasions out a little bit, when I have a man like that where I want him.* The bitterness of it made me scream out as though someone were stabbing me.

I suppose Oisin and his household had an uneasy life, with me around.

One night, as I lay in the gray half-sleep that consumed most of my life, I heard voices outside my room. Oisin's and someone else's. A woman's voice.

"She'll go like the other one did. And then what?" I heard Oisin saying. "I need sons. The other one couldn't give me sons, and now this one can't."

"Master Oisin," I heard the woman reply, "Why do you come to me with your troubles. Don't you worship the Lady Goddess, as our masters bid us?"

"Yes, but you know I worshiped the Sea Child in my youth. My mother used to bring me to you. I don't know where to turn. She—my wife—I think she worships the Children. I think her protector is the Sea Child."

"It's very dangerous for me to be here, Master Oisin."

"I promise you no harm will come to you. Just see her and find out if there's something you can do with her. I can do nothing with her. She screams. I think the grief of the baby's death has made her run mad. I don't know what to do. By day, I'll pay my respects to the Lady Goddess, as is my duty. But right now, go to her. I promise you no one will know you've come here. I'll make sure no one knows or sees."

The woman murmured some kind of assent.

I heard my husband's heavy feet, diminishing away.

The door opened, and a woman came in. Through the dim light filtering through the window, I could see that she was old. She drew up a stool beside my bed and sat down on it heavily. She picked up my hand and held it close.

"Dear one, beloved of the Sea Child. You are very troubled."

I turned my head away. *Where were the Children when I needed help?* I thought bitterly. Fylkir and Stefan might have been worshippers of theirs, but it didn't make them good or honest or kind. As for the Lady Goddess. My mother had believed in Her. *Help us, Lady, when no help is near.* That was the prayer she'd taught me. In spite of my mother's sincere belief and her own gentle ways, the Lady Goddess didn't help me at all, just as She hadn't helped my mother. The priest of the Lady had participated in the selling of me to this man as if I were an ox or a horse.

"Great wrong has been done to you," the old priestess whispered. "I can sense this. And I know what Oisin is. He is not that bad a man. At least, he doesn't mean to be. He's as good as the people around him are, and no better. I've known him from his boyhood. But he has no under-standing. His first wife died as you are dying. She died of despair. I beg you, dear child. Don't give in to him and to those like him. Fight."

Now I turned to look at her. Fight? All the fight in me was gone.

"They took away my daughter. They tell me my hus-band, whom I love, is dead. They sold me to this man. And now my baby by him is dead, too."

"But they don't own you, my daughter. They may tell you they do, and try to make you think they do, but they don't. You own yourself."

Where had I heard those words before? I had heard them from Wat, from my friends in the Rising, from

Diera herself. And deep inside myself, I had known them to be true.

"What must I do?" I whispered.

"There's a journey you may undertake, if you're strong enough to do it."

"What journey?"

"North of here, an outcropping of rock juts out over the sea. Cut into the rock, a hermitage. The Sea Child's farwydd lives there. Yes, the very one. She is older than I am. Far older. She is very wise. Go to her. Ask for a vision. If anyone can help you, she can. The Sea Child is your protector and mine, and this is our farwydd. But before you can go to her, you must get strong enough, because the journey is hard."

"How can I leave? I'm a prisoner here, or just as good as," I said, turning my head away again.

"Are you? Are you indeed? I can't help you there, my daughter. There you must help yourself. Here is a parchment." She put it into my unresponsive hand.

After a moment, I closed my fingers over it.

"Don't lose it. As you get stronger, ponder it. It's a map that will lead you to the farwydd. But you must want to go there, and you must become strong enough to go there. It's not magic, you know. Or rather, it is magic, but magic that lives inside you."

I turned back to her. I tried to thank her, but my cracked lips wouldn't make the words.

"Bless you, dear one, beloved of the Child of Sea," she said, and kissed me on the forehead.

She stood up and glided out of the room.

"How is she?" I heard Oisin say to her, just outside. "Can you help her?"

"We prayed together," said the priestess. "Now it's up to her."

I pushed the parchment she had given me underneath the mattress of horsehair on the bed. I promised myself I'd look at it in the morning. I promised myself I'd really sleep, and in the morning, I promised myself I would eat.

I'd get stronger. I'd make the journey. I'd find a way.

# Chapter Nine

# Getaway

That's what I did. I made myself stronger. The very next morning, I began forcing myself to eat. Oisin's two bondservants were overjoyed. I worried that perhaps he'd had them beaten when I wouldn't eat before. I didn't dare ask them, though. I needed to keep my plans a secret from everyone and make no alliances in this household. But I did need to eat, and that couldn't be kept hidden very easily.

Early in my time in Oisin's household, I had thought about trying to turn the bondswoman, Wera, into my ally. When Oisin beat me that first day, her appalled reaction made me think she sympathized with me. That wasn't the way of it at all. She'd heard the gossip that I had practiced witchcraft.

The beating didn't appall her.

I appalled her.

And I soon realized Oisin had set her to spy on me.

After the Sea Child's priestess left me, Oisin came to my bedside and sat holding my hand. However flawed he was, the priestess was right. He was a weak man but not a deeply bad man. Just a man who believed what he'd always believed about the world, without the imagination to think anything other. A man with few inner resources and no backbone who was trying to survive as best he could in a changing and dangerous world.

When I compared him to Fylkir and Stefan, I saw two different types of people. Fylkir, my own father, played both ends against the middle and sat, self-satisfied, in his remote manor while he profited from the conflict and ruthlessly rid himself of whatever he needed to sacrifice in order to enrich himself. To use whatever and whomever he had in his control to gain power. A daughter, a granddaughter. Probably a wife. I thought of the treatment my mother must have endured at his hands. Stefan was cut from the same cloth. These men were my own father and brother. I shuddered to think that somewhere inside me the materials that made them up lay hidden. Then I reminded myself that my mother had been nothing like the two of them. She had gotten me away from them and had given me a better father and a better sister.

That was the belief I clung to.

The father inside me was Drustan, a good man, and noble. He was an earl, but his nobility lay in the true dignity granted by nature. Even in childhood, when I thought he was a poverty-stricken farmer, I could see that. My mother too was noble. Noble and strong in her nature, though she, Stefan let me know, was a commoner. If she'd only done that one good thing, getting me away from a man like Fylkir, I'd call her noble. She had not let me grow up with Fylkir as a father. She had seen to that. But she did many other good and noble things as well.

Now I knew I had to follow her example. I saw I must take my daughter back out of Fylkir's hands and make sure she knew her true father. Wat was her true father, and he was her actual father, too, but Wat was dead. I'd have to be both mother and father to Keera. I'd somehow have to show Keera what kind of father Wat would have been to her.

I swore to the Sea Child no man would take Wat's place. I knew in my bones no man would ever claim me. Only one ever had, and that was because we claimed each other. Now that man was gone.

I could do this for Keera's sake and for my own. I had the skills to do it. I just had to find those skills inside me again.

Before I could take such a step, I would follow the priestess's advice. I'd visit the farwydd in her hermitage. She would show me the way.

Little by little, I began making my plans. I studied the parchment the priestess had given me. It was a map showing how to get to the farwydd's hermitage. I took a piece of clothing here, a piece there, when I knew it wouldn't be missed. From the bottom of the chest where we kept the things the bondservants needed, I found an old pair of trousers on the small side. They didn't fit our manservant. They must have been owned by some long-ago departed servant, maybe a boy. They'd do fine. I found a worn-out tunic, too. It was much too big, but I could easily belt it.

In our farm shed, I found scraps of leather that I fashioned into a new scabbard to fix to my leg. I found a rusted knife. When the servants and Oisin were otherwise occupied, I oiled the knife, scraped it free of rust, and sharpened it on the whetstone in the farm shed.

I marveled how, all along, I could have done these things. But my despair had run too deep. Now at last I was doing what I needed to do.

Whenever I had a moment alone, I practiced the exercises Wat had taught me, and the ones Torrin, Lorel, and

Conal had taught me. I was so weak. I'd spent the better part of a year in bed. I needed to get stronger. I could tell from the map that the journey would be long.

Summer was drawing to a close. I had to leave before autumn turned the nights colder. Otherwise, I'd have to wait til spring. So now I began secreting food into a pouch I hid under my bed. All this time, I pretended a weakness I was actually beginning to overcome. I pretended I still needed to sleep by myself. I could tell Oisin was growing impatient, so I knew I had to hurry.

I kept hesitating. The time never seemed right. At night I stared into the dark, thinking, *I will miss my chance. I have to act.* Somehow, I knew I had to trust my inner voice. It would tell me when the right time came.

For a fortnight and more, Oisin had insisted I come to the table at night to eat the evening meal with him. I needed to play a fine game, so I was humoring him in that. On a particular night, I made my way into the hall, and when the servingman finished setting up the boards on their trestles, I slid to my place on the bench beside Oisin. He took my hand in his and smiled at me.

I managed to smile back. I could see he was trying, as best he knew how, to be kind. Wera brought us our meat. I picked at the edges of my trencher. I didn't have to feign a lack of hunger. I really wasn't hungry.

Instead, a new feeling began to fill me. I began to tingle from the roots of my hair downward into my limbs. I could barely talk. With rising excitement, I realized. The inner place was opening. It was time.

This night, Oisin was talking on and on about the work of the manor and the trade he was engaged to with the neighbors. "Tomorrow, wife, I'll journey to the south," he told me.

At his words, my eyes leapt to his face, but I remembered in time. Almost always, I kept my gaze cast down at my trencher, so it was easy not to let him see my sudden burst of joy.

"I have business there," Oisin continued, "and also, I need to go to the castle nearby. His Highness King Caedon is in residence there. I can't miss my chance to show him fealty."

"I thought—" I began, then cautioned myself, *go carefully*. "I thought you were King Audemar's man."

"You know little of politics, my wife," said Oisin with an indulgent chuckle. "One year, a man has to swear allegiance to one king. The next year, as it may happen, to another."

I nodded.

"Men know these things," said Oisin. "It is how we keep our women safe."

I nodded again.

"Does this please you, wife? That I am always looking out for your welfare?"

"Yes, husband," I forced myself to say, with the proper degree of meekness.

"Never fear, though. The bondservants have my orders. They'll keep you safe until my return. I'll not be gone long."

"Thanks to the Children," I said piously.

"To the Lady Goddess," he reminded me. His tone was sharp.

"To be sure, husband. Yes. To the Lady Goddess."

"Make certain you keep to yourself that—that thing I did," he said. Now he sounded anxious, even fearful.

"What thing is that, husband?"

"That time I sent the Sea Child's priestess to console you. That was a mistake."

"Oh," I said. "That."

"Make sure you keep that private. I was overcome with grief."

"Yes," I told him. "I'll remember."

"See that you do. Your safety depends on it."

*And yours*, I added silently.

"I'll have you beaten if you ever refer to that incident again. And you know I will do it."

"Yes, husband," I said in an appropriately humble tone. *He's frightened*, I told myself. He had only beaten me that once, at the beginning of our marriage, and I could tell he was so terrified of himself and his own rage that he'd never raised a hand to me since, although from time to time I angered and frustrated him. I felt a kind of contempt for him, tinged with a strange sort of pity. I also felt a bitter regret that I'd ever let this man cow me into a year and more of abject helplessness. That was not going to happen again.

As I made my way to my little bedroom, feigning a weakness I no longer felt, I thought to myself, *Tomorrow is the day*. I wasn't afraid. I was on fire for the morning to come, for Oisin to depart, and then to make my escape. I lay listening to the night noises, the creak of the timbers of the house, the soft cries of birds or animals rousing and then subsiding again into quietness. I barely slept.

In the morning, I helped Oisin into his traveling cloak and saw him to our wagon. He kissed me before he mounted to the wagon seat. I steeled myself not to cringe away from his withered sunken cheek, his reeking mouth, his avid eyes that always reminded me of a carrion bird.

The two bondservants and I waved goodbye to him until the wagon disappeared over the crest of the hill and around the bend toward the road south.

I turned to the servants. "Before he left, our master told me you would need to go to our neighbor over the hill to get seed, Mort," I told the bondsman. He pulled his forelock obediently. "Do that after you have seen to the hogs," I said.

To the bondswoman, Wera, I said, "Our master wants me to become a more accomplished needlewoman. Accompany Mort, please. The goodwife at our neighbor's farm has made me a pattern to copy so that I can embroider a sash for the master." It's true. I was wretched at embroidery. Even Wera knew that wasn't a lie.

"Master says you're not to be left alone," Wera told me anyway. She had a stubborn look in her eye.

"But I say you're to go," I said. My voice was firm. "I am hoping to make a present for the master. If you don't go now, I won't have time to embroider the sash before the master's return."

She dropped me a sullen curtsey.

After an anxious interval, I watched both servants trudging across the fields toward the neighboring farm.

Here was my chance. I whirled into the house, retrieving the map and pouch of food from under the bed. I stripped off my clothing and hid it under the furs of my bed, and then drew on the trousers and tunic, belting the tunic with my own sash so it would not drag down. Last I hiked up my right trouser leg and strapped the knife in its scabbard to my calf. I slit that trouser leg to the knee so that I could quickly draw the knife.

Now I headed to the door. I was about to leave when I remembered something. I remembered my rebec, hanging on the wall in the main hall.

It's a measure of how severely my life had turned that I almost forgot it, the object most precious to me in this world. So I turned back to the hall and went in. I dragged the bench by the door to the wall where the rebec hung, and stepped up onto it. I was just lifting the rebec down when a noise behind me almost toppled me from the bench. I slung the rebec over my shoulder and turned to see Wera staring at me from the door.

"Mistress. You are doing wrong. Master told me to watch for this. You must go into your room. Master told me to bolt you in if you gave me any trouble."

Wera was a big strapping woman. She outweighed me by quite a bit.

I wasn't afraid of her. She'd be easy to gut, and a part of me wanted to do it.

"Wera," I said. "So you see how it is. I'm leaving, and you can't stop me."

"The master will beat me. When he gets back, he'll beat you too, mistress."

"He may beat you, but he'll never put his filthy hands on me again," I said. A hot rage was rising in me.

She came at me then. She stopped dead when she saw me at a crouch, my knife in my hand.

"Don't take a step closer, Wera. The Child knows I don't want to kill you. But I will if I have to."

She hesitated. I saw her steel herself. She clearly thought she could overpower me.

Thinking quickly, I summoned up all my acting skills. It was that, or actually kill the silly woman. I dropped the knife to my side and raised my left hand, gesturing in the air and muttering out some uncanny words. Truth to tell, they were words of the Old Ones I had learned from Caedon long ago, but Wera didn't know that.

"Omnia. . Gallia. . .est divisa. . . in partes. . ." I muttered. Then I screamed out "Tres!"

I could see it in Wera's face. She turned pale and her mouth worked. She backed away, nearly stumbling over a stool. *Witchcraft!* That's what I knew she was thinking. I knew she was remembering all the stories about the Blue Men when I'd first arrived, and how Oisin had beaten the witchery out of me. But now, I could see just by looking at her what she was thinking. *Maybe not!*

She whirled around and was out the door, pounding across the fields to the neighbors. I could have stopped her. I stepped to the door and watched her run. I could have gone after her, cut her down. Wat would have. *Do it.* Wat's voice in my head. Eris, Wat's half-sister, the one who betrayed us all, would have reached back with the knife and hurled it powerfully end over end forward, to bury it between Wera's shoulder blades.

I raised the knife. Hesitated. Lowered it again. Slowly I re-sheathed it. I picked up my rebec from where I had laid it down, and I walked out of there. By the time Wera was back with help, I'd be gone. Letting her live was a risk, and it had whittled away the time I'd need if I were going to get myself far enough away to be safe, especially if the neighbors came after me on horseback. But it was a risk I had to take. I had killed three men in my flight from the burned-out village on the coast, during the retreat of Audemar's army, and I'd killed the assassin sent after me and Wat. Those killings were almost too much for my conscience to bear. Some nights those killings kept me awake.

Things like that never kept Wat awake at night, yet he's a gentle man. And then, I thought with pain, there was my father, the gentlest man I knew. The kindest. The most loving. The assassin from whom Wat learned his skills.

I can't explain my actions then—or lack of them. Just the same, whatever Wat might think about it, I wasn't going to add Wera to the list of my dead.

*Whatever Wat might think about it.* As if he were still around to think it.

# Journey

Heading west from Oisin's farm, I cut diagonally across the waste land stretching past our fields into the rugged country at the foot of the range of increasingly steep mountains beyond. The land was ragged and uneven, with no tree cover, just leagues of undulating uplands scored by deep gullies and patches of lower-lying bog.

Far away to the right between me and the start of the mountainous terrain, I spotted a lone figure, probably a peat-cutter. Behind me, Oisin's farm, the turf-clad big house and all the outbuildings, were dwindling away. I kept looking over my shoulder nervously until I nearly fell into one of the gullies slashed across my path. *That's all I need*, I thought. A twisted ankle. I'd be brought back to Oisin in disgrace and might never get the chance to escape again. For that matter, I might be stoned as a witch once Wera had finished telling her fantastical tale.

It was hard to concentrate, knowing that by now Wera had reached the neighboring farm to raise the alarm.

Shading my eyes with my hand, I studied the land before me. The gullies were getting deeper, effectively herding me ever closer to the peat cutter. But he wouldn't know who I was. He'd take me, no doubt, for some vagabond. So I didn't worry as much about him as I worried about mounted pursuers coming up on me from behind. I trudged on.

Not a candle measure later, some impulse led me to look back the way I'd come. There, unmistakably, horsemen appeared over a little rise, and they were frighteningly close behind.

The treacherous land meant they weren't gaining on me fast, but they were gaining. These pursuers obviously knew the land and how to pick their way across it. In a panic, I realized that if they were visible to me, I must be visible to them. But I'd be too far away for them to make me out exactly. They wouldn't be sure I was the one they were after.

For that matter, I wasn't sure this party of horsemen was after me, either.

I didn't dare start to run. If I did, that would only con-firm for them that I was the wayward wife they were hunting. If they indeed were. And I might break my leg into the bargain.

As I stood thinking over my choices, the riders halted. I could distinctly see one raise an arm to point at me. Then they resumed their steady progress in my direction.

As if casually, I changed the course of my path, zigzag-ging across the landscape, but still they came on. At one point, I took the risk of leaping across a deep gully, al-most a crevasse, that slashed through to the edge of the bog where I could see the peat cutter bent over his work. I landed in a forward roll on the other side of the gully, just as Wat had taught me, thanking the Children or, more accurately, my own good sense, that I hadn't tried this journey in skirts. I was still weak from a season and more of inactivity, but I stumbled to my feet none the worse for my leap.

That should slow my pursuers down. Even a good horsewoman like my poor dead rebel friend Lorel wouldn't leap that gap on horseback. The horse would go down on such treacherous boggy ground. The riders would have to go around the crevasse, which slashed across the rugged landscape a good long way, and when they did, the lay of the land would hide me from their line of sight, at least for a bit. But they'd still catch up to me, and soon.

I looked desperately around me for a hiding place. "What's this, now."

It was the peat cutter, standing directly in my path, his mattock and spade slung across his shoulder.

Without thinking, I made that sign we all make. The sign of the Children. My heart was pounding. I tried not to look frightened and guilty.

"That were a leap, lad," he said, frowning. "Thought I'd have to drag ye home behind me, broken to bits." He took a step forward, his eyes widening. "Ye're a lass." Then he reached to lay a warning hand on my arm. He stepped to the crest of the slough where he had been working with the peat and then back to me.

But I'd knelt on the boggy ground, trying to prepare myself to be taken. Trying to decide whether to fight, and how hard. I knew I could keep myself from being taken, if I was ready to take the fight to extremes, but if I were killed, what would become of Keera?

The peat cutter came back to me. "I see how it is, lass." He took me by the shoulders. "Stay low," he said. "They'll not take ye, vile liver-eaters that they be." He pulled me forward and into the strip he'd been working. He pushed me face-down into the furrow and began piling the blocks of turves on top of me, pressing me flat. I pulled my hands to my face to make a hollow so I could breathe, and I curved my body protectively around my rebec.

I heard voices above me. The peat-cutter sliced through the peat, the blade of his spade just missing my ear.

"Fellow, a woman came past not too long ago. Which way did she go?"

"Nay," I heard the peat-cutter say. "I saw none."

"Come, come, my man. We spotted her heading this way."

"Oh, aye? I've seen naught but a stripling lad pass by."

A different voice. "That's the one. Wera said she's in men's things."

"Oh, indeed." That was the first who had spoken. I tried to make out the voice. Was it the householder from the neighboring farm? I couldn't tell. I hadn't had much to do with the man. "That's the one we are hunting, fel-low," he said to the peat-cutter.

"That way," I heard the peat cutter say.

"Our thanks, good man. There's witchery afoot." That was the second voice, another of the pursuers. I tried to calculate how many of them there might be. Two voices, but I'd seen more horsemen than that. Three, maybe four, I guessed. "Master Oisin will reward you well for your information," this other voice was saying. "Present yourself at the manor on the next full of the moon, when he holds his assizes. This is his runaway witch-wife we're after."

"Danger, my masters," I heard the peat cutter say. "If this lad I saw be a witch, I want nothing to do with 'ee."

"We'll take her. And you'll get your reward. Don't be frightened, man. You've done well," said the voice. Then I heard the horses moving off.

During this exchange, I thought I would suffocate, pressed down into the peat, but at last the jingling and creaking of the horses' gear began fading away.

"Don't get up yet, mistress." The peat-cutter's voice, quiet, just above me. Then, after a time, "Safe now, mistress."

I struggled to my feet while he shoved the blocks of peat off me. I was coughing and brushing the crumbling bits of peat out of my mouth, nose, and hair.

"Runaway wife," he said now, scrutinizing me. "Witch, too. I took you different. There have been some of them men over the way lately making off with our village maids and leaving them ruint. I thought ye were one o them maids." He looked at me skeptically.

"Oh, good sir, I'm no witch. I'm a widow my father has forced into marriage with that man Oisin, and he took me away from my daughter. I have to find her. My father will sell her too." Then I burst out, "She's still a small child, good sir!"

"Oisin, he be one o the big landowners about here."

I thought then he'd probably run after my pursuers and turn me in to them now.

Instead, he spat into the ground at his feet. "They're trying to force us off our land and take it for theirselves, them big men," he said. "Buying theirselves brides, is it? I'd sell no daughter of mine, nor give her, neither, not to the likes o they. I'd sell no babe."

"I wish my father thought as you do, good sir."

"How will you find your girl, lass?"

"A priestess of Sea told me, seek out the farwydd. She'll tell you how."

He made that sign. He put a hand on my shoulder and stared into my face. I thought for a moment he wouldn't believe me. How far-fetched my story must sound. A runaway wife is a dreadful thing. She must be punished and brought to know her duty. Everyone thought that. And I was a witch besides.

But the man stepped back. "Go to her, lass, the farwydd, and pray for me and mine there in her halls. May the Child go with ye."

"I will, good sir. How can I ever thank you? You have saved me from men who meant me ill," I told the peat-cutter, dropping him my best curtsy as soon as I could breathe easy again.

"Lady-likers," he said, and he turned aside and spat on the ground. "Lady-likers and landlords. But as for ye, mistress, ye're no witch. I see the Children watch over ye."

I stared at him. Then I realized why he had believed me. When I rose from the earth after my tumble across the crevasse, I was so startled I'd made the sign of the Children. I saw it had saved my freedom, because this man believed me, not them. It may have saved my life, if my pursuers had taken Wera's tales of witchcraft seriously. Witches died by stoning.

"I'm no witch," I told the peat-cutter. "The fisher-bird is my friend."

He made that sign now. "Sea Child keep ye on your journey," he said, "and may She protect ye from all such ill-doers as those ones." He clapped me on the shoulder. As I turned to go, he stopped me. "Mistress, my goodwife keeps a warm hearth should ye wish to shelter a while."

"My thanks, good sir, but I have a long journey ahead of me, and I fear for my daughter."

He raised his hand in blessing, and I walked on. When I looked back over my shoulder a way down further across the moor, he was bent again to his ridge of peat with mattock and spade.

I slept rough that night, wrapped in my warm cloak, thanking the Children—and luck, but the Children too— for my delivery. Strange to tell, I slept soundly. My cloak was a bright blue. I had hesitated to take it, but I needed protection from the weather, the farther north I moved and the shorter the days grew toward autumn. I found that if I wore the cloak inside out, with the fur to the outside, I'd blend in with my surroundings. This night, I made a little ceremony of eating the one lump of bread I allowed myself. I huddled in my cloak and spread my neckerchief out before me. I placed the lump of bread in the middle. I raised my hand to the sky, thanking the Child of Sea. Then I raised it again, thanking the peat cutter. I ate the lump slowly. My food might have to last me a while.

By now I had made my way up a long green hill, almost a mountain. The bog stretched out far below me. I was exposed on the hill, but at least I'd be able to see any pursuers. None appeared. The sun set west of me in brilliant bands of color. Before it got full dark, I needed to find a stream. Over the crest of the big hill I found one, trickling down from an outcropping of rocks. I threw myself to the ground beside it, drinking the cold water in deeply. Then, under the shelter of those same rocks, I wrapped myself fur-side inward in my cloak. The darkness would hide its brilliant blue, and the furs would keep me warm while I slept.

The next morning dawned clear and warm. I groaned as I unkinked my stiff limbs. I had let soft living get to me. That was over now. I went about the morning's business of setting my traps. Soon I'd caught a fat rabbit. I trussed it and slung it over my shoulder with my rebec.

No one had seen which direction I'd gone, and to go north would seem madness to most. I'd learned well from

Torrin and Lorel, my teachers, how to dissolve into a landscape so cleverly that even a keen-eyed watcher might not know I was there. That skill had helped with my flight with Keera away from the burning village far away over on the Western Isle, and it helped me now.

I encountered no one along the way. The further north I went, the less likely I was to see anyone at all. No one lived up here. The landscape was too rugged for farming, and the cliffs at the sea too steep for fishing. I doubted my pursuers were persisting, once the peat cutter had misdirected them.

Besides, if my pursuers hadn't gotten discouraged and were still trying to track me, they'd think to overtake me by going in a different direction entirely. The most likely path Oisin and any other pursuers might think I'd take would be west, toward the coast. Toward my daughter. They'd put out word about me among the seamen and wait there to take me.

Oh, I'd get Keera back. But to do that, first I must go far to the north, here on the mainland. Still, I was cautious. Hunters might be about.

As I made my way north, the land steepened. Even with the exercises I had been doing, my legs were aching by mid-morning, and my breath came short. This journey was going to harden me. I needed that. On the second night, I risked starting a fire with my flint and steel. I roasted and ate my rabbit. Once again, I slept soundly.

On the following day, when the sun rode high in the sky, I stopped to sit under the shade of a boulder overlooking a high meadow. I reached into my bag and brought out a piece of bread and a piece of cheese. These would do. I was used to eating little. After I had eaten, licking my fingers of crumbs, I made my way to the verge of the surrounding forest and found another stream that ran through a forested glen. Upstream were rapids fed by a small waterfall. I picked my way out into the stream, balancing carefully along a series of downed mossy logs, and stepped out onto a large flat rock. I bent over, cupped my hands and drank from the stream. The water was fresh and cold.

Around me, the trees were thick. Not very tall, as our trees far to the south of here were, in the Riverlands where I grew up. These northern trees were gnarled and stunted. In their forms, I saw how the winter winds blew fiercely over them. The landscape was bleak, but it had its own sere beauty.

For the first time in many turnings of the moon, a song rose to my lips. After a while, I unslung my rebec and accompanied myself softly as I walked along. The risk seemed small, and playing music comforted me. *This is what I am born to do,* I whispered to myself. I had been divided from this deep inborn gift. No more.

That night, as I settled back against a tree trunk to sleep, a wave of melancholy overpowered me. I sang the song I had been trying my best all day not to sing.

> *I saw the old moon yester night*
> *with the new moon in his arms;*
> *if you sail out to sea, my love,*
> *you'll never more come home.*

I couldn't stop the tears running down my cheeks. My husband. My daughter. But then I pulled the cloak more closely over me, with the fur on the inside now that it was dark, and I gazed up at the stars. Hanging by their golden chains from the inside of their sphere, they were shining down on Keera. It's possible, I thought. It's just possible they were shining down on Wat, even in the Land of the Dead. The Children shone down on us all. Then I sang one last song before settling myself to sleep—the seventh verse of the song that Johnny the Traveler, Wat's brother, had taught me so long ago:

> *Seven for the seven stars over us.*
> *Green grow the rushes oh...*

I peered up through the branches, trying to make them out, the stars many call the Seven Sisters. I had sung the song on my wedding day, the same day as

Diera's coronation. *This is a song for you, Wat, I whispered.*
*Earth Child keep you wherever you may dwell.*

I was comforted. And I slept.

# Chapter Eleven

# Hermitage

Now, several days into my journey, after I had walked until mid-day, I began thinking I was making real progress. When I looked at the priestess's map and compared landmarks I had passed, I thought I might be nearing the farwydd's lair. In the distance, I heard the pounding of high seas against rock. But I couldn't be sure.

The further north I walked, the more my optimism drained away. The more I began to battle a down-hearted feeling. Maybe the map was too vague. Maybe I'd never be able to find the place where the farwydd had her hermitage. The sound of the sea gave me some hope. The priestess had told me the farwydd's hermitage was in a rocky cave overlooking the sea. But the land was vast, and so was the sea.

High above me on a grassy slope, sheep grazed. I raised my hand to shade my eyes. I gasped. There was a man up there. I'd spent such a long time as the only person in the landscape that I had gotten careless. Now, my heart pounding, I dodged behind a boulder and peered up at the man.

He was rounding up the sheep, nudging them with his staff to the path downward.

The boulder was the only shelter on the entire exposed ridge. I'd have to stay there until he passed. He seemed busy with the sheep, and I was confident he hadn't spotted me. He wasn't looking in my direction. He didn't seem alarmed or alert to me in any way. I settled in to wait.

He took his time picking his way down the meandering path from the top, reaching out with his staff every so often to keep a sheep with the rest of the flock and not wandering off toward some tasty-looking mouthful of grass.

As he came closer, my heart rose into my mouth. He was accompanied by a small black and white dog who harried the sheep by the heels and helped to keep them in line.

I'm not comfortable around dogs. The only dog I'd known was Bogo, the village beadle's mastiff, and only from a safe distance. He lived in my childhood village far to the south in the Riverlands. Bogo's task was to run down malefactors. He caught them and bit them. He killed some of them by ripping out their throats. We children knew to stay away from him.

But as soon as the shepherd and his flock got near, the little dog with him dashed down the path ahead of them and around my boulder, where he stood stiff-legged, barking loudly. I shrank beside the boulder and thought of running.

The shepherd came around too, to see why his dog was barking. He looked astounded when he saw me, but then he relaxed. With a whistle, he summoned his dog to his side. "Never fear, lad . . . or mistress, is it? Jakke here won't bother you. He's just curious."

I nodded to him, hoping he, his flock, and Jakke would go on their way.

"So, mistress. Are you here to see the farwydd, then?"

Now it was my turn to be astounded.

"You come up here, all of you, some from great distances," he went on. He was a short, stout man with a gray frizzle of hair, dressed in stained and well-worn rawhide. "You come to see her, our farwydd, although I hear it's not allowed now by the man who is our chief, or our . . . how do you say that? Our . . ."

"King?" I supplied.

"King, eh. Well, I didn't cast my lot at the moot for him."

I smiled at him. "Can you lead me to her, the farwydd?" I asked him.

"Of course. These are her sheep, aren't they? Follow me," said the man, who told me his name was Gur.

Thank the Children. I followed, although I was still apprehensive of Jakke, who left his master to trot alongside me.

At first, the way was pleasant. We moved down a gorge between two peaks. In the distance between the peaks, I could see the sea unfurling its shining length. Underfoot, the springy, grassy path felt good. My sore feet were unaccustomed to so much walking and climbing, even though I had made sure to make my getaway in my stoutest shoes.

After a time, we began to climb again. Until I got used to the pace, my breath came hard. We were going high. Gur stopped to pen the sheep up in a stone enclosure, and then we continued further up the path, which wound to a broad, flattened meadow.

I drew in my breath. All the way up, we'd made our way around rock outcroppings, boulders, meadows strewn with rocks. But these stones at the path's end were different. They were tall slabs that stood sentinel in a double row, forming a lane that led to a circle of smaller round stones. Gur moved to the center of the circle and stood quietly, making the gesture of the Children. I followed and imitated him, just in case it was expected of travelers to this high and wind-swept spot. Another double row of standing stones led away from the circle, and Gur followed these to the other side of the level place. As we neared the edge, I realized we stood on a high cliff overlooking the sea. From far below came the hollow booming of mighty waves dashing against the cliff.

The path of stones abruptly stopped at a gaping pit at the edge of the cliff face. A stream meandering across the level meadow at the top poured over the lip of this pit. Gur strode up to it. He popped down it. Jakke stood stiff-legged at the ragged margin, barking at me where I hesitated. He disappeared over the lip into the pit, then bounced back out again, barking and wagging his little sweep of a tail, then dashing at me, shoving at me with his snout.

I yelped in fright, leaping away from him.

Gur's head reappeared over the lip of the pit. "Bless ye, lass, Jakke's a herd dog. He's herding ye in. Come on, then." His head disappeared down the pit again.

I stepped gingerly to the edge and craned my neck to look. The pit led straight down to the sea below. Beside me, the silver strand of the stream dropped in a long twining veil to turbulent waters. A narrow rocky path wound down into the pit. I put a hesitant foot on the path, holding on as best I could to the cliff face on one side. As I crept down this path cut out of the rock of the cliff face, I avoided looking over the edge, although that was hard to do, since the path was so narrow. On my left hand, the sheer cliff soon towered far above. On my right, a straight drop-off, a dizzying fall to jagged stones and the wild sea below. If I missed my footing, I thought, I would have no more worries left in this world.

Gur and Jakke sped nimbly along, waiting at every sharp turn for me to catch up.

Abruptly, the path stopped. We were still far above the sea, clinging to the rocky side of a vast inverted broken funnel. The pit, the funnel's narrow mouth at the cliff's edge, had led us down into the widening part of the funnel, an enormous space curved back under the rocky land, carved by wind and weather out of the cliff face. One side sheared away, opened to sky and sea. Far below at the bottom, I saw the race of the sea boiling underneath the cliff into an opening, some kind of passageway or underground river.

Close beside the spot where the path ended at the sheared off rock face of the cliff, a natural window opened outward high above the sea and inward onto a cave hollowed out by the fierce weather into the rock. Far above, the underside of the pit at the end of the meadow of standing stones arched outward over us. The ledge directly to the right of us acted as a sort of broad window-sill projecting over the abyss. When Gur and Jakke got to the end of the path, they leapt from the path's end over a gap onto the ledge and into the cave. They looked back at me, waiting for me to do likewise.

The gap wasn't that wide, but the consequences of missing my footing were high. A drop to the rocks and the torrent below, which rushed over a series of rocky ledges outward to the sea and inward, underneath us, who knew where, would be death.

*I can't look down*, I told myself. I knew if I did, I'd freeze. So I made the leap. Once again, I thanked the Children for all the acrobatics Wat had taught me, back in the day when we were posing as poor strolling players.

I tumbled into the cave. Gur put out a hand to steady me, and I got to my feet. The interior of the cave was dim. I made out a small figure huddled at a fire toward the back. The smoke drifted to the opening and up and out into the air.

"Your Ladyship, here is someone come to see you," said Gur to this figure. He stepped aside and motioned me closer.

This tiny woman was the farwydd. The farwydd of the Sea Child. There is only one like her in the entire world. I looked into her face, and when I did, it was as if I had dropped down a deep well. Her face is as wizened as a dried up nut, and the same color. Her hair stands out around her head in a white halo like thistledown. There's something about her I can't describe, something so full of dominance and might that it made me want to bow low to the ground in her presence. People who make the mistake of thinking those of small stature are weaker than others should meet the Sea Child's farwydd. She is one of the most powerful persons I have ever encountered.

When she saw me, she got to her feet and moved toward me, holding out her hand.

I'm not tall, yet I towered over her.

But when I bent over her hand and kissed it reverently, a power flowed from her that over-awed me. I felt as if I were in the presence of a giant.

I curtseyed.

"Come to the fire, child, and sit by me," she said in a deep voice. Her voice almost seemed as if it were the source of her power, so big it was.

Gur pulled his forelock.

"Dony is my shepherd," the farwydd told me. "He brings me all the strays."

Gur murmured sidelong to me, "Dony was me great-grandfather, the first of us who served her. She gets us confused, sometimes." Then he dropped the bag of needments he'd brought the farwydd to the cave floor, and he and Jakke bounded back out the cave's vast window the same way they'd come in.

I was speechless.

"And you, child. You have lost the ones you love, and you've come to me for help."

"Yes," I whispered.

"I can point you the way, but I can't take you there. You must do that for yourself."

"I know where my daughter is," I said, "but not how to get her back from the people holding her. And my husband is—" I couldn't say it, so I temporized. "He may be dead."

"Yes." She nodded. "He may be. Perhaps the Sea Child will give you an answer. Perhaps she'll show you how to get your daughter, too."

"How do I ask Her?" I didn't think to wonder how the farwydd knew so much about me. She did. That was all that mattered. Then I worried I wasn't showing her the proper respect. I made that gesture of the Children and bowed to her. "I beg you to show me how to ask Her," I said.

"Follow me," she said, turning to a narrow crevice at the back of the cave. She slipped through it. I stared after her in despair. I didn't see how I'd be able to fit through that cleft in the rock.

I squeezed after her into the crevice, which soon went almost horizontal. My heart began to beat faster and my breath came short. I felt as if tons of rock were imprisoning me, sylvestran, and would never release me. I felt as if all the rock in the world were above me, and all the rock in the world were below me, and those enormous weights of rock were squeezing together. I forced the panic down and continued sidling along the crevice. It led to a small hole in the rock. Feet first, the farwydd popped down it, raising her hands so she'd be able to fit through. As for me, I spent many moments wedging myself through the tight little aperture, sure I'd get stuck there forever. At last I was through. I fell trembling to the floor of another, lower cave and crouched in the dark. I knew that out in the air, the sun shone and the sea pounded. Not even a dim ray penetrated to this place, and not a sound.

"There now," said the farwydd. Her voice came from right beside me. I heard flint sparking against steel. A flame blossomed. The farwydd shielded it with her hand and lit some wisps of grasses in the bowl of a soapstone holder affixed to the wall.

The farwydd and I were in a small chamber, almost circular. Across from us on the floor was yet another hole, but this one was too small for even the farwydd to fit through. A lazy tongue of smoke rose from it, meandered across the ceiling, and found the aperture we had come down. It rose through that, too.

The farwydd motioned me over to the hole in the floor. I followed her lead to sit cross-legged before it.

"This," she said, gesturing, "is the Sea Child's portal to the other world. Each of the Children has Her portal. The Earth Child's portal is far to the east, on a sun-warmed promontory. Her farwydd sits there on her tripod. People go to her from all over that southern sea to ask her questions and take her answers back to their people. The Sea Child's portal is here, almost forgotten. The Fire Child's is to the north of us, in the bowl made by a mountain of fire. The Sky Child's is to the west, somewhere in the vast lands that lie beyond the Great Sea. As for the other three, no one knows where they are or what Child commands them."

"When the Children fell from the heavens to the earth, these places are where they fell?"

"Yes," she answered me. "But they fell beneath the earth, not on it. They fell inside."

"And this cave leads to the place inside, the place where the Sea Child fell."

"You could say that," said the farwydd. "But I don't mean a place you can dig to or tunnel to. I mean inside all that is, not on its observable surfaces."

"I don't understand," I said.

"Don't worry, dear child. You are not meant to. No one understands. These things are felt, not understood. We might come to them in dreams or in sudden flashes of insight. You, I see, might come to them through music." She was looking at my rebec, which I had carefully carried, lifted, eased through the tight crevices of the cave. "But here at this portal," she continued, "we can connect to them in a deeper way."

"How do we do that?"

The farwydd didn't answer. She just leaned closer over the hole in the floor and inhaled the smoke deeply. Then from a pouch at her waist she took herbs and a small bowl. She shook the herbs into the bowl. With her flint and steel, she set the herbs alight. They soon burned down to a fine ash, which she stirred with her finger tip. Then she tilted the bowl over the hole and let the ash trickle into the hole.

"As you saw me do," she said, "lean over the hole and breathe in the vapors. Close your eyes. Don't think. Let yourself drift with the smoke."

I leaned over the hole and breathed in.

# The Garden

I was in the cave. Then I wasn't. I was somewhere else. An endless sea lapped at my feet. A shore stretched away from me in both directions. A full moon shone down on the waves as they crested and came rolling, roaring, foaming in. The moon laid its long reflection, a silver spear, across the water. Out of that glory, something came walking.

It was not a person. I don't know what it was. I do know who it was. It was Wat.

He reached out to me with a heart full of love, and I reached back, but we didn't touch. We couldn't touch. We were on two different planes.

I felt a terrible grief.

Then a voice above us both, a whisper across the waters. *Do not grieve.*

Everything in me shrank and concentrated itself into a small jeweled space. My limbs transformed. I could fly. I skimmed the waves, singing my sad song. And as I sang and flew, the waves calmed and stilled until the sea was a flat sheen beneath me. I was flying in a silver space pressed between silver sea and silver sky. The wind blew past me. My body shaped the wind and was shaped to it. I flew high. With my small brilliant eye I looked over the curve of the earth. I was flying over a vast green plane. I spiraled down and down into the even more vibrant green of a walled-in garden where a young girl sat yearning beneath a pear tree. Every pear on the tree glowed with a bronze-gold light. The girl's hair was flame. I came to rest on a twig above her. She reached up her hand. I sang to her, and all around me I felt a misty presence of someone else there too.

*This is our daughter, the seal of our love.* Those were the words that formed and came from my beak as if they were pearls or rich jewels. Each word fell into the upstretched hands of the girl. She closed her hands around them.

There was another presence it was harder for me to make out—a small bright orb that zigzagged through the trees and never came to rest. But the core of this orb was a pure flame of love.

I hovered in the garden. I wanted to stay there forever, enfolded by love. Time stretched out endlessly in all directions. Eventually (who knows when? A day later? A year? An age?) from the compact being I was, I felt myself began to elongate.

The trees began their whispering.

Whispering. Whispering.

I came to myself on the floor of the cave. The farwydd was praying, her eyes closed, her words whispering. Whispering.

I sat up slowly.

"You have been gone a long time," said the farwydd. "I was wondering if you were going to come back. Some never do."

"I was in a beautiful place."

"Did you get an answer to your questions?"

I nodded. I couldn't put into words what that answer was, the way you can't put into words the powerful feelings roused by a dream, but I knew I had been answered. I was weak. I sank down again. For a long time, all I could do was lie on the floor of the cave. The farwydd sat patiently beside me, waiting. I felt hollowed out. I wanted to cry, but I couldn't even do that.

Many candle measures later, or maybe even days, I managed to pick myself up. The farwydd supported me, and then we crept back out.

The journey back through the crevices to the main opening of the cave was even more difficult than it had been when I was trying to get down to the inner chamber. My limbs felt like water. With the farwydd's help, though, I finally made it. I collapsed to the hard-packed dirt floor of the cave. The farwydd helped me closer to the fire and covered me with warm furs, settling my rebec beside me.

"There, child. I know you'll be anxious if you can't see it and stroke it. You do well to keep it by you always. This is the source of your mana."

"Mana?"

"You might call it power. The manifestation of your inmost being, drawn from the deep well of the world."

I reached out my hand to touch it. She was right. Just touching it gave me an abiding comfort. I had let it go from me for far too long. No wonder I was weak from those long years in Oisin's house. Three years.

"Child, don't blame yourself," said the farwydd. It was as if she could read my thoughts. "You were having a baby. Then you lost that baby."

"I despised that baby's father."

"Yet a deep part of you loved that baby, and you have never grieved for him."

Tears leaked from the corners of my eyes. I closed them. I was so tired. The farwydd was right.

"Suppose, dear child . . . suppose this. Suppose there was a young woman, much the same as you, only even younger. Suppose that young woman had had a baby from a husband she had been sold to, as you were. Suppose she loved that little daughter with all her heart. Suppose, just suppose, she fled with her daughter to safety and a different life."

I sucked in my breath. What the farwydd was describing—wasn't that the story of my own life, my mother fleeing with me to the mainland?

Now the farwydd fussed over me, putting a hand to my forehead, feeling the muscle in my arm. "This will never do. You've been gone too long, and you weren't in the best shape to begin with." She stepped to the cave entrance and looked out. She put her fingers to her mouth and a surprisingly loud and shrill whistle burst from her lips.

I dozed. When I woke, Gur the shepherd was there, and he and the farwydd were talking. He leapt from the cave, and Jakke leapt with him. Soon he was back with leathern bags draped around his neck. He put them down by the fire, and the farwydd opened them up. In one was a leather bottle. She took it to me and held it to my lips. It was milk. I drank deep. Then she propped me up, while Gur brought a small box to her. She opened it and fed me its contents. It was cheese. "These are from our own sheep," she told me.

It was almost as if the farwydd were pouring life back into my spent husk of a body. Later she gave me water from a bucket Gur brought in. She dipped the gourd into the bucket over and over, and I drank.

During all these trips Gur was making, the dog, Jakke, was close by his side. Now this time Gur made a hand gesture and Jakke sat down, as if he understood perfectly what his master wanted him to do. Gur left again, but Jakke stayed.

My limbs felt boneless. I couldn't move. When Jakke headed toward me, my eyes widened, but I was too weak to act on my fear and inch away from him. He curled up beside me on the furs, resting his chin on my arm. With my other hand, oh very cautiously, I reached out. His fur, which looked rough, was surprisingly silky. I stroked him. He lay with his eyes fixed on mine, almost as if he were speaking to me. He said, *I love you. I will protect you.*

"Jakke has made a friend," said the farwydd, smiling at us.

"The dogs in my village at home were there to bite and savage whomever their masters told them to go after."

"This is not the same kind of dog, though," said the farwydd. "Jakke is a herd dog. His mission in life is to protect and love."

"I know," I said. "He just told me that."

The farwydd nodded. "He can speak as well as you and I."

During the coming days, Jakke, Gur, and the farwydd tended me until I got stronger and was able to sit up, even to help a little. The farwydd soon realized I knew about herbs and roots. I began helping her compound them into potions that she would send out to the priestesses who visited the sick. And so the time went by, a whole season and more. Outside the cave, the wind screamed, almost a demented thing. Inside the cave, we were warm, dry, and protected.

One evening we were sitting by the fire. Jakke's head was lying in my lap, and I was stroking him. My rebec was at my side.

"Child, I've never heard you play this instrument of yours. Will you play and sing for me?"

I picked up the rebec. Then I hesitated.

"You're afraid," said the farwydd.

"Yes."

"Tell me why."

"Playing and singing has always been my greatest comfort." She nodded encouragement. I went on, groping for words. "But now," I said. "Now there's only one song that comes to my lips, and it is so sad that I can't play it without crying."

"Play it and sing it to me."

So I put aside my fear and sang.

> *I saw the old moon yester night*
> *with the new moon in his arms;*
> *if you sail out to sea, my love,*
> *you'll never more come home.*

*Now good Sir Ceyx, he loved his wife,*
*and she was Alcyone.*
*He'd drive his ship to gates of hell*
*but he would come back home.*

*Weep, O weep, Alcyone,*
*by waters wap and wan,*
*hold out your silver mirror,*
*hold up your golden comb.*

*Oh long she sits in tower high*
*at window o're the sea.*
*Come back to me, my own dear lord.*
*But never more will he.*

*I saw the old moon yester night*
*with the new moon in his arms;*
*If you sail out to sea, my love,*
*you'll never more come home.*

*O forty leagues off rocky strond*
*'tis fifty fathoms deep;*
*And there lies good Sir Ceyx adrowned,*
*Alcyone's heart to break.*

*He calls her ghostly on the wind,*
*and then she knows he's gone.*
*I may not live, O Child take me.*
*My grief it is too strong.*

*The Children, they look down from high*
*with pity in their gaze.*
*They change her into Halcyon,*
*the bird that stills the waves.*

*Halcyon, oh fisher bird,*
*Wife forever true,*
*weep for me and fly to me,*
*and I will weep for you.*

*I saw the old moon yester night*
*with the new moon in his arms;*
*if you sail out to sea, my love,*
*you'll never more come home.*

"These are your deepest fears, child," the farwydd said to me, when I had finished.

I nodded.

"But," she continued, "they are also your deepest hopes. The wife in the song becomes transformed into the halcyon, the bird of peace. She reunites with her love."

To that moment, my experience in the inner chamber of the cave had stayed locked inside me. With her words, the entire vision, or whatever it may have been, came rushing back to me. "Yes," I said.

"I'm thinking," said the farwydd, "that when you breathed in the smoke of the Sea Child's portal, she told you this."

"She did." I realized this. The Sea Child had given me Her answer.

"Now you must act on what She told you."

"You said that to me, when I came to myself."

"Yes, but then you were too weak. Now you've grown strong again. You must take this message from your Child out into the world with you."

"So many bad things have happened, out there." I thought of what Caedon had done to me. What he did to Wat. I thought of his malicious smile, as he hinted at what he must have done to Jillie.

"Bad things do happen. You are right. They've happened to you and people you love," said the farwydd. "But good can grow out of the bad."

"It just seems that bad produces more bad, and more, and more," I said. I stroked Jakke's fur, envying him the simplicity and directness of his love.

"Only if you let it," said the farwydd, responding to my sad thoughts. "Shall I tell you a story?"

"Yes, please."

It was a story very like the one she had told me when I had first come to her cave, but this time, she filled in the details. "I'll tell you a story of a brave young woman. She grew up on the coast of the Fire Isle. Her parents loved her and her sisters and brothers, but bad luck struck them down. Plague visited their house. Her mother and her two sisters died, and the father lost most of his livelihood the next year, when his crops failed. He had been a prosperous farmer, but now they were poor. The two brothers had to hire themselves out to other men in order for the father and the little daughter to eat.

"One brother hired himself to a hard master. This man was solitary. He had no one except a small boy. His wife had died in childbirth, but the man's baby boy had lived. He was at odds with his neighbors. With his own brothers, even. This man told his hireling, the son of the poor farmer, that he wanted to buy the farmer's little daughter for a wife. *Sell me your sister*, he told his hireling, *and I'll make sure your family becomes prosperous again. I've seen your little sister playing in your dooryard, and I want her.*

*But sir*, the hireling responded, *my little sister is still a child.*

*Soon she'll be a woman. Sell her to me*, said the man. So the hireling took the hard master's offer to his father, and finally the father consented. Otherwise, he knew he'd have to stand by and watch his little daughter starve."

I was listening intently now. I was beginning to realize the farwydd was talking about my mother and how she became wife to Fylkir. I thought hard about this—my mother's father, the farmer, had sold his little child. I shared blood with that man, too.

"My grandfather. He sold my mother to Fylkir."

"I see you are understanding me, child. Your grandfather was not a bad man," the farwydd said. "He had no choice. He couldn't watch his daughter die. Surely you've seen families afflicted like this?"

I thought back to my childhood village in the River-lands, and to the villages on the mainland's coast, where I had wandered so long. I'd seen it in both places there. My own desperate thoughts came back to me now. I remembered the time when I thought Keera might die in my arms. I prayed that anyone, even Caedon, would buy us so that Keera could live. "Yes, I have seen this. I've even known it myself. You're right."

"Shall I go on?" said the farwydd.

"Yes. Yes."

"So the transaction was made. The father of the girl soon died, some say of grief and shame, shame because he had given his daughter to the hard and solitary rich man."

Now I felt a deep pity for this grandfather I'd never known.

"So then," the farwydd went on, "Fylkir took this girl, your mother, Elsebet. As soon as she passed the boundary from childhood to womanhood, much too soon, he made her a mother. As for her brothers, one died on the seas, fishing in harsh weather. The other brother, the hireling, enraged and helpless and ashamed of the part he had played, left Fylkir's employ and made his way south. No one knows what happened to him. So now, Elsebet had to live with Fylkir and do whatever he said."

"The way I had to live with Oisin."

"Yes, so you know how hard it was for your mother. Besides, Oisin is weak, but he's not bad at the core. Fylkir, though. . . ."

"I have his blood."

"Blood doesn't mean everything. Elsebet gave birth to you. She loved you very much, and she made sure you grew up with the things she knew deep inside, not the things Fylkir knew.

"One day a traveler, a man from the Sceptered Isle, made the journey to the Fire Isle to see Fylkir. Fylkir is a man who is always wanting to know the news and what that means for his own power. He saw how the king, Ranulf at the time, might help him in his claims against his brothers. So he welcomed this man from the Sceptered Isle as a guest."

I nodded. That was Fylkir, through and through, always trying to find his own advantage.

"They say the worst offense a guest can give to a gracious host is to run off with that host's wife," the farwydd continued. "They say this is the source of some of the world's greatest troubles. They say that long ago, in the east, in the Lyre-Lands, a mighty war was fought over just such an offense. However it happened, this man, Drustan—"

"My true father."

"In many senses, yes. Your true father. So Drustan and Elsebet ran off together, and Elsebet took you with her. Fylkir spent quite a bit of his gold trying to track down Elsebet and his little girl. He had every thought of success. He knew where Drustan lived. Drustan lived on the mainland—"

"On the cliffs overlooking the sea," I said. "Like this, but far to the south." I stepped to the sea window and looked out. Mists closed us in. In imagination, though, I could see the place where Drustan had his lands.

"Yes. But there was a problem," said the farwydd. I came back to sit at her side. "It turns out this Drustan was highly placed. He was an earl. His family was greatly favored by Ranulf. Fylkir nearly gave up. He knew he'd have little success. Then Ranulf died. Fylkir's hopes renewed. But civil war broke out over the succession, and the times were chaotic."

"The rightful heir was murdered by Audemar, the false king his brother."

The farwydd nodded. "And here is where your story intersects the one I'm telling you, dear child. You know the rest. How your family was dispossessed. How you grew up a peasant child in a small village. How you came to know your true heritage as the daughter of an earl. The time you spent at Fylkir's manor on the Western Isle, after his brothers forced him from his ancestral lands."

"Only . . ." I said, thinking hard. "I'm really not the daughter of an earl. My sister Jillian is my father Drustan's true-born daughter."

"Does that matter to you, child?"

"No. I just know," I said, and I could feel my mouth set stubbornly. "In the only ways that matter, I'm Drustan's daughter, not Fylkir's."

"And that is a choice your mother made for you. Now you have claimed it as your own. Blood is one thing. Love is quite another."

"My mother is not the only one who made that choice."

"Indeed, you are right, dear child. Drustan made it too. He freely took you for his daughter. He freely loved you all his days. You, just as much as Jillian, were his true daughter."

Inwardly I smiled to think how the members of the Rising, Avery, Lorel, Conal, Torrin, and even Wat, had all said they saw my father in me.

"But they did," the farwydd insisted. As always, it's as if she could read my mind. "They saw the iron in you that Drustan gave you. The honesty and loyalty. Some of them knew your origins, and some of them didn't, but they all saw the resilience, and they saw the love."

"That's my story, then. Thank you for telling me." I put my hands in hers. "I needed to know these things."

"I'm sure you've always known them, in some sense. But now you have the details. Meanwhile, the civil war you spoke of has widened and gotten much worse. Faction against faction against faction."

"Audemar against Caedon. But Diera's side is no faction. She's our rightful ruler."

"Sometimes the right does not prevail."

I shuddered, thinking of war, the death and destruction that accompanies it. Thinking about Caedon's hurtful words. Thinking about Jillie, what had happened to her, what might happen to her now. Thinking about Wat and how he was taken.

"You saw your husband Walter when you traveled through the portal."

"I think so. I'm not sure I saw him. I felt him. Does that mean—could that mean he's alive?"

"Maybe. Or maybe he visited you from the Land of the Dead."

"Don't you know? You know so many things."

"I only know the things the Sea Child lets me see. She doesn't let me see everything. You have seen more, in this matter, than I'll ever see."

I looked down at the rocky floor of the cave. "I know he's dead," I said.

"Do you?"

"The man who killed him told me."

"What a terrible thing to hear. What terrible words this man spoke to you."

"Another presence was there in the beautiful garden. A small darting thing."

"What was that, do you think?" said the farwydd.

"I don't know. It was made of love. That's the only way I can describe it."

The farwydd said nothing, just watched me.

"Maybe—" I began.

Still the farwydd said nothing.

"I think it might have been my baby son," I whispered.

"Sometimes," said the farwydd, "when a pure soul is born into this world but spends only moments or maybe a few candle measures here with us, our sorrows don't rub off on it and corrupt it. Then it returns to the place it came from as pure as it was when it began its journey toward us."

"So it doesn't hate me because it could not live?"

"No, dear child, it loves you and pities you and wishes you well."

A wound deep inside me was healed then. I was comforted.

Something puzzled me, though. "With my daughter, it was different. In the vision I saw my daughter. I saw her clearly. It's just that—"

The farwydd waited.

"It's just that I saw her as she would be. I saw her older." Now I scrambled to my feet. Jakke leaped around me, barking.

"I have to go to her. I have to get her out, the way my mother got me out. Otherwise Fylkir will do something terrible to her."

"Even now he is planning it."

"What can you tell me?"

"He sold you to Oisin and got the best price for you he could manage." The farwydd closed her eyes. She began speaking as if she were far away. "Oisin is angry, but Fylkir tells him, 'That's not my look-out. Yours was to keep that girl if you could. You lost her. You'll not get a penny of coin back from me.'"

"Suppose he—"

The farwydd went on, serenely. "And now Fylkir has another commodity he can sell. Another girl-child. For her, he'll get a high price. He has the best buyer, a man who has already approached him. If he sells your daughter to this man, he'll get on the good side of someone as powerful as any in the Sceptered Isle."

My mouth dropped open in horror. "Caedon."

"That's the man. Now the time has come at last. You are strong and ready. Go to your daughter, and may the Sea Child go with you."

# Chapter Thirteen

# The Garden

I moved as nimbly as a forest creature through the trees on the hills above Fylkir's manor in the Western Isle, sending up a prayer of thanks to those brave women of the Rising, Lorel and Torrin, who taught me the ways of stealth. I knew where Fylkir would likely be keeping Keera. Probably in the same small bedroom we shared three years ago.

Three years. Keera would be a big girl now. She likely wouldn't recognize me. Suppose, when I got to her, she wouldn't follow me. My heart froze with fear. Resolutely, I pushed these thoughts away.

I knew the lay of all the inner rooms of the manor house. I also knew the enclosed garden on the side of the manor. The garden of my vision. It was a real place, once for a brief time my refuge, but later, one of the worst places of my life, haunting my memory. I shuddered as I recalled Caedon's body on mine, his malicious laughter, the devastating words he spoke to me. Yet in the vision, the little garden was a place of beauty and peace. A place of love.

Something, maybe my second sense, told me that's where I'd find Keera. I knew not to over-rely on this sense of mine, despite Oisin's fear of it as witchery. I could never force it, this knowing outside and underneath knowing. But sometimes the feeling was so strong I knew it was not playing me false. I had that feeling now. Keera would be in the garden. She'd be standing under the pear tree where its branches hung over the wall. I edged to that side of the manor.

I still remembered the routines of the manor pretty well. Judging from the sun, it was about noon-tide, the time when everyone gathered for the midday meal, the gentles inside the manor and the bondservants and other workers in the kitchen building past the manor. I waited.

Pretty soon I saw the bondservants in twos and threes trickling down from the barn and the other out-buildings toward the kitchen house. I knew Mistress Berit would still be inside the manor hall, serving Fylkir, Stefan, and any of their friends who had happened by. Keera, though.

Would she be required to eat with them at board? She was still a child.

Again, I shrugged off all doubts. When no more servants appeared, and they were all inside the kitchen house, I decided I could risk moving from the shade of the trees out to the wall enclosing the garden. I darted to the wall and pressed myself against it. There was no shelter. I'd be spotted right away if anyone looked out or if some straggling servant came down the path. Or if Mistress Berit had to go to the kitchen house to—

There was the thud of a door closing. I froze. Edging to the corner of the wall, I looked cautiously around it.

Mistress Berit, walking down the path toward the kitchen house. I ducked back out of sight. She appeared to be deep in thought. She hadn't spotted me.

I made a silent leap to the branches of the tree overhanging the wall and pressed myself against the trunk. I knew the branches were swaying and crackling under my weight. Holding my breath, I peered down.

Mistress Berit had reversed course; was coming closer to the wall, rounding the corner, staring up into the branches.

*Sea Child be my friend*, I prayed. *Don't let her see me.*

With my drab clothing, with the heavy foliage of the tree, she didn't. The Sea Child helps those who help themselves. Or luck.

She was moving closer, peering into the branches. She would have seen me then, surely she would have, when a call from the main house snapped her head in the other direction. "Coming," she called. She glanced up into the branches, shook her head in puzzlement, and continued her way to the kitchen house. I waited. I heard her tread, coming back. Soon I saw her on the path beneath me. She carried a pitcher and a basket of bread along the path the way she had come, and entered the manor hall.

Now I settled myself more comfortably into a fork in the tree, where I could look down into the garden. It was empty.

But the feeling from deep inside me intensified. I waited. Quite a while I waited.

I laid my head against the sun-warmed bark of the tree's trunk. My eyelids were growing heavy. Just as I was starting to worry about falling asleep on my perch, maybe actually falling out of the tree, a noise from below roused me. I stiffened and peered down through the branches. Two men came out into the garden. Fylkir and Stefan. Their voices filtered up to me through the foliage.

"It's done, then, Father?" This was Stefan's voice.

"Yes," said Fylkir. "They'll take her to Caedon's castle tomorrow. But we won't give her into his hands until we get the chest, and open it, and make sure of its contents."

They were speaking of Keera. I was certain of it. The Sea Child—or luck—had brought me to this place at the last possible moment. The thought chilled me.

"And the ceremony?"

"There will be no ceremony."

"No? But we'll be given the bride price?"

"Caedon has already married."

"Then why—" Stefan began.

"It doesn't matter. We'll get our price. That's what matters."

"But he shames us in this."

"Son, this does not matter. He can't shame us. He doesn't have the power to do that. We have something he wants. He's willing to pay for it. Meanwhile, our own power grows."

"But he's king." Stefan's voice was stubborn. "He has ultimate power, and he'll not relinquish the throne. Audemar, they say, is nearly done. And as for that niece of Audemar—"

"Diera," Fylkir supplied.

"—her forces are broken and scattered. She's no threat at all. I don't see how we fit in this. If Caedon had taken Keera to wife, then—but now you're telling me he won't."

"Diera has powerful relatives across the Narrows from the Sceptered Isle in the Eastern Baronies," Fylkir said.

"And you think they'll come to her aid?"

"No, of course not. She's weak, and as you say, her forces are broken and scattered."

"What, then?"

"Her cousins in the Baronies will see this as their opportunity. While Caedon and Audemar continue to fight, they'll invade on the pretext of either helping Diera or avenging her death, as the case may be. They'll use the strip of land they control on the edge of the Sceptered Isle's mainland as their base. Then they'll take the Sceptered Isle for themselves."

"And that will benefit us?"

"I already have emissaries in their court, in Lutetia, that tremendous city of theirs."

"Father!" I heard the marvel in Stefan's voice. "Well-done, Father."

*To be sure*, I thought, *Fylkir is canny. Whether that makes him a political genius . . .*

Fylkir was continuing. "And then, when we are their allies, we'll turn our attention to our own lands in the Fire Isle. Backed by such power, we'll take action at last. Forget the child. She's naught but a girl-child, after all, and when the Baronies take over, we'll be glad there's no direct tie between us and Caedon. But he'll still pay us the price we negotiated with him. We'll have Caedon's gold, and that's the most important thing, not the child."

"Have you heard from your brothers?"

"Olaf Redbeard is dead. Naturally, Sigismund has seized our lands. But I know Sigismund. He is weak. We'll easily overcome him and take back what's ours."

Through their conspiratorial murmurs, I waited impatiently. But I couldn't help catching some of their plans. Diera. They'd written her off. Her own relatives, the ones who were supposed to be helping her, were treacherously betraying her. And these two. I scoffed inwardly. These two thought they'd outwit Caedon. I knew what came of such foolishness. While they thought they were outwitting Caedon, he'd be planning a dire fate for them. He was already planning it.

But Caedon had taken a bride. That was news. They were selling my daughter to him anyway. Fylkir, her own grandfather, and Stefan, her own uncle. They were selling her as a concubine. Maybe even a bondswoman. My daughter. They'd not get away with it. My rage rose and rose as I braced myself in the fork of the tree. I seethed with it. Burned with it. It was a palpable thing. I was amazed Fylkir and Stefan didn't feel its scorching breath and come to the base of the tree to investigate.

I had to keep quelling this rage of mine because I needed to be clear-headed in the desperate time to come.

Below me, my father and brother were finishing their conversation.

"The child must not know until we hand her over," said Fylkir to Stefan. "See to it, Son."

"Indeed, she's a fiery one. She'll kick and bite. Clearly she's our kin. I don't want to give her to him, Father. You know what they say about him and . . . and young girls."

"Young girls and boys, both," said Fylkir below, in the garden. His tone was sour with distaste. "But you'll do as I say, son."

"Yes, Father."

I felt a sudden dread for Jillian. If she were still with Diera, what would happen to her when these enemies crushed Diera? I felt dread for Diera, too. My stomach turned over in a sickening lurch, compounded by my fear for Keera. I must not fail.

"If that worthless daughter of mine had given me a grandson—but she didn't." Fylkir's voice threaded up to me from beneath the trees.

"Where is she, Father? That girl?"

"You mean Mirin? Who knows. If she's ever found, we'll deal with her then."

Those words of theirs made me bite back a small sound of derision.

Still talking together, they made their way back into the manor, while I could feel my teeth clench and my tension rise. I knew what they said about Caedon was true. Caedon's terrible words to me about Jillie, words spoken in this very garden, scoured me like a corrosive poison, and I was remembering, too, my time back at the manor house Caedon had owned on the mainland. I was remembering the children he kept there. That must not be Keera's fate.

I forced myself to relax. I had to. Keera was close. I could feel it. I needed all of my attention on her. They'd not sell her. She'd not become one of those lost children Caedon kept for himself. He would not take her.

I'd take her.

As I was thinking this, Mistress Berit led her into the garden. I drew in my breath. My beautiful daughter. Her hair was fire-red, falling in coils about her slender shoulders. Her skin was creamy, her lashes dark and lush. It was a bit hard to see from my perch, but as she looked up into Mistress Berit's face and I gazed through the branches down at her, I saw the blue eyes of her infancy had given way to gray-green, with flecks of gold. Mistress Berit was telling her something, and she was listening intently. Then Mistress Berit turned on her heel and left Keera in the garden.

Here it was, the moment I needed. I prepared to spring from the branches of the pear tree into the garden. I hesitated. When I leaped out of the tree, would she cry out in fright? Surely she would. Would she know who I was and why I had come? Surely she wouldn't. When I grabbed her to carry her with me back over the wall, wouldn't she call out in terror for help? I had left her when she was two years old.

Before I could resolve to move and risk everything, Keera moved under the tree and looked straight up into my eyes. "Mother," she said, in a voice as clear-toned as the bell in the chapel of the Lady Goddess near the manor grounds. "You've come for me at last." She reached up her hand to me, and I took it. Bracing myself against the trunk of the pear tree, trying to be as gentle as I could, I drew her up into the tree with me and buried my head in the soft hair, against the curve of the soft beloved cheek.

"I've come for you, little daughter," I whispered in her ear. Then I swung her with me over the wall, took her hand, and we both ran for the shelter of the forest skirts.

Once there, I bent for many moments embracing her and smoothing her hair and murmuring words of love into her ear. I did not think, *How could this be? How could she know me? How was it she had made herself ready?* I just drank and breathed and loved her in, sending up prayers to Sea Child and Fire Child. For once I was sure of it. Luck had nothing to do with this.

# Chapter Fourteen

# Metamorphosis

"We have to move fast," I told Keera. I hoisted her onto my back. She held on around my neck. We sped together through the scrub of trees surrounding Fylkir's manor and turned north. I knew I had only moments of lead time. Mistress Berik would be out soon to check on her charge, and then she'd raise the alarm, and then the searchers would fan out.

I headed not toward the road or the fields but for the north-west and the sea cliffs. As we neared the cliffs, I felt my strength begin to go, but I did not dare allow it. I must find the extra strength I needed.

In my ear, Keera whispered, "We're nearly there, Mother."

How did she know? I didn't have time to ask myself. From somewhere, a surge of energy filled me, and I rushed us to the edge of the cliffs, where a narrow track led down from dangerous heights to a small shingled cove below. This I had discovered during the painstaking seasons of exploration and discovery I had undertaken after I left the farwydd's cave. Pulled up far below us onto the shingle, there was a little blunt-nosed boat, a wicker frame covered with cowhide, the kind called a currach.

I held Keera's hand as we edged down the path. "Are you afraid?" I said. The sea pounded far below us.

"No, Mother," she replied. "You're with me now."

We reached the currach, and I helped Keera in. I shoved us off the shingle, leapt in after her, and un-shipped the oar I had stored underneath the seats. Now I rowed us out into the big breakers, angling the little craft through and around the headland where we could no longer be spotted from the cliffs.

How did I know to do these things? I had help, the help of Gur and Jakke. The farwydd had sent them with me when I left her cave. We had spent many turnings of the moon by the sea. There Gur taught me all he knew of the sea-ways. He'd been born in a seafaring land, I discovered, and only later in life, after many trials and adventures of his own, had he come to serve the farwydd, as his father and grandfather and great-grandfather had before him.

I learned well and fast from Gur's teachings. The sea is my friend, my protector. As my father had often said to me, my true father Drustan, "Mirin, you are half-fish." The sea is my element, and I took to it because it is my nature.

So now, with Keera in the currach beside me, I pulled for the headland that would cut us off from the sight of any watchers on the cliffs above. My muscles strained with the effort, but I pulled for the headland with joy. My hair streamed away from me in the stiff sea wind, and it tumbled Keera's curls around her eager little face.

Once we had rounded the headland, I angled our craft back toward the shore. The beach there is wide and sandy. The bottom of our currach grated on the sand and I leapt out into the surf, guiding the light little craft up onto the beach. I helped Keera out onto dry land and then pushed the currach further onto the beach. I up-ended it and covered it with the cut boughs I had hidden there earlier. From the top of the sea cliffs, no one would spot it. But no one would think to move over the rough landscape at the top of the cliffs to the remote place from which it might be visible, either. The cliff's edge above us was near-inaccessible from land, broken and crevassed. And no one would think about an escape by sea.

Now I took Keera by the hand and led her to a cave under the cliffs at the sea's edge. At high tide, the cave would flood near half its length. I led her far back into the cave where it was always dry. There a fire was already built and blazing. Gur and Jakke waited for us there. When they saw us, Gur leapt to his feet and Jakke came rushing forward to frolic around us, jumping up and licking Keera's cheek.

She exclaimed in delight.

Gur threw warm fur cloaks around both of us and led us to log seats by the fire.

I embraced him and we stood smiling at each other, filled with the satisfying glow of a hard task taken to completion. Through the difficult part, anyway. The rest of our flight away from Fylkir and his venal ways would simply require patience. I settled Keera down and then sat beside her on the hard dry shingle of sand.

"Mistress, I'll leave you now while the tide is out," he said. "But Jakke—you stay here with Mirin." Gur seemed to melt back into the darkness and out of the cave. Jakke curled around and nestled down at our feet, while Keera stroked his silky ears.

I put my arm around Keera and drew her close. "We're safe here now," I told her.

"I know, Mother," said Keera, looking up at me with her wide somber eyes. "I have prayed to the Fire Child, and also to your Sea Child, and they've told me you will keep me safe. They told me you would come. Both of them did."

Beside the fire, I told Keera many things, her story and mine. She was so young. But in her face I could see she was older than her years. Much older. So much older that I nearly shuddered at her.

"Don't be afraid, Mother," said Keera. "Everything will be fine now."

Somehow she knew this.

As we talked, I began to realize something that sent a chill up me. The vision I had had of the garden, known only to me and the farwydd, was known to Keera, too. She had been there, she herself, not just in my vision. She had seen and experienced it all.

"Only one thing I don't understand, Mother," she told me. "Someone else was there with us. Someone who loved me."

"That—" I began, hesitating. "That was your father. He loves you very much."

"I could see you, but I couldn't see him. I just knew he was there."

I hugged her close, staring into the flames. This must mean Wat was a figure from the Land of the Dead, as the farwydd had suggested. Not a living presence. And I remembered how I couldn't touch him. How it seemed we were on different planes. Why is it each new manifestation of this knowledge filled me with grief, as if I were somehow hoping it weren't true?

Keera put her hand on mine. She knew I needed comforting. "This will help you, Mother," she said. She pulled something from underneath her cloak and handed it to me. It was an oilskin bag.

As I took it from her, I understood what it was. My rebec. It had been slung over my shoulder when I leapt into the pear tree, but after that, I hadn't given it a thought. During the entirety of our escape, I had forgotten it completely. Somehow, though, Keera had kept it for me.

"Play that song for me, Mother," said Keera.

I drew it from its bag, and tucked it against me. Keera reached into the bag and handed me the bow, too.

I began to play and sing, not caring how loud, not caring how Keera knew. My voice soared and echoed through the recesses of the cave. At first, I was afraid. The sorrow the song roused in me was too powerful. As I sang, though, the words came out different, the song itself transformed.

> *I saw the new moon yester night*
> *with the old moon in her arms;*
> *you'll sail out to sea, my love,*
> *and then you'll come back home.*
>
> *Now good Sir Ceyx, he loved his wife,*
> *and she was Alcyone.*
> *He'd drive his ship to gates of hell*
> *but he would come back home.*

*Weep no more, Alcyone,*
*by waters wap and wan,*
*hold out your silver mirror,*
*hold up your golden comb.*

*Oh long she sits in tower high*
*at window o're the sea.*
*Come back to me, my own dear lord,*
*may waters carry thee.*

*I saw the new moon yester night*
*with the old moon in her arms;*
*You'll sail out to sea, my love,*
*and then you'll come back home.*

*O forty leagues off rocky strond*
*'tis fifty fathoms deep;*
*the waves bear up the good Sir Ceyx,*
*Alcyone, do not weep.*

*He calls her ghostly on the wind,*
*and then she knows he's near.*
*O Child of Sea preserve him now.*
*O Sea Child pray thee hear.*

*The Children, they look down from high*
*with pity in their gaze.*
*They change her into Halcyon,*
*the bird that stills the waves.*

*Halcyon, oh fisher bird,*
*Wife forever true,*
*Sing to me and fly to me,*
*and I will wait for you.*

*I saw the new moon yester night*
*with the old moon in her arms;*
*you'll sail out to sea, my love,*
*and then you'll come back home.*

As I ended the song, something inside me had changed too. I wanted to think it was a message of hope telling me Wat wasn't really dead, and I knew that couldn't be true. But I was sure of one thing. He loved me, and he loved our child. The spent old moon was not holding the new moon in his arms any longer, burdened down by a terrible sadness. The new moon was cradling the old moon and releasing herself into new life.

I put my rebec carefully down at my feet. Keera stole her hand into mine. We sat leaning against each other as the tide came in with a roar of foam and filled the cave almost to the place where we sat. I was not afraid. The sands almost to our feet bore evidence of the great sea washing in and out over many multitudes of years. But here at the back of the cave, everything was dry as whitened bone. No waters had ever touched this place. Here

we were safe. Fylkir, Stefan, even Caedon could not catch
us here, even if they knew where to look.

"But they don't," said Keera. She read my thoughts just
as if I had spoken them aloud. "And now, tell me about
my father."

So I did. As I described each dear detail of him, Wat
came alive for me. I couldn't believe he was dead. He was
too real.

We stayed in that cave for many days. Gur had stocked
it with food and water. As if I could see it myself, I knew
what was happening on the cliffs above us. Fylkir, Stefan,
Caedon. They were all searching. But they were baffled.
It was as if we had vanished. As if we had eluded them
through a powerful magic.

And so we had.

How long would they search? I wondered. But as the
tide retreated on the last day of our stores, Jakke began
to bark and run toward the mouth of the cave. Soon Gur
appeared, smiling.

He said little, just waited as we bathed in the sea and
made ready for the next leg of our journey. This time, Gur
and Jakke accompanied us in our currach. We launched
it from the shingle, and Gur and I both rowed. We went
far out to sea, but I knew by now to trust Gur's skills. He
rowed us wide to the north, and once we were well away
from the coastline, Gur and I hoisted a small hide sail

onto a little mast he had stepped into our currach. We set a northeasterly course.

Gur knew of a tiny island quite close to some of the outermost larger islands west and north of the mainland, islands held in perpetual contention between the Sceptered Isle to the south of them and the Ice-Realm to the north, the kingdom ruled by Hakon Hardaxe.

The Sceptered Isle held possession of these scattered specks of land to the west and north of the realm's northmost mountainous reaches, but Gur assured me hardly anyone from the populated south of the Sceptered Isle came there.

Out on the water, I remembered the Blue Men, and shivered. But the sea was tranquil. The Blue Men stayed away.

Gur set us down on an unpopulated island in a remote cluster of these isles. While Keera and I had been hiding out in the sea cave, Gur discovered a way for us to start a new life without exciting any suspicion. He'd found this strip of land lying barely above the waves that pounded it, and he had stored provisions in a small turf hut used by salt makers who visited the isle once a year.

Gur and I angled our currach through the surf and beached it on the isle.

"Here's where Jakke and I must leave you, Mistress Mirin," he told me. He tousled Keera's head. Like any five-year-old, she clung to his leg and clung to Jakke.

But I knew better. She was not any five-year-old. I wasn't sure what she was, only that she was my daughter.

"Jakke and I must leave, little Keera," Gur told her gently. "Don't cry. We'll see you again in after times." Then he turned to me. "I've found out this is where a ferry brings salt-makers from the neighboring isle. They're due within the space of a full moon or so. At the end of the season, the ferry returns to take them back with their makings. You'll stay with the salt-makers and then go with them when the ferry comes to take them to the bigger isle east and north of here. Take this. It's a coin for the ferryman." He pressed a metal disk into my palm. "There's a town there, and people."

"What under the Spheres do I tell him, and these salt-makers? Won't they wonder what I'm doing here?"

"No one will wonder. I'll stop at the town on my way back to the farwydd, and when I do, I'll make sure everyone knows I've spotted a poor castaway woman and child. From the town, mistress, you can plan where best to go next. But you'll be safe in these isles. No one knows much about King Audemar here, or King Caedon, or whoever thinks he is our king. No one cares, and the land is too poor to attract the attention of any king."

"Thank you, dear Gur. Thanks for lending us Jakke. He was a comfort to us both."

Gur gave us a big gap-toothed grin. "Any message for the farwydd?"

"Our most heartfelt thanks for her help and her mercy. I don't know where we'll go from here, but we'll be safe, as you say, and I think that will be enough for us."

"The Sea Child be with you both," said Gur. He whistled to Jakke, and they shoved off. Keera and I stood on the shore and waved to them until they rowed into a bank of mist Gur told me was called the harr. Gur hoisted up the craft's little sail, and he and Jakke sailed out of our sight.

"Let's look at this hut, shall we?" I said to Keera.

She just stood on the shore, shaking her head.

I knelt beside her. "We'll miss Gur and Jakke, won't we?"

"We'll never see them again," she said, and threw herself sobbing into my arms.

*Sea Child and Fire Child help me*, I prayed then. I suppose Keera had made a believer out of me when no one else could, even after my experiences in the farwydd's cave. I'd need all the help I could get, raising a child like this, a child who saw things no one else could or did. That's what I thought then, and circumstances proved me right.

Keera's far-seeing was the least of it. Her powers made me wonder at her, and they made me fear for her. Sometimes I thought I was the mother of an elf-child, some enchanted changeling out of song and story. Then she'd turn right around and act like any other little girl,

delightful and challenging and interesting and infuriat-
ing and dear.

When Gur and Jakke sailed away from us, leaving us
alone on the salt isle, Keera allowed me to comfort her.
Hand in hand, we slogged through the sands to the salt-
makers' turf hut and shoved our way in. The door had no
lock, but the wood of it was warped from exposure to
wind and driving rain. Once inside, though, we found
Gur true to his word. He'd left us a sack of dried peas,
leathern bottles of sheep's milk, leathern boxes of sheep's
cheese, a big haunch of mutton, fishing lines, and a fire
starter box. Draped across the bench before the hearth
stones were four or five soft, thick fleeces. A large soapstone pot stood by the fire, and one corner of the hut was
stacked with turves of peat.

I looked around the hut with pleasure. "We'll be fine
here, daughter," I told Keera. I set to work building up a
peat fire in the hearth ring, I struck a flake of fire from
the flint with my fire steel onto the char cloth in the little
box, and soon I had a blaze going.

"Now let's look for water," I said.

We spotted an old wooden bucket in the corner of the
hut and went out to make a circuit of the island. It didn't
take us long. The island was only a league or two across,
and only about as wide. In the center, we found a small
spring of fresh water and filled our bucket.

By the time we returned to the hut, the fire was burning well. Keera and I both had a drink from the bucket and I used the rest, and the peas, to make porridge in the soapstone pot. After we'd eaten the porridge, we also ate some of the cheese, and I had Keera drink from one of the bottles of milk. Then I bedded her down in one of the sleeping niches built into the wall of the hut. I lay one of the fleeces on it, and settled her in with another fleece and her cloak.

"Stay here," I told her. "I won't be long. You're not afraid, are you?"

She shook her head no. I gave her a quick kiss on the forehead.

As I made my way back to the spring with the rest of the milk and cheese, to keep it cool there, I realized that the same trait making Keera such a challenging child—her uncanny second sight, far stronger than mine—was the trait that made her seem almost fearless. She didn't just trust that she'd be safe alone while I was gone. She knew she would be. That trait, as I was to discover, made her reckless, too. Her second sight wasn't always perfect, and she sometimes misinterpreted what it was telling her. Even worse, she sometimes acted on what it told her without thinking the consequences through. She was five years old and a thousand years old, a dangerous combination.

When I got back to the hut, I kissed her and made up my own bed in the wall niche across from hers, so she could look across the smoldering peat and see me there. So we drifted off to sleep, and after all our exertions and anxieties, we slept well too.

The days went by uneventfully.

Our provisions lasted us a good long while, and I supplemented them with fish from the sea. I taught Keera how to fish. She never became as comfortable around water as I am, but then, the Sea Child is my Child. The Fire Child is hers. Just as we were running out of everything but fish, we spotted the ferry on the horizon one misty morning. By noon, the harr had lifted and the ferry, a sturdy little cog, had come to shore. The salt-makers had arrived.

We took Gur's advice, throwing ourselves on their mercy, and they seemed to believe we were who I claimed us to be. The salt-makers were an incurious lot. The bondsman who oversaw their work questioned me, though.

"Thanks for your kindness, good man," I told him, accepting a small piece of bread and cheese from him. In return, I handed him a string of fish. "I'd be a poor sort of fisherman's wife if I didn't know how to fish," I told him with a sad smile, drawing on my acting skills. "As soon as my daughter Keera and I saw you and your people coming in, we fished for you, hoping to trade our catch for kindly treatment."

He gave me a skeptical look.

"We're not from around here, my husband and I. The fishing around our own village failed us, failed all of us," I went on, spinning out for him the story Gur and I had rehearsed. "Many of us began to starve. My man heard the fishing banks here are rich. He brought us here, me and the wee one, and left us on the island while he headed out to sea in his currach with his nets and lines. I wove his nets myself, good sir. Wait here, wife, he told me. You and the wee one. Wait for me here. He knew we'd have shelter here. He'd heard about you salt-makers. But he has never returned for us. Now our food's all gone, and we've waited so long . . ." Here I drew hard on my acting abilities and began to cry. Soon I was crying in earnest. The tale Gur had concocted was too close to the truth: the waiting wife, the husband gone off to sea who'd never returned.

His eyes softened then, and he put out a clumsy hand to comfort me. My tale was the usual story in these parts. He had known many with the same story as mine.

"I figure I can't wait any longer, good sir. The wee one and I have been occupying your hut, but when we saw your boat, we moved ourselves out of it. We don't want to be any trouble to you. But when you return to your town, I beg to go with you. Else I'll never be able to feed this wee one. I have payment for the ferryman," I added, to forestall any objections he might raise.

"That's best, then, mistress," the man told me.

By then, many of the salt-makers had gathered around us to listen. Once they had heard my sad tale, they murmured a few sympathetic words and went back to their work.

It was slow work, but not very hard. Soon Keera and I were helping too. We dipped up sea water into pans and then, over fires on the beach, evaporated the salt crystals out of the brine and scraped it into hide buckets. Generations of salt-makers from their village, the others told us, came out to this island where brine pools along the low-lying coast provided a handy source for the precious salt. When the ferry brings the salt-makers and their product back to the town, they told us, the fishermen's wives use it to salt down their husbands' catch into barrels stored to feed the people of the island throughout the year, even beyond fishing season. So the community thrives, in a modest way, even though farmland on the island is rocky and yields little. In the life of the community, the salt-makers play their part.

Fishermen lost at sea, leaving behind wives and children—such sad occasions happen all the time, in these islands. When the ferry came to take the salt-makers back to their town, Keera and I hurried to it with the rest of them. By then, we'd become part of their community ourselves, sleeping in a rough lean-to on the beach, as they did, earning respect from them as we helped them with their work.

Now as the little cog stood in to shore, we moved down the beach with the others to meet it. I searched in my apron for the piece of cloth where I'd tied up the coin Gur had given me, for safe-keeping. I handed it to the ferry-man for our passage.

He looked at the coin with interest. "A coin from the Old Ones," he said. "I don't often see the likes of this."

I could hardly make out his thick accent, different from the one on the Western Isle, where Wat and I had tried to make a home; where Keera had been born. Different too from the accents of the northern mainland, where Oisin had kept me.

I worried for a moment that the ferryman wouldn't take the coin.

"Look at it," he said, showing me. "A pretty thing."

I hadn't really looked at it, just tied it into the bit of cloth after Gur had given it to me, and made sure to keep it safe. Now I did look. On the coin was stamped the visage of a man with some type of leafy wreath about his head. I really looked at it now. Although I pretended not to recognize them, I saw right away that the words on the coin were in the language of the Old Ones. Caedon had taught me a little of this language years ago, when I lived in his house as his prisoner. He hoped to train me to betray the Rising, and he used Jillie to coerce me. Thank the Children, or luck, it had worked out otherwise. But I still remembered most of what Caedon had taught me. Not for the first time, I wondered how it was that a man who loved knowledge so much, an educated man, could be so cruel.

"Where did you get such a thing?" the ferryman asked me now, peering again at the coin.

I shrugged. "My husband left it with me, in case I needed it."

"Maybe he knew he might not come back, the poor fellow."

I nodded. My eyes filled with tears. Silly, I know. Tears for someone who wasn't even real. But in my mind, this fictional husband lost to the rough seas was Wat.

"Come aboard, then, mistress, you and your bairn," the ferryman told me. "There's work for the willing, back in the town. You and your bairn will not starve."

I must confess, that's as far as I had thought through my situation, mine and Keera's. Get her away from danger. Take her someplace safe. Live a quiet life.

Over the next few years, that's what we did. Since my talents lay that way, I set up as a healer. It turns out the town needed one desperately. The only real healer had died some turnings of the moon before our arrival, leaving only a superstitious old crone in her place. And that's how I finally learned the skills of the midwife as well.

There were only a few on the island who knew much about it, other mothers who had been through childbirth themselves. Babies were being born all the time. I knew as much as the rest, and thanks to Old Cwen, my teacher long ago, I knew a little more. As I practiced midwifery, I learned fast.

As Keera grew, she learned, too. She learned from me about herbs and the skills of healing. She became my assistant, young as she was. Everyone knew it; she had a special touch.

There was something uncanny about it, though, and others sensed it. Sometimes I noticed people crossing the narrow cobbled street to avoid Keera's too-direct gaze, wise beyond its years. That worried me. Sometimes I feared for her. Some in the isle believed in witchcraft. But the people who came to us sick or hurt, like as not, recovered and were grateful to us. For the most part, we did live a quiet life, there at the very remotest top of the Sceptered Isle. I think we would have lived out our days there.

Then something happened to change everything.

# Chapter Fifteen

# Blatant Beast

As I went about my daily rounds, preparing potions and salves, administering them to the sick and injured, and now even delivering babies, Keera and I were happy. We never seemed to yearn for more. A few village men paid suit to me, but I stayed apart from them. Keera played with the other village children, and at home, she learned her letters from me as I had learned them from my own mother.

It was understood between us that we wouldn't speak of such things in the town. No other girls learned their letters, and only one or two of the boys. As our quiet life went on, I gained an increasing appreciation of my own mother, why she had always seemed to keep herself separate in spite of enjoying the high regard of her neighbors.

*But I'm not like you, Mother, because you had Father by your side*, I thought bitterly. I tried to drive those sharp pangs of envy away. What my parents had between them was precious, and I myself was the beneficiary of their love. I could never begrudge them that. But I wanted Wat, and Wat was dead. My terrible ache had no outlet.

There were others I yearned for. I wondered often about my sister Jillie. I had found her and then lost her again. That was bitter to me as well. And now, after the terrible words Caedon had spoken to me about her, I feared the worst for her. Caedon had kept Jillie pent up in his fortified manor along with other hostage children. When circumstances freed me from my own cell there, and I couldn't get back to her, I was frantic. Then came that miraculous day, the day of Diera's coronation and my wedding to Wat. As if those happinesses weren't enough, a new happiness arrived to crown everything, a lost child found. My sister Jillie.

Yet now I began to ponder, and to worry. I never did find out her story, only bits of it. Only suspicions. She was too damaged. Too silent. Before I could gently try to win her confidence, she went with Diera across the Narrows to the Eastern Baronies. Wat and I fled west. What had happened to her those years in Caedon's cages? What might he have done to her there?

Now I had a pretty good idea.

And what had become of her once Diera's army had been defeated?

As for the others in the Rising, only a few of my old friends were left, and I didn't know where they were. I hoped they were still alive, but they might have died when Diera's army was destroyed. And Diera herself, where was she?

Worst of all were Caedon's malicious and gloating words to me about Wat.

These fears and memories accompanied me always, even though I could stave off the thoughts by filling my day with tasks and obligations.

At least I had my daughter safe with me. And my rebec, the source—according to the farwydd—of my mana, my power. The way to my second sense, that deep well of knowing that would open to me sometimes, and tell me things I'd never be able to fathom on my own. During our escape into the sea cave, I felt I had retrieved my power. The transformed song had transformed something inside me, and now I could play and sing again, a source of great solace. I didn't play and sing to others, though. Only to Keera.

Whatever my power was, it lay useless inside me as a tool for improving our livelihood. To draw attention to myself in that very public way would be too dangerous.

Sometimes I practiced the moves that Wat, Conal, Lorel, and Torrin had taught me. I had needed these skills once, to rescue myself and then my daughter. I didn't need them now. In fact, I had started to imagine a life where I'd never need them again and only be what I seemed to be, a mild-mannered young mother living a quiet life. Not a trained killer.

Sometimes, though, the world chases you down.

I found myself, one day, in a tavern. I recalled a time I played and sang in taverns to earn my keep. Those days were in the past. Taverns with their buzz of news were alien places to me now. But at The Silkie's Rock, frequented by fishermen and sailors, the tavern keeper had developed a painful boil that must be lanced. Lanced and drained and cleansed, and then a healing salve applied. Otherwise, the Dark Ones might invade the site of the boil on his neck and spread throughout his body and kill him. I left Keera at home for this visit to the sick. The tavern was full of rough men, no place for a young girl like Keera, rapidly becoming a beauty.

As I walked through its door, smells and sounds familiar to all taverns battered at me, comforting and threatening both. The smell of piss and stale, spilled ale. The mouth-watering odors of roasting meat. The rough

sailors and their wandering eyes and hands. The invigor-
ating burr of talk—lands and voyages and news and
politics. The warmth of the big central hearth.

On my arm I carried my basket of supplies. The tavern
keeper's wife ushered me past all the hubbub to the inner
part of the building, the room where the family lived one
wall away from the noisy activities of the tavern, where
her man sat wincing, his hand shielding the red painful
swelling on his neck. As I followed his wife in to him, he
looked around her at me, his eyes walling in apprehen-
sion.

"Now, my good man, you're in a lot of pain, and yes,
I'll give you a little more, but then it will be over," I said to
him in as soothing a voice as I could muster.

"Don't let her touch it," he said to his wife, in a high
whining unnatural voice.

"Don't be a baby, Kot. Let the goodwife look at it," said
the woman, swatting his hand away from his neck and
summoning me closer. The boil was huge, an angry red.
It must be intensely painful, I thought, giving him a sympathetic glance.

Somehow, the look that passed between us settled the
man down. Then his eyes wavered to the sharp piercing
tool I had devised for operations of this sort. He rose to
his feet from the joint stool where he had been sitting,
kicking it over in his haste to back away from me.

Between us, the alewife and I were able to settle him back down on the stool and hold him steady long enough for me to pierce the boil. An ugly yellow pus spattered his shoulder.

His howl of pain and outrage stilled the tavern roar in the outer room. After a moment of shocked silence, the chatter out there began again.

"There now," I said to the tavern owner. All three of us—me, the tavern man, and the alewife—were breathing hard.

"It feels better," he snuffled.

"Yes, and now I will clean the wound so the Dark Ones can't get in."

He nodded and sat quietly while I cleansed the deflated boil.

"You'll need to change out of this shirt into a clean one," I told him as I applied salve and began bandaging his neck.

"I'll get your good shirt," said his wife to him.

"Make sure to wash this one well, in the hottest water you have," I told her as she pressed coins into my hand.

"What are you paying her," the man said, rising to look. "How much— Nine Spheres, woman—"

His wife gave him a long exasperated stare.

He settled back obediently on his stool.

Turning to me, the alewife said, "Ignore Kot's bad manners, goodwife. You've done us a fine service, and we thank you. Both of us." She shot her man a hard look. He managed a sheepish smile. "It's a raw day. Step into the tavern for a bowl of my good broth. Fresh made," she said. "On the house." Over her shoulder she said to her husband, "Take a lie-down, Kot. I'll see to things in the other room. That man," she said to me, shaking her head as she hustled me in front of her to the tavern part of their house.

The wind was sharp that day, so I gratefully accepted her offer. I sat in a secluded corner of the tavern and put my hands around the soapstone bowl she placed in front of me. The warmth was gratifying. The alewife wiped a spoon off on her apron and handed it to me, patting me on the shoulder before she headed to her post at the barrel of strong drink she had no doubt brewed herself.

As I downed the hearty soup, where bits of fish floated, and pieces of vegetable, I started to relax. The scene was familiar to me. I felt comforted.

But I couldn't help paying attention to a man who had gathered a knot of boisterous tavern-goers about him. The blatting and blithering of their chatter was giving me a headache. I was about to rise to go when something about them stopped me. I settled back into my corner.

"Tell us the news, Piet," one man was saying.

The man called Piet looked the very picture of a sailor who had traveled far beyond quiet villages and towns like ours. He was burly, scarred in every visible place, and missing an eye. Around his neck he wore a string of exotic beads that might have come from the far-off towns of the Trade Route Fortifications, or perhaps even farther, all the way from the Great City of the Lyre-lands. "It were a mighty battle, that it were," he said, settling down on his bench to wrap a massive, knuckle-beaten hand around a cup of ale. He drained it and tossed it at the serving wench, who caught it expertly and bore it away with her to the kitchen shed in the rear of the tavern.

"Tell us, Piet," called several from the crowd forming around him. One handed him a new mug of ale. I knew Piet's type well from my earlier days as a tavern singer. A big-mouth muckspout, spreading gossip and news and lies and rumors wherever he went.

"Our king had defeated that other one, that—"

"Audemar," another man supplied.

"Right. Audemar. And he had fled with only a few companions. No one knows where he went. That left only the young queen, the beautiful maid. But she were no match for our king, however beautiful."

Listening to this talk, my heart sank. I knew what this man Piet was talking about. I knew the king he meant was Caedon.

Once all the legitimate heirs of King Ranulf the Fourth were dead—the crown prince Artur, assassinated by his brother Audemar, who had then killed Artur's young sons and also his younger brother Avery, leader of the Rising against his treachery—Ranulf's cousins in the Eastern Baronies backed Diera, Artur's only surviving child, against Audemar's tainted claim to the throne.

But Diera is a woman. By law, no woman may rule.

When the crown had come, however briefly, to Avery, he set aside that law about women rulers. He knew he'd not live long. He made sure his niece's right to the throne was protected. Her relatives in the east honored Avery's new law. Or seemed to. Then, because wealth and politics and power rule all underneath the Spheres, these relatives turned on Diera and took back all their fine words.

Meanwhile, Caedon, a nobody, had come to power and had defeated Audemar, his former master. Now, or so it seemed, the venal and grasping relatives of Ranulf in the Baronies were throwing their support to Caedon against the claims of their own blood. One of the most powerful, the Baron Gilles de Rais, was backing him. I knew Caedon came from his lands, but how that meant this baron was standing by some upstart commoner, I failed to see.

"Courageous, though, I'll give the lass that much," Piet was saying. "He'd defeated her before, our king, and sent her packing back across the Narrows, but now here she comes again, she and her army. Not as big an army as before. Only a piddling few. Some say her cousins, those foreigners, were helping her. If they did, they didn't help her much. Our king killed them all, those soldiers, as he had killed the ones before."

"A drink to the king!" cried a man.

The news-giver paused while the lot of them drank, and the others stood him another round.

"Go on, now, Piet. And then what?"

"It were all over for this queen," said Piet, clearly reveling in the attention. "Young and beautiful though she be, that were not enough to save her. Our king caught her and captured her. And took her companions with her. And now she is dead. They're all dead now."

"Death to the king's enemies!" cried the same loud man, and the roar from the rest sounded to me like the snarling of beasts of dogs, a pack of them, closing in on some helpless prey. There was a new round of drinking, while I lowered my head onto my arms and couldn't help myself. I began to weep. In the commotion and the roistering, no one paid me any mind.

"And is it true, do you think, Piet? She's dead?"

"Aye, man. My cousin saw her led through the streets of the big town on the northern edge of the realm, near where our king caught her and defeated her. That's where he tried her. That's where he set up his scaffold."

"How was she caught?" someone prompted. "Tell us that part, too, Piet."

"It's treachery, they say, that did it. She were betrayed by someone in her own household, and she were taken," the seaman Piet said, to smiles and nods. It seemed that they'd all heard this news before, but now they had an eyewitness, and they hung on every grisly word.

*Eight for the foul betrayers. Eight for the foul betrayers.* The mocking verse of Johnny the Traveler's song echoed in my memory.

Piet went relentlessly on. "She were led through the streets right enough, that young queen, and there stood the headsman with his big axe, and then chop, off with her head." Piet concluded his tale with relish, making chopping motions with his hands to the cheering of the others. "As for the rest of them rascals, they say our king devised brave tortures for that lot."

I pulled my hood up over my head, pulled it well around my face, grabbed my basket, and sidled past the drinkers. I slipped out of the tavern and leaned for a moment against the side of it, trying to compose myself. I failed. I strayed crying down the street to the door of my own little cottage and let myself inside.

Keera was there to comfort me. Had she known of this before, or come to know it as I was being told it? I wasn't sure, but I knew as I entered the house that she'd be there to give me comfort. I knew she'd know without being told. I only hoped she hadn't realized the tortured rascals of Piet's account included her father. And then I flinched away from my morbid imaginings. Suppose Keera could see my own thoughts too? Was this witchcraft she practiced? Some would say it was. By now she was ten years old.

After I heard about Diera's execution, the next few days passed in a blur.

Luckily no one needed my services. No baby was born. I made sure I saw no one. I took to my bed. It was neglectful of me.

Keera could take care of herself, though. And she took care of me in addition. There were times I thought I was the child, and she was the mother. This was one of those times.

Days later, seemingly out of nowhere, as Keera was sitting beside me stroking my hand, she said, "In the beautiful garden, you were there, Mother, and my father was there, too."

*Good,* I thought. *This is the only memory Keera has of her father, and it is a wonderful one. If you can even call it a memory,* I amended silently.

I realized another thing. This vision she and I had shared. It had happened years earlier. Wat couldn't have been there at Diera's defeat. He couldn't have been among those Caedon's army had captured and tortured.

He might not have even made it to Diera's side, I thought, barely able to raise my listless head from my bed shelf where I had wrapped myself away. Caedon must have taken Wat long before Diera's brave attempt. I didn't know the details, only the horrible insinuations of Caedon that night in the garden.

Whenever and however it had happened, all of them were dead now, my friends and those who bore King Ranulf's sacred blood. Diera was dead. Wat was dead.

All dead but Audemar the usurper. The only surviving member of the royal line. Where was the Children's justice in that, I wondered. Any last hopes of the brave Rising now were over. Almost all of its members were dead, and all of the Six. Every one of the leaders. I myself was one of the few survivors of the Rising, an unlikely survivor at that.

I doubted I'd ever get up from my pallet again.

But after a few days, I was needed at a childbirth, and after that, a fisherman was gravely injured by a falling spar, and after that—

So, gradually, I re-entered my life again. But I was not the same.

I took to haunting the taverns, sitting for candle measure after candle measure with a mug of ale in my hands, listening to seamen bringing the news, goading the great yelping beast of rumor before them.

Why did I even care any longer? I really didn't know. I was hungry for news of Caedon and the evil he perpetrated on the realm. That's the only thing I could tell myself, when the question rose to haunt me.

Not that anyone in the taverns thought of it that way. To them, he was the distant king, the leader of the realm, their king. They cheered his victories, as remote from them as children's tales told around the fires at night.

Any hardship they suffered wasn't because of him. They never connected it to him. To be honest, most of their hardships really weren't his fault. His corrupt ways may have infected the mainland and even the big Western Isle, but here in these remote northern islands, his ways touched few. All around me kept living the same hard, hardscrabble lives they had always lived.

Most believed in the Sea Child, and no one from the populated areas of the Sceptered Isle bothered to come up here to gainsay them. Most of these people scorned those who worshipped the Lady Goddess as Lady-likers, but there were a few who worshipped Her.

Keera and I were as safe here as we had always been—safe from Caedon, anyway.

Just the same, from the time I heard of Diera's death, everything felt different.

A vision of Diera as I had seen her last kept haunting me. Diera, young and beautiful, surrounded at her coronation by those who wanted to see justice done her. My wedding day, too, the happiest day of my life, the day Wat and I bound ourselves to each other as one, past all the stars, through all eternity.

Whenever I got too downhearted, I gazed on my daughter, the product of that love, and was comforted.

So the news of Diera's defeat and death was the first thing that disrupted our quiet life in the northern isles.

The other was much more troubling, because it wasn't distant bad news. It affected our lives directly, and in the worst possible way.

# Chapter Sixteen

# Witchery

On the little isle where we had sought refuge, people were beginning to notice Keera—her beauty, and also her uncanny powers. She let them slip out in unwary moments, using her powers for good but also sometimes for other reasons. I had to remind myself she was still a child.

The miraculous healing that came, I knew, from her, that was a good thing. Everyone else, even I myself, had given up on a patient, a woman. Then Keera stepped to her side and put a hand on her head and said some words

. . .

But there were times she wasn't so wise in the use of her gifts.

One day, Keera rushed in from playing, her face like a thundercloud.

"A boy has been mean to Skag, Mother," she told me. Skag was one of her friends, the son of a woman who wasn't married to the man she lived with. She had six children by three or four different fathers, and this current man wasn't Skag's father. The family were poor, much poorer than we were. I worried Skag wasn't getting enough to eat. Whenever he came into our yard to play, I was in the habit of slipping him something to eat, even if it was only an apple.

"They tease Skag and call him names." Keera was practically seething with indignation.

"That's very wrong," I told Keera.

"Auban yells at him and calls him a dirty bastard, and now some of Auban's friends are doing it, too." Keera glowered at me through her tears. "Why are they doing that, Mother? What's a bastard? It sounds like a bad word, Mother."

I sighed. It was hard to separate out the things Keera knew from the things she didn't know. I decided to tackle the more important question first and save the bastard issue for later. "Sometimes people are mean to each other," I told Keera, picking my words carefully. "We must both be especially nice to Skag, so he'll know he has friends and that not everyone is a mean person." I wondered whether I should speak to Auban's mother, but knowing the woman, I thought it would do little good. And it would call down unwanted attention on me and Keera. "Let's show him how kind we can be," I said.

Keera tossed her curls and gave me an angry look. "That won't help much," she said. Her voice was scathing. She marched out of the house. From the window, I saw her straight little back and determined stride, heading away from our house toward Skag's.

I sank down on the bench at our hearth and sighed again. Not for the first time, I regretted how harshly I had sometimes judged my own mother. But I had failed Keera with these halfhearted words of mine.

I thought little enough of the incident as the days went by.

Then, perhaps a sen'night later, Keera ran into the house sobbing and buried her face in my lap. Her hair was damp from the snowflakes beginning to fall thickly on that dreary winter afternoon.

"Where's your cap, Keera? Have you lost it again?" But I saw how genuinely distressed she was, so I stopped scolding and held her, stroking her hair and rocking her back and forth the way I used to do when she was younger and unhappy. "Tell me what's wrong, Keera," I said at last, making my voice deliberately gentle.

"Auban fell through the ice into the pond," she choked out.

"Good Lady save us!" I exclaimed. "Is he safe? Is he hurt?" I jumped to my feet to look for the little leather sack I kept by the door for emergencies.

"I think so," said Keera, turning her face away from mine. "They went to Goodwife Mathilde with him."

"Don't worry, Keera. I'm sure she'll know what to do for Auban." Keera and I both knew that was a lie. Goodwife Mathilde called herself a healer, but she was a dirty, superstitious old crone whom I'd as good as driven out of business, a thought which caused satisfaction in one part of me, and great uneasiness in a different part.

"She won't," Keera spat out. "She won't know what to do, the dirty thing."

"Is the lad all right?" I asked, fear gripping me. "It's freezing. Did they get him out of the pond right away? Did they wrap him in something warm? Did they—"

"He'll be fine," Keera muttered. She still wouldn't look at me.

"You've seen this?" I said. I sat back down on the bench beside our hearth. "Well, then, daughter, calm yourself now. All's well after all."

"No, it's not," said Keera, and then she began crying again.

I felt a sudden chill.

"Keera," I said, trying hard to keep my voice steady. "How did Auban fall into the pond?"

"I did it, Mother!" Keera burst out. She buried her face in my lap again.

"Holy Lady," I said. "But accidents happen. We'll go together to pay him a visit once they've warmed him up. Then you can tell him you're sorry."

Keera muttered something into my skirts.

"What's that? I didn't hear that."

Keera leaped to her feet. "It wasn't an accident!" she shouted, her face red and scrunched up.

"You pushed Auban into the pond," I said slowly.

"No," she bit out.

"How did Auban get into the pond?" I asked her, trying to keep calm.

"He was on the ice, sliding around and saying whee, look at me, and the ice cracked. And he fell in."

"It sounds like an accident to me," I said, my voice careful.

"I made the ice crack," she told me, staring up at me with big scared eyes.

"You thought about it, it happened, but that didn't mean you made it happen," I said, trying to convince myself as much as I was trying to convince Keera.

"I did make it happen," she said quietly.

It was unworthy of me, I know, but then I said something shameful to her. "No one knows that but the two of us," I said. I was desperate. Keera needed to be held accountable for her powers, especially if she used them for ill, but she and I needed to stay safe.

"They know," said Keera.

"How could they possibly—" I began. Then I stopped myself. "Keera, tell me exactly what happened."

"We were sliding on Auban's farm pond. We were having fun. Skag came over and began to slide, too. Then Auban pushed Skag down. He said no dirty bastard was allowed to slide on his father's pond. And then they all laughed. And Skag cried. And then I said—"

"Then you said you wished the ice would break and Auban would fall in?" I said, hope rising in me.

"And then I said, Break, Ice, and drown Auban," said Keera.

"Under your breath?" I asked, stilling my trembling hands by twisting them into my apron.

"No, I shouted it at him."

"And he heard it?"

"They all did."

"Just children?"

"Oh, Mother!" Keera sobbed into my lap. "I really didn't want Auban to drown. Just scare him. I was mad, Mother, and I—" She began sobbing so hard then that I couldn't make out the rest, but I'd heard enough. I stroked her hair until she grew calmer. Then I drew her up so we were eye to eye.

I knew what Keera had done would prove very dangerous to our lives in the village. But I also knew something
more disturbing was taking place, and I knew this other
thing was more important. The nature of Keera's life depended on it, her inward life, not just our physical safety.

I made Keera look at me. "Keera, I love you more than
life itself. More than all the stars hanging by their golden
chains from the Spheres. You know that, right?"

She nodded.

"It is an admirable thing, your wanting to defend your
friend Skag. But what you did to Auban was wrong. Do
you understand that, my darling?"

"Yes, Mother, I do," she said.

I looked into her eyes and I saw she did. I thought back
to my own wicked little experiment, as a girl, to create a
charm that would inflict harm. "Keera, you have powers
others don't have."

"Yes, Mother."

"If you don't learn to control those powers, and never
to misuse them, you'll end by hurting yourself. And you'll
hurt those you love, too."

"Yes, Mother."

"Hear me, Keera. I'm not talking about physical harm.
That, too. But I'm talking about a harm you will do to your
inmost self. And if that were to happen, you'll bring terrible grief to those who love you and wish the best for you.

You'll bring terrible hurt to yourself. Do you understand?"

"Yes, Mother, I do understand."

I saw she did. I hugged her.

"Tomorrow, we'll pay a visit to Auban and tell him we're sorry he got hurt."

She flinched away from me, but she nodded. Then she asked, "Will I say I'm sorry I did it?"

I sighed. "In a perfect world, you would. But we don't live in a perfect world. We'll make what amends we can, but don't say that to Auban and his parents. They won't understand, and you and I will be put in danger."

Keera burst into fresh sobs. "I'm sorry, Mother! I'm really, really sorry."

"I'm sorry, too, Keera, but I'm enormously grateful the boy has avoided serious harm." *If he has*, I thought anxiously to myself. What would Goodwife Mathilde do to the boy? And what did it mean that Auban's parents went to her instead of to me?

The next day, it was perfectly clear what that meant. As Keera and I approached the door of Auban's house, we saw his father standing in the doorway. He wouldn't let us in.

"Get away from our house, you and that witch-spawn," he said, as we came near.

I could see Keera wanted to explain and apologize, but I turned her around and nodded over my shoulder at the man. "I worry about the boy's lungs, after a plunge into icy water in this weather. I've made him a potion. I'll leave it here." I bent to put it down beside his gate and pulled Keera after me.

"Keep walking," I told her. "Say nothing."

"We don't want your potions, mistress. Get off my land," the man yelled after us.

"Oh, Mother," said Keera to me, stricken.

"These are the consequences," I said to her, between gritted teeth. "Better to learn this hard thing about your powers now, before anyone gets really hurt."

As we let ourselves into our own small house again, though, I had to chase away the grim thought that we hadn't seen the end of the incident. And of course we hadn't.

No one called upon me for healing now. No one came to our house, and I didn't let Keera out of the yard. I was starting to worry how I'd feed us. I knew what the villagers were thinking. Witchcraft. And really, who could blame them?

I heard later that even some of the salt makers, women I'd counted among my first friends on the island, had begun whispering things, unsettling things they'd noticed about Keera during that early time we'd spent on the tiny offshore isle of the brine pools.

By spring, though, very gradually, we put the incident behind us. Around the time I seriously began wondering whether we'd be able to eat, I was called upon to deliver a baby under difficult circumstances. The family had sought Goodwife Mathilde's aid first, but when things began to go wrong and she piously consigned mother and unborn baby to the will of the Lady Goddess, the panicked father ran all the way to my house and pounded on my door. I was able to save mother and baby, and then my reputation was partly restored. It didn't help Goodwife Mathilde that she was a Lady-liker in a village where most worshipped the Children.

But I was very careful after that with Keera. I no longer allowed her to assist me. I barely allowed her out of the yard. We both grew thin and pale. She knew I was trying to protect her, but she was just a child. She wanted to play.

The people of the village were afraid of her. Auban became a different boy, which was an irony. From a blustering little bully, he became withdrawn and cowed. If Keera and I passed anyone in the village lane, I saw how they cringed away from her. If they couldn't avoid her small self, they avoided her direct gaze.

I was brooding over one of these shunning incidents one evening when Keera got up from a seam she was sewing, put her work aside, and came to lean against me. She whispered into my ear, "But I am not a witch."

I took her two hands in mine and sat her across from me at our small table. "So then, my darling, why did you know I was thinking that very thought?"

She looked confused and colored up. "I don't know, Mother. I just did."

"That's what troubles people, Keera. That's why they think you're a witch. And that's dangerous."

"Do you think I'm a witch, Mother?"

"No," I said, squeezing her hands. "I suppose there may be witchcraft." I thought uneasily again of my charm. "But you're no witch. I do believe the Fire Child has given you powers beyond most people's. Beyond mine."

"You have powers, Mother."

"I suppose I do. I've always thought I did. My father told me so."

Keera shuddered. "Grandfather Fylkir?"

"No. My true father."

"Grandfather Fylkir isn't your father?"

"Yes, he is, and your uncle Stefan is my half-brother. That means he had a different mother."

"I know about that," she said, making a dismissive gesture. "Like Skag."

"That's right." I nodded.

"I don't understand," said Keera stubbornly. "Why isn't Grandfather Fylkir your true father?"

I laughed and tousled her hair. Putting it that way, "your true father," I saw right away she knew the answer to her question. She just wanted to hear me say it. "You know why. You do understand. There are fathers, and then there are true fathers. There are mothers, and then there are true mothers."

"Tell me about your true father."

"He adopted me as a small child, when my mother—your grandmother—fled with me away from Fylkir to a safer place." We were getting ready for bed then. I began banking the fire.

"As you fled with me, Mother, when you found me in Grandfather Fylkir's garden."

"Exactly right," I told her, taking her by the hand and leading her firmly to her bed.

"But you and I didn't flee from Gandfather Fylkir to my true father. Who is my true father, Mother?" Keera said as I tucked her into her fleeces.

Again, she wanted to hear me say it. She knew the story already. "The name of your true and only father is Walter, son of Ranulf the Fourth, King of the Sceptered Isle," I told her, making my way in the dim light to my own bed. "Walter, adopted son of his half-brother Avery, the noblest man I've ever known." I stopped for a moment, gazing up in the dark, to ponder the riches I had been given. "Well, along with other noble men, noble and good. My own father, my true father Drustan. And your own uncle, a man named John. And your own father—"

"You knew lots of noble men, Mother."

"I had that privilege. Not all were men. The good queen Diera. And there were others." I thought then of Torrin and Lorel. I thought of Conal and Rafe. Some were born into the nobility. Others were not. Nobility, then, was about quality of mind, not about lineage.

Fylkir and Stefan were born into the nobility, but they were not noble. They were, in fact, ignoble.

"But he is dead. My father." Keera's voice came at me in the dark again, breaking into my thoughts.

"Is he?" I asked her. Then I bit my tongue. If she did have the power to penetrate to this answer I sought, would I want her to use it? Would it damage her? Drain her? *Why am I even asking*, I thought dully. *I already know. Caedon told me.* His voice, his gloating smile, swam back into memory. How much he had enjoyed killing Wat. How much he had enjoyed telling me.

"Don't worry, Mother. I can't see the answer."

A chill took me. I reached out to the wall to steady myself. I kept my voice even. "But you felt him, that time. And so did I." We both knew what time I meant. The time of the vision of the beautiful garden.

She nodded.

"Were you afraid?" I asked her. *After all*, I thought. *Surely he was a presence from the grave. A ghost father.*

"No. He loved me. He meant only love to me."

I jumped out of bed to hug her fiercely. "You must stay safe, Keera. You must not flaunt your powers around people who don't understand."

"I promise, Mother," she said, but in the dim light I saw she looked troubled.

"What is it, my darling?"

"Your powers. You can show them without fear. It's not fair."

I thought she meant my second sight, the flickering awareness that came upon me sometimes and just as quickly left.

"Not that," she said. "Your mana."

"Ah," I said. She meant my rebec. "Let's have some music," I said. "It will get us in the mood for sleep. You need to sleep, Keera." I swear to the Nine, Keera talked all day and if I let her, she would talk all night. I took my rebec down from the peg where it hung, and played and sang to her, and we both settled into contentment.

But afterward, as I pulled her sheepskins around her in the bed shelf, she grabbed me by the hand. "What did Auban mean, Mother, when he called Skag a dirty bastard?"

"All that to defend your friend, and you didn't even understand the insult," I said, laughing a little.

"I don't know everything. Just some things."

"I know," I told her. "Well, then," I said, sitting down on the hard-packed dirt of the floor beside her and stroking her hand. "That's a bit difficult to explain. I doubt if Auban really understood what he was calling Skag, although I'm sure he knew it was something hurtful." Privately, I thought it was something he'd heard his parents say about poor little Skag. "Strangely, the word isn't really insulting. It's how people say it that's the insulting part."

"I don't know what you mean, Mother." In the dark, Keera sounded fretful. I could just make out her expression in the dim light of the banked peat fire on our hearth.

"Let's start with something easy, then. You know how a man and a woman make a baby, right?"

"Of course," said Keera scornfully. "Everyone knows that. It's just like when the bull gets a calf on the cow, or the ram getting a lamb on the ewe."

"Yes and no," I said.

"What does that mean? How is it different?"

"It's a bit hard to explain. The cow and bull come together, and afterward there's a calf. Or the ram tups the ewe and they make a lamb together. But the ram and the ewe don't have special feelings for each other. They may never even see each other again, and that's just fine with them. People are different. If a man and a woman have a baby together, often it means they have special feelings for each other. They want to love and protect each other, and stay with each other. Often. But not always."

"You and Father wanted to love and protect each other and stay with each other."

"Yes," I said.

"But you couldn't, because Father died."

"Yes," I said. "And that makes me very sad. Anyway, this is a common thing with people. Often, when people decide to love and protect and stay with each other, they get married. They go to a priestess of one of the Children, or if they believe in the Lady Goddess, one of Her priests—"

"Lady-likers," Keera said with scorn.

"Never say that," I told her. "Both of your grandmothers worshipped the Lady Goddess."

"Grandfather Fylkir did, too," said Keera. "And so did that awful man who was going to take me away with him."

"That's true," I told Keera, thinking with relief that our conversation was now about to veer off into theology, and I could explain bastards another time. But no.

"What does that have to do with bastards?" Keera said.

"Nothing," I admitted.

"So?" she prodded.

"So," I continued, taking a deep breath. "Marriage is usually a good thing. It usually means that two people care about each other. Maybe they love each other, the way your father and I did. The way my true father Drustan and my mother, your grandmother Elsebet, did. Maybe they want the protection they can offer each other, or the comfort, or the security, and not much else. That happens, too. You know that I was married to a man when you were little, after your father died, don't you."

"Grandfather Fylkir made you do it," Keera said.

"Yes. That's not the good kind of marriage. But no matter why two people marry, the law has some rules they must follow."

"What rules?"

"Different rules for different countries, even different kinds of people, like kings and commoners. But usually it means that if the two people have any children, the law declares those children to be legitimate."

"What does that mean?"

"It means the children have certain rights because they were born of a marriage. A son inherits his father's land when his father dies. Things like that."

"So when Grandfather Fylkir dies, you'll get his land?"

"No, your Uncle Stefan will get it, because he's a son, and I'm just a daughter."

"That's not fair," said Keera.

"I know. If there hadn't been any sons, I would have gotten it. My sister Jillie has inherited my true father Drustan's lands. Or should have." I trailed off. Who knew what had happened to those lands.

"Why not you, Mother?"

"It's complicated," I told her. "Anyway, I don't want them. I don't want anyone's lands. Just to stay safe here with you."

"If your baby boy by that man had lived," Keera said, "then he would have inherited that man's lands."

I sat rigid in the dark beside her.

"My little brother."

"I didn't know you knew about him," I said, trying to make my voice calm and even.

"Of course I do," she said. "He was there in the garden, too, when we were all together. But he wouldn't hold still. I wish he could be with us now, Mother."

"I do too," I said.

"But about bastards—" Keera persisted.

I blinked away the tears, glad that she couldn't see them in the dark, and soldiered on. "Two people don't have to be married to have a baby," I explained, "and if they do have one anyway, the law declares that baby a bastard. It just means the baby doesn't have any rights to anything of its parents. It can't inherit the father's lands or other property unless the father makes special arrangements. And that's all a bastard is."

"Then why is it so bad to call someone that?"

"Why, indeed?" I said, more to myself than to Keera. "Anyhow, now you know what a bastard is, and now it's time for you to sleep."

"But Mother—"

Inwardly I groaned. I knew that explanation wasn't going to satisfy Keera. "Listen, Keera, some people think it shameful that a man and a woman have a baby when they aren't married. I don't know this for sure, but it could be that Skag's mother wasn't married to Skag's father when he was born. Calling someone a bastard as an insult is taunting them that they don't have inheritance rights."

Keera was silent for a moment. Then, out of the dark, I heard her say, "Well, that's just silly."

"Yes," I told her. "It is. So now, go to sleep." Then I made the big mistake of casually saying, as I climbed into my own sheepskins, suppressing a yawn, "Your own father was a bastard."

We didn't get much sleep that night. I had a lot of explaining to do.

But at least our lives settled back down into their ordinary pattern as the incident involving Auban faded into the past. I began letting Keera leave our yard to play with her friends again, although some were still afraid of her and avoided her. I wouldn't let her help me assist with sick people any longer—what if someone died and the family blamed her?—but I did let her gather herbs for me.

Everything was normal again.

Not for long.

Late that spring, a farmer north of town came out of his cottage one morning to find his three sheep dead. They had been fine the day before. Now they lay stiff, their poor legs pointing at the sky.

It was clear to me the Dark Ones had touched these sheep with pestilence. When the neighboring farmer's sheep died the same way a few days later, I knew it to be true. The Dark Ones invade—no one quite knows how—but once they do, the sick often pass their dis-ease on to others, usually animals or people nearby. It was a natural process, not witchcraft.

That sen'night, Keera had gone out to gather herbs for me. Someone had seen her skipping and singing past those two farms. So now the whispering began.

She'd put a curse on the animals, some said. She'd sung a curse as she passed by, and now the animals were dead. It was a warning, they said. Cross Keera, and you might find yourself dead next, or your children.

I found this out when a woman appeared at my door. She was the woman whom Keera had miraculously cured. No one in the sick room ever talked of what had happened that night. How we were preparing her family to face the death of their beloved mother, wife, aunt—and then Keera's cool touch on her forehead, the few soft words she spoke. Then the woman herself, rising from her bed a candle-measure later, in perfect health. They'd called in the coffin-maker already. They'd had to send him away.

The woman had been grateful. But Keera and I also saw she was afraid. She had avoided both of us ever since.

Now here she was at our door.

"Mistress Mirin," she said. "I must speak to you."

"Please come in, Mistress Gerta," I told her, holding the door wide.

"Is she—is the little girl about?" Gerta's eyes darted around my cottage fearfully.

"No, she's out playing with her friends." I led Gerta to the hearth fire. It was a chilly morning. I pressed a warm cup of milk from our goat into her hands.

"I see you're in difficulty, mistress," I told her finally, when she only sat passing her hands around and around the mug. "Is there some way I can help you?"

"It's your girl. She's in trouble," Mistress Gerta said, all in a rush, as if she needed to get the words out before she lost courage. "They say she's a witch. They say she killed Nagbard's sheep, and Pona's."

"What in the Nine Spheres!" I couldn't help exclaiming.

"Mistress, your girl saved me. I know that. But now they are saying these things. They're coming for her, mistress. They're afraid of her." Mistress Gerta gulped down a mouthful of goat's milk. "I'm afraid of her, too."

"Sea Child save us."

"You know what she is, your girl. Is she—"

"Of course not," I said. "You'd better leave."

She got up in such haste that she kicked over the mug and goat's milk spread across the beaten earth floor of my cottage.

"I mean no harm to you or your girl. I've just come to warn you before—" She whirled out of the cottage, banging the door behind her. From the window, I saw her running down the street.

*I should have dealt with her more gently*, I thought, looking bleakly after her. Without her warning, a terrible fate might have come upon us. Now it wouldn't. I owed her a great debt.

I set my mouth in a grim line. I never believed this day would come. I thought we were finally safe. But the day I feared was here. At least I was prepared. I'd had to shake myself out of my complacency after the incident with Auban. Now I climbed the ladder to the loft and felt into the niche between stones where I concealed my scabbard and knife. I strapped it to my leg and pulled on a pair of trousers under my kirtle. On my way back through our tiny main room, I grabbed up my rebec from its peg, my cloak from the neighboring peg, and a small sack of supplies I always kept ready—flint and steel, a bag of oats, a bag of dried peas, my trapping and fishing lines. I headed out in the direction of the house where Keera was playing.

"Keera," I called to her over the fence of sticks enclosing her friend's cottage.

She came running to me. I saw in her face she knew what was happening.

Then I spotted them. A knot of them, people from the village, standing by the door of the cottage. Their heads were together; they were conferring about something. They looked up and saw me, and I could see in their faces: Keera was in danger.

I gathered my skirts and vaulted the fence, running to Keera. At a shrill cry from her mother, Keera's friend went pelting back to her cottage.

Keera and I stood in the center of the little fenced in patch of land that served these people as a place to keep their pigs and grow a few vegetables. Around the corner of the cottage came others. And then, down the lane from the village, others.

"Mother."

"Stand by me, Keera. We need to leave."

"I know," she said. She looked down at her shoes. "It's because of me, isn't it."

"That doesn't matter. We need to act fast. Do exactly as I say."

"Yes, Mother."

By now, though, we were cut off from the path. The group of villagers came closer.

"We mean you no harm, Goodwife Mirin," called one man across the gap between us. "We just want the child."

"She has done nothing wrong, you know that, Beathan," I called back. "She's just a child. Let us go by."

"She's a witch," shrieked someone from the crowd, a woman. I knew her now. Auban's mother.

Keera edged closer to me. "Tell her I didn't mean to hurt Auban," she pleaded. "Tell her it was an accident. I just wanted to scare him, I—"

"Hush." Then I called back to the woman, "My daughter's no witch."

"But Mother, if you tell them the truth, then—"

"That's not going to help us now," I said, not taking my eyes off the woman, and a few of the others, who were coming closer. *The truth*, I thought bitterly. *The truth will just confirm it for these people.* Then, the memory of the farwydd's words, *Sometimes the right does not prevail.* "Listen to me carefully, Keera. Stand behind me. Keep one hand on my skirts. We must not get separated. Do you understand?" I handed back the bag with my rebec for her to hold.

"Yes, Mother." She grabbed on to the back of my kirtle.

I had seen something. I'd seen the woman who had shouted witch, and a few others, bend down and pick up rocks. Smooth rocks from the yard.

The man called Beathan was tossing a large stone from one hand to the other, and he was leading the group forward.

"Keera," I told her, making my voice as quiet and even as I could, "We're going to back up. Slowly. We're going to back up toward that breach in the fence, where the farm is closest to the trees. Don't stare, but glance behind you and tell me that you see where I mean."

"I do, Mother,"

"That's right, then. Back up. Slowly."

But the people from the village had seen what we were doing, and now some on the edges were fanning out to encircle us.

"We don't want to hurt you, Mistress," the man named Beathan called out again. "But we want the girl."

"No," I called back to him. I stepped backward, and behind me, I could feel Keera doing the same. I'd need to get my body between her and those stones, I thought.

Someone from the back of the group lifted his stone and heaved it at us, but it fell short and rolled harmlessly between us and the group. That unleashed something, though. I could see it in their eyes. They were raising their arms now, those with stones. Those without them were bending down to find stones of their own.

"We may have to run, but keep backing up," I said to Keera. I felt the bleak bitter feeling I'd lost the battle to keep my daughter safe.

An amazing thing happened then. The Children, protecting us? Or luck? Neither, as it turned out. But someone toward the crowd looked back at the village and let out a ragged scream.

"Fire!"

Everyone turned. People dropped their stones and began running toward their homes. As they were stalking us, the whole village behind them blazed up into fire.

"Run, Keera," I told her. We turned on our heels and ran for the breach in the fence, and we didn't stop until we got to the trees.

The woods were thick, and we headed up the steep slope behind the cottage into the deepest part of the forest. When I thought we were far enough away, I signaled to Keera to stop. We dropped to the ground, winded.

Now I raised myself on one elbow and tried to see through the trees. They were too thick around us, though. But I could smell the smoke.

"Was that—" I paused and chose my words carefully. "Did you send up a prayer to the Fire Child, maybe?"

"No, Mother. I promised you I'd stop doing things like that."

"Then why—" I fell silent. If this were a stroke of luck, it was the luckiest stroke I'd known in my life, almost as lucky as the moment Caedon failed to kill Wat on that hillside above the massed armies of the civil war before Keera was even thought of. But today, I felt even luckier, because this event, this fire, coming at exactly the right moment, had preserved our child, Wat's and mine. How many strokes of luck can one life expect to hold?

I hugged her to me. "If you can start fires in the nick of time, though, I think just this once you could have made an exception."

"But I didn't."

I hugged her again. She was getting agitated, starting to cry.

"Don't worry, my darling. Let's just think about getting away from this place. We'll have plenty of time, later, to think what to do about these powers of yours."

I bedded us down for the night then, because it was getting dark and chillier. We had our cloaks for coverings, and I had also removed my kirtle by now. Wearing trousers around the village would have just confirmed to the villagers that I was an alien and unnatural presence. But now the trousers were practical. And my discarded kirtle gave us one extra layer of cloth against the cold.

Keera lay snuggled against me. I could tell by her breathing she was finally asleep. I couldn't sleep, though. The thoughts whirling around in my head were too disturbing. *How. Why. If I had my suspicions about how the fire started, the villagers would take it as simple truth. More of Keera's witchcraft.*

I also remembered something I had left behind, something important. It was a small pouch of coin, maybe enough to buy us passage off the island. It would be safest for us if we left the island entirely. I thought the isle was big enough, and our village remote enough, that people in the port city on the other side of the island weren't likely to hear anything of this incident, but I couldn't be sure.

The moon had risen. I sat up. I knew I'd have to go back to check.

"Mother." Keera was awake.

"I won't be gone long, darling. If I don't come back, I want you to promise me something. We need to get to the port city. That's north. Can you find your way there? It should take about two days, and I have the provisions."

"You'll come back."

"You sound sure of that. That's good. But just in case—"

We got up from our nest of cloaks and I led her to a clearing. I crouched down and pointed, guiding her to look along my arm into the sky. Fastened to their sphere, the patterns of the stars would show she was traveling north, and I made sure she could recognize these patterns.

"You'll come back. But you don't need to go."

I looked down at her shadowed pale face, peering up at me.

"I have to go."

"Because you have to know."

"No, I believe you. I just need to get the pouch of—" I stopped. She was right. The main reason. I had to know for sure what had started that fire. I paused and thought hard. I'd be risking my daughter's well-being, maybe her life, on what could easily be a fool's errand. And I did believe her. At least, I didn't believe she had started the fire intentionally. But suppose something she had thought—

"Go, then, Mother. You'll be back, and I'll be fine."

"But if I can find that coin, we'll be better off. Safer." I felt guilty, saying that, because it was the truth but it was a shading of the truth, and Keera knew that.

She reached up and twined her arms around my neck, and I kissed her.

"I won't be gone long," I told her.

"I know," she said.

So I slipped away down the hill, circling around to the village. I waited in the shadows the village granaries made, and assessed my chances. The whole village was a smoldering ruin. Little knots of villagers stood in the street, gazing at their houses in despair.

One group came walking by, and I shrank back further into the shadows. They were talking among themselves.

"That Gerta, she never did have any sense," one man was saying. I recognized Beathan's voice, or thought I did. "And her man has less."

"He beat her when she came running back from warning the Witch-Mother," said someone else. I didn't recognize this new voice. But that's when I realized that despite Beathan's assurances, the whole lot of them did mean me harm. Me and Keera both. "Then he fired the Witch-Mother's thatch," said this other person. "And then it spread to the entire village, one thatch to the next. Now look."

"It's still witchcraft, however it happened. She laid a curse on us for sure, the Witch-Mother, and the little Witch too," said Beathan. "She made us burn our own village down. Everything I have is gone."

*So*, I thought. *Not luck. Not the Children*. Just human fear and stupidity. When the group of them had moved on, I stepped out of the shadows. My own house was burned all the way to the ground. I could see it from where I stood. Maybe I'd be able to comb through the ashes. Maybe I'd find the coins. But the chances weren't good in the best of circumstances, and I wouldn't have the advantages of broad daylight and a lot of time.

So I stole away, back to the place I'd left Keera. I felt that human fear and stupidity were my own lot, too. I should have trusted Keera and stayed away, not taken the risk.

When I got back, though, Keera threw her arms about me. "You know now," she whispered. "Now you feel better."

"Better, and also worse," I told her, giving her a rueful smile she probably didn't see in the dark.

In the morning, we moved on. I knew we were safe. The villagers had an entire season of work ahead of them, trying to repair their burned-up lives. They were combing through their own ruins right now, not thinking about chasing us down.

We were careful, though. It had been a cold wet spring, and the soggy ground might keep an imprint of our boots. We could still be followed.

"Keep to the stony ground," I told Keera. Fewer footprints to follow.

I made us turn our cloaks inside out so the bright color wouldn't signal our presence. Then, with my knife, I cut a low-hanging fir branch. As we went on, I scrabbled the mud behind us with the branch. That would erase any footprints.

But as we made our way across country, the need diminished, and we just trudged on. This spring morning was bright, not sodden, and my mood started to lift. My child was safe.

"To the port, Mother?"

"That's right, Keera. It should take us all day to walk there, and part of the next."

It did. At the port town, larger than ours, no one knew us. No one had heard of the outcry we had left behind. I spent the next fortnight going from tavern to tavern, playing my rebec, until I had enough coin to buy us passage across to the next island. Things seemed safe here. But I wasn't going to leave anything to luck.

And so we left our quiet life behind.

# Something Bad

The isle where we landed was further north and quite a bit bigger than the small isle where we'd been living, an outpost of the Sceptered Isle. Our new refuge was called the Northmost Isle, the realm's largest center of population and trade in that region. It was the linchpin between two realms, our Sceptered Isle and the Ice-realm, and also served as a way-station for ships traveling to the smaller Fire Isle further away.

The Northmost Isle had changed hands back and forth many times between our realm and the Ice-realm. Living in Fylkir's house and listening to his outraged scheming about regaining his patrimony, I discovered that the Fire Isle, his original home and the place of my birth, had had a similar history. The Fire Isle had at times been the outpost of the Ice-realm, just as our Western Isle had been our own realm's outpost. During other times in its history, as now, the Fire Isle was independent. At present, the Fire Isle belonged to no one but its powerful landowners, but everyone knew it was only a matter of time before Haakon Hardaxe, monarch of the Ice-realm, would descend on it to re-claim it.

I set myself the task of finding out as much as I could about the political goings on in our new home. Keera and I had moved out of danger on the tiny isle where we'd sought refuge, but now we'd moved much closer to the center of Caedon's power. I needed to keep us both safe.

Around here, as on the smaller isle we'd fled, the tavern regulars were still buzzing about the latest and, I had to think, last campaign of the Rising. With Diera's execution, surely all hope was lost. Around here, the tavern windbags and muckspouts were saying Diera's powerful relations in the Baronies had only made a pretense of supporting her. These tavern talkers were saying Diera was dead, her forces defeated, because her Baronies relatives had decided the future belongs to Caedon. Besides, Diera was only a woman. So they sold her out, as many men in this world sell women. To most of the men in the taverns, the big talkers, this reasoning appeared to be perfectly understandable.

Not to me.

To me, the betrayal of the eastern barons was not only immoral and vile, it was short-sighted. I sat in the taverns listening to this talk and smiled to myself, a bitter smile. Whatever the other ills they may be perpetrating, they were doing the one thing that would come back to bite them. They were doing what so many before them had done and continue to do: underestimate Caedon. I knew too much to underestimate him.

I know how Caedon thinks. *Which of these two rivals do I take on first, the east or the north?* he must be thinking. *If I don't, they'll take me on, maybe in alliance together. So I'll divide and conquer.*

And I know why Caedon is so clever. Of course he has natural ability. Caedon is a very intelligent man. But I know where Caedon gets his ideas. I had spent too many candle measures in Caedon's library. Books line it, precious books, several written by a famous general of the Old Ones, the very general who subdued our lands in the far-distant past. In his books, this general tells how he did it. He analyzed his enemy, using his intelligence just as Caedon uses his. *All these lands are divided into three parts,* this general wrote long ago, in their old language that Caedon knows how to read. In the same book, this old general explained how he conquered our forebears. He went on to make himself king, at least for a while, until his followers turned on him and stabbed him to death.

Caedon read the general's book and was preparing, even now, to follow its plan.

I could only hope someone would rise up and stab Caedon to death as the general of the Old Ones had been stabbed. But I knew that was unlikely.

Why should Caedon try to defeat his two rivals? Couldn't he establish peaceful alliances with both the Eastern Baronies and the Ice-realm? That's what many in the taverns were speculating about. I was sure Caedon was making a pretense of doing exactly that. Knowing him too well, as I do, I was sure about Caedon's real intentions. He was biding his time before he turned on one or the other—eventually both. He was too shrewd to take them on both at once. He had studied the books of the old general well.

What will Caedon do with a realm that big, once he has conquered both the Baronies and the Ice-Realm? When his lands stretch from the northmost to the easternmost parts of the world? I thought about that, and I thought back to the coin I'd given the ferryman, the coin of the Old Ones who had ruled our realm long before Ranulf, and Ranulf's father, and his father's father.

We all know the Old Ones were real. They aren't just stories. We find their coins when we plow the earth. We walk the roads they built. In the cities, they say, people still drink water from their great aqueducts. These are marvelous lanes for water that bring it down from the streams and into the cities. I've only heard about them. Someday I may drink from them myself. I'd like to do that.

After many ages of rule, though, the Old Ones' grip on our part of the world weakened, and they retreated back to their lands in The Southern Primacy. But before they did, they marked our realm in many ways.

It is said the realm of these Old Ones, once the general and his descendants had made their conquests, stretched from our lands to the lands far to the east, encompassing almost the entire world, even parts of the mysterious Forgotten Kingdom. The mother of Eris, the betrayer, Wat's half-sister, came from one of these eastern lands. The entire world! Caedon, studying the general's words, has decided he will do likewise.

Almost the entire world, I should say. There is one part of the world that the Old Ones never conquered: the unknown western lands. I don't mean our own big Western Isle on the edge of our realm. That they did conquer. I mean lands far beyond our isle, far across the tempestuous sea, the gray-green whale roads stretching off the Western Isle's coast. No one knows where these far-off realms are, exactly, or how big they are, or who rules them. Everyone knows they exist, though. Everyone in my world. Over there on the mainland, no one knows about them, but I kept hearing things on these little isles in the north. Fishermen gone astray come back, if they do, with tales of these savage lands and their savage inhabitants, and they talk about them in towns like the waterfront city where Keera and I found our latest refuge.

These are the things I heard on this biggest of the isles, where sailors bring their strange tales and the politics of the world gets traded around from mouth to mouth as the tavern-goers down their ale.

And so, in spite of our poverty and our status as runaways, Keera and I began leading a productive and interesting life on the biggest of the northern isles. We felt ourselves at the crossroads of the world.

I was finding it difficult to take care of the two of us, though. I had spent all my saved-up coin to buy us passage, and now I was having a hard time getting work. Here I had no reputation as a healer, and I worried too much about Keera to allow her to go alone into the woods to find herbs to sell. She was blossoming into a desirable young girl.

There was only one thing for it. I resumed my practice of taking my rebec from tavern to tavern and playing for a bite of food and whatever coins the tavern-goers dropped in my lap. At least our brief stay in the port of the island we'd fled had gotten me back into practice. I'd learned some new songs.

As for shelter, at first we slept in an abandoned turf shed for animals. Shortly after our flight to this island, the spring weather made the turn into summer, thank the Nine, so we didn't suffer too much from cold nights, even this far north. But it would be only a matter of time before someone in authority discovered us. Then I didn't know what would become of us. So I had to think of something fast.

The Children stood by us, though. Or luck. At one tavern, the Sun-Stone, the tavern owner's wife Teasag was so taken by my singing and playing that she offered me a tiny room and food in return for my services as an entertainer.

"Stay here with us, mistress," said Teasag. "I'll give you room and board if you do."

"But Goodwife Teasag, I have a child," I told her.

"Bring her. She won't be in the way."

The tavern owner looked over at his wife as if she'd lost her mind. "This tavern's no place for a child," he growled.

Looking around at the rough sailors in from some long sea voyage, ridding themselves of their ill humors by boisterous behavior, I had to agree with him.

"Nine Spheres, husband," huffed Teasag. "Don't our own grandchildren visit us here? Mistress, I'll see you and your wee one are safe."

I looked around me again. Really, I had no choice. I accepted her offer, hoping it would not be a mistake.

It wasn't. The coin dropped into my lap from exuberant sailors feeling generous was mine to keep, and Keera and I were sheltered, fed, and protected. As before, I carefully hoarded any coin I came across. By then, I knew. No matter how safe we felt, some untoward turn of events might send us fleeing again.

The Sun-Stone was down by the docks. It was perfect in one sense, because there I heard everything, all the news the seamen brought back from their travels. It was not perfect in another sense, because I had to fend off over-eager or drunk sailors every day. Luckily, the tavern owner was strict with such people, and Teasag his wife was larger, meaner, and stricter. No one bothered me while she glowered at them from her position at the front of the tavern, her powerful red arms bulging from their sleeves, a heavy crock at the ready. She used to throw it at customers who displeased her, and then beat them over their heads with it, or the shards of it if their heads were hard enough to break it. Nothing displeased her more than men who tried to put their hands on me.

I knew I could take care of myself, but of course I didn't want anyone to see how well. Or leave any inconvenient corpses for the beadle's men to find.

I worried for Keera, though, in spite of Teasag's reassurances. It was a rough place. She stayed cooped up in that little room above-stairs. Her beauty was flourishing more every day, and I knew how restless she must be feeling.

Or I thought I knew.

I didn't. How could I? Every afternoon, as the sailors and fishermen began filling the tavern and my services were needed downstairs, she wriggled out the window, clambered over the rooftops, shinnied down off a low-hanging eaves, and romped off to the meadow stretching past the waterfront to play. And every late evening, as I climbed the steep little staircase to our attic room under the eaves, she was there waiting for me. After all, she was just a child. She used her powers to know when I'd re-appear.

Then, as if she'd been waiting for me all day, she'd settle down with me to share the ample hearty food the tavern keeper's wife sent upstairs with me. We ate these meals very late, because the sailors stayed in the tavern until Teasag threw them all out, and they wanted to hear my songs as long as she let them stay. Keera and I were used to eating when others had long ago gone to their beds. Afterward, we made up our own beds on our pallets, gazing out the slit of a window at the stars and the moon while I sang her softly to sleep. Then we'd wake late, and the entire cycle of the tavern would begin again.

Keera's not a deceitful child, not at heart. She wanted to play, she wanted to explore, and she wanted to protect me from my fears. Because she was a child, she had the idea she could possess all of her conflicting desires without having to sacrifice any of them.

She succeeded. I didn't know what she was up to.

As before, our lives assumed a pleasant routine. I didn't pine for finer surroundings. In fact, I gave such matters no thought at all. I had Keera, we had a roof over our heads and food in our bellies, and that's all I needed.

Meanwhile, during the mornings before the tavern got busy, I taught Keera. She mastered her letters with ease. My only problem was how to feed her insatiable hunger for more. Where could I get books for her? I thought of Caedon's library with longing. Keera and I made do. We thought up stories for each other, and every time I could find a scrap of parchment and bring it home to her, Keera began writing her stories down.

Somewhere along her roaming path through the city, while I played and sang thinking she was safely stowed away, Keera—I later discovered—came upon a school. It was a school for boys who were studying to become priests of the Lady Goddess. And yes, the Lady Goddess had made her way to our town at last. The worship of the Children was banned. No one bothered with the ban, though, no matter how much the Lady's priests ranted and threatened.

Keera couldn't get into that school, being a girl, for one, and a stray street urchin, for two. She found another way. She befriended one of the boys and persuaded him to let her see his slate where he wrote out his lessons. Once, she even persuaded him to sneak her into the schoolroom, when everyone was away, so she could look at the schoolmaster's book chained to its pedestal. Afterward, as often as she could, she sneaked into that room and read that book, page by page. She didn't let the boy know she was doing it, though.

But soon she was helping this boy with his school work and learning faster than he did, wielding slate and stylus far more skillfully. Soon after that, a number of his friends were sneaking out to the little piece of greensward where she waited, and she was helping them all with their school work. No one told on her. The dullards threatened to beat anyone who did, because this way, they avoided their own beatings by the schoolmaster. The schoolmaster was astounded. Never had he taught such a class of bright boys.

Keera even learned that strange language, the language of the Old Ones that Caedon knows so well. I marveled at this, when I finally found out. My own daughter!

I would have been proud back then, if I'd known, but I would also have been terrified, so she wisely kept this piece of information to herself.

Why wasn't I surprised when something happened to disrupt this peaceful life of ours? Something always did.

As before, a piece of news upended my world. The news that Caedon was making a journey to treat with King Haakon Hardaxe of the Ice-realm. This was hardly unexpected. I thought back to the visit Caedon had paid to Fylkir's house when Keera was just a baby. What jolted me was the path he'd need to take to get to Haakon's realm. Caedon would have to travel by sea, of course, and his sea-voyage was taking him here.

The news chilled me to my very bones. Caedon in the world—always a threat. Caedon in the same town, though. That turned me to stone.

Then I settled myself down. Caedon would never come to such a low tavern as this, and even if the sailors of his ship did, they knew nothing about me. *But*—a voice insisted—*they might know something of a beautiful child with unruly curling fire-red hair, a child Caedon considers his own property, property he's been cheated of.*

*And you*, the voice went on, refusing to stop its insistent whispering. *He thinks you're his property too.*

I thought I'd been holding Keera in seclusion, but even I knew how hard she was to keep totally out of sight. She was impossible to miss. Heads turned as we walked through the town's lanes together, and those heads were not turning to gaze after me.

That same voice inside me warned, *We'll have to run. We'll have to run again.*

After worrying about this all day long, the day I heard about Caedon's official visit, I climbed back up to our little room to find Keera waiting for me. She accepted the bowl of stew Teasag had made up for her, and we sat down together to eat.

When we'd finished, she set both bowls aside and took my hands in hers. She looked up at me with those gray-green eyes of hers, eyes that saw so far and so deep. "Mother," she said. "You're not to worry. Nothing bad is going to happen to me."

"Are you sure of it?" By now, I believed her when she said such things to me.

"Yes. But something bad will happen to you."

My hand flew to my mouth.

"You must see this Caedon. You must."

"That's very dangerous, Keera."

"I know, but you have to do it."

"But why?"

"Something important will be revealed when you do," she told me.

"But what?"

"I don't know," she said. "I'm not told what it is, just that it's so."

*Told by whom?* I wanted to ask her. But I knew if I did ask, she wouldn't be able to answer me. She knew what she knew, and she knew how she knew it, but she could never explain it in a way I could understand. It distressed her if I pressed her about it, so I knew not to.

"I'm afraid," I told her.

"I know, Mother."

But I knew she was right. If she was telling me this, then yes, I had to do it. This may sound strange to any other mother. I challenge any other mother on this earth to live with my daughter for seven years and see how well she deals with it. How many things she'll end up doing that she'd never do if she were of sound mind and possessed of good sense. Those I had apparently lost long ago.

So I knew I'd do it. Now I had to figure out how.

"I don't have to walk right up to him and let him take me, do I?" I tried to make my tone light as I asked this, but the dread must have risen up past my intention not to alarm her.

"I don't think so," she said, and began to cry.

"Think, my darling. Can you see past this incident? Will we be separated?"

"I don't know," she said, as the tears streamed down her cheeks.

I looked at her thoughtfully, remembering how my music, years ago, had summoned blackbirds. I never had much control over them, and not for long. Then, once my task was complete, not at all. The Children's wishes are obscure. They have their own higher plan, and all we poor mortals can do is use their gifts as best we can. "Hush now," I told Keera. "I'll do it, this difficult task. I'll do it in my own way, and it will be fine." Then I took down my rebec and played the song to her, the one that always soothed both of us and made us know things would work out for the best.

And sure enough, as if it were a sign to us, when we looked out our tiny attic window and up into the night sky, that's what we saw. The new moon with the old moon in her arms. The new moon just aborning in a sliver of silver, cradling the ghost-sight of the old darkened full moon within her crescent.

# Chapter Eighteen

# Something Worse

The whole city was agog with the news of Caedon's arrival. The main part of town was decked out in banners and flowers. Everyone dressed in their holiday attire. I had spent a long time thinking how I would encounter Caedon. In the end, Keera solved my problem for me.

"Dress as a man, Mother."

I laughed. "Did you know that at one time I did do that? I pretended to be a boy, while your father and I roved all over the countryside as entertainers. I played and sang."

"What did my father do?"

"You don't know?" I was never quite sure what Keera did and didn't know. "He was an acrobat. A juggler. He's very good at it, too."

"My father is an acrobat?"

"Among other things." In spite of myself, I felt my mouth quirk up into a smile.

"But that's not what he is, mostly."

"No," I said, pulling her in for a hug. *What is he, mostly? I wondered. A bastard. An assassin. The son of a king. A warrior. A tender lover.*

I felt a warm uprush of memory and feeling. Later, I realized it was because we were talking about Wat in the present. *What he is.* Not *What he was.* As if he were still alive.

"You love my father," said Keera, looking me over carefully.

"Yes, more than anyone in the world besides you."

"More than me?"

"The same as you. Well, not exactly the same. When you love a person, you love that person and those circumstances surrounding that person and everything that makes up that person and all the features that only that one person possesses. So no love is ever exactly the same. But I love him fully. And I love you fully. And I don't love anyone else in the world that fully."

"Not even your mother and father? I love you fully," Keera said to me.

Keera was hard to talk to as if she were the child she is. "I did love my mother and father fully. Now they're dead."

"And your little sister?"

"Yes. And Jillie."

"But Jillie isn't dead."

"No," I said. "That's the one thing in all this—" Here I found myself waving my hand vaguely about, but Keera seemed to understand it—"the one thing that gives me hope."

Keera's face changed. From bright, it grew dark. Somber.

I felt a thrill of alarm. "What is it? What do you know?" I took her face in my hands and tilted it up to mine. No wonder people who didn't know her thought she was a witch. She was hard to be around, sometimes, given the things she knew. Given what was inside her.

"I don't know." She looked away.

"You really don't? Or you're afraid to tell me. Is Jillie dead?"

"No," she said. "I don't know. I'm not sure." She clamped her mouth into that little familiar line and stopped talking.

It was hard not to press her. I knew I shouldn't. It wasn't fair to her. Still, I couldn't help myself. Tears rose in my eyes. "Something has happened to her. She's dead."

"No," said Keera. "That's not it. But I don't know what."

"Something bad," I whispered to myself.

"I only have a feeling," Keera said.

"I have feelings like that, sometimes," I told her.

She nodded, as if she'd known that all along.

"I don't know how far to trust those feelings. My father called them my second sense."

"Your true father."

"Drustan. He would have loved you, Keera. And so would your grandmother, Elsebet." My heart twisted in pain.

We sat for a while in the little attic room, watching the moon come up. I pulled her close to me.

"But Mother. You must dress as a man."

"That was easy when I was a thin slip of a girl," I said. "Not so easy now."

"I'll help you."

I stopped trying to second-guess her then. She had seen something. I knew the feelings she had were a lot stronger and more trustworthy than my second sense, even though they weren't perfect. I believed she had somehow seen me as a man, in the presence of Caedon.

We got some sleep. In the early morning, before my duties were to start in the tavern, I slipped downstairs to tell Teasag that Keera was sick and I needed to be with her. By then, I was such a valued employee that I knew Teasag would accept it, and she did, murmuring sympathetically that she would send a bowl of soup up later.

"Best leave it outside our door," I told her. "In case there's infection."

Her eyes widened with fear, and she nodded agreement. Teasag was afraid of nothing, but she was afraid of plague. Of course we all were.

Then I rushed back upstairs. Using my sharp knife, Keera hacked off my hair.

"What will I do, later on, when I need to sing in the tavern? Oh well," I said. "I'll just wear my headcloth to sing." That would look odd. When I sang, I let my hair flow free. It was an accepted thing, for tavern singers.

"You'll think of something. A scarf, maybe. A hood."

My hair fell in waves and wisps about my feet. I felt a chill, remembering how Wat and I had turned me into a boy so many years ago. Keera and I swept my shorn hair up, and Keera hid it all under her pallet. Then we ripped an old cloak of mine into long strips and used these to bind my breasts so my woman-figure wouldn't show. Luckily I'd never had what might be called an ample figure, not even after childbirth and nursing.

But it was fine. My figure. I had to stop for a moment and smile, because I was remembering some things between me and Wat. Things only the two of us need to know. Things about our love-making. *Not need. Needed.* I shook off the familiar twist of grief, a knife to my innermost self.

I concentrated instead on the task of getting ready for my masquerade. After Keera and I bound my breasts, it was a simple matter to strap my knife to my leg, get into trousers and loose tunic, wrap my cloak about me, pull the hood up to shadow my face, and I was ready to go.

"Wait," said Keera. She rushed to the window and threw open the shutters. Where the smoke from the tavern's fire-hole had made everything sooty, she scraped some off and smoothed it over my cheeks. The smoke from the fire-hole rose directly from the main room of the tavern. But our attic was built over the room where Teasag and her husband slept. Otherwise, our attic would have been too smoky for us to sleep in. We kept warm with plenty of furs and blankets.

"There now," said Keera, once she had smoothed the soot on my cheeks. "Mother, you have a little bit of a beard. It looks like you'll need to shave sometime soon." We both laughed and fell down on the pallets, stifling our merriment so no hint of it would filter down the spiraling stairs to the bottom level and make Teasag wonder. Keera scooped some more of the soot up into a little pouch I used for potions and handed it to me.

"I'm not sure how long I'll be away," I said uneasily, realizing why she was doing this. I could be gone for days. I didn't want to leave her alone.

"You have to, Mother," she said, reading my mind as easily as if I had spoken the words aloud. As usual.

"It's a strange mother-daughter relationship we have, you and I, Keera," I muttered.

"Is that bad?" Her little face looked anxious.

"No, my darling. Just—unusual." I thought of all the things my own parents had kept from me, to protect me. There was no keeping anything from Keera.

A snatch of song came to me from somewhere, a song about a changeling child who leads her mother on a merry chase. Who knows where in the Nine Spheres I'd heard it. *Come all you mothers, listen well to me!* I hummed. *A woman had an elf child, an elf-child so had she. Come to catch your elf child, elf child, elf child, Chase your naughty elf child underneath the sea. . . .*

We waited now, keeping ourselves still, listening at the door until we heard the bustling noises that burst from the tavern when its first customers rollicked in from their long sea-voyages, hungry for a bowl of stew and thirsty for a mug of ale.

The moment had come. "It's time, Mother," said Keera.

As my last act before I left on my perilous errand, I took my rebec down from its peg and laid it in her arms. "If something happens to me—" I began.

"But nothing will," she said.

"You said something bad would happen to me."

"Not like that, though," she assured me. "A different kind of bad."

"The thing I'll find out?"

"Yes," she said.

I gave her a quick hug, slipped out the door, closed it tight behind me, and stole down the staircase. I peeked around the corner. Teasag's broad back was turned as she labored over her barrel of ale. The tavern keeper himself was nowhere to be seen—probably out behind the tavern, turning the large spit skewering the pork and beeves he'd need that day to feed his customers.

I strode to the door with, I hoped, a manful gait and shouldered past some sailors coming in.

"Watch where you're going, lad," snarled one.

*Good,* I thought. *I'm fooling him.* Now I must only hope to fool Caedon and his men. *Suppose the something bad I find out is that Wat is truly dead,* I thought. My mouth was dry with fear. I pushed the thought away. I already knew that. *Suppose, though ... suppose I find out exactly how he died, in terrible detail, the way Caedon threatened to tell me.* That thought, too, I pushed away. I had to. I had too much to do to entertain such fears.

I headed for the center of the town to join the celebrating throngs. As I made my way along the docks, I saw Caedon's ship in the harbor, banners gaily fluttering, the wolf's head insignia blazing gold on his sail. Before the ship headed out on its voyage northward to the Ice-realm of Haakon, Caedon and his retinue would disembark, and he'd spend a night being entertained by his viceroy in the islands. Ours is the vice-regal city for the northern isles, shabby though it is. Caedon would ride through our crooked, dirty streets, graciously throwing coin to his eager subjects scrambling in his wake. His procession would wind up the hill, the highest point in all the isles, to the fortified manor house of the viceroy.

"He's coming! He's coming!" Shouts from the crowds further toward the docks alerted me. I pushed to the front of the crowd, where I could see Caedon as he rode past. I didn't want to. I would as soon have come face to face with one of the fabled poisonous serpents of the Realm of the Asp.

Gradually the crowds parted to either side of the street. The black horses I remembered Caedon always favored came in view, and the richly decorated open cart behind them. High on a seat in the back of the cart, Caedon. Beside him, a veiled lady, probably the wife I'd heard about. The one who had displaced Keera as Caedon's bride. I shuddered, remembering what could have happened to my precious daughter if the Sea Child hadn't led me there at the right moment to intervene.

*There*, I thought. *I've said it.* I've credited the Sea Child, not luck. Because if it were mere luck, it certainly came in a miraculous package.

The wagon rolled past my station on the street. Caedon's pale, sharp-featured face blazed out over the crowd. Almost mesmerized, I looked up into his deep-sunken wolfish amber eyes as he rode by. I couldn't help myself. *Who are you, and what made you the way you are, ruthless and cruel?* What would happen if he looked down into the crowd and recognized me? My heart beat harder. But of course he didn't. To him, we must seem a sea of upturned rapt faces, all of us mesmerized. He must be feeding on our mass adoration. But he wouldn't be picking out individuals in the crowd.

If he were scanning the crowd for me at all—but he wouldn't be—he'd be looking for a woman.

As the carriage swept past, the cheering rose to a crescendo. Our tiny outpost, honored by a visit from the king himself! People were on fire with excitement. I saw, riding on either side of the cart, hard-faced guards, their weapons at the ready. Caedon was taking no chances. Some in the crowd might not be as excited to welcome him here as others.

Caedon loves flattery, but he is a realist. He loves flattery not because he believes it but because it is a sign to him how much power he wields over the flatterers. He loves how much he makes them fear him, underneath all the cheering and the flowery speeches and the obsequious little offices.

That there were some who hate the flattery they pay him, some who might call up the will to oppose him, even fight him? He loves that too. He loves nosing them out and crushing them.

He loves traitors and treachery. As I had found to my own distress, he loves coercing people into acts of treachery by putting them into impossible positions and enjoying it as they vainly try to wriggle out of the traps he has set them. Some say he used his own bride this way, to betray Diera. They say she had been a member of Diera's own household, before Caedon got his hands on her. Some say he coerced her with threats, even torture. Others say she willingly participated in Diera's betrayal.

I thought back to the assassination of King Ranulf's rightful heir, Artur, betrayed by his own wife. Many argued that Caedon was the architect of that particular plot. He had perfected himself in its use.

That's what he loves. The power, the intrigue, the fear.

I knew Caedon well. Much too well.

The cheering rose in waves and subsided, then rose again well down the road away from me. Those around me began flowing away again, back to their tasks as apprentices, farmers, seamen, ale-wives, fish-wives, coopers, smiths.

I stood standing in the road, looking after the procession in a daze.

Then I shook myself awake. I needed to follow the procession. I needed to get close to Caedon. Beyond that, I had no real plan. It was a little bit crazy. A twelve-year-old girl had told me I must do this, but not the reason why, and it was dangerous, and I was doing it. More than a little bit crazy.

I just knew there was something I needed to learn. Something important. Keera didn't know what it was, and I certainly didn't. But something important enough to risk my safety, maybe my life, to find out.

I quickened my steps in the wake of the procession, edging off the road, following along down back lanes. I didn't want to seem too conspicuous. That's the only thing that made any sense at all in the whole insane enterprise. Keera knew I was capable of doing things like this, sneaking, acting. Dangerous things. She trusted it. I had never told her much about my life with Wat during the Rising. Some of it she somehow knew, I had no idea how much. But of course she had witnessed my skills when I rescued her from Fylkir, and again when we fled from the witch-accusers, so she had first-hand knowledge, not just her uncanny sight into unknown matters. She trusted I knew what I was doing.

If only I trusted myself as much.

The day was getting warm, and the binding about my breasts was starting to chafe me. When I wiped sweat from my face, my hand came away covered with soot. I needed to keep moving. I wasn't sure how long my disguise would protect me.

Eventually I found myself at the very back of the procession as it began to toil up the hill toward the fortified manor of the viceroy. I had a surprisingly easy job blending into the crowd of retainers and servants and following along.

The back of my neck prickled as we all surged through the gates into the manor grounds. If I were spotted as an imposter, the guards surrounding Caedon would bring me down on the spot, no questions asked.

But I got onto the grounds of the manor without incident. Looking around me, I saw that many of the retainers who milled around the manor grounds had been hired on for the occasion. They were all young men. They didn't know each other and they didn't really know much about the tasks they were meant to do. That stood me in good stead. I was as confused as the rest and—Keera must have seen this—I was a young man. Apparently.

As we came through the gates, identical yellow tabards were thrust into our hands, and we put them on. Now we all looked like a single cadre of servants. It was a pretty effect. I realized the viceroy's household had been overwhelmed by the news of Caedon's progress north, and the time to prepare had been short. The viceroy had had to hire on a lot of servants and, for the sake of his own prestige, create the illusion they were part of his staff. He hadn't had time to pick and choose.

*Dangerous,* I thought to myself. *If anyone wanted to assassinate Caedon, how easy would this haphazard collection of young men make such a deed?* I wondered if I should have known to try it. Could I have succeeded? I was no assassin. That was something in me I had to face, I thought now. I had to be honest with myself. In spite of all the dreaming I'd done about someday killing Caedon, in spite of the killing I'd been forced by circumstances to do, I don't think I could have done it, not plan out and coldly kill a man, even Caedon.

Wat could have. He would have. I suppose that makes Wat sound bloodthirsty and hard. If Caedon had hurt Keera, though, that would change everything. Not just for Wat, if he were around to see it. For me, too.

I did realize one important thing about Wat. Caedon's men, maybe Caedon himself, had cut my family down, but I hadn't been there. I hadn't watched, just witnessed the horrific aftermath, which was bad enough. But Wat. Wat had watched. He was there as Caedon's men killed his six-year-old brother Aedan. And his mother. Later on, Wat had done his utmost to save his older brother John from Caedon, but had gotten there too late. When he did, he had seen. Experiences like those could transform a peaceable person into a killer. They could transform me.

"Don't stand there lollygagging, boy. Get to work," barked a voice in my ear. I jumped. A high-ranking servant of the court was staring at me, his face red with irritation. I scurried for the kitchen shed before he could get too close a look at me. Many of us temporary servants congregated around the shed, where the kitchen helpers thrust platters of meat and small kegs of wine and ale into the hands of us lesser servants. I was shaking.

"Steady," said a kind-looking man in the viceroy's livery. "Just do your job, lad. Naught to fear." He handed me one of the ale kegs. I took it gratefully, ducking my head in obedience, and also making sure he didn't get a clear look into my face.

Carrying my keg, I followed a line of yellow-tabarded servingmen into the manor house itself. We lined an entryway.

"He's coming, the king is coming," said the same kind-looking servant. His livery told us he was someone meant to be there, one of the viceroy's real servants. "Wait until I give the signal. Then bring the food and drink into the back of the hall."

We all nodded earnestly, we servingmen, this head servant's yellow-clad underlings, and we all pulled our forelocks.

I watched what the others did and did likewise.

Now there was a commotion at the door. The viceroy himself came through. I had only seen him once before. He was a stalwart man sumptuously dressed in furs, his tunic banded with the finest silk, his richly-ornamented sword belted at his waist. In his left hand he carried, upraised, his ceremonial mace of office, glistening with gems. He nodded graciously at us all and swept past. His personal servants, even higher in the chain than our own head servant, led him to the banquet table. His family followed him: his plump wife, dressed as richly as he, his half-grown son, his two young daughters, the older looking to be around Keera's age. I gazed after them with interest. The younger daughter seemed lively. A mischievous grin kept appearing on her face, despite her mother's surreptitious efforts to settle her down. I couldn't help smiling a little at that. It was an impulse I recognized well. The older daughter was better-behaved. I craned my neck for a closer look at her. Her eyes were serious, her features fine and sensitive.

"Pay attention, lad," muttered the servant on my left. "Those girls are too high and mighty for the likes of ye." I gave a guilty start. I mustn't seem so obvious. "The older one, now..." I saw that his own gaze strayed to the older daughter and rested on her appreciatively. "Here they come," he said suddenly. A pushing and jostling at the door told me something important was happening. I straightened up and held my keg out, trying to look like I belonged there.

"The king! The king!" The murmur swelled into a glad roar as Caedon himself strode through the door. His guards accompanied him. I saw these hard men scanning us for threats. Maybe it wouldn't have been so easy to assassinate Caedon here after all. I pressed myself back against the wall, shielding myself against scrutiny with my keg hoisted up, partway hiding my face.

Caedon paused to acknowledge the cheering. Then he reached behind himself, held out his hand for his lady wife. She minced through the doorway, her head held high. Her rich veils trailed over her shoulders.

Caedon was in his usual black, although his robes were sumptuous with furs and silk bands picked out in gold, a gold band about his brows. He didn't look a day older than when I'd seen him last. He was the same lithe and wolfish person who had attacked me in Fylkir's garden, the same person who had held me in his cell, the same educated and intelligent person who had taught me to read the language of the Old Ones, to speak the language of the Baronies.

My eyes turned from him to the little wife beside him. She was hardly more than a girl. *The way Caedon likes them,* I thought in pity. My first impression of her was a resplendent splash of color, rich reds, blues, and yellows.

Caedon led her past me.

How can I speak it, this dreadful thing, even to myself?

Our eyes locked, this little wife's and mine. I couldn't help it. My arms sagged down, the keg lowered. I stared. Her eyes widened, but she said nothing. The moment was over, the royal party swept past, and we servants, after depositing our burdens, filtered back into the sunlight of the manor grounds. We were supposed to go back to the kitchen shed to make ready to carry out another course for the banquet.

Instead I staggered against the wall of the shed, horror-struck, and supported myself with a hand before I could go on. I tore off my yellow tabard in a sort of agony and dropped it at my feet. If anyone noticed, they were too harried to do anything about it. I made my way out of the gates then. No one stopped me. I felt my way as if I were a blind person, or someone very old. At the bottom of the hill, I tottered and nearly fell. I had to sit down. I leaned my head down between my drawn-up knees. I felt as though I might faint.

Caedon's young wife. She was my sister Jillian.

# Chapter Nineteen

# Dis-ease

Late that night, after wandering the streets in a daze, I returned to the Sun-Stone. The moon had set. The tavern was barred against entry by now. I huddled against the tavern wall to wait until morning. During that time, a shearing wind swept in off the sea, and it rained in torrents. I was soaked through. I pressed myself against the stones of the wall, sliding down it to sit against it on the cobblestones, letting the rain wash over me, lifting my face to the dark mists of sky where no star shone. Wishing I could melt away.

Without realizing how I'd gotten there, I was lying full-length, one cheek pressed to the cobblestones, heedless of how they scratched my face. I might have slept. I was in some gray area between sleep and waking.

Eventually the rain eased up and the skies began to lighten in the first glimmer of dawn. I lay in a heap on the cobblestones. The first sailors off-ship, heading to the tavern, stepped over me. They probably thought I was some drunken lad. They may have thought I was dead.

The morning wore on, and still I lay there. When the throngs of sailors were at their loudest and most distracting, I felt Keera's hand on my shoulder. She helped me up and took me a devious way in through the back door of the tavern building. Teasag and her man were busy. They didn't see us. Leaning on Keera, I climbed the steep stairs to our room. She pushed open the door and led me to my pallet, where I collapsed, shivering.

As I came to know the bad thing Keera had foreseen, so, somehow, had she.

We didn't say anything. She just sat beside me, holding my hand and making sure I was warm.

Later in the day, she went downstairs to let Teasag know she'd recovered from her illness. But now, she told the tavern wife, "Mother has the fever. Has it bad."

So I could stay secluded in the little attic room. A nice ruse, except that what Keera had told Teasag was only the truth. I shivered, and then I burned. Sometimes I raved out of my head. During a lucid period, we decided we'd tell the tavern wife Keera had had to cut off my hair, my fever was so high. That would quell any suspicions Teasag would have when she finally caught sight of me.

I didn't tell Keera my fear, that I might not recover.

"You will, Mother," whispered Keera in my ear. "You've just had a bad shock and caught a bad chill, out there in the rain in the night."

She withheld her other message from me. She knew it would distress me too much. In time, when I was better, she told it to me. "Someone is coming for you, and you'll have to go with him."

"Who?"

"I don't know."

I brooded over that, as I lay fighting the fever. Another message, another dangerous task. How much longer would I be able to muster the strength to face these difficulties?

Another thing about Keera's message worried me. Maybe the someone coming for me was Caedon, or one of his men. If my sister really had recognized me, even though she hadn't cried out, supposing later she told Caedon. Supposing the stories were right, that Caedon hadn't coerced her into betraying Diera at all. That she'd done it willingly. That she was his instrument. So then, what would she tell Caedon? And then, would he send his men to take me?

As I thought about this possibility, I shuddered to think exactly how Caedon had made her his instrument. How he must have damaged her, willing or not.

Nevertheless, the news filtered up to me from the tavern below that Caedon and his party had sailed on to the Ice-realm. Nothing had happened to me. Nothing yet. Maybe nothing would. Keera's message was vague. There was no *when* attached to it. There was no *who*.

A few days after Caedon's departure, I felt well enough to pick my way downstairs, where Teasag exclaimed over me and seated me in a warm corner of the inn to feed me and fuss over me, especially over my shorn hair.

"But it couldn't be helped. The bairn said your fever was that high."

"I don't remember much of it," I told her. "I was very sick."

"Child be praised, you lived through it." As with most in this city, no one thought a thing about invoking the names of the Children. Caedon had come; he had gone; the viceroy ruled in his name, but he was no fool. The viceroy, as everyone knew, was a Lady-Liker, as he had to be, but who knew what his real beliefs were? He kept out of local politics and local beliefs. It was better for everyone that way.

"Soon I'll be well enough to sing," I told Teasag. "You've been very kind, keeping us when I haven't been able to do you any service."

"Oh, but the bairn has. She has helped out a great deal. Now I don't know what I'd do without her, truth to tell."

Teasag was right. While I slept my way back to health, Keera had stepped into the role of all-around tavern helper and kitchen wench. She did it cheerfully and discreetly. I tried not to worry when I saw the glances rough sailors sent her way as she stepped through the tavern bearing mugs of ale and bowls of stew.

She was twelve years old. When I was twelve, I was already helping out at home by hunting and fishing. Dangerous work, too, especially as it was forbidden to girls. I knew I'd have to let go my grip on Keera. Soon she'd be a young woman. Only a few years older than she, I'd lived a vagabond life that ended in fear and violence, imprisonment by Caedon, wandering, suffering, risk. I didn't want such a life for Keera, so as much as I could, I kept my grip. Of course I didn't realize how far it had already loosened.

"That bairn of yours is even helping the goodman with the accounts, fancy that," said Teasag. "I can't think where she learned to do it, but she's good at it."

"She's—"

"She is a remarkable child, she is that," said Teasag, whisking away to confront a fisherman getting a bit too belligerent for her tastes.

As the seasons went by and no bad incident occurred, I began to relax my worries about what Keera's message could mean. I resumed my singing; my hair was growing back in, and I began to look normal again. I could discard the scarf I had begun wearing around the tavern.

I also resumed my career as a healer. As before, it happened by chance. Two sailors got into a fight at the Sun-Stone, one of them near killed the other, and the victorious man ran away.

Teasag stood over the injured sailor, twisting her hands in her apron. "This fellow will die, and the beadle will be on our doorstep," she moaned. Her jowls wobbled in her distress.

I was just returning from a quick trip to the docks to see if new strings for my rebec had come in. Gone were the days when I made them from the guts of rabbits I trapped myself.

I looked down at the shattered sailor over Teasag's meaty shoulder.

"I can help the man," I told her.

She looked skeptical, but I set to work, picking broken crockery from his head wound and binding up the worst of his gashes while Teasag and Keera held him down at my direction. Last of all, over Teasag's protests, I poured a measure of her best hard cider into the head wound. "It will keep the Dark Ones out," I told her. Her eyes widened and she took a backward step, loosening her hold on the cider flask.

Then I stitched the head wound up. Keera had appeared at my side with needle and thread. I secured it with a bandage.

The man lived, and my reputation spread. Soon Keera and I were as busy as ever with the healing arts. I worried Teasag and her husband the tavern keeper would disapprove of my sideline. Instead, they were proud.

By then, Keera and I were accepted members of the tavern keeper's household. He and Teasag were like grandparents to Keera, and the sailors who frequented the tavern knew to leave her alone if they didn't want a stunning blow from Teasag's mighty arm.

Underneath the calm, though, I was uneasy. It wasn't just Keera's message that someone would come for me. It was the message of my whole life. As soon as I got comfortable in a place, something happened to jolt me out of it, and I'd go on the run again. This time I made sure not to let complacency rule me. I found time and private space to practice my skills, the throwing of knives, drilling with the short sword, acrobatic moves that had saved me in the past and might again. I made sure to keep a pouch of supplies and the proper clothing at easy reach and this time, a bag of coin.

As the summer came on, I found myself unusually busy. There was illness about, and it was bad. People started dying, no matter how I tried to help them. They died in clusters, along the bank of a small stream meandering through the town. This stream trickled down from a wellspring within the grounds of the viceroy's manor. It was uncanny, how illness followed the course of that stream. I couldn't understand it. When the townspeople murmured the Dark Ones were to blame, I found myself agreeing with them. What other explanation could there be?

I ministered to the sick as well as I could. The illness would start out with maybe some stomach pains and cramping, so the poor sick ones told me. Then—and this is around the time they'd call on me—they'd get dizzy and fall very ill with a high fever. Many went out of their heads. Sometimes they broke out in spots. Most of the healers in town, worshippers of the Children as well as Lady-likers, resigned the sick to the mercy of the gods and waited for the illness to run its course. Many died, although if they could make it past the crisis point, which happened around the third sen'night of their illness, they had a good chance of living.

The saddest cases were the little children. This terrible scourge from the gods hit the little children hard. Funeral processions around that part of the city became all too common, and all too often, the corpses shrouded in their grave clothes were small, followed in procession by grieving parents and placed in the shallow rock-lined rectangular pits of the burial places.

I, like all the other healers in the city, could only stand by helplessly and try to make the sick more comfortable. My herbs and potions helped a great deal with this, but they didn't keep death away. Nothing seemed to do that, as long as the gods willed the sick ones to come to Them.

I walked slowly back to our small tavern room in a bleak mood after one of these heart-wrenching vigils at the side of a dying child. Keera stroked my hair. I worried I might bring infection back with me, and I saw Teasag worried about that too.

But now in this second turning of the moon since the scourge had struck the city, I sat down in our attic room to think quietly over what was happening, the first time I'd allowed myself any respite in a turning of the moon. I sat with my back against the wall, under the tiny window, and I just thought. After a while, Keera came to sit beside me.

Finally I spoke. "We're not in any danger here."

"Why is that, Mother?" said Keera. She hadn't seen.

"This illness happens in only one or two places in the entire city. We're far away from there. Teasag can rest easy."

"But Mother," said Keera. "Remember the plague, when I was little?"

Indeed I did. It was brutal. I gave thanks to the Children that Keera and I were spared, because death from that dis-ease was far more certain than this one. The illness didn't touch either of us at all. We were among the lucky ones. Out of around three hundred, sixty or seventy in that village had died.

"The dis-ease took people from all over the village," said Keera.

"I'm amazed you remember that," I told her. This plague had struck our village back on the first island, the one we'd fled as witches. Keera had been very young. I thought about her words. "And yes, you're remembering correctly," I said. "It was hard to tell who would be struck down and who would escape that sickness. It seemed a matter up to the Children." *Or luck*, I amended silently. "But this sickness is different," I said. I took up one of the lumps of charcoal Keera used in practicing her letters and began drawing a diagram on the boards of the floor. Bright moonlight shining in through the window illumi-nated it.

"See?" I told her. "Here's the viceroy's manor. And here's the little stream. All the illnesses have been along this stream."

"Is the water cursed?" said Keera, her eyes big in the moonlight.

"Maybe," I said slowly. "Maybe it is."

"By a demon, a naiad?"

"Nonsense. No naiads infest the waters," I told her, smiling. That was a belief in my village back home. But we of the Sea Child know that's silly. Then I shivered. I remembered the sharp teeth and avid glinting eyes of the Blue Men.

Keera was pursuing her train of thought, though. "Maybe not by a demon," she said. "Maybe by a witch."

I looked over at her. "Keera, you know you're not a witch. You know you have nothing to do with this illness."

She nodded. Ever since we had to flee our former village, ever since she'd called on the ice to break and that boy to fall through it, Keera had been troubled by her own powers. She nodded in agreement with me, but I could see she was still worried.

"Remember the people who thought you had cursed their sheep?" I asked her.

"Yes."

"You had nothing to do with those sheep, did you?"

"No."

"The sheep died from some natural process, not from a curse."

"What natural process?"

"I don't know," I admitted. "But I think—" My mind flitted to the sheep, to the plague, to the illness happening in this town now—"I wonder whether it might not be the same natural process, or similar processes, that cause all of these illnesses. No curse. No will of any god."

Keera looked down at my diagram. "Something in the water," she said. "But not a demon or a curse."

"Something," I said slowly. "But what? Well, it's a mystery hidden from us by the gods, I suppose. Stay here." I made my way down the stairs to the ale shed behind the tavern. That's where Teasag brewed the enticing liquid that kept sailors from all across the Northern Sea coming back to this tavern, the Sun-Stone, over and over again. I knew I'd find her there, even though the night was drawing on toward dawn. She always brewed furiously when she was troubled.

Sure enough, by the light of soapstone oil holders, she was brewing. When she saw me at the door, she cringed.

"Teasag," I said. "I know you've been worried. I've come to tell you something about this illness. It won't come here."

"How do you know that?" Her tone was skeptical.

"I've figured it out. The illness comes from the water of that stream, you know the one? The one that runs from the viceroy's manor down the hill? Think about it, Teasag," I said, when she looked unconvinced. "Has anyone else sickened? Anyone beside those poor people who live alongside the stream?"

She shook her head no.

"Our water is just fine. We won't get sick."

"The demon could jump from their water to ours," said Teasag, her mouth set in a stubborn line.

"It won't," I assured her. "See? I have a charm. I'll put it in our well." I held up a bundle of herbs I had grabbed up at random. I'd come to know Teasag and her way of thinking. As I left our room, I'd made sure to take the herbs with me.

Teasag brightened. "Thank the Sea Child for you, Mirin. Put the charm in the well!" She followed me out to it and we stood over it together. The moon was going down.

Child forgive me. I said then, "Teasag, we must wait until the moon is gone before I can throw it in."

She nodded. We sat down to wait. Not very long after, the moon edged back down under the horizon.

"Now," I said.

We stepped to the well. I raised the bundle of herbs high, and I intoned, "Gallia est omnis divisa in partes tres." Turning to Teasag, I said, "I must say it three times." Thank the Child the darkness hid my expression.

She nodded again with a sharp intake of breath. "Tis a powerful charm you're making, Mistress."

"Gallia est omnis divisa in partes tres," I said again. Then, louder and slower, "Gallia est . . . omnis . . . divisa in partes . . . TRES." I dropped the herbs in the well. "We'll pray," I whispered to Teasag. We dropped to our knees. "Sea Child protect this well with words of power," I prayed. We raised our arms to the sky.

"There," I said, helping hoist Teasag up from her knees. She was a robust woman, but once she went down, she had a hard time getting back up again.

"No sickness will come here. I thank the Child for you, mistress," said Teasag, folding me in her big sweaty arms and releasing me. I couldn't see her face by then; it was too dark. But I knew by the sound of her that she was beaming.

When I got back to our room, Keera was waiting for me.

"Mother!" she exclaimed. Her voice was accusing. Of course she had been listening in. "That's not a charm. That's the general of the Old Ones explaining his strategy in his great book."

"Why aren't you in bed?" I said, not explaining. Parents, if they remember nothing else, should remember this. Distraction. Diversion. Misdirection.

But my daughter Keera was well-nigh impossible to distract, divert, and misdirect. "I do know some words of the Old Ones," I muttered, guiding her to her pallet and gently pressing her down on it. "Caedon taught me."

"How did he do that?" Now curiosity had replaced outrage in Keera's voice. *Oh, no,* I thought. And then we were in for it.

# Chapter Twenty

# Words of Power, Book of Might

Someone might say I had flimflammed Teasag with some words of half-remembered mumbo-jumbo. That someone would be right. My life with Wat as a vagabond, performer, and spy had turned me into a practiced cozener. My ruses worked on everyone but my own daughter.

As I lay on my pallet beside Keera, trying to get some rags of sleep into my tired body before I had to rise again and go out to the sick people who lived along the little stream, I was thinking hard. The water. The people who lived along the water. Something in the water.

Finally I drifted off to sleep.

In the morning, all too soon, I made ready to set out again. I'd have to be back at the tavern before late afternoon, when the ships would come in.

"Did you get any sleep at all, Keera?" I asked her, as she rose pale and drawn from her pallet. I heard her shifting around after our long conversation about Caedon and the language of the Old Ones and what I had been doing in Caedon's custody, all those years ago.

"I couldn't. I was thinking," she said.

"Me too. But Keera, you must not feel troubled about Caedon and . . ." I hesitated. " . . . and what he did to me. That's in the past." I hadn't told her everything. I hoped she couldn't see everything.

"It's troubling, Mother, for certain. But that wasn't what kept me awake."

"What, then?"

"I was thinking about the water."

I looked at her, astonished. "I was, too. Well, I must go out to those poor people and do what I can."

"I'm going to help Teasag with the last of the brewing," Keera said.

We hugged, and I set out.

I went from cabin to cabin up the stream, comforting those with terrible fevers and giving them willow bark

potions. I sat quietly beside those too far gone for potions, as they picked at the bedclothes and talked
nonsense. It really did seem to all of us, me, their families, as if a demon must possess these people. The
priestess of the Sea Child visited for some final prayers,
or sometimes the priest of the Lady Goddess.

Later in the morning, as I made my way up the lane to
the next cabin, I was pressed to the side of the road by the
viceroy's guards, making way for the viceroy and his family. I craned my neck to look. As he passed by, the viceroy
looked as if someone had beaten him. As I knew from my
masquerade as one of his servants, he was a vigorous
man in early middle age. Now he looked ten years older,
bowed down by sorrow. His wife, walking behind him,
was wailing with grief, supported by a maidservant.

*Oh, no*, I thought. The sickness had reached even the
halls of the viceroy's manor. No one escaped it, high or
low.

Servants bore a longish package behind the sorrowful
parents. I could tell by the shape and size that the dead
one must be their son. I scanned the procession for their
daughters but didn't see them.

As the procession went past me, one of the servants
darted into the crowd of onlookers and seized me by the
arm. I felt a rush of pure fear through my body.

"Mistress. Mistress. You're the healer, aren't you?" he
said.

Sagging with relief, I nodded.

"Mistress Mirin, is it?"

I nodded again.

"The viceroy has heard of your work with the sick. After the ritual for the dead, follow us back to the manor."

I fell in behind the others at the rear of the procession.

It wended down the hill and through the town to the sea. There, on a high bluff, we all stood looking out over the gray waves where the harr was hanging ominous now, out in the bay, like a great gray curtain, obscuring the peaks of the mountains far across on the opposite shore. The priest of the Lady Goddess had a lot of words to say over the body of the dead boy. Then the viceroy's servants settled it gently into a narrow little boat.

The viceroy drew a rich sword from his scabbard and laid it lengthwise on the body of his son.

The servants raised the boat on their shoulders and took it to the newly-dug grave pit at the edge of the sea cliff and lowered it in. One by one, members of the vice-regal household stepped up to throw clods of dirt down on top of it. Her maidservant supporting her, the lady of the viceroy stepped to the edge of the grave. Her lips trembled. The servant guided her hand over the grave. From her fingers fell a single clod of earth.

Last was the viceroy himself. After he had dropped his clod of earth onto the body of his son, he stepped back and looked up at the louring sky and out to sea. Then he turned his eyes on us, the onlookers. "May my son have a good voyage to the Land of the Dead," he said, his voice husky. "I will erect a stone here memorializing his life. Thanks to the Lady Goddess for all Her mercies."

The procession broke up then, some going one way, some another, but the family of the viceroy stayed together, and I with them. As we turned to leave, I saw, out of the corner of my eye, the viceroy making the sign of the Sea Child over the grave of his son. I looked quickly away. We few remaining mourners made our way across the town and back to the viceregal manor on the hill.

When we reached it, the lady of the viceroy swooned. I made my way over to her, but her servants had already scooped her up and were making off with her to the family's sleeping quarters. That was the best thing to do for her, after all. I stepped back quietly.

I stood at loose ends while various important people came to the viceroy, knelt, and offered their condolences. Stony-faced, he accepted them all. I could tell he was near collapse himself.

Finally only the viceroy and his servants were left in the hall. And me.

"My lord," said one of the servants, the one who had grabbed me. "The healer is here." The servant nodded in my direction, and the viceroy looked up.

"Thank you," he said to the servant. He came to me. "Mistress, I need your services."

"I will do anything in my power, my lord," I said, dropping him a curtsey.

"Probably that's not much," he said. He nearly snarled it.

I knew he was overcome with grief and didn't know how to show it.

"Perhaps not, my lord. But with the help of the Children—" I stopped suddenly in terror. What had I said? These people worshipped the Lady Goddess, and worship of the Children was forbidden. No one paid attention to this law except, of course, the viceroy himself. And if he were directly faced with someone flouting this law, what was his duty?

I quailed back. Then I remembered the sign he had made.

With no word, he took me by the arm and guided me toward the family's sleeping quarters. We stepped inside.

"My daughters," he said simply.

Two beds were ranged beside the hearth, and in them two small huddled shapes.

The lady of the viceroy stood beside one of them. Her servant was hovering near. I was glad to see it. The poor exhausted mother could be overwhelmed again at any time.

The viceroy went to stand beside his wife, and after hesitating a moment, I followed.

"How are you, my daughter?" he said, looking down at the thin girl trembling under furs in the bed. She stared up at him with hollow eyes. Even in the depths of her illness, I recognized her. The older daughter.

"Fiona! Fiona!" moaned her mother.

The viceroy moved to the other bed, where an even smaller girl lay with her eyes closed. Fiona's little sister, I surmised. My heart twisted with grief. All her mischief was snuffed out of her now.

He looked up at me, but I knew he wasn't seeing me. "Well, they're daughters only, after all," he muttered. "Only daughters." A low sound was wrung from him. I couldn't tell at first what the words were. Then I understood. "My son . . . my son . . . " he was saying. But suddenly he had knelt at the bedside of his little daughter and had pulled her limp little form into his arms. "Sorcha!" he cried out. He buried his face in the furs covering her.

I wanted to lay a comforting hand on his shoulder, but I knew I dared not.

The servant was leading the children's mother from the room. Now the viceroy got to his feet, dashing tears from his eyes. I looked away and stepped quietly back.

When he had composed himself, he approached me. "My son is dead," he said. "And the illness seems determined to take my daughters too. Can you help us, mistress?"

"I'll do what I can," I said. "There's very little any of us can do."

He nodded and bowed his head. Then he reached out and pressed my hand with his. "Try to comfort them," he whispered.

"My lord, I will," I said.

He turned on his heel, summoning his wife to follow him, and rushed from the room. I saw he was borne down by grief and terror.

I was alone with the two children. I went to each of them and felt their heads. They were both burning with fever. The older, Fiona, seemed a bit stronger than the little Sorcha, but they were both terribly ill.

A servant came into the room. I called for water and began setting up my supplies of herbs and potions.

"Mistress," said the servant, as she brought the bowl of water I'd requested, "your assistant is here. Shall I show her in?"

I looked up, startled, and there, lingering with a guilty look in the doorway, was Keera.

She came to me and crouched down beside me. "Don't be angry with me, Mother," she whispered.

I knew that in at least one case, Keera had brought a woman back from the brink of death. I looked at her hard. Did I want her to use her powers again, knowing the terrible cost she paid?

Keera shook her head. "I don't see anything I'm given to do for these two girls," she told me, keeping her voice low. "Or I'd do it, Mother."

"You can't cure the entire city," I said to her in despair.

"I'm not given the power to cure anyone," she said.

I nodded. It was just as well.

I saw then that her powers, while much stronger than mine, were a lot like my powers over the blackbirds, back during the risks I took to save Diera. They came to me when the Child gave them to me, and not before, or not at all, if the Child decreed otherwise.

*But what in the Nine Spheres can I do for these two poor dying children but keep vigil at their bedside*, I thought.

"Why are you here, Keera," I said to her, sighing inwardly.

"I found something out, Mother," she said.

"And it couldn't wait?"

"No. It can't wait."

"Well, then," I said to her, trying to keep the exasperation out of my voice, "What is it?"

"It's about the water, Mother. I know what's wrong."

I sat up then, looking into her eyes. "Your Child told you this?"

"No, I—well, I suppose She could have helped, but I figured it out for myself."

"Tell me," I said.

"I want to show you instead," said Keera.

"You'll have to wait, then, until I've tended to these poor girls," I said. Together, Keera and I bathed their foreheads and lifted their heads to spoon my willow bark potion into their mouths. We sent the servant to get fresh garments for them and changed them into the lighter cleaner clothing. We sat beside them quietly, murmuring comforting words to them. I sat beside the little one, Sorcha, and Keera sat beside the older, Fiona.

"That's all I can do for now," I told the servant, rising from Sorcha's bedside and pressing her little hand.

"Don't leave," she whispered between parched lips.

"Don't worry," I whispered back. "I'll return soon. The potion should help you sleep, and sleep will restore your strength." I doubted she understood what I meant, but I hoped that my soothing tone of voice would reassure her. I got to my feet. To the servant I said, "I'll come back in a candle measure or so to see whether the potion has brought the fever down, and to give them more of it."

Keera looked over at me then from Fiona's bedside, then back down at her charge. I saw that Fiona's eyes, glowing in her pale face, were fixed on Keera's. There was some profound connection I hesitated to break. At last, reluctantly, Keera stood. She'd had Fiona's hand in hers. I saw Fiona convulsively grip Keera's hand, then loosen it. Her hand dropped back listlessly and she turned her head away.

Keera bent down to Fiona then and whispered something in her ear.

The servant nodded and showed me and Keera to the gate. "See that Mistress Mirin is admitted when she returns," said the servant to the guards at the gate. "And her assistant." They looked us over carefully and assured us they'd let us in.

"You and the older girl seem to have grown close," I said to Keera.

"As you and the little one have, Mother," she said.

I had to know. "Did you whisper words of the Children to her, as we left?"

Keera shook her head. I could see she was exhausted, troubled, close to tears. "Only that she should have patience, and not give up, and that I'd be back beside her soon," she told me. "Only that I was her friend, and would be always."

"You need sleep, Keera," I told her as we walked into the courtyard of the manor. Our way led past the central well for the manor, fed by the little stream that meandered through its grounds.

Keera stopped and seized my arm. "See there, Mother," she said. "I didn't really know, but now I've seen. Look over there now."

I stared the way she pointed. A bit upstream, just by the walls enclosing the manor's grounds, was the shed that served as the manor's jakes.

"The jakes," said Keera.

I looked at her, uncomprehending.

"Let's follow the stream," she said. She seemed to have shaken off all her weariness. We made our way to the manor gate, and I nodded to the guards. They knew us now. They let us through.

"Keera," I said. "You should go home. You need sleep."

"No, Mother. I need to show you what I've found out."

"Very well. Show me," I said. I was terrified that Keera might somehow grow ill herself, so tired she was, but I knew that tone of voice. She was onto something.

I thought of the small terrier who lived behind the tavern. Once he had a rat, he shook it and shook it until it gave up any hopes of escape it might have harbored and succumbed to its fate. Keera was like that when she got hold of an idea. It was useless to try to pry that idea away from her. The idea was going to succumb to her. She was going to shake it and shake it until she mastered it, trampled it, bit it in half, and romped with it triumphantly down the lane.

"Follow me," Keera said. We went from cabin to cabin up and down the little stream. I stopped in to see about the various sick people as we went. But at each cabin, Keera showed me something, something that turned out—Nine Spheres, it really did—to be very important.

"Look here, Mother," said Keera, taking me behind one of the tiniest cabins. "These people are so poor they have no jakes. And so—" She led me to the side of the stream, where I was almost overcome with the odor of human waste.

At the next cabin, she showed me the well behind it, and how close it was to the jakes.

At the next. . .and the next. . .and the next.

After the fourth or fifth, Keera and I looked at each other. "Their water is fouled," I said.

Keera nodded.

"Something from the foulness is poisoning the water," I said, "and that's making these people sick."

Keera nodded again. "They wash in it. They drink from it or from the stream, and see, they're downstream from the place those people shit," she said, matter-of-factly. "They wash their food in this water, too, and prepare their food with it. Stir it into their porridge."

"Dark Ones take it," I breathed. "This is it. You've found it, Keera."

"And I'm guessing the manor's well is built much too close to the manor's jakes," Keera concluded. "I'm guessing the manor's well is where it all starts."

"But how are we going to get all these people to see that you are right? How are we going to convince the viceroy that he himself is the source of the foulness?"

"You'll think of something," said Keera. She gave me an impish grin. "The language of the Old Ones?"

I saw at once what needed to happen. I thought about Teasag and what I'd done to reassure her. I'd played her. I needed to play on the viceroy, too, but he was a lord, not some simple ale-wife. I needed an act that would convince him. I needed, I thought, a kind of theater.

"What are you thinking, Mother, when you smile to yourself like that?" said Keera.

"I don't know," I told her, startled. "Remembering," I said. I thought for a moment.

"I need a book," I told her, and then I began to worry. I needed a book in the language of the Old Ones. Where in the Nine Spheres would we get such a book? But I knew we had to convince the viceroy to fix his own well first and then, after that, he'd decree that the people along the river obey us. Move the jakes away from the well. Don't shit in the river.

He'd never just take my say-so for it. A poor woman like me, a person who lived above a tavern.

"I can get you a book, Mother," said Keera.

I was struck with a sudden suspicion. Something that in the heat of the moment the night before, I hadn't thought through. Keera had known I was making up my charm for Teasag out of language from the Old Ones, but how did she know? Here's the problem with mothering a girl like Keera. If she knows something she can't possibly know, it's all too easy to ascribe it to her powers. But she may have gained knowledge of that thing through very different means. Very different means indeed.

Before I could act on my suspicions and grill her about this book she was somehow going to find for me, Keera had whirled away. "I'll be back soon. I'll bring it to you in the manor," she called back to me over her shoulder.

Very soon, I was back in the manor, tending to the sick daughters of the viceroy. The willow bark was working. Their fevers were down. Old Cwen had shown me long ago, when I was not much older than Keera, how a potion made from willow bark can allay the fever.

But willow bark and some of the other potions I used—these helpful substances didn't cure anyone.

No.

What they did was this: they gave the body a chance to cure itself.

The little daughters of the viceroy were exhausted trying to fight off a powerful enemy, their dis-ease. The willow bark gave them the relief they needed to fight on.

And they did. Late that afternoon, the moment of crisis came. I had had the servant summon their parents, in case they moved across the border into the Land of the Dead. Then their parents would have a chance to bid them a last farewell.

But instead, the two girls fought a mighty battle and prevailed over their enemy. Fiona, the older, sailed over the barrier and back to herself. Sorcha struggled over it, but she made it, too.

"They'll live," I whispered to the viceroy and his lady.

I stood back while the parents rushed to each young daughter, embracing and kissing and smoothing hair back from cooler foreheads.

Later, the viceroy summoned me to his audience chamber. I stood before him.

"Mistress Mirin, what I owe you can never be paid. You have saved my daughters," he exclaimed, rising from his carved chair and taking my hands in his.

"Your words are kind, my lord," I began carefully. "But my lord, I must tell you something. I didn't save them."

"The Children did," he burst out. We both ignored that forbidden profession of faith.

"That too, my lord, but let me explain something to you. This illness comes from the water."

"A demon," he breathed. I could see he wasn't as credulous as Teasag, though.

"No, my lord, not a demon. We poor mortals don't know what it is, but something in the water poisons it, and then the people who drink from it are sickened."

I could see he was trying hard to suppress a skeptical look. He was giving me the benefit of the doubt. After all, he thought I'd just brought his daughters back from the brink of death, and he was grateful.

"Think about it, my lord. Who has gotten sick? In all your city, only the ones who live along the little stream that runs below your manor. And where does that stream come from? Here on the grounds of your manor."

He was paying me begrudging attention now. "Humph," he grunted. I could see he didn't believe me. "Nevertheless," he said at last, "I credit you with the cure."

I curtseyed to him. I knew I needed to convince him, or the sickness would just continue. But now that his own daughters were out of danger, I didn't know how much compassion he'd have left over for the poor folk living in his household's shadow.

"Name your reward, mistress. I'll give you anything in my power."

I thought about all the riches and acclaim he was ready to give me, but truly, the safety of my daughter was all the riches I wanted. If he could have brought Wat back from the dead, I'd have asked for that.

Before I could answer, a servant interrupted. "Your assistant is here with the Book of Might," he told me, his eyes huge.

Here's where I had to summon all of my acting skills to my aid. "The . . . Book of Might. Indeed. Let my assistant approach," I told him grandly. "With your permission, my lord," I said to the viceroy.

"Of course."

I saw how impressed the viceroy was looking. *So, I thought to myself, not so very different from Teasag after all.*

Keera staggered in with a book so large it nearly bowled her over. From it dangled a silver chain.

I went to her. "What in the Nine?" I muttered to her.

"Follow my lead," she murmured back.

I had an unsettling sense I'd heard those words before. I took the folio from her.

The viceroy clapped his hands together, and the servant ran forward with a small pedestal table. I plunked the book down on the table, which swayed perilously under the weight of the enormous volume.

The viceroy stood back, eyeing me intently.

Playing for time, I leafed through the book as if looking for an important passage. I was in a state of despair. Now that I had the prop I needed, my confidence fell in pieces at my feet. My lessons in the language of the Old Ones were so far in the past, and had been cut so abruptly short, that I doubted I could read a thing. The book was in the language of the Old Ones, though. Keera was right about that.

Now a new fear caused a thin trickle of sweat to run down the back of my neck. Suppose the viceroy himself could read the language of the Old Ones? I glanced up at him, his soldierly stance, the shields and swords mounted on his walls. No, clearly the viceroy was reared as a warrior, not a scholar of the Lady. Only the rare highly educated man like Caedon could read this old language, unless he happened to be a priest of the Lady.

Now I stopped at a page, my finger pointing at a paragraph. I looked up at the viceroy. "The healing properties were well known to the Old Ones," I told him.

He nodded as if he were thinking, or wanted me to think he was thinking, *yes, of course.*

"They have written about it in this treatise. For here they proclaim—" I cleared my throat and began to say, as if I were reading it, because, truth to tell, when I looked at the page, I could make nothing at all of it, "Gallia est omnis divisa in partes tres." I looked back up at the viceroy. "That is to say, my lord, in our own language, 'Thou shalt not build thy jakes next to thy well. Neither shalt thou build thy jakes next to any stream.'"

"Really?" said the viceroy. "The Old Ones were concerned about matters as low and coarse as that?"

Keera stepped to my side. "Mother, may I remind you that on page three hundred and forty-eight. . ." Here she reached around me and began flipping over the big folio pages. I stood aside and she stepped up to the pedestal. "Here it says . . ." and she began reading in an impressive voice,

naturalis autem decor sic erit, si imum omnibus templis saluberrimae regiones aquarumque fontes in iis locis idonei eligentur in quibus fana constituantur, deinde maxime Aesculapio Saluti, quorum deorum plurimi medicinis aegri curari videntur. cum enim ex pestilenti in salubrem locum corpora aegra translata fuerint et e fontibus salubribus aquarum usus subministrabuntur, celerius convalescent. ita efficietur uti ex natura loci maiores auctasque cum dignitate divinitas excipiat opiniones. item naturae decor erit, si cubiculis et bybliothecis ab oriente lumina capiuntur, balineis et hibernaculis ab occidente hiberno, pinacothecis et quibus certis luminibus opus est partibus a septentrione, quod ea caeli regio neque exclaratur neque obscuratur solis cursu sed est certa inmutabilis die perpetuo.

"And what that means is," I said to the viceroy, trying to preserve the fiction that I understood everything Keera just read, "the Old Ones knew that good health depends on a good, healthy water supply. It must be free of fecal material especially."

The viceroy looked blank.

"Shit," Keera supplied.

"Oh," he said.

"Shall I read on, sir?" I asked.

"No, that will be sufficient," said the viceroy. Then he said, "I see." And then, "What do you recommend?"

Our ruse was successful. The boon I begged of the viceroy for successfully healing his daughters was his promise to dig new wells on the properties of those who lived along the stream; to relocate their jakes; and in the case of peasants too poor to have jakes, to build each of them one. He made good on his promise, and he started with the manor itself, renovating his own well and his own jakes.

Here's something strange. The dedication of these new facilities to the Lady Goddess (although we all really knew they were dedicated to the Children) was one of the proudest moments of my life.

But when I got Keera home that night, she had a lot of explaining to do, and a lot of maneuvering to sneak the enormous folio of the Old Ones back into the school of the Lady Goddess and reattach it to the podium by its chain.

Later she came to me, shamefaced. "Mother, I need to tell you something. You know how I learned the language of the Old Ones?"

"Yes," I said. "You explained all that." We'd had a very uncomfortable session about her sneaking into the school to learn.

"I helped all the students, too. I helped them with their schoolwork."

"I'm proud of you, then," I said to her.

"But Mother, I just got them all whipped."

I sighed. "Tell me, Keera."

"The priest in charge of the book got in trouble when it disappeared. His master had him whipped. So he blamed it on the scholars. When the book reappeared, he was glad, but he was sure it was all a schoolboy prank to make him look bad. And he whipped them all."

"Those poor boys," I said. "The poor priest."

"And now I can't go there any more," she said, not meeting my eye.

"Do they know? Do they know about you?" I was aghast.

"One of the boys must have told on me," she said. Then, before I could panic, she said, "Don't worry, Mother, I gave them a false name."

I looked at her skeptically. False name or not, anyone who looked like Keera really stood out. The viceroy and his entire household had seen her, and they wouldn't soon forget a slender red-head spouting the language of the Old Ones from a book bigger than she was.

"It's done now," I said at last. "And the greater good was served, so I suppose . . ."

We left it at that. Public sanitation had triumphed. Dis-ease was at bay. No one knew, at least not yet, that Keera had anything to do with it.

# Friends

At the dedication of the new well and jakes, an event leading me to suppress a smile—such an official to-do over such humble structures—the viceroy and his wife proudly brought their daughters up to me and Keera.

I looked them over carefully. They were still thin and pale, but they looked to be out of any danger.

The two girls dropped curtsies to both of us and thanked us prettily. Keera and I hastened to make our deep curtsies to them and to their parents. Then we all stood for the official blessing of the well, and yes, even the blessing of the jakes. Afterward, servants circulated among us with sweetmeats.

Only a few of us attended this ceremony—the viceroy and his family, the two of us, a very few others. I understood. In a way, the building of these facilities was a little embarrassing to the viceroy. But he was still grateful, and I could see he was determined to show it.

I put out a hand to Keera as soon as I politely could, and gestured to her to come away. We were humble people. We needed to accept the viceroy's gracious gesture, and then we needed to get out of there. I needed to make sure Keera wasn't receiving too much attention, and that she wouldn't come to the attention of anyone who might get curious about us and investigate our origins.

After all, it was odd that a tavern singer would know the language of the Old Ones, and odder still that her young daughter would.

What conclusions might the viceroy draw, once he had a chance to think about it? And besides, now there were people in town, like the priest whose book had been stolen, who might raise uncomfortable questions. Dangerous questions.

A servant was at my elbow. He was deferential but insistent. "Mistress Mirin, my master and mistress have a request."

A request from the viceroy. I knew it for what it was. An order.

I curtsied politely to the man.

"Their older daughter has taken a fancy to your daughter, mistress."

My heart sank.

I remembered my days as a boy singer, and how the wife of a mighty earl had simply commandeered me into her service.

"How flattering," I whispered.

"The viceroy requests that your daughter stay here at the manor as his daughter's companion," said the servant.

"I—" I hesitated. "My daughter is my apprentice in the healing arts. I need her," I said desperately.

"The viceroy says you may visit her whenever you like," said the servant, not answering my objection.

Now Keera pushed past him and flew into my arms.

My heart was pounding.

"Mother," she whispered in my ear. "It will be fine. I'll be safe here. But they're not going to let me leave, you know."

I stood aside from her and stared at her, my eyes welling with tears.

"This means riches for you, mistress," said the servant, seeing my distress.

Keera fixed her eyes on mine and nodded slowly.

I curtsied to the viceroy and his family and somehow made my way back through the city streets to the tavern. Without my daughter.

When I got back to the Sun-Stone, I fled into Teasag's arms, sobbing into her ample bosom. I alarmed her horribly. She thought Keera must be dead; thought maybe the sickness had gotten her.

When she extracted the truth out of me, difficult because I could hardly speak, or anyway, not in any sensible form, she just sat on the bench outside the tavern, holding me and letting me cry, darting a dirty look at any sailor or tanner or fisherman who stopped and stared at us. Any man under sentence of Teasag's disapproval quickly hustled himself away, including her husband the tavern keeper, who stepped outside to see what was keeping his wife from her customers.

Afterward, I was all cried out. I lay dully against her bulk as she stroked my hand. "Mistress Mirin, ye know—" she began hesitantly.

"I know. I know what you're about to say. This will be the making of Keera. She'll know luxury and riches," I said.

"Aye, and the making of ye as well, Mirin. Ye know that viceroy has been looking to do a good thing for ye. Ye know digging a well and a jakes wasn't going to be enough for the man, not he, a lord."

"Taking my daughter away from me is doing a good thing for me?" I said, sitting up straight, my hands balling into fists at my sides.

"Most would say yes, ye know they would. Most any-one in this town, they'd say, Please, my lord, please take my daughter and let her live like a rich person."

"That's not what I want," I said.

"Ye're a strange one, Mistress Mirin, if ye don't mind my saying so," said Teasag.

That made me smile in spite of myself. "You're right," I told her. *And you don't know how strange*, I added silently.

Then she said something that surprised me.

"I'll miss her help around here, that I will," she began. "But mistress, this tavern is no place for a beautiful young lass, and both ye and I know it."

"Yes," I whispered. "I do know that."

"Ye've told me a little, how ye had to flee hard times with the lass, barely a babe. But she's nigh a woman now. And I may be a simple woman my own self, but I have no-ticed something. That girl of yours, she's lonely. Ye keep her pent up here, and I know well that it's only because ye love her so and fear for her. But she's lonely, I tell ye. And now she's found a friend."

We sat for a long time in silence then.

Finally I raised my eyes to hers. "You're right," I said. I thought back to Keera's expression. I saw sadness in her eyes, but I saw something else, too. Excitement, maybe.

"I've been her only friend," I said. "That's not right." My own girlhood had been so out of the ordinary it hardly qualified as a girlhood. My friends had been assassins and conspirators. I'd had no one my own age to exchange secrets with, to giggle with, to be a girl with.

I didn't know how to be a girl, and the way I was bringing Keera up, she didn't know how either. From the moment of the incident involving the boy who fell through the ice and the charges of witchcraft, I'd kept her away from friends, at least as best I could.

"Not her only friend," said Teasag, echoing my thoughts.

I jerked my head up and looked at her sharply.

A little smile played over her lips.

"You knew! About the boys!" I said.

"Aye, it was our little secret, Keera's and mine. I caught her going over the roof one day, and then she told me." Teasag started her deep rumble of a chuckle, and I found, despite all my fury, that I was starting to laugh as well.

"You knew where she learned how to keep accounts," I fumed, but it was hard to keep a grip on my anger. "Oh, mistress," I said, mimicking Teasag's voice. "Keera has helped out with the accounts. I don't know where she learned them but it helps us out, me and the goodman."

"I did know, mistress," said Teasag, wiping the tears of laughter off her plump cheeks. She put a placating hand on my arm. "That I did. But it were no less wonderful for all that, mistress. What other young slip of a girl would go running off to play and come back with her letters and numbers all learnt? I ask ye now."

Teasag and I sat side by side on the bench, both of us swelling with pride.

"No one is like Keera," I said.

"No one," said Teasag.

After a moment, she said, in a different tone, "So then, mistress, it's time ye let her go. Let her see what she can learn over yonder at the viceroy's. Let her make a friend."

I nodded. I was weary. I gave Teasag a smile and a hug. Then I headed to my tiny room, which seemed immense without Keera in it, and I lay down to try to sleep before my evening set in the tavern.

I thought with regret that I'd had no mother of my own to help me let go. I thought with grief of my poor mother, her children and husband and her very life shorn from her in one brutal moment.

I thought with gratitude of Teasag, and I sent up a timid prayer to the Sea Child for her. Finally, I prayed to the Sea Child for myself. I was already lonely, and I'd only been parted from Keera for a few candle measures.

And then I had to laugh at myself. Teasag the simple ale-wife indeed. She'd taught me a thing or two for sure.

I lay remembering the times her own grown-up daughters had trekked to the tavern from their outlying farms. She had three, each with large broods of their own, a troop of lively boys and girls who came with their mothers to visit Teasag and the tavern keeper, their grandparents.

And they'd had a son who had gone to sea and died out there one stormy night. All their hopes had rested on that boy. He was the one they were working hard for. He would have inherited the tavern, and then their hopes were dashed.

Still they kept on with their work, and they even had the time and compassion for two strays, me and Keera. Now Teasag was helping me learn to be a better mother.

I lay remembering the longing looks Keera cast at Teasag's grandchildren, the rare times they came to visit. They were friendly children, including Keera in their games. I remembered how down-hearted she was when they left to return to the countryside.

I lay in my bed gazing out through the slit of a window. I knew I should be comforted. But I was afraid.

The viceroy was as good as his word, at least. I saw Keera once a sen'night, usually alone.

But sometimes Fiona came with her to the garden where we walked. Fiona was shy and quiet. I'd seen this a little as I watched her during Caedon's visit, and I'd seen a little of it, too, as I nursed her through her illness. But I also saw that she was serious and kind. I saw it in her manner to the servants and her response to me.

With Keera, she shone. She came out of herself. She and Keera were both growing into beautiful young girls, Fiona's grave dark beauty and Keera's fiery joyous beauty, side by side. They were quite a sight together. Heads turned as they walked past.

But I worried. Fiona would soon be of marriageable age. She'd soon be given to some lord as his bride. Then where would Keera be?

Sometimes I felt resentment when I looked at Fiona. *Keera's blood is as good as yours. Better.* I whispered this to myself sometimes.

But then I'd catch myself. True nobility didn't come from blood. It came from deep inside. I knew this. I had to remind myself, when I had thoughts like those.

I feared for Keera, too. What if she revealed her uncanny powers to Fiona and frightened her? The old witchcraft charges still gave me a chill of fear.

And I feared Caedon. What if he came back to this part of the world? What if he visited the viceroy? What if he spotted Keera there?

I decided I'd have plenty of warning if that danger were looming. I'd be able to get Keera away. One day I talked to Keera about it.

"That won't happen, Mother," she told me.

Then I felt a little better and tried my best not to think about it any longer. I was partly successful.

I relieved enough that I didn't think about the thing I should have been thinking about all along.

And Keera was so happy and occupied—the viceroy had agreed that she and Fiona should be given tutors as

if they were boys and taught together—that I suppose
she wasn't thinking about it either.

So it took me completely unaware, the bad thing Keera
had foreseen so many turnings of the moon before.

# A Barrel

The epidemic of dis-ease, trying to understand how it happened, my amazing daughter figuring it out and figuring out how we could do something to change the filthy conditions of the town—those thoughts were gratifying, but they took up all the space in my head. During those hectic seasons, and then afterward, with Keera's move away from me and the turmoil of my feelings following that circumstance, I hadn't paid any attention at all to her dire prophecy. That I'd be taken. Besides, I really did feel well prepared. I had my bag of supplies ready at hand.

When the long-delayed moment finally came, though, I couldn't get to any of it. Those careful preparations came to nothing. I was taken, and neither I nor Keera saw it coming.

I had gone out into the town to get some supplies I needed to compound my potions. It was a more time-consuming task now that Keera wasn't helping me. I remembered my apprenticeship with Old Cwen, back in my girlhood. She had taught me all I knew, and now I had thought I'd be passing the knowledge along to my daughter. But Keera had learned a lot, and what she lacked was more than made up for by her ability to think through a problem and come up with a solution. As far as I'm concerned, that is the main thing a good healer needs. Keera might be a little unorthodox in her methods, but . . . And then, of course, there were the extraordinary insights that came to her from the Children at times.

I wasn't thinking of any of that. I was just thinking, on this particular day, that the afternoon was coming on toward evening. That I needed to hurry if I were to fulfill my tavern duties. In spite of Teasag's good will, I never wanted my tasks as a healer to interfere with the running of the tavern. She gave me a roof over my head, and more. She gave me love and care. I would help her to the best of my ability.

So on this particular day, I was feeling a bit panicked that I might be late and let Teasag down. I was paying attention only to that. Otherwise, I might have felt something, some kind of warning from my Child. Maybe. Maybe not. Whatever the case, if there was a warning, I didn't notice it. Later, looking back, I decided there would have been no warning.

I took a short-cut down a narrow alley between two towers the town had built for armories at the edge of the docks. I was almost to the main roadway along the harbor when someone hit me from behind. Before I could react, I was down. A rough bag was thrown over my head and a man was kneeling on my back, binding my hands behind me.

"Easy, mistress," a voice said. "Struggle, and it will be worse for you." Then, to someone else, he said, "Bring the wagon over to the end of the alley."

Another voice: "Who cares if we grab some doxie on the wharf? Who's going to stop us?"

The first voice: "She's famous, man. Where have you been? This is the woman who saved the town. No one must see we have her."

We waited there. I was fuming, but I was also struggling to breathe. I tried to think. It was no use. There was a clattering, probably the wagon being drawn up. I was hoisted over someone's shoulder and thrown roughly into the wagon. Then the jolting over the cobbles of the street leading down to the docks.

I did the only thing I could. I beamed a thought out to Keera. Who knew if she picked up on such things? But she might. Frequently, if I knew something, she did, too. She might realize what was happening to me now. She wouldn't be able to do anything, but at least she'd know I hadn't suddenly disappeared from the face of the earth. At least she'd know I was still alive. Teasag might get word to her too, once she realized I had disappeared.

I was sure the people who had taken me were Caedon's men. Who else but Caedon? The wagon stopped and the someones who had taken me hauled me out. I went limp, trying to make it as hard as possible for them, but that only earned me a thump to the head.

"Careful, you idiot," said a voice. "This one needs to stay alive." Then, fainter, "I don't know why, man. I just do as I'm told."

I was wrestled aboard what I realized, in terror, was a ship. If they got me out to sea, no one would ever know what had become of me.

I slumped against the side as sailors stepped over me, preparing to put out from the harbor. The plunging of the deck let me know we were indeed on the water. After a candle measure and more had gone by, one of the sailors leaned over me and tore the bag from my head. As I gulped down fresh air, he untied my hands. I sprang to my feet, but then staggered. The ship was under sail.

Glancing around, I saw no land anywhere. I had no idea where we were or where we were heading.

"Easy, mistress," said the sailor, a rough-looking man with a wiry beard and a scarred cheek. He put out a hand to steady me. "Soon you'll have your sea legs."

"Where are we? Why have you taken me?" I was enraged.

He laughed at me. "Spitfire, are you? We need you, mistress. Our chief needs you."

"Your chief?"

"You'll meet him."

"How could this man possibly need me?"

"He needs healing. Our seanchai said it's you would help him."

"Your seanchai? What's that?"

"One who is a far-seer. He knows. It's you."

"That's rubbish. How can I possibly help this man, this chief of yours? I've never met him." Then a worrying thought caught at me. Suppose this still involved Caedon somehow. Or Fylkir. "I haven't met him, have I?"

The sailor shrugged. "I doubt that indeed, Mistress. But he needs healing. You're a healer."

"He'd be better off using a healer who knows him well, not some random stranger."

The sailor shrugged again. "They've tried. Failed. The seanchai says, *Bring this one, the one who worked the miracle* at the viceroy's house. He means you, mistress. He says, says he, She won't come if you tell her nicely. So take her."

The sailor ambled away, leaving me speechless at the rail of the knarr. This was what Keera had warned me about. Now it had happened. I looked off over the open water. Life by the waterfront had taught me a few things. I could see from the design of the ship that it was an ocean-going vessel, made for long voyages. We weren't going island hopping. My heart sank.

Two days went by. The weather was mild, and on the second day, I was allowed on deck in the fresh breeze, not stuck down in the stuffy bottom of the ship with the cargo, where they forced me to stay during most of the first day. At first I thought the ship was simply a cargo transport, and I was simply the strangest part of the cargo they transported. But gradually I began to understand. These sailors were outlaws. Pirates.

On the third day, we neared an island. Hope rose in me. I was a strong swimmer with none of the usual fears about water. If we got near enough to shore, I could jump off and swim for it. But the sailors grabbed me and thrust me down with the cargo again, shoving some planks over the opening of the alcove. I heard the groaning of the ship's rudder. We were turning.

After a time, I heard warning cries. I felt a great thump and a jarring, as the ship encountered some other big object. I started to wonder if we had run aground, maybe on a hidden rock. I started to fear we would sink.

Then came shouts, the clatter of weaponry, feet pounding above me, more shouting. Louder shouting. A raw scream. The ship lurched. A man fell face-down on the planks overhead. Peering up, I could see he was dead. Blood dripped down onto me even as I flinched away. After an eternity of clamor where I sat huddled into the farthest corner of the alcove, the ship rode calmly again. A sailor shoved the planks and the body away and helped me back out onto the main deck. Now I saw the carnage. Three men lay dead, two of them men I had never seen before. We'd been in a sea battle, and this was the aftermath.

Without being asked, I got to work helping the wounded.

"I need water here. I need clean water," I told one of the seamen wringing his hands and hovering around a wounded man. "Don't just stand there. Move. And find me a clean shirt." In moments I had the supplies I'd asked for. I ripped the shirt into strips to make bandages.

"Step back and give this man air," I ordered. "You'll do him no good hanging around him like that. Do any of you have willow bark?"

They looked at each other in confusion. Then one man, a young man, really just a near-grown boy, said softly, "I have willow bark, mistress." His features made me think he might come from far away. His accent, too. Although I couldn't place the accent, I knew he was not from these isles. All the others were big strapping red-bearded or blond-bearded fellows. This young man was darker, slighter, clean-shaven. But his shoulders were broad, and his expression was intelligent.

I stared up at him for a moment. "Get it," I said.

He did, and I began compounding the willow bark into a potion for the two men in the most severe pain. I shook my head as I worked, though. The Dark Ones would enter these wounds. There was no way to keep them clean. The deck was filthy, splintering, slippery with blood.

I did what I could.

Then I turned to the hardest task, the man with the most severe injury. Someone had laid his leg open with a sword, it looked like. Someone else had nearly finished the job with some heavy object they'd dropped on that leg. He was bleeding badly.

First, I gave him some of the willow bark. It was little enough. He needed more.

The sailor I'd met on that first day shouldered to me with a leathern bottle. He uncorked it and held it out to me.

I sniffed it. Some kind of strong drink. I held it to the man's lips, which were starting to turn blue, and he drank it down gratefully.

"Set up those planks on some barrels," I said to his fellows. "We need to get him off the deck." Soon I had him lying on his back before me. Luckily, none of the red blood lanes were spurting out his life's blood, because then he was a dead man for sure. But I knew what I had to do. If the blood wasn't spurting now, it would be spurting then, and I needed to do something to forestall it.

"I need two knives. One, the longest and sharpest you have," I told the men surrounding me. "One, it doesn't matter."

They came to me with the knives. I turned to one of the men. "Heat this over the fire," I said, nodding to the protective iron cage forward on the deck, where a fire was always kept burning. I handed him the duller of the two knives. "Keep it in the flames. When I need it, I'll call for it, and you bring it to me then. Mind," I called after him. "Handle it carefully. It will burn you badly when you pick it up out of the flames if you don't take care. Now," I told the others. "I'll need three or four of you to hold this man down." I leaned over the wounded man. His eyes were walling in fear. "Goodman, I am sorry for it, but I'll need to take this leg. You understand, don't you? If I don't, you'll die."

He nodded.

I held the bottle to his lips again, and he sucked the rest of the drink down.

I took a narrow strip of leather and tied it tightly around the man's leg just above his terrible wound.

"Give this man something to bite down on. Not that," I told one man, who was holding out his dagger. "That will break his teeth. Something leather."

One put a leather strap between the man's teeth.

"This will hurt you badly," I told the poor man on the planks, "but I'll make it as quick as I can. Bite down against the pain. Courage."

He nodded.

I hefted the long, sharp knife in my hands. Then I made the cut.

I do think I was quick. As I was sawing the man's leg off, it didn't seem to be quick. I hacked through muscle and gristle. I hacked through bone. Blood flowed over my hands, up to my elbows. Afterward, with the knife that had been in the fire, I cauterized the stump to stanch the bleeding. I released the tight strap around his leg and hoped for the best. No blood spurted. I stepped back. It was all I could do.

I was exhausted and covered with blood.

The poor amputee had fainted dead away. Pain? Fear? Loss of blood? Probably all of those. "Keep him warm," I told the others. They lifted him from the planks. Gently, too. They were rough men, but I could see they loved their comrades. They took him to a sheltered area of the ship and made him as comfortable as they could.

A few of them came up to me later to lay a hand on my arm and speak a few words of gratitude. The young man with the willow bark did. He was well-spoken. I wondered briefly what he was doing there, in such rough company.

Other crew members nodded at me, letting me know in this way that they were glad I had helped. I nodded back at them. I'd done what I could. I had my doubts whether the poor amputee would survive, and I don't think I ever found out whether he did.

*You didn't foresee this one, Keera,* I thought. *How could you? How could anyone?*

I earned respect from the crew that day, but I also learned what they were. Brigands and rascals and thieves. As I was going about the work of patching up the wounded, I looked out over the rail behind us. Far to the rear, the wreckage of a vessel was slowly sinking. Looking around me, I saw new barrels and boxes crowding our deck.

In spite of the one death and the grisliness of the amputation, the crew were in a celebratory mood. They'd prevailed. By the end of the day, they were all drunk. But none of them offered me any disrespect. They wouldn't do such a thing, not now.

They were happy men, bringing the loot of their endeavor back with them to their chief. I realized that two of the dead were sailors from the vessel they'd destroyed, but many more probably went down with the ravaged ship in our wake to watery deaths. Peering out to sea, I made out no survivors clinging to the wreckage.

As for me, I spent the rest of that day trying to scrub the blood off me.

Although I didn't realize it at the time, our voyage was almost over. On the fourth day, I spotted a small rocky island in the middle of the vast emptiness of the sea. Amazingly, the young man seemed to be the one in charge. He called out orders. Two hefty seamen leaned hard on the ship's rudder, while others pulled on the tack spar, moving the sail to catch the wind. We headed toward the towering hunk of rock in the middle of the sea, pulled the ship up to a stone pier, and dropped anchor.

A small boat nuzzled up to our knarr, and a sailor helped me over the upper strake of the knarr into it. Soon other sailors were hoisting me up onto the stone pier. "Wait here, mistress," one of these sailors told me. "Someone from the fort will be here soon to take you to the chief."

I had no choice, so I waited, leaning against some of the crates off-loaded onto the pier and trying to regain my land-legs. Behind me, a commotion on board caught my attention. Shouting.

I peered over at the ship, trying to make sense of what I was seeing. The men were rolling a barrel down planks from the knarr into the small boat and then pulling the barrel up onto the pier. They upended it and gathered around it, looking in. One of them, the young dark-haired man, reached down and pulled out a bedraggled looking figure.

A slender bedraggled figure with bright red tousled hair.

# Had ye seen them, ye would have surely thought

"Keera!" I cried. I rushed to her, pushing the young sailor away from her. He stepped back from me, his eyes huge. I gathered her into my arms. She clung to me, crying. "Someone get water. Something to eat," I commanded, and the sailors did what I told them to. I suppose I'd trained them to obey me during our dangerous voyage.

I cradled Keera against me, holding her head so she could drink from a cup the young dark-haired sailor handed me. When she looked a bit more alert, I gave her a piece of hard bread from the young man, and she ate some of it.

I didn't ask her anything or upbraid her. Time for that later, the whys and the hows and the how-could-yous. She told me later that she drank a trickle of rainwater that came into the barrel on the one day at sea when it rained a bit.

One of the crew members looked into the barrel again. He reached down and pulled out an oilskin bag, the bag that held my rebec. He held it out to me. "Is this the young lady's?" he asked.

"It's mine. She has brought it to me."

"Maybe we'll keep it, mistress, as payment for your passage," he said, beginning to laugh. But the younger dark-haired seaman strode up to him and gave him a sharp buffet to the side of the head, and the others looked at him sidelong. The mariner who had laughed then hung his head, ashamed. He knew I'd done them all good service. He handed my rebec out to me by its strap.

The dark-haired seaman grabbed it up from him and brought it to me. I took it from him and stared at him hard. He fascinated me. He was not like the others. And his accent. I couldn't place it. He had some kind of authority on the ship. But he was so young.

"Thank you," I said. He nodded.

The sailors stood aside now, as a craggy-featured, bent-over man made his way down the pier, leaning on a stick. "Is this the healer?" he asked them. When they nodded, he came to me and took my arm.

"No, take your hands off me," I said, panicked. "My daughter is ill."

"We'll tend to her, mistress. Let's get her to the shelter of the fort." He glanced at the sky. "A storm is blowing in."

So between us we helped Keera up the rocky hill that crowned the island. The first flashes of lightning and cracks of thunder were ringing out as we reached the top. There, a passageway led straight into the rock. The fort of these outlaws, these pirates, was hewn directly from the rock. The man with the stick led me through a narrow passage out of the weather and handed me off to a silent woman.

"Isla will take care of you," he told me. "You and the girl. Make ready, though. I'll bring you to the chief shortly."

"Thank you," I said, dropping him a curtsey. "If I can help this chief of yours, I will. But I don't see how I can. I'm afraid you're in for a disappointment after all the. . ." I felt my mouth curve into a wry smile ". . .the trouble you've gone to."

"No," said the man. "I've seen it. You'll help him."

So this man must be the seanchai, I thought. Their far-seer.

"Then you know more than I do."

"Until later, mistress," he said only, and left us.

The woman he called Isla led us through a warren of rooms, big and small, to a small bedchamber with a bedstead. No fire. She left us there without a word. I made Keera comfortable on the bed, pulling the furs well around her. The chill of the rocky walls was penetrating.

"Mother, I—"

"Shhh, my darling. Just rest. You've had a terrible ordeal, much worse than mine. We'll talk about it later."

I tucked the furs about her and sat holding her hand and stroking it.

Isla brought soup in, then. I helped Keera sit up and spooned the broth into her mouth. Isla returned with a bowl of water and a rag. Using them, I tried my best to put myself to rights, and Keera too, without rousing her too much. She was drowsing in the furs, utterly exhausted.

Afterward, Isla silently reappeared with fresh clothing, an underdress and kirtle, and a mantle, all of them very fine cloth. I shuddered as I put them on. Probably they'd been ripped from the body of some poor woman the pirates had killed at sea.

"No, Mother," Keera whispered. "Just a sea chest they stole."

I couldn't help smiling at her then, worried as I was. And, I confess, a bit angry with her.

"Don't be angry, Mother."

"But why, Keera? You took a terrible risk. You could have died."

"But you'll need your rebec."

"I will?"

"Yes."

"How, in the Nine Spheres?"

"I don't know."

I knew not to question her further. I wanted her to rest.

Isla had brought fresh clothing for Keera, too, so I laid these articles at the foot of the bed where Keera could get into them when she felt better. She slipped her old stained clothing off under the furs, and I took them and discarded them in a corner. They were fine cloth, beautifully embroidered at the viceroy's manor, now only fit for rags. When Isla returned, she took them away, and my bloodstained sensible clothing, too.

What I really wanted. I thought about this. What I really wanted was a bath. Every sen'night, Teasag, the Children bless her, had heated buckets of water. Then after the tavern had closed in the quiet time between the tail-end of night and the peep of dawn, Keera and I could come down for our baths. I closed my eyes, imagining the heaven of hot water I was missing now.

"Mistress, it's time." The seanchai was at the door.

I opened my eyes and got wearily to my feet from where I was sitting on the rock floor beside the bedstead.

"Mother, wait."

I turned to Keera. "I won't be long, my darling. This man will see how little I can help his chief, and then I'll be back here with you."

"Mother." I followed Keera's gaze to the rebec, propped in the corner of the room.

"I need to take that with me?"

She nodded.

I reached over for it, slung it over my shoulder. As I followed the seanchai from the room, Isla came past us, carrying another soapstone bowl of broth. I was relieved. I hadn't wanted to leave Keera, but Isla was taking care of her.

I followed the seanchai up a steep set of steps circling around the exterior wall of the cavern. At the top I stopped, winded.

"In here, mistress," said the seanchai.

He stood aside, and I entered a vast room with a high rocky roof, one end cracked open to the seas below. From this immense opening, I saw the skies beginning to clear after the storm that had blown up. I saw that the room was actually three-quarters of a natural cavern. A fire warmed the center of it. Past the fire, a man stood, erect and proud, with his back to me. This must be the chieftain of these pirates, I thought. I narrowed my eyes.

There was something about him . . . Might I know this man? I peered at him uncertainly. But how could I?

"My lord. The healer," said the seanchai, and stepped away. I glanced around, unsure what to do next. A few others were in the room. Some were leaning over a table, studying what looked like maps and documents. A few others sat on a long bench down one side of the room. The seanchai made his way over to the bench and sat down.

The chieftain, if that was he, did not turn around. He said nothing. I stood on the other side of the fire, scrutinizing him. In the light from the clearing skies beyond him, I could see that he was a tall, lean man in a long cloak, swept off both shoulders. One sleeve of his tunic, the left, dangled empty. The hilt of a long sword was at his waist. The man's fair hair, caught back in a narrow fillet of gold, was streaked with gray. A kind of bandage was wound about his head.

Maybe he has a head wound, I thought. But he seemed upright. From what little I could observe, he looked strong. *How can I possibly help this man*, I thought in despair. *What will happen to me when I can't? What will happen to Keera?*

The man made a kind of strangled sound and waved dismissively with his good arm.

The seanchai was back at my side now. "Later, then, my lord?"

The man gave a definitive shake of his head.

*Yes,* I thought. *You and I know what this senchai can't seem to see. There's nothing I'll be able to do about a missing arm.*

I turned to go.

The senchai was at my elbow. "His most high majesty may need your services later," he murmured at my ear.

*His most high majesty,* I thought in scorn. Every tinpot ruler was setting himself up for a king these days. But all the vials of Ranulf's sacred blood were shattered, maybe only Audemar's excepted. Audemar's blood, though. That blood was tainted.

I said only, "You see what your lord knows full well. I won't be able to help him." I was beginning to get really angry again. All of this, even risking the life of my daughter, on a fool's errand.

The senchai seemed as if about to answer me, but he was interrupted.

"Mother."

Keera. I turned and moved to shout at her. Keera should not be out of bed. She should not be here. She had pushed me to the brink, with her shenanigans, and now she was about to push me over it.

Keera stood leaning against the door and holding on, but despite her weakness, I could see it in her face. She wasn't going to back down, stubborn child that she was. She ignored my anger. "Play your song. Play the song you always sing."

Something in her face made me pause. I sighed.

"How this will help . . ." I muttered, mostly to myself. But just the same, I unslung my rebec and took out the bow. Shaking off the restraining hand of the seanchai, I tucked the instrument against me and began to play.

I began singing, first softly, then letting my voice ring out.

> *I saw the new moon yester night*
> *with the old moon in her arms;*
> *you'll sail out to sea, my love,*
> *and then you'll come back home.*

*My voice is my power*, I thought. *It is almost a physical thing.*

*Not almost. It is.*

With my breath and my body, I pushed the song out of me in a rising coil of beauty and mystery. I forgot about the wounded man. Forgot even about Keera. The song took me up.

Slowly, as I played, the man on the other side of the fire turned to face me.

What was it seized my attention first? So hard to capture, that first moment of knowing. I think it happened when the firelight caught the glint of the brooch clasping his cloak at the shoulder, the golden brooch with the six proud walkers, the brooch my own father, my true father, had made him and the other five originators of the Rising.

*Six for the six proud walkers.* The song Wat's brother John had taught me burst into memory. *Green grow the rushes oh.*

My song died on my lips. I stood breathless. Looking. Just looking.

He did not look back. His eyes. The bandage around his head covered one eye, the left, but the right eye stared sightlessly past me.

I had no time for more. He was around the fire. He was clasping me to him, his head buried in my hair. Now he was covering my face with kisses.

"Mirin. Anamcara," he was murmuring, and I was holding him fiercely in my arms, and I was planning never to let go.

"Wat," I whispered to him. "Wat. Wat."

That moment in Wat's arms lasted an eternity. Eternity doesn't mean "a long, long time," you know, or even "forever." It means, "a place outside of time." And in this moment we stepped out of time altogether.

When time resumed its ordinary drip, I stood back from him.

"You see I am a damaged man," he said to me.

"I see no such thing," I told him. Then I remembered. I turned to Keera. "Wat—this is—"

Keera was by our sides.

"Father," she said.

"And this is my beautiful daughter," Wat said, bringing her in to him too, crushing us both together. "I saw you," he told Keera.

"And I saw you, Father," said Keera.

"You saw her?" I was dumbstruck. But then I understood.

"In a beautiful garden. And we were all there," he told Keera. "Your mother. And you. And I was there."

"But I couldn't see you!" I wailed with remembered grief.

"Shh. Hush, my darling. You knew I was there."

"Yes," I said, wiping my eyes. "I did know it."

"And I saw both of you. And a strange little zipping light." He stopped, a puzzled look crossing his face.

Time for that explanation later, I thought.

After a moment he said, "Now I can't see anything at all."

"But we're here, and that's what matters," I told him.

The seanchai led us then to another bench, a quieter, more private place by the vast opening over the sea. We sat down there, and I leaned my head against Wat's chest.

He told us everything then. How Caedon had captured him, during one of the earliest battles with Diera's forces.

"Remember that castle? Where you sang? Where we found Diera? Where I tried to rescue—" He stopped, swallowed hard.

Mentally, I filled in the words. I knew what he was about to say. *Where I tried to rescue my brother Johnny. Where I failed. Where my brother died.*

Now Wat went on. "That's where they took me. It's Caedon's castle now. He chased Audemar's people out of the place and took it for himself." It was the place Caedon tortured him. In that place, Caedon told him I was dead.

"Caedon enjoys that," I said quietly.

I knew how Caedon operated. I had experienced it myself. In my imagination, the scene unfolded. Caedon, flinging open the doors of Wat's cell, his cruel smile curling his lips, while he had Wat restrained by his men. Caedon, telling Wat in gloating detail everything he was about to do to him. I knew this as if I had been there. I remembered what Avery had told me long ago, how Caedon had tortured Wat's brother John before he killed him. I remembered Caedon's own chilling words long ago, said to torture me when he first had me in his power. *I killed the little boy. Then I killed the oldest. Only one remains. I'll get him too, and then I'll have the whole set of them, those bastard brothers.* That's how I knew exactly what Caedon had told Wat, exactly how he'd said it.

Someone might call this imagination. Perhaps not. *You think you'll die,* Caedon said to Wat, the Caedon of my imagination, *but, you're thinking, even if I die, at least Mirin is safe. You don't know me, if you're foolish enough to believe that. I've chased her down on that squalid farm. I've had her killed. I watched. It was a pleasure. And now you will die knowing she too died in the agony I've planned for you.* My heart twisted with grief for Wat.

Wat stopped talking. I held him, trembling.

He told us more. I worried whether Keera should be hearing this, but then I stopped worrying, because I knew she'd know it anyway. I thought, maybe for the thousandth time, what a problem it was, mothering a girl with her powers.

Caedon had stood watching while they set to work on Wat. But then, Wat told us, a vision came to him in the depths of his torment, a vision beyond all the pain. A beautiful garden with a beautiful little girl standing in the center, her two loving parents enfolding her. And the strange little darting light.

"I'll tell you about the little darting light later on," I told him. We were all silent for a few moments.

"After that vison, or whatever it was I saw," he said, and he held me tight, breathing in hard, "after that, I didn't care. Let Caedon do his worst. Strange. That made the man angry. I've never seen a man so angry. It was—" he paused. "It was interesting to watch."

"Interesting?" I couldn't keep the outrage out of my voice. "You found that interesting?"

"I know. But that's how it felt. The poor man was thwarted of all his pleasure. I almost felt sorry for him."

"Wat, you know that at times like this I want to punch you, don't you?"

Keera made a squeal of alarm.

"Don't mind your mother, Keera. She gets like this sometimes," Wat told her.

Keera thought about his words for a moment. "Yes, Father. She does."

I sighed. "Go on," I said.

"I didn't observe Caedon's strange reaction much longer," Wat said. "That's when he—When he—" Wat made a gesture toward his eyes, and I shuddered. "But then there was a lot of noise." Wat told us how all that time, while Caedon was enjoying the taunting and the anticipation and the horrifying acts of torture, Wat's companions in Diera's army, the few who had survived their action that day against the castle, were shinnying down the noisome sewer shaft that our companion in the Rising, poor dead Rafe, had discovered so long ago. They'd all burst in. They'd driven Caedon back, and they'd gotten Wat out of Caedon's dungeons.

"Phew, those men stank." Wat smiled reminiscently. "So did I, by the time they got me out of there. I'd like to think Caedon stank, too. That's too much to ask, I suppose."

"Wat. How are you still alive?"

"The Children stood by me," he said.

"Or luck," I told him, getting an eerie feeling I'd said those words before.

"No, Mother. It wasn't luck," said Keera, tucked between us.

"I suppose not," I admitted.

Then Wat told us how, with the help of those good friends, he made his way here, to his rocky refuge in the far north. How, when he learned of Diera's death, he rallied the few in the Rising who were left, and they began using the island as a base from which to harry Caedon's shipping.

"It's all we can do. It's very little," he said.

"It's something," I told him. "What of Audemar?"

"He's still out there, somewhere. You know he's now the legitimate king, don't you, if the succession proceeds by blood and legitimacy?"

"I'll never call him king," I said. "Caedon has run him off. No one knows where he is." We sat there contentedly together. I looked around me at the men busy at the long table with their maps. Every so often, one or the other smiled in our direction. I could tell they were careful to let us have our privacy. When their gaze turned to Wat, their eyes shone with respect and devotion. "These men think of you as their king."

"They do. Am I? What does that even mean?"

"The blood of King Ranulf runs in your veins."

"And is that enough to make a man a ruler?" Wat smiled a little. "You know, it's a funny thing. Poor Artur, Avery's older brother. And Audemar's. And mine, actually, although I hardly knew him. Artur was a strange man. The rest of us, Avery, John, your father, me later on—and Rafe, Mirin. Rafe is a man I'll never forget. I'll have to tell you about him sometime. We were all together, and Artur was always set apart. Lonely. I wonder what kind of king he would have made. But we would have died to see him on his throne, and most of us did die, avenging his assassination.

"So I wonder. Caedon styles himself king now, and he has the military and political power to back up his claim, although it's no claim at all in law. He's a commoner. Yet he has talents, intelligence, everything a great king might need. And still, when he uses them, he uses them all for ill. I suppose that's the only reason we fight on. Not to defeat him because he's a commoner. To defeat him because he is evil. Caedon has won, but if there's anything we can do in this world to take that power back, we must do it."

"Wat—" I wasn't sure I should go on. Suppose Wat didn't know. It would add to his pain. I took a deep breath, and I continued. "Do you know the one he took to be his bride? Do you know who betrayed Diera?"

"Yes," said Wat. His mouth set in a grim line.

"This is as hurtful to me as anything I've ever known," I said. "Almost anything. When I thought you were dead, though, that hurt went much deeper."

"But I'm not dead. At least not most of me."

"Caedon tried his best to kill you."

"Caedon can try. Nine Spheres, girl. . ."

I finished the thought for him. "You're hard to kill."

"He's still trying. He knows I'm out here somewhere, and he's looking for me. When he finds me, then he will kill me."

Keera spoke up then. "He won't be able to do it," she said. "And Father. You'll see again."

Wat laughed. "That I doubt, daughter."

I looked down at Keera, her set stubborn chin. "Wat, if Keera says you'll see, believe it. You will see."

"What's this, then?" said Wat, reaching down to her and stroking her cheek with his finger.

"Keera has . . ." I began carefully, thinking how in the Nine I could ever explain her.

"I have powers, Father. And I know how to use them," said Keera. "And I don't use them for ill. At least not most of the time." She shot me a guilty look.

Wat smiled at her and shook his head. "I don't ask for anything more than this," he said to us both. "This is my power, right here. Right now."

"They brought me here to heal you," I told him.

Wat laughed. "That good man"—and here he nodded in the direction of the seanchai—"said he'd heard of a wondrous healer on the big island, and he'd fetch her to me. I told him he was out of his head. That no one could. We weren't talking about my arm or my eyes. We were talking about . . ." he fell silent. "There were times I wanted Caedon to find me and finish the job. I thought you were dead."

"Did you know those rascally followers of yours kidnapped me?" My voice grew indignant, and my indignation grew as a wry secret smile begin to play across Wat's lips, a smile I knew very well.

He tilted my face up to his and kissed me until I stopped fuming.

"I told them I wouldn't be able to heal their chief, as they kept calling you, but they didn't listen. So they brought me here entirely against my will to try to heal you anyway."

"And so you have," said Wat. "I don't know how they found you and I don't know how you did it. But you're here, and that's all the healing I require."

Later, in the early evening, we both led Keera back to her bed and saw her safely nested in the furs. We kissed her goodnight, as ordinary parents might, taking boundless delight in that one simple act.

"I'm too old for this," she complained. "I'm a girl nearly grown, Father."

We ignored her and smiled at each other over her head. Wat couldn't see my smile. I knew he could feel it, though. I reached across Keera to smooth his hair back off his face. It was strange to see him wearing it long again. I had a hard time not touching him. I wanted to touch him all the time, to keep my hands on him. I think I thought if I removed my hands from him, he'd disappear.

We came back to the main room and stood at the great savage slash in the rock face. I gazed out into the deepening twilight, watching the sun set over the waves, grieving that Wat couldn't see the brilliance of the moon's silver crescent as it rose over the waters.

But he caught me to him, and we shared that moment in some deeper place, all bitterness left behind. We'd plowed to the end of the furrow, and now together we could rest. There we stood entwined. The alchemists speak of transmutation, where the base metal of the world turns into precious gold. It seemed to us then we were transmuted to one person, beating with one heart, seeing with one inward eye—man, woman, melded into one magnificent single creature never to be parted.

For a long time after that day of transformation, the three of us lived in our rocky refuge, content with our lives. I had my rebec. Keera had more books than she'd ever imagined reading. Wat had his heart's desire, and so did I. The halcyon flew over the waters, dropping from her beak the pearls of tranquil life and deepest love.

But one thing nagged at me always. One terrible thing. My mind shied away from it.

It was Jillie.

Wat's men brought back the news that she was dead. They say she fell from a vast height into the sea and was killed.

*How?* I kept asking myself this, over and over again. Did she throw herself into the sea? Did someone—Caedon, maybe—push her? I didn't know the answer, and I still don't.

If someone were to suggest a solution to my worries, a cruel little solution, I'd tell that person this. Don't ask to know of it from my daughter. I won't allow it.

I have only one glimmer of insight. Oh, I don't want to think about it. And now I see I must. Otherwise, the thought will hound me until I give it room.

It's this.

When Keera came to me with her directive, *You must go to Caedon. You'll find out something important there*, and I undertook that insane task, I think I misunderstood her message. Keera herself was just the intermediary. She didn't understand the message at all, not in the deep sense.

It's a bit like what I learned in my vision at the portal in the farwydd's cave. When I came to myself, I had no idea what I had just seen. Only later did it flower in my mind into a message of hope. And only in these latter days have I come to know its fullest meaning.

What I learned about Jillie is maybe the opposite of that. Instead of a message of hope, it's a message of despair.

In the hall of the viceroy, when Jillian and I locked eyes and I staggered back to the tavern devastated at what I had learned, I'd thought that was the message. *Your sister has done this thing. Your sister the traitor. She is lost to you forever. Mourn it. Know that you come from the same mother. Fear it.*

That was not the message. Or if it was, that was only a small part of the message.

The message was not for me. I was just one more intermediary.

After many seasons of thinking, I am just beginning to realize the message was not for me at all.

It was for Jillian.

Sometimes it made me cry out in anger and anguish against the Children. I'd failed my sister. In a cruel irony, They made me the instrument of Their message to her. We were both punished.

The bad thing I learned was very bad for me. I'm beginning to see now, after what I've been told of her death, that the bad thing to learn, while it was terrible for me, must have been more terrible for her.

We came face to face. She saw what she was. And then maybe she did what she needed to do.

Just a thought. A dark one, too.

Emissaries from Haakon Hardaxe came to visit us soon after we received the news about Jillie. These emissaries wanted alliance. They wanted to know about Caedon, anything we might tell them about him, because they saw they'd soon be at war with him.

And one of the emissaries asked for a private audience with me. She wanted to know more about Jillie. I brought Keera with me. By now, she knew Jillie's story, at least as much of it as I knew.

"Don't ask me about my sister," I told this woman, Haakon's ambassador. "Perhaps I could have saved her from Caedon. I kept trying to do that, and I kept failing." I had to fight to keep the bitterness from my voice. Early on, the Rising had sent to Haakon for alliance, and Haakon, thinking us weak and bound for failure, had rejected our plea. Haakon's failings, and my own failings too, were not this woman's fault.

She was a woman in Haakon's household, the Lady Jehanne, Haakon's concubine, but she was also his trusted confidante. She was sent with the others to us, I soon realized, because she'd had a deep connection with my sister. I found out some terrible things about the Lady

Jehanne later. Before she'd been Haakon's, she had been Caedon's. She knew things. She'd lived under Caedon's control. As it turned out, she had been Jillie's only friend. She'd feared for Jillie.

A servant brought in a tray of sweetmeats.

"I'm so pleased to meet you, Lady Keera," said Jehanne. "There's a person in Haakon's household who keeps asking about you. A friend of yours. The Lady Sorcha of the Northmost Isle."

"Sorcha!" Keera exclaimed. "She's the sister of my dearest friend. How is she at King Haakon's court?"

"She has married one of our monarch's courtiers," said Lady Jehanne.

I put out a hand to squeeze Keera's arm. I saw her eyes had filled with tears. If there was one difficulty about our lives for Keera, it was the loss of her friend Fiona. She had worried about Fiona terribly. "She'll never know what happened to me, Mother," she whispered to me wistfully, that first day in our rocky refuge.

"Please give Sorcha my fondest love," she said now to the lady Jehanne. "Tell her to send my dearest wishes to her sister Fiona, when next she meets her."

"Who knows?" said Jehanne. "Perhaps our realms will grow closer. Perhaps you'll see her again, Sorcha and her sister too. I believe Sorcha is hoping to find her sister a husband at our court. Her father the viceroy has sent emissaries to us."

"King Haakon is wise," I said. "He entertains an emissary from Caedon's viceroy, and I imagine from the Baronies as well. He'll listen to all sides, I see."

Lady Jehanne bowed her head in acknowledgement.

"Go back to Haakon Hardaxe your master," I told her. I saw what she was doing now—trying to use Keera to build a connection between us and Haakon. "Tell King Haakon to draw his own conclusions about Caedon, about my sister Jillian. Don't look to us for alliance, though. Wat and I, we're finished with war. That's all I have to say about that." I knew my voice was cold.

She curtsied to me silently. I saw she had tears in her eyes.

*She knows about Jillie. She knows something.* It was my second sense, speaking to me. Keera reached out a hand and clutched my arm, hard. Keera saw it, too.

"Forgive me, Lady Jehanne," I said, moving to guide her to her feet. "I see you're moved. I see you're here to speak to me from the heart. I tell you the truth. I know what Jillie did. I just don't know Jillie herself. I knew what she was as a child. I didn't recognize the Jillian I met on the arm of Caedon, the Jillian who became his wife. You, Lady Jehanne, you must have become the sister she needed when I couldn't be there for her.

"It fills me with sorrow that I failed her. I'm glad you were there with her through some of her darkest times. I'm glad she had a friend. So I don't know what to tell you about Jillie when you come to me for answers. You have better answers than I do." I took her hands in mine and pressed them warmly, looking into her eyes.

"I do know this," I told her. "I know the Children are infinitely, immeasurably kind to us small creatures crawling beneath the stars across the surface of the land. When we lose all hope, the Children give us Theirs.

"You're about to undertake a voyage back to Haakon Hardaxe, disheartened because you think you're returning to him empty-handed. You're not. We're never empty-handed. Before you go, let me sing you a song. It's a song of transformation. It has done me good. Maybe it will do some good for you, knowing Caedon as you do, experiencing the hurt he metes out to all around him. Listen.

*I saw the new moon yester night*
*with the old moon in her arms;*
*you'll sail out to sea, my love,*
*and then you'll come back home.*

*Now good Sir Ceyx, he loved his wife,*
*and she was Alcyone.*
*He'd drive his ship to gates of hell*
*but he would come back home.*

*Weep no more, Alcyone,*
*by waters wap and wan,*
*hold out your silver mirror,*

*hold up your golden comb.*

*Oh long she sits in tower high*
*at window o're the sea.*
*Come back to me, my own dear lord,*
*may waters carry thee.*

*I saw the new moon yester night*
*with the old moon in her arms;*
*You'll sail out to sea, my love,*
*and then you'll come back home.*

*O forty leagues off rocky strond*
*'tis fifty fathoms deep;*
*the waves bear up the good Sir Ceyx,*
*Alcyone, do not weep.*

*He calls her ghostly on the wind,*
*and then she knows he's near.*
*O Child of Sea preserve him now.*
*O Sea Child pray thee hear.*

*The Children look adown from high*
*with pity in their gaze.*
*They change her into Halcyon,*
*the bird that stills the waves.*

*Halcyon, oh fisher bird,*
*Wife forever true,*
*Sing to me and fly to me,*

*I saw the new moon yester night*
*with the old moon in her arms;*
*you'll sail out to sea, my love,*
*and then you'll come back home.*

Was that enough, the only gift I could give her? Surely not. The Children had blessed me beyond all expectation, and I was grateful. But I know that all of us struggle along against the darkness doing the best we can to solve the puzzle of our lives, and none of us has all the pieces.

Yet the Children have given us these graces: their music, our minds, and then, if we're incredibly lucky, love of friends, love of family, dearest love between one heart and another. That's what takes us onward in our lives, only that.

# About the Author

I hope you have enjoyed *Halycon*, Book II of the Harbingers fantasy series. Please leave a review of my novel on amazon.com and other web sites for readers and book lovers. I care about what my readers think! Please visit my author page on amazon.com and my author web site, www.janemwiseman.com. Follow my blog about speculative fiction, www.fantastes.com.

*Jane Wiseman splits her time between Minneapolis and Albuquerque. She loves fantasy in all its forms, enjoys her family, reads all the time, and writes in many different modes. As for fantasy, she writes books that she would like to read. She also paints.*

# A NOTE OF ACKNOWLEDGMENT

Thanks to my wonderful daughter, Margaret Govoni, for your editing eye. You steered me away from many mishaps and missteps, Margaret. All the remaining ones are mine alone.

Thanks to Bob, beta reader extraordinaire.

Thanks for all the helpful suggestions I've gathered from a number of online Litreactor workshops, www.Litreactor.com and from other writing workshops, especially the Tinker Mountain Writers workshop, www.hollins.edu/academics/workshops-online-writing-courses/tinker-mountain-writers-workshop-residential/ , and the (sadly now defunct) Taos Summer Writers' Conference. The instructors' comments and suggestions were of course incredibly helpful, but I have valued beyond measure the comments and suggestions of my fellow workshop attendees. Thanks to all of you! You may not have been able to save me from all my writing sins, but you saved me from many. Thanks also to the Anam Cara Writer's and Artist's Retreat, www.anamcararetreat.com, on the Beara Peninsula of Ireland. What a peaceful and lovely place to write! Thanks, Sue!

And finally, thanks to all you Norrathians out there. You are my true battle buddies. You know who you are. You are my fantasy friends in the purest sense of all.

# NOTES ON Halcyon

## from the author

*This novel is a work of fantasy, not historical fiction. Just the same, it is indebted to history. For visual depictions of some of the scenes and ideas in this novel, visit my Pinterest board, Medieval Life—Halcyon. For a play list of songs in the entire Harbingers series, including this book, see* <u>*https://janemwiseman.com/a-harbingers-play-list/*</u>

The time-period of this novel is roughly early medieval, in a realm vaguely resembling several of the Celtic, Viking, and Anglo-Saxon kingdoms vying for power in and around the 10th and early 11th century British Isles shortly before the Norman Conquest. The landscapes of the novel vaguely resemble medieval Ireland, medieval Scotland, and the western and northern isles that stretch between those two lands and Scandinavia.

Twelve Realms:

> The Sceptered Isle stands in for the united Heptarchy (seven major kingdoms) of mainland Anglo-Saxon England, but also includes the northern part of the realm (Scotland), the Western Isle (Ireland) and the northern isles (islands off the coast of Scotland— Inner and Outer Hebrides, Orkney, and Shetland Islands). It does not include the area around Lunds-fort (London), however.
>
> The Eastern Baronies stands in for a loose confederation of powerful feudal lords spreading across medieval France and parts of Germany. In my tale, the Eastern Baronies also

own territory on the mainland of the Sceptered Isle—the land around Lunds-fort (London) and along the eastern edge of the mainland—in addition to their strongholds across the Narrows (the English Channel).

THE SOUTHERN PRIMACY stands in for medieval territories in Italy (as well as Portugal and Spain), the homeland to which the Old Ones (ancient Romans) pulled back as their empire dwindled.

THE LYRE-LANDS stands in for the vestiges of ancient Greece and the lands rimming the Aegean in the medieval era, including that vast metropolis the Vikings knew as "the Great City," Constantinople (Istanbul).

THE REALM OF THE ASP stands in for the ancient Near and Middle East.

THE BURNT LANDS is a vague concept to people of the Sceptered Isle and similar northern realms. It stands in for North Africa and below, through Sub-Saharan Africa, but people in the northern realms know little of these lands.

THE ICE-REALM stands in for medieval Norway and, in a loose sense, the other parts of Scandinavia.

THE FIRE ISLE stands in for medieval Iceland.

THE MOUNTAIN FASTNESSES stands in for the Alpine regions of Europe.

THE TRADE ROAD FORTIFICATIONS stands in for the old Silk Road of the late ancient world through the Renaissance, stretching along the Eurasian steppes.

THE SILK LANDS stands in for China and southeast Asia.

THE FORGOTTEN KINGDOM stands in for the Indian subcontinent. No one in Mirin's world knows much about this place.

ALSO:

UNKNOWN LANDS (the Americas) across the Great Sea stretching to the west. Travelers have come back with tales of these lands but no one knows whether they really exist.

The concept of two competing religious groups , worshippers of the Lady Goddess vs. worshippers of an elemental universe controlled by earth, sea, fire, and sky, is fantasy but based on some actual bits of information about belief systems in the post-Roman British Isles and medieval beliefs in general, especially medieval ideas about the body and healing. (Present-day astrologers have their own settled ideas about these matters. I know nothing about their ideas and don't pretend to.)

The overall concept of the universe  is Pythagorean: Nine revolving crystalline spheres carry the heavenly bodies (sun, moon, stars, planets) around the earth at their center. This idea from the ancient classical Near East was widespread in the medieval period, obviously long before anyone knew anything about the way the physical universe really works.

The rebec is a real medieval musical stringed instrument from around the 10th century. The rebec preceded later stringed instruments such as the lute, the gittern, and the citole. Unlike the lute, which is built of strips of wood, the rebec's bowl was carved from a single piece of wood. It may be the precursor to the violin, but musicologists have had a lively debate about this, and I'm not qualified to weigh in. This web site gives a fantastic overview of the instrument itself: http://crab.rutgers.edu/~pbutler/rebec.html

Mirin's elf child song  is loosely based on Child Ballad 40 (Roud 3723), "The Queen of Elfland's Nourice," ("nourice" meaning "nurse"), a song also known as "Elf Call." Mirin's version changes the story considerably. Steeleye Span has recorded a fairly sinister-sounding version, https://www.youtube.com/watch?v=SvYYVjzy_Qg Mirin also sings snatches of the (repurposed) folk ballad *Green Grow the Rushes, Oh*, as she did in *Blackbird Rising*.

Anamcara as an endearment is actually an anachronism. The actual phrase has no romantic connotations. I'm taking liberties here!

The Halcyon ballad Mirin sings is a hybrid. It's inspired by Child Ballad 58 (*Sir Patrick Spens*), but I've combined it with the myth of Alcyone and Ceyx. Their story of lost love, a Greek tale recounted by the Roman poet Ovid in his *Metamorphoses*, entered the English tradition through Geoffrey Chaucer's *Book of the Duchess*.

Keera is actually the Irish name *Caera*, a name related to fire. Because it is too often mispronounced like *Sierra*, I have silently changed the spelling. Another way it can be pronounced is *Ky-era*.

The Blue Men of the Minch are fabled water-demons that were said to infest the narrow strait ("the minch") between the northern Outer Hebrides and the Scottish Highlands, especially around the Shiant Islands north of the Isle of Skye. The Blue Men are said to call out a couplet of song to the mariners of a ship crossing their path. If the mariners can't respond with the right response in a couplet of their own, the Blue Men seize the ship, dash it to the bottom of the sea, and kill all on board. Read more: https://www.scotsman.com/whats-on/arts-and-entertainment/scottish-myths-blue-men-minch-1483877

The currach, a small Scottish lightweight vessel made of hides stretched over a wicker frame, was used on rivers and even at sea and was known as far back as Pictish times. It is closely related to the Irish currach or curragh and the Welsh coracle. While usually propelled by oar, it was sometimes outfitted with a sail.

Fresh water on small islands in the ocean occurs because sea water is heavier than rain water. When rain falls on such an island and seeps into the ground, it makes a "lens" of fresh water floating on top of the sea water. Here are some sources:
http://www.learnz.org.nz/argofloats142/bg-standard-f/properties-of-the-sea%3A-salinity-and-temperature
https://www.quora.com/How-is-it-possible-for-small-islands-to-have-fresh-water-springs-uncontaminated-by-salt-water-from-the-ocean

**Typhoid Fever** is a life-threatening disease that was almost as horrible a scourge to medieval people as the Black Death (bubonic plague). It's a disease spread especially by poor sanitation.

**Credit where credit is due!** I have taken Keera's reading of the "Old Ones'" treatise on a healthy water supply from the ancient Roman Marcus Vitruvius Pollio's famed *De Architectura*, Book One, text and translation posted on www.penelope.uchicago.edu/Thayer/L/Roman/Texts/Vitruvius/1*.html#2.7
The text doesn't exactly say what Keera and Mirin claim it says, but then, that's all part of their scam. Still, if you really want to find out what Vitruvius had to say on the topic of aqueducts and water supply, the University of Chicago site is a handy place to read it. Since my own skill in reading the language of the Old Ones is more akin to Mirin's than Keera's, I am grateful for the translation.

**Apologies for my petty thefts!** In this book, I stole from Geoffrey Chaucer (and Ovid), a little bit from Anglo-Saxon poetry such as *Beowulf*, a lot from the Child Ballads (traditional ballads from Scotland and England first collected by 19th century folklorist Francis James Child), and also from ancient Greek traditions about the Delphic oracle and the Trojan War, Julius Caesar's *Commentaries on the Gallic Wars*, William Shakespeare, John Donne, Edmund Spenser, and William Wordsworth. I admit it—I also made brief nods to *Monty Python and the Holy Grail* and *Deadwood* (and . . . just whispering this for anyone in the know, *Sylvester and the Magic Pebble*). Lawyers! When I use the word "theft," I am making a joke. I am actually using the literary device known as "allusion."

As in *Blackbird Rising,* I have shamelessly cribbed at the end from one of the great works of English literature. In *Blackbird Rising,* I robbed Milton. In *Halcyon,* I've plundered the original (1590) conclusion of Book Three, Edmund Spenser's *Faerie Queene,* with a pinch of Donne. Not such a petty theft after all. I'm consoled only because Spenser made a lot of raids on existing material himself. They're so far above mine in every way that I hesitate to bring it up. Since he is one of the founding great-great-grandfathers of present-day fantasy, though, I am proud to take a small stand in that tradition. I'd be thrilled if these words led anyone to read *The Faerie Queene*, that neglected masterpiece. My advice: don't try to read it cold. Get some help. Just saying.

As for the rest, go for them on your own: *Beowulf* (unless you happen to be a scholar of Anglo-Saxon, read it in translation—I like Seamus Heaney's), Chaucer (with footnotes and librarius.org, you can read it in the original! Much better than translation!), Shakespeare, Donne, Milton, Wordsworth.

And a big thank-you to Warren Robinett, the inventor of the easter egg.

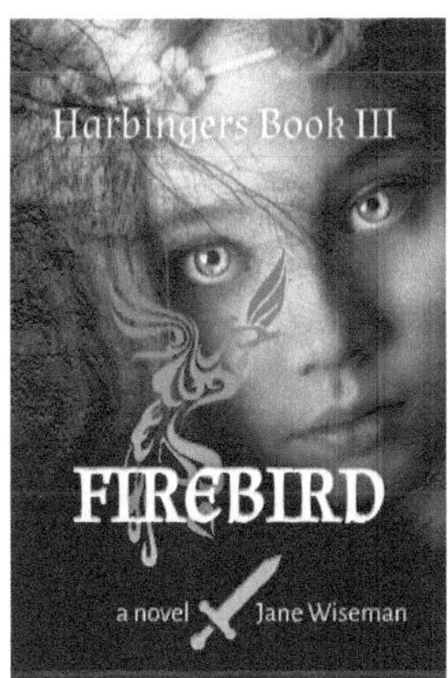

*What is a riddle for? A riddle is a test, it's a space for insight, it's a place of power. A riddle is a maze made of words. When the gods give you a riddle, you must walk the labyrinth until you wind into its heart.*

# From Chapter One:

*The ravenous wurm of the mountain*
*devours the great streets of men.*
*Battle storm of Hildr, life-harm of the hall,*
*the hound of the forest with its hot mouth*
*swallows every house; fell dog*
*of willow, ash, yew, oak*
*casts its baleful eye on the yard-gate.*
*Woe, that red-gaping hound of the wood.*

*Firebird the True, carry her on your back*
*to the isle of the thousand suns.*

My troubles started with a riddle. Shall I tell you what happened when I lost my powers?

I suppose I have no choice. The farwydd of the Fire Child compels me to tell you.

Why you? Who are you, and why are you the one I have to tell? I see I have more questions than answers, and I don't even know you, lady. I can barely make you out. Your outlines are kind of fuzzy, and your voice is wispy. Yes. That's it. If I had to describe you and your voice, I'd say you were kind of wispy.

If it were up to me, I wouldn't be sitting around telling some strange wispy person like you the story of my life, and I certainly don't see how you can offer me any good advice about my predicament, especially now I've lost my powers.

But the farwydd, Dark Ones seize her, has made me take you on as my companion. In fact, she's made this a condition for regaining my powers.

And I must regain them.

I must.

Having no choice in the matter, then, I will make you my Companion, and I will tell you everything you think you need to know. I'll exercise my duty to you faithfully, whether I understand the why of it or not, even though that wicked old crone compels me.

What? I didn't catch that. Speak up.

What? Am I really hearing what I think I'm hearing?

You shut up! You take liberties, my lady Companion. You do. Who are you to scold me? Yes, I really did say that. I'm going to say it again.

Ready?

*Dark Ones take that farwydd of mine, she's a wicked old crone.*

What a coward you are, Companion. What a fopdoodle, cringing away from me like this. I've a mind to say it over and over again, just to watch you cringe.

Oh. I see.

Don't cry.

No, really. I'm starting to understand you a little better.

I apologize.

We're both in her control, that wicked old thing. Our fate is in her hands. That's what I hear you telling me. If we don't behave, she'll punish both of us. Is that what I'm hearing? Is it really?

Hmmm. Wait a moment while I think this through.

It seems to me you're my punishment, Companion, and I'm yours.

Strange that it should be so. I'm a Child of Fire, and so the Fire Child's farwydd is my farwydd, and it makes sense that she'd try to control me. I'm not sure what I did to deserve her punishment, but if someone is going to punish me, it would be she.

You, Companion, or so you tell me, are a Child of Earth. The Earth Child's farwydd should be the one attending to you. So how is it you've come under the Fire Child's control?

No, I agree with you there, Companion. I don't understand it, either.

Well, here we are, then. It doesn't make any sense, but here we are, both of us under the thumb of the Fire Child and her nasty old farwydd. It's just as well we straightened that out, right here at the beginning of our journey.

Now, then. What do you want to know about me, Companion?

Very well. We'll start there.

I will say to you first, my name is Keera. I am my parents' true daughter, and their real daughter, too. My father is his most sacred majesty Walter the First, the exiled monarch of the Sceptered Isle, and my mother is the king's beloved wife, Lady Mirin of the High Sea Cliffs. I live with them on a rocky island in the middle of the Northern Sea, where they can defend themselves from their enemy, Caedon the Usurper.

My hair is red as fire, and I bear the Fire Child's mark on my shoulder.

Would you like to see it? Here. Look. A little flame, and the firebird rising from it.

I'll tell you about my firebird later, maybe.

You already know about my red hair. After all, you can look at me and see it for yourself. So you may be wondering why I bring it up, and why it's so unusual. My father's hair is as fair as the ripe barley in the field, although now as a sign of his troubles it's streaked with gray. My mother's hair, he tells her, remembering, running his fingers through it, is spun bronze. His protector is the Earth Child; hers is the Sea Child.

Earth Child and Sea Child are not incompatible. But Fire Child? Out of those two? Not the usual thing. If you were to meet my Grandfather Fylkir, though, and my Uncle Stefan, you'd see where my red hair comes from.

You'd understand more about the delicate matter of what is true and what is only real. You'd see how it eats at me.

True and real. Remember that, if you please.

I have set myself two tasks. The first one is hard. It's to make my father see again, and I'm not sure how I will do it. My powers would have helped me, but now they're gone.

The second task? That one is easy. It's just this.

I am going to kill Caedon.